*"**Hanging Curve** is a rare blend of suspenseful mystery writing within the milieu of 1920s black baseball. Hanging Curve has the lively snap and speed of a Satchel Paige pitch."*
—Roy Campanella II

And praise for THE MICKEY RAWLINGS SERIES:

"Mickey Rawlings bats .250 on the field and 1.000 as an amateur detective. Troy Soos does a red-letter job of mixing the mystery into a period when all baseball was played on fields that had real grass."
—*St. Louis Post-Dispatch*

"The Mickey Rawlings mysteries feature authentic old-time baseball atmosphere and absorbing stories. Troy Soos captures the period perfectly."
—*Lawrence Ritter, author of The Glory of Their Times*

"A perfect marriage between baseball and mystery fiction. The Mickey Rawlings mysteries are among my favorite crime fiction discoveries in recent years."
—*Mystery Readers Journal*

"A delightful mystery series."
—*Kalamazoo Gazette*

"You don't have to be a baseball fan to love this marvelous historical series."
—*Meritorious Mysteries*

"A charming series ... Soos tells riveting tales of murder and mayhem on the historic ball fields of the early twentieth century."
—*Killer Books*

TROY
SOOS

Hanging
Curve

KENSINGTON BOOKS
KENSINGTON PUBLISHING CORP.
http://www.kensingtonbooks.com

This book is dedicated to Cool Papa Bell, Oscar Charleston, and all the other Negro League stars who showed how the American game could be played at a time when much of America refused to see.

ACKNOWLEDGMENTS

It is a pleasure to thank Kate Duffy, my editor, for her invaluable guidance and encouragement; my agent, Meredith Bernstein, for her continuing efforts on my behalf; Janice Rossi Schaus, for her splendid cover design; and Sara and Bob Schwager, for their fine copy-editing.

I am also indebted to Negro League historian Jim Riley, for reviewing the manuscript; James Murray, of the National Association for the Advancement of Colored People, for historical information on civil rights issues; and Mark Potok, of Klanwatch and the Southern Poverty Law Center, for material on the Ku Klux Klan.

Providing valuable research assistance were Scott Allen, Steve Kelner, Bernie Rosenberg, Nat Rosenberg, Dean Hargett of the State Historical Society of Missouri, Vanetta Ellis of the Society for American Baseball Research, Debbie Mize of the Seminole County Library, the staff of the St. Louis Public Library, and the staff of the Indiana Historical Society.

I am deeply grateful to all of these individuals and institutions for so generously sharing their time and expertise.

CHAPTER 1

Springtime. The enchanted season of rebirth and hope, when every wishful dream seems destined to become reality. The exhilarating time of year when career .200 hitters imagine winning the batting championship, dead-armed pitchers feel strong enough to win thirty games, and St. Louis baseball fans believe that this will be the year the Browns finally capture an American League pennant.

The postgame crowd straggling out of Sportsman's Park certainly had the seasonal fever. As I lingered near the Dodier Street gate, I overheard confident predictions of a championship. According to some, the Browns would be powered to success by the bats of George Sisler and Ken Williams. Others put their faith in the pitching arms of Urban Shocker and Dixie Davis. Not one mentioned the name Mickey Rawlings, but since pennant hopes rarely ride on a team's utility players, I was accustomed to being overlooked.

A few fans claimed that the city's National League Cardinals, managed by Branch Rickey and sparked by the hitting of Rogers Hornsby, would also win their first title. If so, the entire 1922 World Series would be played right here in north St. Louis, in the classic ballpark that both teams called home.

I began to drift along with the crowd toward Grand Boulevard, where packed trolleys slowly shuttled fans home. I sidled close to a group of men near me, eavesdropping on their optimistic discussions and hoping their fever would prove contagious. Because, so far, I didn't have it. Spring was arriving late for me this year.

The traditional signs of early April were abundant. Robins sang in the elms and sycamores that lined the street, and daffodils bloomed in the city parks. Mild weather had relegated winter overcoats to the closet, and most of the automobiles crawling by were open-topped touring cars and roadsters.

But, of course, the true harbinger of spring is the start of a new baseball season. Here, too, the outward indications were all positive. With the Browns' opener four days away, the roster was the strongest in the club's history, and the team was already on a winning roll. Today's 6–3 victory over the Cards, before a record crowd of almost thirty thousand in the final game of the city series, gave us the championship of St. Louis and a 20–1 record for the preseason.

By any objective criteria, everything looked promising. However, the *feeling* of springtime—the internal buoyancy that lightens every step—eluded me.

So, in my mind's eye, I jumped six months ahead, imagining that today's game had indeed been a preview of the World Series, and trying to envision myself playing in my first Fall Classic. I could see the packed stands draped with bunting and streamers, and hear the cheers, and smell fresh-roasted peanuts. But I couldn't conjure up an image that included me in any part of the *action.* All I could imagine for myself was watching the Series from the bench. Well, at least that would be an improvement over the way any of my previous seasons had ended.

Could that be the problem? Perhaps it was the experience of seasons past that kept me from getting my hopes up about this one. After ten years of big-league ball, with six different teams, I'd been through enough Aprils and enough Septembers to know that the promise of spring is a hollow one. I wasn't going to win a batting championship—hell, I'd be lucky to end up within a hundred points of the champion. And if I managed to last the entire season with my new team, would I end up playing in my first World Series? Unlikely. I'd already played for some of the best clubs in baseball history, and never got to fulfill that dream.

So here I was, a thirty-year-old utility infielder, in a new city, with a new team, but no reason to believe that the new season would bring a change of fortune.

Stepping more quickly, I was about to catch a streetcar for home when a gruff voice behind me called, "Hey, Rawlings! They don't even let you play in a game that don't mean nuthin'?"

I turned to see a hulking, bareheaded man of about forty approaching. His homely face was familiar, but I couldn't quite place him. "I know you?"

He smiled, exposing several brown teeth and a great deal of barren gum. "Chicago. 1918."

It took another moment, then I pictured him in a Cubs' uniform. "Wicket Greene," I said. "I'll be damned." His hands remained jammed in the pockets of his ill-fitting Norfolk jacket, and I didn't offer mine. Our acquaintance wasn't one that I'd ever hoped to renew.

Greene's dark eyes seemed to withdraw deeper into their sockets. "Nobody calls me that no more."

"Oh, sorry." When we were teammates on the Cubs, Greene had picked up the "Wicket" tag because of his knack for letting ground balls roll through his legs at third base. His real name didn't come to mind.

"It's 'Tater' now," he said, sounding proud of the new nickname. He probably got it because his balding, lumpy head resembled a spud, but at least it was no slur on his playing skills.

"What are you doing now?" I asked. Greene had remained on the Cubs' roster during the Great War primarily because he was too old to be drafted. As far as I knew, his baseball career had ended when the Armistice allowed younger players to leave the battlefields for a return to the ballfields.

"I'm in the automobile business," he answered. "Monday to Friday, anyhow. Weekends, I still play ball." He gestured to a row of curbside pushcarts, where vendors were aggressively hawking their last sausages and pretzels to the dwindling passersby. "You want a dog?"

I was tempted, but shook my head no. Margie would have dinner waiting at home.

"I'm gettin' one." As we walked over to the cart, Greene said, "I play in East St. Louis. It's only semipro, but the club's a good one—better than a lot of minor-league teams I seen." He flipped the vendor a dime for a hot dog with kraut. "Always room for improvement, though—and you can help with that."

"Me? How?"

Greene hooked one of his remaining teeth into the frankfurter and tore off a bite. As he chewed, he spit out the answer. "Want you to play for us."

I stifled a laugh. "Why would I want to go from the St. Louis Browns to a semipro outfit?"

"We'll give you ten bucks to play in one game. Tomorrow afternoon."

"Sorry, can't do it. Fohl wants us rested for Opening Day." Browns' manager Lee Fohl would fine me a lot more than ten dollars if he learned that I'd hired myself out to another team.

Greene snorted, and a piece of bread fell from his lip.

"Browns give you any more rest, you might as well trade in your mitt for a pillow."

His comment hit me like a kick in the stomach. It was an accurate assessment, and it probably explained why I couldn't catch the spirit of the season: It's hard to dream of batting .400 when they won't even let you in the batter's box. The Browns weren't giving me enough of a taste of the game to be teased into hope.

"Besides," Greene coaxed, "the Browns won't find out. You'll be wearing our uniform, and you won't be using your real name."

"You mean—"

"What the other team don't know won't—" His mouth gaped open in an ugly grin. "Come to think of it, if you play good, it *will* hurt them."

I was flattered that they wanted to bring me in as a ringer, and mulled it over for a moment. I could use the practice, after all, and maybe some game action would give me that spark of spring fever I so badly needed. But I wasn't convinced that it was a wise idea; if Fohl got wind of it, I might not get into a Browns' game for a very long time. "Sorry. Wish I could help you, Wick—uh, Tater."

"We could really use you," Greene persisted. "We're going up against a helluva club, and need to field the best players we can find. Got a lot riding on this game."

As much as I liked being counted among "the best players," I again declined.

"Might be something a little different for you, too. Team we're playin' is colored. You ever play against coloreds?"

"No. Always wanted to, though." I'd wished for years that I could get in a game with Negro players. Since it didn't appear that such a game would ever be played on a major-league diamond, this might be my best chance.

"Them boys can sure play ball," Greene said.

"Yeah, I know. I've been to their games." I'd seen some of the Negro League's best teams—Kansas City Monarchs, Chicago Giants, Indianapolis ABCs, Detroit Stars—and was impressed by their talent and their style. "I'd like to," I admitted. "But I'm not sure . . ."

Greene pulled a pencil and scrap of paper from his pocket and scribbled a number. "Gimme a call tonight." He sounded confident that he had me.

Remembering some of the colored pitchers I'd seen, like Bullet Joe Rogan and Dizzy Dismukes, I imagined myself stepping to the plate against them. And I knew he had me, too. "You sure nobody'll find out?" I asked.

"Hell, you think we want 'em to know we had to bring in ringers?" He handed me the paper. "By the way, it ain't just your bat and glove we need. You still know how to use your dukes?" Greene had had some experience with my fists when we were on the Cubs; his and mine hadn't been a friendly relationship.

"I can fight if I have to," I said. "But if I go, it's only to play ball."

"There's been some bad blood between the teams the last few years." He gave me a playful punch to the shoulder. "Expect to be doing both."

Half an hour later, I hopped off a streetcar in the western part of the city, a few blocks north of Forest Park. During the short walk home, I looked around with curiosity at my new neighborhood.

I was still getting acclimated to the Mound City. When the year began, Margie and I had been living in Cincinnati, expecting that I'd be playing another season with the Reds. Then, for the third time in three years, I was sold to another club in another city.

Tired of the repeated uprooting, I wanted to sell the furniture we'd bought for our Cincinnati house and look for furnished rooms in St. Louis. But she convinced me to have our old furniture shipped so that the new place—a four-room flat on Union Boulevard—wouldn't seem quite so foreign.

As I opened the door and stepped into the parlor, I knew that once again Margie was right. It was comforting to see the familiar things from our last place: Margie's bronze mantel clock above the fireplace, her mahogany Victrola in the corner, my rolltop desk by the window, and, across from the overstuffed sofa, my throne—a Morris chair of solid white oak and soft burgundy leather. While I'd been at the Browns' spring-training camp in Mobile, Alabama, Margie had turned this apartment into a home.

I was hanging up my straw boater when she came in from the kitchen, wiping her hands on a dish towel. At the sight of her, I thought that as nice as it was to see the old furnishings, what really made this place a home was having Margie here with me.

She brushed a few unruly strands of chestnut hair from her face. Her long, curly tresses were always out of control, but I liked the old-fashioned style and hoped Margie's hair would never fall victim to the bobbing fad.

"How was the game?" Margie asked. She tucked the towel into a pocket of her blue-and-white-checked gingham dress.

"Good. We won." There was no need to mention that I hadn't played. Margie was aware that I'd been relegated to the dugout for most of the spring. That's why she'd elected not to come to today's game; she claimed it was a protest against the Browns for not playing me, but I knew she really wanted to spare my feelings—it was embarrassing for me to ride the bench when she was in the stands.

After a hug, and a kiss that didn't seem nearly long enough, Margie said, "Dinner's just about ready," and bustled back to the kitchen.

I watched as she walked away, thinking that the sway of her hips was tremendously appealing. Baseball hadn't kindled a feeling of springtime for me this year, but the sight of Margie always did—I loved her big brown eyes that glowed with intelligence, the mischievous smile that came so easily to her lips, and even the little hitch in her step that she'd acquired after a mishap during a moving-picture stunt. The attraction wasn't merely because the only company I'd had for the last six weeks was that of my teammates. I simply felt more alive whenever Margie was near.

From the kitchen wafted the aroma of Margie's special spaghetti sauce, which included a great deal of garlic and a number of secret ingredients which I preferred not to know.

I walked up behind her as she drained the pasta. With the stove unguarded, I swiped a fingertip through the simmering red sauce and brought it to my tongue. "Mmmm, almost as good as army food."

Margie gave me a playful swat with the dish towel. "Go set the table."

I obediently went back to the parlor, got the dishes from the sideboard, and began setting them on the small dining table near the fireplace. As I did, I thought about how much I enjoyed sharing my life with Margie. Although we'd never formalized our living arrangement into that of husband and wife, I wanted to come home to her always.

I called to her, "I asked a couple of fellows at the ballpark. They say the Marquette Hotel has a good dance band."

"You still want to go?" she asked hopefully. We hadn't had a Saturday night together since February.

"Of course. But probably not too late. I, uh, I might have a game tomorrow."

Margie brought out the spaghetti. "I thought today was the last one until Chicago."

"For the Browns it was. Tomorrow's game is in East St. Louis."

She put the bowl on the table and turned to give me a quizzical look.

"A fellow I played with on the Cubs, Tater Greene, came to see me. He's with a semipro club now, and he offered me ten bucks to play for them tomorrow."

"Do you need . . . ?"

I shook my head. "No. In fact, Phil Ball gave us each a hundred-dollar bonus for beating the Cards." The Browns' owner wasn't known for his generosity, so winning the city championship must have meant a lot to him. "It's funny: I just got a hundred bucks from the Browns for doing nothing, but I really want to play with this semipro club."

"Why?"

It wasn't for the money, of course. Partly it was because Greene thought I could help his team win, and it was a refreshing change to be wanted. With the Browns, I was starting to feel like the kid who always gets picked last. "Just thought I could use an extra workout before the season starts," I answered.

Margie knew there was more to it than that, but didn't prod. She ducked back into the kitchen and returned with a loaf of bread and a bowl of sauce. "The Browns will let you?" she asked.

"They won't know about it. This team's bringing me in as a ringer; I'll be playing under a different name."

She frowned. "I don't know . . . If you have to hide who you are, it can't be right."

"Local clubs bring in ringers all the time—it's almost expected."

She gave me a look that showed she didn't think much of my argument.

As we sat down to eat, I said, "The other team is colored. I guess that's another reason I want to go. Some of them are damn good ballplayers, and I've been wanting a chance to play against them for a long time.''

"Won't it be a problem if the Browns find out?" Margie asked.

I shrugged, but didn't answer. It occurred to me that the Browns weren't the only ones who might object. Judge Kenesaw Mountain Landis, beginning his second year as commissioner of baseball, was quietly letting it be known that he didn't approve of major leaguers appearing in games with Negroes. But he hadn't issued any explicit restrictions, so I could always plead ignorance.

"Well, think about it before you make up your mind," she cautioned.

I shrugged again and cut a slice of bread.

Margie could tell that I'd already made my decision. "Okay. I'll go with you."

I remembered what Greene had said about possible fights. "That might not be a good idea," I said. "There's been some trouble between the teams in the past. Could be more of it tomorrow."

She smiled but said nothing. Her mind was made up also.

"I'll call Greene after we eat," I said, "and tell him I'll— we'll—be there." At least Margie would have a rare opportunity to see me play. And against semipros, I was sure to have a great game.

CHAPTER 2

The rattling trolley felt too much like a roller coaster for my comfort. It wobbled its way eastward across Eads Bridge, carrying us from St. Louis, Missouri, to East St. Louis, Illinois, while horns and whistles of barges and steamboats echoed eerily from the Mississippi River below. Gusting winds buffeted the car, causing it to rock and shudder so much that I envisioned all of us being spilt into the water.

Next to me, Margie, wearing a new spring dress of green silk with white embroidery, appeared as comfortable as if we were sitting in our parlor. Of course, considering some of the things she'd ridden in the past, she was unlikely to be perturbed by a trolley ride, no matter how turbulent. Back when she was a moving-picture actress, Marguerite Turner had specialized in action serials, riding elephants and camels, wrestling crocodiles, and taming lions and tigers. I wasn't quite so adventurous; I didn't play with any animal larger than a dog, and I liked solid ground beneath my feet.

Staring out the trolley window, I watched the sun struggle to break through a swirling cloud cover. The fight was toughest on the East St. Louis side of the river, where the clouds were reinforced by a yellowish exhaust spewing from a forest of smokestacks.

City boosters liked to call East St. Louis the Pittsburgh of the West, although it was more often referred to as the Hoboken of St. Louis. The city's economy was based largely on providing a home to industries that St. Louis didn't want on its side of the river: stockyards, packinghouses, chemical plants, and metal refineries, all of which contributed to a foul atmosphere and dreary landscape. This was my first visit to East St. Louis, and even before we touched Illinois ground, I was already hoping it would be my last.

Once off the bridge, the trolley crawled through a maze of tracks and sidings. An enormous billboard welcomed visitors to the city and boasted that *More trunk line railroads pass through East St. Louis than through any other town of its size in America!*—proving that, with a little effort, every city can find something to brag about.

Next we entered the downtown area. Or what was left of it, anyway.

"Jeez," I said, pointing out the window, "would you look at that."

Margie leaned over and followed my gaze. "Is this from . . . ?"

"Must be." Scorched brick shells of gutted shops and offices were surrounded by vast rubbish-filled lots once occupied by wood-frame homes. "So this is where it happened."

Five years earlier, in the summer of 1917, a mob of white townspeople decided to drive out the colored population. They did it by burning entire blocks and shooting the Negroes as they fled.

"This looks like some of the villages I saw in France," I muttered. But unlike what I'd seen during the Great War, this destruction hadn't been caused by an invading army. These scars were self-inflicted; the city's own residents had destroyed part of their hometown and murdered scores of their neighbors.

There was another difference between the war in Europe and the massacre that had taken place here. No Armistice had been declared in the racial battles. Every summer since 1917, riots had erupted in cities across America—Chicago, Tulsa, Detroit, Washington. East St. Louis still had the distinction, though, of being the site of the worst race riot in the nation's history.

I turned from the window, the same way people avert their eyes from maimed veterans. There are wounds you don't stare at too closely. And horrors you try not to think about.

Cubs Park, home of the colored East St. Louis Cubs baseball team, was located more than a mile from the area of destruction. The quaint wooden ballpark at the corner of Broadway and Twenty-second Street occupied an entire block in a mixed neighborhood of single-family homes and small businesses.

A yellow, two-story clapboard building housed the park's ticket office and concession stands. I paid the ticket clerk fifty cents for Margie's admission, and told him I was a player, holding up my bat, glove, and spikes to support the claim. There was no need to ask which team I was with; he simply pointed out the gate to the field, and said, "Third-base side."

Margie gave me a good-luck kiss and went to get a seat, while I headed for the third-base dugout, which turned out to be just a bench.

My new teammates wore gray uniforms with *ENOCH'S ELCARS* in red block letters on the jerseys. They were in the early stages of loosening up, tossing baseballs around and running sprints in the outfield. On the first-base side, the Cubs, wearing white flannels with navy trim and lettering, were similarly occupied. Not one player strayed onto the other team's half of the diamond. It was as if an invisible barrier stretched from home plate all the way out to the center-field flagpole.

I spotted Tater Greene engaged in a four-way game of catch. "Hey, Tater!" I called. "Where's the clubhouse?"

He left the others and walked over to me. "*Clubhouse? Where the hell you think you are—the Polo Grounds?*" He spit a stream of tobacco juice. "Lucky to have a bench in this dump."

The field was actually better maintained than most minor-league diamonds I'd seen. The earth was smooth and clear of rocks, the grass neatly trimmed, and the fences in good repair. "Then why not play at your park?" I asked.

Greene spit again. "Ain't got one." He touched my arm with his mitt. "Come on, Ed's got your uniform."

I was led to a short, potbellied man who bore a striking resemblance to Giants' manager John McGraw. He'd even adopted the Little Napoleon's aggressive stance; he stood with his arms akimbo, surveying the players.

Greene said to him, "Ed, this is Rawlings, the one I told you about."

The Elcars' manager stuck out a hand. "Ed Moss." From his crushing grip, I could tell he wanted no doubts that he was in charge. "Glad you could join us. What name you gonna use?"

"Welch," I answered. Since I'd been christened "Mickey" after the old New York Giants' star Mickey Welch, it seemed fitting to borrow his last name, too.

"All right, Welch, you'll be playing second base." Moss pointed to a satchel on the bench. "Got your uniform there." As we walked over to get it, he added, "You get your ten bucks after the game."

"Don't want it," I said.

"Why the hell not?"

"If the Browns find out I played today, I want to be able to tell them it was just for practice."

Moss shrugged. "Fine by me. I don't care *why* you play,

as long as you help us win." He opened the bag and handed me a uniform and cap, both of which were stained with dirt and sweat.

I ran a fingertip over the lettering on the jersey, and read aloud, "Enoch's Elcars." An Elcar, I knew, was a boxy automobile manufactured in Elkhart, Indiana.

"Automobile dealer," Moss explained. He pointed to a dapper, gray-haired gentleman in the front row of the stands. "That's the man you're playing for: Roy Enoch. He sponsors the team."

Tater Greene spoke up, "Most of us work at his car lot."

"Hey, you better suit up," Moss said.

"Where?"

"Either the men's toilet or the back of a car."

I opted for the former, a tiny room with bad ventilation next to the concession stand. Knowing that I was going to have to change at the park, I'd dressed casually in old duck trousers and a soft-collar shirt. I quickly swapped those for the Elcars' uniform, cinching my belt tightly because the pants were a couple of sizes too large. The cap was too small, but I preferred it that way—it looks dramatic to have your cap fly off when you're making a play.

When I returned to the field, the Cubs had taken over the diamond for batting practice. The Elcars milled about in foul territory, impatiently awaiting their turn. While I stashed my street clothes under the bench, Tater Greene introduced me to some of the other players, giving my last name as "Welch."

I paced around, getting used to the new uniform and letting my cleats get a feel for the turf. As I did, a sense of familiarity began to course through me. I had spent most of my teenage years traipsing around the country playing for company teams like the Elcars. Although there's a grandeur to major-league ballparks, and donning a big-league uniform is like wearing the robes of royalty, I still had a fondness for small-town baseball. There's something special about intimate parks like this one, and local teams made up of working people. It's closer to the roots of the game, the one we all played on sandlots as kids.

I stopped for a few minutes to watch the Cubs practice, and thought that if we were still kids, on a vacant lot somewhere with no one looking, maybe we'd even choose teams the way it was supposed to be done: in order of ability. Here everything was strictly by skin color, for both the players and the fans.

Open, single-deck bleachers ran along either side of the diamond, with wire fences separating the seats from the playing field. Behind first base, the crowd was all colored; behind third base, all white. Both stands were already filled, and altogether there were at least two or three thousand people on hand.

One similarity between the black and white crowds was that they were almost all male. It was easy for me to spot Margie seated among a dozen or so other women behind our bench. She was looking in my direction, so I touched the bill of my cap, and she waved back.

Looking over the rest of the crowd, I noticed a number of armed men in khaki police uniforms positioned on the white side of the park. Their eyes were directed across the field, and the way they carried their shotguns they looked like sentries defending a fort against attack.

The Cubs left the field, and Ed Moss yelled for us to take fielding practice.

I grabbed my mitt and trotted alongside Tater Greene. "Looks like somebody's expecting a war to break out. What's going on?"

Greene answered, "I told you there might be trouble."

"Yeah, but *why?*"

"It's been bad ever since the riot. Didn't play each other at all for two years afterward. And when we did play again, every close pitch and hard slide was an excuse to throw punches." His mouth cracked open in a homely smile. "So watch yourself."

It was my fellow infielders that I watched during practice, trying to familiarize myself with their ranges and moves. Tater Greene, older, slower, and about thirty pounds heavier than when he was a major-league third baseman, now played first base—the place where elephants go to die. At third was J. D. Whalen, a powerfully built man with short legs and a cannon for an arm; he liked to show it off, delaying his throws to first to make the plays close. The shortstop, Brian Padgett, was a wiry, freckle-faced youngster with terrific range and a deft glove that was almost big-league caliber.

After batting practice, Ed Moss called the team in and gave us the starting lineup. He read name after name without getting to "Welch," then finally announced, "Batting eighth: Welch, second base."

I couldn't believe that this semipro team had me so far down in the order. Why the hell would they bring in a major leaguer and bat him *eighth?* I grumbled to Greene about it, and he explained, "Ed has to live with these guys every week. He's not going to piss them off by letting an outsider bat ahead of them."

Still seething, I looked around at the crowd while Moss launched into a pep talk. Spectators had overflowed both stands and were lining up along the fence all the way to the outfield. There were also many more police officers, shotguns at the ready, obviously expecting violence.

So was Ed Moss. He concluded his remarks by saying, "We're gonna win this game, goddammit! And we're gonna stand up for ourselves. Any of them Cubs gets out of line, any of them starts trouble, you give it right back to him. We don't take no crap, and we give back double." He pointed to the bats laid out in front of the bench. "And if worse comes to worst, grab yourself one of those."

* * *

Through the first two innings, all was peaceful as the pitchers dominated the action, providing few opportunities for conflict between the other players.

Tater Greene was the game's only base runner; he'd gotten on board in the second with a bloop single, and was left stranded there when Cubs' hurler Slip Crawford struck out the next three batters in a row. For us, Leo South was almost as impressive; the hard-throwing righty gave up only a bunt single and two walks to the Cubs while striking out four.

I got my first shot at Crawford when I led off the top of the third. From the coach's box, Ed Moss hollered, "Let's go, Welch! Get it started!"

As usual with a pitcher I'd never seen before, I intended to use his first pitch more as a learning experience than a hitting opportunity. I wanted to pick up the rhythm of his motion, and see what kind of pace and movement he put on the ball.

Crawford's cap was tilted back on his head, leaving his chocolate brown face wide-open for study. But I could detect nothing helpful from the lanky left-hander's placid expression. His eyes, almost hidden behind high cheekbones, looked sleepy, and his wide mouth was partly agape. He appeared as relaxed as if he was throwing batting practice. I wondered if part of the reason I couldn't get a read on him was that I'd never faced a colored pitcher before.

His delivery was equally mystifying. Crawford went into a slow, elaborate windmill windup, his long rubbery limbs appearing to move in every possible direction. Just before sending the ball to the plate, he hesitated, leaving me completely off-balance and unable to do anything but watch it go by.

Even if I could have recovered in time, I couldn't have hit the ball. Crawford's hesitation move would have been a perfect setup for a fastball, which is what I expected. Instead, the pitch was a slow curve that floated up high before taking a downward dip.

"Strike one!" barked the plate ump.

The second pitch was right where I like them: knee-high on the outside corner. I stepped into it and swung hard to drive the ball into right field. I was sure I'd have a double at least, maybe a triple. But at the moment when I should have felt the impact of ash on horsehide, all I ended up with was a disheartening *swish*. The damned ball must have *wiggled* its way around the bat barrel.

"Just get a piece of it!" Moss yelled.

With a two-strike count, Crawford should be wasting the third pitch, but by now I knew I had to be ready for anything. He served up another slow pitch like the first, high and slightly off the plate. I held back until the last possible instant. Determined not to let him sneak another one into the strike zone, I lashed out, wanting only to make contact. This time the ball twisted away from me, and I almost threw my back out reaching for it. Strike three.

It was a long walk back to the bench under the glares of my teammates. Ed Moss, contempt visible on his ruddy face, let loose with some profanities that would have made John McGraw proud.

The Elcars who followed me to the batter's box were also mowed down by Crawford, but that was no consolation. I was a major-league baseball player, and to be fanned so easily by a sandlot pitcher was humiliating.

The game was still scoreless when the Cubs came to bat in the bottom of the fourth. The cries from both bleachers were becoming more raucous as the fans tried to stir their teams, but they remained shouts of support with little heckling of the opposing nine.

To the delight of the colored fans, Leo South started the

inning by walking the Cubs' leadoff man, who trotted to first base as if running across hot coals. I was surprised to see that although he was a full six feet tall, his dark face had the wide-eyed innocence of a twelve-year-old.

The next batter gave me my first fielding chance, driving a hard grounder to my left. I darted back on the outfield grass before lunging with my mitt. As I snared the ball, momentum carried me behind first base. With a sidearm flip, I got the ball to Tater Greene barely in time for the out.

I moved back to my position, pleased with the play, but curious as to why the cheers I was hearing were from the Cubs' fans. Then I saw that the runner from first was now standing on third. What the hell did he do, cut across the pitcher's mound? Not even Ty Cobb could have made it from first to third that fast. The kid must have cut the corner at second.

I ran to second base, planted my foot on the bag, and called to Leo South for the ball.

The pitcher looked at me blankly.

"Gimme the ball!" I repeated. Instead of a runner on third with one out, we were about to have two outs and the bases empty.

South stepped off the rubber and tossed me the ball. I held it up and appealed to the base ump, expecting him to call the runner out for missing second. As the ump gave the safe sign, the kid suddenly dashed home. I was frozen, first from surprise and then with amazement at his phenomenal speed. I'd never seen a human being move so fast—I half expected him to become airborne. The ball was still in my hand as he scored the first run of the game.

While cheers exploded from the colored side of the park, Ed Moss bolted from the bench and lit into the umpire, claiming a base runner can't leave the bag during an appeal. But Moss was wrong; the ball is live, and a runner can advance. And this one sure did—he effectively scored from first base on an infield groundout.

Brian Padgett shrieked at me, "How the hell could you give them a run like that? You goddamn busher!"

I moved away from the apoplectic shortstop, and he shifted his anger from me to the umpire. Moss and Padgett both cussed the umpire more than they'd be allowed to get away with in the big leagues. I noticed for the first time that both umpires were white, and wondered why there wasn't a representative in blue from each race.

Tater Greene came over to me from first base. "Don't worry about it, Mick. I might have tried the same thing."

"Thanks," I grunted. I didn't know which was worse: scorn from Padgett or commiseration from Greene.

He added with admiration, "Damn, but that boy can fly."

"Like Ty Cobb with his feet on fire," I said. "What's his name?"

"Beats me. I just call 'em all 'boy.' "

When the inning continued, the colored team went on to score two more runs before J. D. Whalen caught a foul pop-up to end it.

Back at the bench, Roy Enoch's teenage son was meticulously recording the totals in a scorebook. Out of curiosity, I checked the Cubs' lineup for the name of the speedster who'd scored their first run. It was listed as *Bell, J,* and he was playing center field.

Due to bat third, I turned my attention to studying Slip Crawford. Everything about Crawford and his pitches involved changes in motion—stop and go, twist and turn, float and flutter.

Our lead-off batter worked him to a full count before striking out, then Brian Padgett took his turn against the tricky left-hander. With a two-two count, Crawford served a tantalizing lob. Padgett scooted up in the box and knocked the ball deep to left-center. He raced around the basepaths as the ball rattled off the fence. The speedy Bell fielded the carom and threw to third base in time to hold Padgett to a triple.

The white crowd was roaring, making the most of their first chance to cheer an Elcars' scoring threat. Many in the female contingent were waving their handkerchiefs and calling Padgett's name.

Now it was my turn. I went up to the plate thinking that this was my chance to show what a big leaguer can do. And to make up for my blunder in the field.

Okay, I thought, with a runner on third, Crawford can't afford to go into an elaborate motion; if he does, Padgett might steal home. And if I stand in the very front of the batter's box, his slow breaking balls won't have a chance to move much either; I could hit them as easily as teeing off on a hanging curve.

That's where I took my stance, as close to Crawford as I could get.

The Cubs' catcher didn't like it. In a gravelly voice, he said, "You looking to shake hands with my pitcher, or hit against him?" When I looked down at the massive backstop, he added matter-of-factly, "Pitchers tend to get nervous when you crowd them."

I knew what that meant. But I couldn't back down; I had to remain where I was—and be ready to duck.

Slip Crawford, appearing completely indifferent to Padgett dancing around at third base, stared in for the sign. Then he went into an abbreviated version of his windmill windup and threw the fastest pitch he'd delivered all day—right at my chin.

I tried simply to lean out of the way, not wanting to give him the satisfaction of seeing me hit the dirt, but the unexpected speed of the pitch had me so surprised that I went tumbling on my rear, dropping my bat as I did.

A few hoots of delight went up from the colored seats, and a lot of loud grumblings from the white side. I got to my feet as if nothing had happened. Crawford had gone by the book: I'd crowded too close, so he brushed me back.

I went to pick up my bat, but the Cubs' catcher had it in his hand. He held the handle end out to me, then paused to read the name stamped on the barrel: *Mickey Rawlings*. He looked at me with big impassive eyes. "Popular model," he growled.

I sheepishly took the bat, embarrassed that my cover was blown so easily. I'd sure make a lousy spy, I thought.

The ominous noises from the white fans died down, defused by the catcher's gesture. Then I realized he probably hadn't returned my Louisville Slugger out of courtesy. He'd wanted to get hold of the bat to prevent me from chasing his pitcher with it.

I stood a little deeper in the box for the second pitch, a low curveball that broke straight down. A cloud of dust went up as it passed the plate, and the Cubs' catcher spun around to retrieve the wild pitch. Brian Padgett sprinted for home.

Too late, I realized what *hadn't* happened: There had been no sound of the ball hitting the ground. I yelled at Padgett, "Back! Back!" but he kept coming.

The catcher calmly turned around, the ball secure in his mitt. He'd used an old trick: tossing a handful of dirt when the pitch arrived to make it look like it was going past him.

Fury came over Padgett's face when he saw the ruse, and he charged in with his spikes high. At impact, however, the cleats did nothing more than clatter against the big catcher's shin guards, and Padgett slumped to the ground where he was tagged for the second out. I helped him to his feet, and the shortstop went unsteadily back to the bench.

Crawford then put three straight curveballs, each breaking in a different direction, past me to notch another strikeout and close the inning.

* * *

By the end of the fifth, the Cubs had increased their lead to 5–0. One of the runs came on a homer by their catcher, whose name I learned was Denver Jones.

After Leo South issued two walks in the sixth, Ed Moss decided to make a pitching change. J. D. Whalen took over on the mound while South moved to third base. Whalen's control was sharp, but he directed so many fastballs at the Cubs' heads that he was always behind in the count, and gave up two more runs.

The head-hunting by Whalen was only one sign of the Eclars' growing frustration. Impotent with their bats, they put their mouths to use, loudly attributing the physical abilities of the colored team to "all them years living in the jungle," and urging them to go back to Africa "with the rest of the monkeys." I was tempted to point out that we were losing because the Cubs were playing smarter than we were, but I knew it would have no effect on my new teammates. They didn't merely want to play stupid, they wanted to sound stupid.

So did the white fans, who followed the Elcars' lead and directed the vilest slurs at the Cubs' players.

In the colored bleachers, the fans cheered their team and stamped their feet. As the taunts from the whites grew louder, so did the chants and cheers from the other side, as if trying to drown them out.

Then a hush fell over the colored crowd, followed by low murmurs. Some of the Negroes pointed toward the left-field corner.

I looked in that direction to see four open touring cars that had pulled up next to the fence. The occupants, at least a dozen of them, were garbed in the white robes and pointed hoods of the Ku Klux Klan.

One of the Klansmen held aloft a large Confederate flag. Three of them, standing on running boards, brandished rifles. All of the men kept their faces hidden, and the eyeholes cut in their masks looked more frightening than any facial expression could.

This was crazy, I thought. It was no surprise that there were Klansmen in the area; the KKK had become well established in the Midwest over the past few years. But for them to come out in full regalia, waving a Confederate flag, was something I'd have expected to see only in the Deep South. I stared at the fluttering Stars and Bars with disbelief. We were in Illinois; wasn't this the *North?*

Slip Crawford might have been disconcerted by the new arrivals, or maybe he was simply tiring, but he walked our leadoff batter in the seventh and gave up a double and single to the next two men to face him.

I batted next, and got solid wood on his first pitch, hitting a line drive up the middle that should have been a single—except that Bell in center field raced in to make a shoestring catch.

The rest of the Elcars kept the rally going. The Cubs' lead had been cut to 7–4, when J. D. Whalen went up to bat with two on and two outs. For the first time that day, Crawford looked flustered. He paused a long while, peering at Whalen. Then he threw another rare fastball—at Whalen's head. It was justified, considering how Whalen had been using the Cubs' heads for target practice, but Whalen didn't view it that way.

Bat in hand, Whalen stalked out to the mound, the catcher, Jones, close on his heels. Crawford took a couple of steps in and said something that halted Whalen in his tracks. He stared at the pitcher for half a minute before turning around and going quietly back to the batter's box.

It looked like the fight was out of Whalen. He took two called strikes and flailed weakly at the next pitch to end the inning and the Elcars' threat.

Whalen got his fire back when he took the mound again. He threw twice at Bell's head, but was frustrated when the youngster easily dodged both pitches. Then he drilled him in the hip, and Bell was awarded first.

Denver Jones was next up. He, too, dodged a couple of knock-down pitches before Whalen decided to throw strikes. On the second pitch that Whalen put over the plate, Jones pushed a bunt up the first-base line. I knew it wasn't a sacrifice attempt—the Cubs' catcher wanted Whalen to have to field the ball.

Sure enough, as Whalen ran to pick up the slow roller, Jones took only a couple of steps, waiting until the pitcher was in his path. As Whalen turned to throw to first base, Jones plowed forward, knocking him off his feet.

Whalen promptly sprang up swinging, and Jones returned the blows. Other Cubs jumped off the bench to join in, and the Elcars came from their positions as reinforcements. Brian Padgett raced past me and jumped on Jones's back. Tater Greene squared off with Slip Crawford.

I reluctantly tossed my glove on the ground, obliged to join in the fight. There are some things you have to do when you're part of a team, even if only for a day. Then I remembered that the ball was live, and looked for the runner. There was Bell, flying for home, about to score from first base on a bunt.

My admiration for his base running was interrupted by a punch to the side of my head. I couldn't tell who threw it, so I started sparring with the nearest Cub I could find.

The two umpires tried in vain to restore order while the brawling teams continued their battle unabated. Then a gunshot exploded, and punches halted in mid-swing. We all looked around to see where it came from—and to see if everyone was still standing.

One of the police officers behind the Elcars' bench had his shotgun pointed to the sky. He pumped the weapon and let off another blast. "Play ball!" he ordered.

The umpires quickly got the game under way again. But before Whalen threw another pitch, I looked over at the Klansmen. Their rifles weren't pointed up; they were level, aimed in the direction of the Cubs' bench. Glancing back and forth between the white stands and the colored crowd, I felt like I was standing in no-man's-land between two warring armies.

I fervently wished the game would end soon, and didn't care whether we won or lost.

It finally did end, with the Cubs taking a 9–5 victory. There was only polite applause from their fans; too much celebrating might anger the side with the guns. As it was, some in the white crowd hurled bottles and rocks at the departing Cubs.

I grabbed my street clothes from under the bench and ran to the men's toilet, where I hurriedly changed clothes. All I wanted was to find Margie and get us safely out of East St. Louis as quickly as possible.

At the Elcars' bench, I gave Ed Moss back the uniform. And he gave me a few sharp words about how useless I'd been to his team.

"At least I played for free," I said as I left.

"Yeah, and we sure got our money's worth!" he called after me.

Margie was standing near the ticket booth gnawing on her lower lip. The two of us ran hand in hand for the tracks and squeezed aboard an already full streetcar.

As the packed trolley began to crawl west, I looked back at the ballpark, at the thousands of people still milling about, and at the shotguns and rifles conspicuously targeting some of them.

Ugly as the events of the day had been, I thought, we'd been lucky. One spark could have set off a riot. What was supposed to be an exhibition of the National Pastime could easily have turned into another episode in a national tragedy.

CHAPTER 3

Three days and three hundred miles later, I was in another ballpark—one that seemed a world away from East St. Louis. Home plate had the same five-sided shape, and the bases were still ninety feet apart, but otherwise there was little similarity between the semipro field where the Cubs and Elcars had battled and majestic Comiskey Park, home of the Chicago White Sox.

The modern, steel-and-concrete stadium was dressed up for the start of the new season, swathed in red-white-and-blue bunting, with flags and streamers flapping in the wind. The grass was neatly manicured and the dirt dragged as smooth as a billiard cloth. Even the flattened water hoses that served as foul lines wore fresh coats of bright white paint.

An overflow crowd of almost thirty thousand was also in holiday dress for Opening Day, the men wearing suits and derbies, and the women in bonnets and pastel frocks. Around the perimeter of the field were blue-uniformed patrolmen—but unlike the officers in East St. Louis, these were on hand as part of the pageantry, not because of any anticipated violence.

My attire for the occasion was the gray-flannel road uniform of the St. Louis Browns. I stood with my teammates, lined up in front of the visitors' dugout, as a military brass band thundered its way through ''The Star-Spangled Banner.'' Holding the brown-billed cap over my heart, I kept my eyes on the American flag in center field, and began once again to feel the pride that comes with being a major-league baseball player. Millions of men all over the country played this game, but only a lucky four hundred got to compete in a big-league ballpark. And I was among them. I might not get to play often, but when I did, it was on diamonds like this one.

By the time White Sox owner Charles Comiskey threw out the ceremonial first pitch, I was starting to think that even if this season turned out to be no different from the ones before, it would still be special. Every day as a major-league ballplayer was something to relish.

That's what I kept telling myself as I picked a spot on the bench to spend the next nine innings.

Marty McManus, our starting second baseman, sat down next to me. The tall, skinny youngster was the main reason the Browns had acquired me. I was supposed to teach him what I knew about playing in the big leagues, and in return I'd get to spell him in the lineup every now and then.

McManus was a former bookkeeper who'd been drafted during the Great War and somehow ended up serving in Panama instead of France. He was also a ''prospect,'' which meant he was being groomed to be a ''star.'' He'd done well enough last year as a rookie, but had some rough patches in the early months; the Browns were counting on me to help him get off to a good start this season. He was a likable enough kid, but served as a constant reminder that I had never been a prospect— nor a star. In ten years, I'd progressed only from utility infielder to veteran utility infielder.

Chicago hurler Red Faber toed the rubber to face the top of our order—an unenviable task, for the Browns had the hardest-hitting lineup in baseball. All three outfielders—Ken

Williams, Baby Doll Jacobson, and Johnny Tobin—posted .350 batting averages last year, first baseman George Sisler had once hit over .400 to break Ty Cobb's string of batting championships, and catcher Hank Severeid was coming off a .324 season.

Faber shut down our hitters in the first, though, and McManus picked up his glove before running out to second base.

"Don't forget to check the ground," I reminded him.

"Why? It looks fine."

The kid was supposed to take my advice, not question it. But I explained, "This park is built on a city dump—and they didn't clear it too good before making it a baseball field. Junk works its way up from the ground sometimes. Check it out."

The groundskeepers had done a good job, but I wanted McManus to get used to looking for himself whenever he played in Comiskey. More than one infielder had been victimized by a bad hop from a half-buried piece of nineteenth-century trash.

I then settled back to watch Urban Shocker, ace of the Browns' pitching staff, take the mound against the White Sox. He and Faber were among only a dozen or so veteran pitchers permitted to use the recently banned spitball for the remainder of their careers. Shocker was a true master of the wet pitch; his spitter had helped him lead the league in wins with twenty-seven last year. Hopes were high that this season he would use it to lead St. Louis to a pennant.

Many savvy baseball people favored the Browns to win the championship, in part because the teams most likely to challenge us were hurting. The White Sox, once the league's powerhouse, had been decimated after the 1919 World Series scandal resulted in eight of their players, including Shoeless Joe Jackson, being expelled from baseball. Although a few of the untainted stars—Faber, Eddie Collins, Ray Schalk—remained, Chicago was no longer a pennant threat. The defending champion New York Yankees were expected to be our main competition, but here, too, we had an advantage. The Yankees, opening today in Washington, with President Harding throwing out the traditional first pitch, were temporarily without the services of Babe Ruth and Bob Meusel. Commissioner Landis had suspended them for the first month of the season because they'd gone on a barnstorming tour after last year's World Series.

In my view, the Browns didn't have to rely on weakened opposition. They were one of the best clubs I'd ever seen, strong enough in every area to take on any challenger and prevail.

I looked around the field, at my teammates in their positions. They might be the players who would take me to my first World Series. For a chance to play in the Fall Classic, I would willingly spend the regular season playing second string to Marty McManus. Besides, teaching the youngster might be good preparation for the coaching and managing I hoped to do when my playing days were over.

After Shocker retired the White Sox in order, McManus trotted into the dugout and sat down next to me again. He nodded toward the mound, and asked, "What's the best way to hit Faber?"

"First off," I said, "what do you smell?"

"Huh?"

"What's the air smell like?"

He lifted his head and inhaled deeply. A sour expression wrinkled his young face. "Like a latrine."

"That's the stockyards," I said. The infamous Union Stockyards were only a few blocks from Comiskey Park. "They're behind home plate, so that means the wind is blowing out."

"Good. Means a fly ball will carry."

"You'll get some more distance, yeah. But this is a big ballpark—you try hitting home runs here, and you'll just fly out. It's the *pitcher* who has the advantage when you smell the stockyards. Breaking balls will break sharper when he throws them against the wind."

"Huh." McManus rubbed his nose. "So what do I do with Faber?"

"Well, his best pitch is a spitter, and the wind will make it even better. He's also got a helluva curve you got to watch for. I'd say hold up on the breaking stuff and wait for a fastball."

"What if he don't throw me a fastball?"

That had me stumped, but I wasn't about to admit it to the kid. "Then close your eyes and swing, and hope the ball hits the bat." Hell, if I really knew how to hit pitchers like Red Faber, I'd be in the starting lineup myself.

I cast a wistful glance at my bat lying on the ground in front of the Browns' dugout. Then I picked up my mitt and began absently toying with it. One hundred and fifty-four games would be an awful lot to watch from the bench, even if it did eventually lead to a World Series appearance. I wanted to *use* my bat and glove, to hit and catch and throw. As troubling as the experience in East St. Louis had been, at least I'd gotten to play.

I looked to the pitcher's mound, but Red Faber wasn't the object of my attention. My thoughts kept drifting to little Cubs Park, and I imagined myself in the batter's box, again facing Slip Crawford.

I had tried to shake off the memory of that game as soon as Margie and I crossed to the St. Louis side of Eads Bridge. With packing for the road trip, and then leaving for Chicago the next day, I'd pretty much succeeded. Until now.

What came to mind now was the fact that Crawford had beaten me every time I faced him. I'd gone 0-for-4, striking out three times. There had to be a way to hit him, I knew, but what the hell was it?

I pictured Crawford peering in for his sign, then going into that herky-jerky windup of his, and finally delivering the pitch—probably a dancing curveball.

Okay, I told myself, all that flailing about during the windup is a distraction—just as Crawford intends. So don't look at his limbs. Keep your eye on the bill of his cap until he releases the ball.

I replayed the scenario a couple more times in my mind until I knew what to do about that darting curve of his: stay up in the batter's box to hit the ball before it breaks. If he brushes me back, fine—it's a called ball. And if he keeps doing it, eventually he'll either walk me or have to put one over the plate. If he decides to simply plunk me with the pitch, that's fine, too—it puts me on first base.

As Urban Shocker and Red Faber went on with their duel in Comiskey Park, I continued to think about playing against Slip Crawford and his teammates in East St. Louis. I wanted to face the colored pitcher again. I wanted to beat him.

Shocker got the win in this day's game, 3–2, to get the Browns off to a good start on the season. Unfortunately, it was only a start. There were 153 games to go.

We never even got to suit up on Friday. Twenty-five Browns' players, the manager, and coaching staff, all sat around the visitors' clubhouse of Comiskey Park for nearly four hours, waiting for the weather to clear. Some read *The Sporting News* and local papers, others played gin rummy. I spent the time polishing my spikes, honing my bat, and oiling my glove, even though all of them were already in perfect condition. The intermittent rains of morning grew heavier and more frequent, until finally the third scheduled game with the White Sox was postponed. At least it meant we would remain undefeated in the new season.

When we returned to the Congress Hotel, I stopped at the front desk for my room key. The clerk reached into the pigeon-hole behind him and handed me a note along with the key. It read:

Miss Margie Turner telephoned.
Asks that you return her call.

The message didn't say "urgent," but it didn't have to. I called Margie every day from the road, and she knew I'd phone again tonight. Something must have come up for her to call the hotel.

I used the lobby telephone, and while the long-distance operator made the connection, I thought maybe there wasn't anything wrong; perhaps Margie was just eager to talk with me again. It had been difficult leaving for this road trip; after being apart all spring training, we'd been together for only a few days before I had to hit the road again.

Margie sounded surprised to hear from me so quickly. "Aren't you at the game?" she asked.

"Rained out. Is everything okay?"

"Well ... no." She promptly added, *"I'm* okay, don't worry." I heard her take a deep breath. "But something's happened."

"What?"

"The colored pitcher ... the one you played against in East St. Louis ..."

"Slip Crawford? What about him?"

"He's dead." Her voice cracked. "They hanged him."

"What? Who hanged him?"

"It looks like the Klan. Maybe because he beat a white team."

"Nobody's going to kill someone over a baseball game," I said. As the words came out of my mouth, I knew I was saying them not out of confidence, but because I wanted to believe they were true.

Margie continued in little more than a whisper, "He was found hanging from the backstop in Cubs Park Tuesday morning."

"Jeez." I pictured the little ballpark where I'd played less than a week ago, and recoiled from the image of a body dangling above home plate. "Hey, you said Tuesday. It just made the papers now?"

"I didn't see anything in the newspaper. Karl called this morning and told me."

So my old friend Karl Landfors had heard about it in Boston. "How did he know Crawford was killed?"

"From somebody in St. Louis. Anyway, Karl's going to tell you all about it himself. He's coming for a visit."

As much as I liked Karl, a visit from him was generally not something to look forward to. I turned back to the death of Slip Crawford. "Did they catch the guys who did it?"

Margie didn't answer, and I realized there was no need to "catch" them. If this killing was anything like what had been going on in the South in recent years, the perpetrators would be bragging about it, not trying to hide. Dozens of Negro men and boys were lynched every year with impunity—because lynching wasn't considered a crime.

"I'll call you again tonight," I said. "Are you going to be all right?"

"Yes." She sniffled, then whispered, "Hurry back. I miss you."

"Miss you, too."

After hanging up, I walked in a stupor across the lobby and sank into an overstuffed wing chair.

Mental images jumped before me like a kaleidoscope. I pictured the living Slip Crawford going into his windup and throwing me one of his tricky curveballs. Then I saw him hanging dead in the same ballpark. And I thought of the hooded Klansmen who'd shown up at the game and imagined them standing around Crawford's body as if they'd bagged a trophy. Then Karl Landfors came to mind, and I wondered what his interest in Crawford's death could be.

* * *

It was the death of a different baseball player that had the attention of the Saturday crowd at Comiskey Park. The game was briefly delayed as tributes were paid to legendary slugger Cap Anson, who had died the day before at age seventy. Anson's remarkable career had spanned most of nineteenth-century baseball, including twenty-two seasons with the National League Chicago White Stockings.

When the game began, the American League White Sox played like they'd had the life taken from them, too. We romped all over them for a 14–0 win and a sweep of the series. I even got into the game—after we had a ten-run lead—and hit a solid single in my first time at bat.

My teammates were jubilant at the victory and left for the hotel vowing that the upcoming Cleveland series would be equally successful. I was unable to share their joy and didn't return to the hotel with them. Instead, I wandered the South Side streets near Comiskey Park, alone with my thoughts.

I had walked these same blocks three summers ago, in August of 1919. More accurately, I'd patrolled them.

I was back from the war in Europe that summer, discharged early by the army, and playing baseball again with the Chicago Cubs. But then, on July 27, the city exploded in a race war.

A melee started on the beach near the foot of Twenty-ninth Street, and spread to the city streets with so much violence that it looked like the death toll would exceed that of the 1917 East St. Louis riot. For days, white and colored mobs battled each other as buildings burned. The governor belatedly sent in six thousand troops, including reactivated veterans like me, to restore order.

For one week, in full combat uniform and Springfield rifle at the ready, I patrolled the streets near the stockyards. It was like being back at war, but a civil war. My greatest fear was that I would have to use my weapon on a fellow citizen.

It came as a great relief that I didn't have to. The conflicts eventually subsided, and the troops were sent home. Some newspapers printed the death counts like they were game scores, the final one reading: *15 White, 23 Colored.* The white population of Chicago called that a victory.

After that experience, I tried to ignore the annual race riots. Every summer they would flare up in a few cities across the country, and then they would die out until the next year. I couldn't fathom the hatred behind them, and didn't want to think about it enough to gain such an understanding.

I suddenly realized that I'd been walking for a while and checked my watch. I'd barely have enough time to get back to the Congress Hotel and pack before joining the team at the train station.

After hailing a cab, I once again found myself dwelling on questions I preferred not to ponder: What makes someone want to burn a family out of its home? Or drive around in hoods and sheets, terrorizing a neighborhood? Or kill a colored baseball player for beating a white team?

Was that really why Slip Crawford had been lynched? I hoped not. I didn't want to believe that a man could be murdered because he had a good curveball.

As the taxi neared the hotel, I looked off in the direction of Lake Michigan and recalled the incident that set off those two weeks of terror in 1919. A colored boy named Eugene Williams had fallen asleep while floating in a tube. When he drifted over to a section of the beach traditionally off-limits to Negroes, white bathers woke him up by throwing stones at him. Then they continued to stone him until he was dead.

CHAPTER 4

The Cleveland Indians put an end to our winning streak, easily taking the first two games of the series in League Park. One of them was a 17–2 thrashing that served to remind us that we needed to concentrate on winning in April instead of making World Series plans for October. We came back strong in the finale this afternoon, and exacted some measure of revenge by pounding five Cleveland pitchers in a 15–1 romp.

I got to play in both of the high-scoring games, replacing Wally Gerber at shortstop when we were behind by a dozen runs, and filling in for third baseman Frank Ellerbe after we were ahead by ten. Apparently, Lee Fohl would only risk allowing me onto the field when my presence couldn't affect the final outcome.

The long game meant that we had to take a later train out of Cleveland, and we didn't pull into St. Louis until after midnight. It was another half hour for a cabby to drive me to Union Boulevard.

I unlocked the door as quietly as I could and stepped softly into the parlor. Margie, wrapped in a red floral kimono, was nestled in a corner of the sofa, fast asleep. She'd let down her hair, which curled about her shoulders and flowed down almost to her waist. A chintz throw pillow was tucked under her chin; she hugged it like a little girl cuddling a teddy bear.

Tired as I was, I didn't want to go to bed yet. Instead, I eased into the Morris chair across from the sofa and simply watched Margie sleep for a while.

Before we started living together, the best thing about coming back from a road trip was checking the mail that had accumulated. Now I had Margie, who always tried, and usually failed, to wait up for me. Knowing she'd be there when I got home almost made the long separations tolerable.

Before the sound of her rhythmic breathing could lull me to sleep, I got up and walked over to the sofa.

The kiss I planted on Margie's forehead failed to wake her, and the subsequent ones on her cheek were no more effective. It took a couple on the lips before she stirred and looked up at me, her brown eyes foggy. "Mmm," she purred. "That was nice. If I pretend I'm still asleep, will you do it some more?"

I kissed her again, long and deep enough to show there was no need for her to feign sleep. "Let's go to bed," I said.

She stretched. "Okaaay." The word turned into a yawn. "Oh, I kept some supper for you in the icebox. Want me to heat it up?" Her puffy eyelids slipped down a notch.

"No, I ate on the train. Thanks, though." I put my arm around her waist and steered her toward the bedroom. "All I want is a pillow."

We were almost to the door when Margie said, "By the way, Karl got in tonight."

"He's *here?*" The mere thought of Karl's presence took a lot of the joy out of the homecoming.

Margie smiled at my reaction. "No, he called. He's staying with another friend—a writer, I think he said."

I let out a sigh of relief. "Did he say when he wants to get together?"

"Tomorrow. I'll bring him to the game, and we'll have dinner afterward."

"Okay. I'll leave a couple passes for you at the gate." I was so tired, I didn't even want to think about the fact that we had another game in about twelve hours. But I felt better when I remembered there was little likelihood that I'd have to play in it.

I woke with a start in the dark of night, not sure where I was. It was a common sensation for me, a result of all the travel I did as a ballplayer. Whenever I awoke, it took me a while to determine whether I was in a Pullman berth or a hotel room or at home. Another challenge was to figure out what city I was in.

There was no rumble of the rails, so I knew I wasn't on a train. After a few moments, I got my bearings and realized I was in my own bed. *Our* own bed. Margie murmured in her sleep and shifted her head, pressing it heavier on my shoulder. Her movements were probably what had awakened me.

I made no effort to slip out from under her. With my eyes wide-open, staring into the darkness, I savored the feel of having her next to me. Despite a slight numbness that started to work its way through my arm, I wanted to remain like this all night.

For the first time in my life, the thought struck me that I could give up playing baseball if I should ever have to. But I wanted to keep Margie Turner forever.

That idea stayed with me until dawn started to paint the room in warm shades of orange. By the time it brightened to yellow, I was again contentedly asleep.

CHAPTER 5

The teams were the same, but the roles were reversed. This time it was the Browns' home opener, and the Chicago White Sox were the visiting club.

Sportsman's Park was festooned with all the decorations traditional for the occasion, and a shrill marching band paraded around the outfield, displaying little sense of rhythm in either its music or its footwork.

American League president Ban Johnson, a close friend of Browns' owner Phil Ball, was in attendance, seated in Ball's private box. Dozens of local politicians were also on hand, eager to be seen by prospective voters as fans of the National Pastime.

The only aspect of the event that might have been a disappointment to the politicians—and to Phil Ball—was the size of the crowd. Nearly half of the park's twenty thousand seats were empty. Attendance had always been a problem for the Browns, although the club generally did draw twice as many fans as the rival Cardinals. A year and a half ago, ticket sales for the Cards had been so sparse that they had to abandon their own ballpark and move into Sportsman's as tenants of the Browns.

When the band stopped its noise, St. Louis mayor Henry Kiel took the mound to throw the ceremonial first pitch. Not wanting to give the mayor all the glory, the president of the Board of Aldermen carried a bat to the plate, intending to hit one of Kiel's deliveries. It probably sounded like a good idea in the planning stage, but to the vocal amusement of the crowd, whenever Kiel managed to put the ball over the plate, the alderman failed to get any wood on it. As they continued their exercise in futility, I looked around the park. When I spotted a cluster of black faces in the right-field bleachers, I was reminded that, as in East St. Louis, fans were segregated in Sportsman's Park; Negroes were only permitted to sit in that distant bleacher section. After more than a dozen pitches, the alderman finally popped weakly to catcher Hank Severeid, and I stopped thinking about the ballpark's seating arrangements.

Once the real baseball game began, my teammates fared little better than the politicians. The way they played, they must have been as tired as I was from the late arrival the previous night. Chicago took advantage, and got back at us for spoiling their opening day by ruining ours with a 7–2 win. Since the score didn't make it into double digits, I never made it into the lineup.

In the clubhouse shower, I decided it was probably just as well that I got to rest on the bench. Because I had an ordeal waiting for me after the game: Karl Landfors.

Karl's body was almost obscured by the strand of spaghetti he was slurping into his mouth. He would never die, I thought— someday he'd simply complete the gradual transformation from human to skeleton that he'd been undergoing ever since I met him ten years earlier. And he wouldn't even need to be laid out; Karl's pale, bony frame was already draped in the kind of severe black suit favored by corpses and undertakers.

"You're looking good," I lied. "What have you been up to?"

"A little bit of everything," he said. "You know me—there's always a windmill somewhere in need of someone to tilt at it."

I certainly did know him. Karl, a muckraking journalist and diehard Socialist, championed just about every Progressive cause that came along, especially the hopeless ones. And he'd gotten me involved in more than one of them.

A mustachioed waiter came by, holding a straw-shrouded bottle. "More grape juice?" he asked in a thick Italian accent.

Karl nodded, and the waiter filled Margie's and Karl's wine-glasses with Chianti. The "grape juice" pretense was the restaurant's only acknowledgment of the Volstead Act. Here, in the Little Italy section of downtown St. Louis near Columbus Square, Prohibition was paid little serious attention—just as in most American cities.

The waiter turned to me. "Another root beer?"

I said, "Please," and he soon brought me a fresh lager.

Margie asked Karl, "Have you written anything lately?"

"I have a piece coming out in the next *American Mercury*." Karl pushed his black, horn-rimmed spectacles higher on his long nose. With his balding scalp, sunken eyes, and pinched cheeks, the nose and glasses were the only things that kept people from mistaking him for a skull. "It's on the need for antilynching legislation."

"I'll look forward to reading it," Margie said.

I was aware that the National Association for the Advancement of Colored People was trying to get a federal antilynching bill enacted, but didn't know that Karl had taken up the issue. "Will they pass the law, you think?"

He sipped his wine and dabbed his lips with a napkin. "I'd like to believe so. It's finally through the House of Representatives. But the Senate will be quite a challenge. Those Southern senators . . ." He shook his head. "In any event, I've been trying to get state legislatures to endorse the bill. It appears that Massachusetts will pass a resolution of support next week."

Margie asked, "What brings you to Missouri?"

"I'll be doing some work with Congressman Dyer's staff." The St. Louis representative, I knew, was the antilynching bill's chief sponsor. "And with a friend of mine," Karl added, "a lawyer who works with the NAACP."

"What about the Sacco and Vanzetti appeal?" I asked. "And unionizing coal miners?" Those had been his most recent projects.

"Those battles are all secondary to this one. There is no benefit to having the right to vote or speak or assemble if you are not alive to enjoy them." He waved his fork, dripping tomato sauce on the tablecloth. "The Declaration of Independence says 'life, liberty, and the pursuit of happiness.' And it's in that order—life comes first. Without that unalienable right there can be no others."

With Karl Landfors, dinner-table conversation often turned into speechmaking.

He appeared to notice it himself. Karl put down his fork, and asked, "How are you two enjoying St. Louis?"

Margie and I exchanged looks. She spoke up first. "We're still getting settled. Mickey's been out of town for most of the time we've lived here. And I'm going to be looking for a job— or maybe school. I'm thinking about nursing school."

She hadn't mentioned that to me. The last I'd heard, Margie was interested in becoming a horse trainer.

It was my turn to report. "I'm doing all right. The Browns are a good team—may go all the way." I smiled. "And I'm leading the team in hitting, believe it or not." My two singles in four at bats gave me a .500 batting average.

"Not," Karl said with a laugh. "Remember, I've seen you hit."

We chatted a while more, then Margie excused herself to go to the ladies' room.

Karl and I both watched her walk away. "She looks prettier every time I see her," he said.

"To me, too." My eyes followed Margie until she was gone from view.

"Is she really going to be a nurse?" Karl asked.

"Dunno. She's looking for something to do with herself. It's got to be boring for her to be alone half the year."

Karl toyed with his glass for a few moments. "Mickey, there's something I need to speak with you about."

"I have something to tell you, too."

Karl hesitated. "You first."

I took a deep breath. "I'm going to ask Margie to marry me."

A warm smile spread over his usually humorless face. "It's about time! When are you going to pop the question?"

I was relieved to see that he obviously thought it a good idea. "Well ... I have to think about it. I mean, I have to figure out *how* to propose. What words to use, where to ask ... Jeez, I don't even know her ring size." I hadn't given any thought yet to the realities of engagement—or marriage. I just knew I wanted to be married to Margie Turner.

Karl held up his glass in a salute, and said, "I know you'll figure it out. And I know you and she will be very happy together."

"Thanks, Karl." Since he'd let me tell him my news first, I felt obligated to ask, "What was it you wanted to talk to me about?"

"It's ... well ..." Karl was rarely at a loss for words, but he couldn't find them this time. "It can wait until later," he decided.

Margie came back and sat down. "What did I miss?"

I shot Karl a warning look that he'd better not let on what I'd told him. "We were talking about dessert," I said.

"Let's have it at home," she suggested. "I have an apple pie in the icebox."

Karl and I agreed. I was in no hurry, though. I had the feeling that once we got there, Karl would get around to the matter he wanted to discuss with me. And I was pretty sure I knew what it was.

By the time we arrived at the apartment, I was eager for Karl to tell me what was on his mind. He kept grinning at Margie and me like an antsy kid bursting to tell a secret, and I worried that he'd reveal my proposal plans.

Karl's demeanor remained the same as he wolfed down three pieces of pie and two glasses of Moxie. Several times he appeared on the verge of a giggling fit, and once nearly choked on a bite of the dessert.

I finally reminded him, "You mentioned there was something you wanted to talk about."

"Yes." His expression gradually darkened, and he fastidiously brushed a small mountain of crumbs from his tie and vest. "Some*one*, actually: Slip Crawford."

I thought so. "Margie told me he was killed."

"Lynched," Karl corrected.

Out of curiosity, I asked him, "How did you hear about it? I don't think there's been much in the papers here. How'd the news get all the way to Boston?"

"I received a phone call from the lawyer I mentioned, the one with the NAACP. The colored community here is really up in arms about this—almost literally. Slip Crawford was a popular figure. He was not some obscure semipro player; he was a pitcher with the St. Louis Stars of the Negro National League."

Huh. So the East St. Louis Cubs had brought in a ringer of

their own. I felt some small relief that at least it was a professional pitcher who'd bested me.

Karl pushed up his spectacles. "When I learned that a St. Louis ballplayer was killed, I decided to call you and see if you knew of him. Then Margie . . ."

She finished, "I mentioned that you played against Crawford in his last game."

"And that gave me an idea," Karl said. "I'd like you to ask around, talk to some of the other players from that ball game, and see if you can learn anything about what happened."

"Isn't it obvious what happened?" I said. "Crawford beat a white team, so the Ku Klux Klan lynched him. They were there at the game, all decked out in their hoods and robes, and carrying rifles."

Karl nodded. "So I've been told. However, there is some question as to whether the Klan was really involved. They're usually quick to take credit for their atrocities—it's a way of flaunting their 'power' and helps intimidate anyone who might cross them. But this time they haven't." He leaned forward. "All I'm asking you to do, Mickey, is talk to some of the other players on the white team. See if they've heard anything. That's all."

"There's nothing useful they'd tell me, Karl." I didn't see much point in talking to the Elcars; after the way I played for them, they were unlikely to share any confidences with me. And, there was another reason to avoid them. "I really wasn't supposed to play in that game. If I go asking questions, and it gets out that I played as a ringer, I could be in serious trouble."

"What would the Browns do to you?" Karl asked.

"Suspend me, at least. And it's not just the Browns. Commissioner Landis doesn't like major leaguers playing against colored clubs; who knows what could happen if *he* found out."

"Do you seriously believe he'd punish you for playing in a baseball game?"

"He just suspended Babe Ruth a *month* for playing exhibition games without permission. If he'd do that to Ruth, who knows what he'd do to a"—I almost said "nobody"—"to somebody like me."

Margie suggested, "You don't have to tell them your real name. You could still go by 'Welch.' "

"What about the police?" I asked Karl. "Aren't they looking into it?"

Karl sniffed with disdain. "The police haven't ruled out the possibility of suicide."

"Huh?"

"It's nonsense, of course. Crawford had been beaten before he was hanged. But that's the official police position."

"Jeez."

"It is important that we learn what happened," Karl said. "In the South, the Klan has been carrying out more and more lynchings the further the antilynching bill progresses through Congress. We want to know if their violence is spreading to the Midwest."

"You know what I don't understand?" Margie said. "Why is it called 'lynching'? It's *murder*. Why not arrest the lynchers for murder? Then you don't need an antilynching law."

Karl nodded. "That is one of the arguments opponents use—that the crime is already covered under state homicide statutes. Legalistically, I can see the point. But the reality is that if a mob of fifty men gets together to hang a Negro, it is virtually impossible to determine afterward which men were actively involved in the killing, which were accomplices, and which were bystanders. No prosecutor is going to charge all fifty with murder, and if he did, no jury would convict them. With so many participating, it effectively diffuses everyone's degree of responsibility. When charges are filed in a lynch case, the most serious charge the killers typically have to face is disorderly conduct." Karl pulled several newspaper clippings from his jacket pocket and selected one of the articles. "I've been carrying these with me for the last couple of months. This one spells out the real reason the antilynching bill is being opposed." He adjusted his glasses and read aloud, " 'During debate in the House, Representative James B. Aswell of Louisiana took to the floor, and declared, *White people of the South have a right to lynch a Negro anytime they see fit without interference on the part of the Federal Government.*' "

Margie and I were both speechless.

Karl handed me one of the other clippings. "They've been exercising that 'right' with a vengeance."

I read the headline:

65 PERSONS LYNCHED IN 1921

Sixty-five. I stared at that number for a long moment. Then I thought of Slip Crawford, and imagined him on the pitching mound with sixty-five other colored men on the field behind him.

"I'll talk to Tater Greene tomorrow," I said. "I'll find out whatever I can."

CHAPTER 6

I'd heard it said that the only people who lived in East St. Louis were those who had to. If somebody did have to live there, I thought, Washington Park, in the northeastern part of the city, appeared to be one of the more desirable neighborhoods.

From a slow-moving trolley that rolled down the center of Kings Highway, I looked out at well-kept homes with spacious yards and stately shade trees. Farther toward the outskirts of town, the houses gave way to businesses. When I spotted the one that belonged to Roy Enoch, I pulled the stop cord and hopped off.

The auto dealership was about three miles from the ballpark where the Elcars had played the Cubs. Sprawling over most of a long block, the gravel lot was divided into two sections, one for new automobiles and the other for an extensive selection of used cars. All of them appeared freshly waxed and buffed, and they were all parked in neat rows. At the back of the lot was a large brick garage, with tire racks and two gasoline pumps nearby.

A wood-frame sales office, the size of a bungalow, was situated in the center of the lot. On a rooftop sign above the office, *ENOCH MOTOR CAR CO.* was painted in the same shade of red that appeared on the team uniforms. The sign also proclaimed:

> *Authorized Elcar Dealership*
> *New Cars! Used Cars! Full Service Station!*
> *"Komplete Kar Kare"*

The last line answered one of my questions, and I was disheartened to learn that I had played baseball for a Klan-affiliated business. Slogans like Enoch's had been springing up on signs all over the Midwest in recent years: *Kareful Klothes Kleaners . . . Kwality Kustom Kraftsmanship . . . Kindly Keep Koming.* I'd even seen a men's clothing store in Cincinnati called Ku Klux Klothes. Three Ks on a sign identified the proprietor as a Klansman, and brought in customers who wanted to support the KKK.

I strolled around the used-car section, wondering what to say to Tater Greene. How could I raise the main question that I wanted answered: Did the Elcars' team decide to kill Slip Crawford because they couldn't beat him on the field?

I was staring absently at a 1920 Hupmobile roadster when a cheery voice called out, "That's a beauty there! Yes, sir, you sure got an eye for fine automobiles!"

Rapidly approaching from the sales office was a wiry little fellow in a green-plaid suit and a porkpie hat. I recognized him as Brian Padgett, the Elcars' young shortstop. He had a breezy smile on his thin, freckled face, and a bounce in his step. His manner was so different from the last time he spoke to me—when he berated me for the botched appeal play—that I assumed he didn't recognize me.

"A real bargain, too," Padgett continued. "Nine hundred and seventy-five dollars. We're practically giving it away. The last owner hardly—" His brow furrowed, and he studied me for a moment. "Say, you look familiar."

Keeping to my fictitious name, I said, "Mickey Welch. Played baseball with you fellows a couple weeks ago."

"Oh yeah, the *pro*," he said derisively. "You in the market for a used car?"

"No, I was"—it occurred to me I might get more information if he thought I was a prospective customer—"I was actually thinking of a new one."

"Let me show you what we have!" His voice and eyes were friendly again.

Padgett guided me to the new models, pointing out every feature of the automobiles and getting in frequent plugs for the Enoch easy-payment plan. As he spoke, I made the effort to appear interested, much as I did when Karl Landfors prattled on about politics.

When he'd finished his spiel, I said that he'd given me so much to think about that I couldn't make a decision on the spot.

"Let's go see Mr. Enoch," he suggested. "I'll bet we can whittle down the price a little. Hell, you played ball with us— that makes you part of the family."

I walked along with him, glancing up at the *"Komplete Kar Kare"* slogan on the sign; I didn't want to be considered even a distant relation to this family. Since Padgett had mentioned the game, though, I said, "You know, I really felt awful that I couldn't help you win. I sure had an off day."

"You sure did," he snapped. His face showed a flash of the same competitive temper that he'd displayed during the game, then he got the emotion in check, not wanting to jeopardize a potential sale. "But don't worry about it. You weren't the only one who played lousy."

His sales manner still needed a little polishing, I thought. "I know it was a big game for you guys," I said.

"Sure was. Would have give my left arm to win it. And Mr. Enoch would have give both of his."

"Players took the loss pretty hard?"

"Hell yeah. That makes three years in a row them black bastards beat us." Padgett spit. "We'll get 'em next time, though."

"Should be easier now that their pitcher's dead."

He shrugged. "They'll get another. Ah, there he is."

A slender, middle-aged man in a chalk-striped blue business suit had stepped out of the office, tugging a snap-brim fedora over his neatly groomed gray hair. When we drew close to him, I saw the lines that creased his weathered face; on some they'd be called laugh lines, but on him they were probably caused by the sour expression that puckered his skin.

"Mr. Enoch," Padgett said. "This is Mickey Welch. He played with us against the Cubs."

Enoch's pale eyes narrowed. "I remember him," he said in a flat twang. "It's not every day I throw away ten dollars."

I was about to protest that I hadn't cost him a dime, but decided not to bother. Besides, the manager might have pocketed the money for himself and never told Enoch that I'd played for no pay.

"He's interested in a new car," Padgett went on. "Thought we might give him a break on the price."

The two of them stepped aside and huddled together briefly. Then Padgett came back to me, and Roy Enoch drove off in a shiny green Elcar.

"Good news!" Padgett reported. "Mr. Enoch says you can take a hundred dollars off any new model in stock—except the Studebakers. Got a big demand for those. And if you decide to go used, we'll take fifty bucks off the price. That would bring that Hupmobile you were looking at down to, uh . . ."

"Nine-twenty-five," I said. "Sounds like a good deal. Let me think it over, and I'll get back to you."

"Sure, sure. I understand. But remember to ask for me, right?"

"Of course. Oh, say, while I'm here I might as well say hi to Tater Greene. He around?"

"Yup, he's . . ." Padgett's attention had drifted to another potential customer browsing the lot, and he started to edge away. ". . . in the garage. Excuse me."

I walked over to the three-bay service building, a modern, well-equipped facility where four mechanics in olive drab coveralls were noisily at work. One of them was Tater Greene, hunched over the partially dismantled engine of a battered Chandler Six sedan. I smiled when I recalled the way he'd said he was "in the automobile business" as if he owned the dealership.

"Hey, Tater," I said. "Whatcha workin' on?"

He glanced up at me. "Magneto on this thing is shot. Along with just about everything else." He stood and wiped his hands on a rag. "What brings you here?"

"Looking for a car," I said, maintaining the pretext. "Brian Padgett showed me a few."

Greene snorted. "That little prick."

"Huh?"

My former teammate brushed the rag over his lumpy forehead, leaving a grease smudge that matched the color of his teeth. "I was supposed to get the sales job, and he took it right out from under me."

"What happened?"

"You remember J. D. Whalen?"

The stocky third baseman who'd pitched the final innings of the Cubs game. "Sure. What about him?"

"He was a salesman here, and he got canned last week. Enoch knew I wanted to move into his spot, but he give it to Padgett instead."

"Why?"

"The old"—Greene looked behind to be sure the other

mechanics couldn't hear—"the old bastard says I don't got a good sales manner. Can you believe that crap?"

Enoch was probably right, I thought, but I did sympathize with Greene's disappointment. Instead of clean work in a suit and tie, he was stuck here in the grease and dirt, breathing engine exhaust and gasoline fumes. "I think you'd make a fine salesman," I said. "Hell, you managed to sell me on playing with you against the Cubs."

Greene smiled at the vote of confidence and went back to work on the engine. "I'll get another chance. Padgett spends more time in the office sparking with Doreen than he does on the lot. Can't sell cars that way."

"Why'd Whalen get fired?" I asked. I wondered if his poor performance against the Cubs had cost him his job.

"Nobody knows for sure. I expect he wasn't selling as many cars as Enoch thought he should. Could you give me that screwdriver?"

I handed him the tool. "You told me most of the team works here."

"They do."

"How many of them are in the Klan?"

Greene froze for a moment. "I wouldn't know. Membership in those kinds of groups is usually secret." I knew he was familiar with "those kinds of groups." In Chicago, during the war, he'd belonged to one of the "patriotic" vigilante organizations that targeted Socialists, pacifists, and those with German surnames.

"Can't be much of a secret if it's part of the company's advertising," I said. "I saw the sign outside."

"That doesn't mean much. Some people just like to do business with a fellow Klansman, same as a brother Elk or Mason."

"So Roy Enoch *is* in the Klan."

"He owns this place; the sign is his. That's all I know."

"Some folks think it was the Klan that killed Slip Crawford," I said. "You hear anything about that?"

"Just that he got himself strung up."

"You think it had anything to do with him beating us"— I hated being included among the "us"—"in that game?"

Greene pulled out a long bolt and put it on the fender with a *clunk*. "Over a *baseball game?*"

"There were Klansmen at the park that day. And maybe some on the team."

"Don't know about the ones outside the fence," he said. "But no ballplayer is gonna kill another player for beating him in a game." He mopped the back of his neck with the rag. "You know how it is: If a guy beats you, you want to beat him the next time. If you kill him, you don't get the chance."

Tater Greene made more sense than I'd expected. But I thought it over for a moment and realized that his line of reasoning applied to professional players like him and me. We had made baseball our lives and understood the nature of competition. Perhaps those who viewed the contest with the Cubs as a racial conflict instead of a sporting event didn't have the sense that Greene had. "Anybody take the loss especially hard?" I asked.

"Not in particular. We were all down about it. Mostly from pride, but some lost money."

"Was there a lot of betting?"

"Roy Enoch bet with some of the other semipro owners. And Ed Moss lost out on a fifty-buck bonus he was promised if we won."

Maybe that's why the manager pocketed the ten I'd passed up. "Moss work here, too?"

"Nah, he's with the police—a desk sergeant."

"Any of the players lose a lot of money?"

He shook his head. "To tell you the truth, none of us was certain enough we'd win to risk much money on the game.

Them colored boys are good ballplayers, and we all know it. Wouldn't have had to scout for ringers if we thought we could win on our own." He began another assault on the stubborn magneto.

"Tater?" I waited until he looked directly at me. "You know anything about Crawford getting lynched?"

He straightened up and answered emphatically, "I don't know nothin', and I ain't heard nothin'."

I doubted that his answer was entirely true, but it sure sounded final, so I left Enoch's car lot and caught a trolley back to St. Louis.

For the most part, I believed Greene, although he probably had some knowledge or suspicions that he chose not to share with me. And I could see the argument against any of the players being involved. I'd had a vague notion that maybe one who'd been especially embarrassed during the game would have wanted revenge. But even so, it would have required several people; no one could have beaten and hanged Slip Crawford by himself.

By the time the trolley crossed Eads Bridge, I was inclined to believe that Crawford's killers were most likely the men who'd been at the game in hoods and robes, not baseball uniforms. Besides, if the motive for killing Crawford was that he'd humiliated an opposing player, that would make me a prime suspect.

The Browns gave me no chance to embarrass myself in Saturday's game against the White Sox. I was again limited to watching from the dugout bench—which turned out to be an ideal spot from which to see our left fielder Ken Williams make history.

Williams was one of baseball's best-kept secrets, despite the fact that last season he'd slugged twenty-four home runs, the second highest total in American League history. Unfortunately for Williams, the person with the most was Babe Ruth, and the Babe so dominated the National Pastime that few fans noticed the players in his shadow.

Unlike the flamboyant Ruth, Ken Williams did little to attract attention to himself. The simple, thirty-two-year-old country boy lived a modest life. His only known activity outside of playing baseball was talking about the game, and he did so at interminable length. Sportswriters actually avoided Williams because he tended to give discourses instead of catchy quotes.

Today, however, his bat spoke so loudly he couldn't be ignored. In the first inning, Williams belted a home run all the way onto Grand Boulevard. He later added two more mammoth round-trippers to become the first American League ballplayer to hit three home runs in a game. Not even Ruth, who had set a new season record of fifty-nine last year, had ever achieved such a feat.

Ken Williams's power display was almost enough to convert me to a fan of the long ball. I'd always been a proponent of the "inside" game exemplified by John McGraw and Ty Cobb, where you relied on your wits instead of sheer strength and used the bunt and the stolen base to play for one run at a time. Watching the drives of Ken Williams, though, I had to admit that there's something awfully pretty about a baseball arcing its way over the fence.

After the game, while reporters were still huddled around Williams in the locker room, scribbling furiously to record his long-winded comments, I left to meet Karl Landfors at the gate.

As the two of us walked to catch a trolley for home, Karl couldn't stop raving about Williams's home-run exhibition. Since I'd been trying for years to turn Karl into a baseball fan, it was gratifying to hear his enthusiasm.

Not until we'd transferred at Delmar Boulevard, was I finally able to give him a full report on my meeting with Tater Greene.

I concluded it by saying, "I don't think Greene knows anything. And if the team was behind Crawford's lynching, he would have heard about it."

"What about talking to some of the other players?" he asked. "If any of them are Klansmen, maybe they know who was involved even if they weren't themselves."

"If they do, they sure aren't going to say so. Besides, why are you so sure it's the Klan?" I still thought Crawford's killers were probably Klansmen, too, but there were a couple of aspects of the lynching that I didn't understand.

Karl frowned. "It seems obvious, doesn't it?"

"Yeah, but you said yourself, they usually brag about it when they lynch somebody. Why not this time? And before now, it's mostly been in the South, right? Why suddenly here?" In the Midwest, the Klan was generally seen as just one more fraternal organization with funny names and secret rituals. It even staged public parades and rallies.

"That's the worry," Karl said. "What if it's spreading here?"

"I don't know." But I didn't want to find out; I had other matters on my mind. "Sorry, Karl. Wish I could have been more help."

"Maybe you—"

I cut him off. "I don't have to get on my knee, do I?"

He blinked behind his thick glasses. "Pardon me?"

"When I ask Margie to marry me. Do I have to get on my knee?"

"I don't know." Karl was clearly at a loss. "They do in the movies . . . but I don't believe I've ever read anything authoritative on the matter."

For the rest of the ride home, Karl proved as useless in advising me how to propose as I would be in advising Ken Williams how to hit home runs.

CHAPTER 7

Karl Landfors paced himself over the next few days. He began by mentioning his lawyer friend once or twice, then a few more times, along with some casual suggestions that I'd probably enjoy meeting the man. Before I knew it, Karl had set a time and date.

Early Wednesday morning, Karl and I were on Market Street, in a predominantly colored section of downtown St. Louis. At the corner of Twenty-first Street, the Comet Theatre was showing Oscar Micheaux's *The Gunsaulus Mystery,* billed as "The Greatest Colored Photoplay Yet Made." Next to the movie theater was an ancient, but well-preserved, brick office building.

We walked into the front office of F. W. Aubury, Attorney-at-Law, and were greeted by his receptionist, a pretty Negro girl with bobbed hair. "Mr. Landfors," she said with a prompt smile, "you're right on time." Reaching for the telephone, she nodded a greeting in my direction, and informed the person on the other end of the line that we'd arrived.

She then showed us into a small office that was sparse on furnishings but flush with papers. They sprouted from the open drawers of an oak file cabinet, and spilled over from above the law books that lined the back wall. There were also teetering stacks of papers on the desk, piled so high that they almost hid the slim colored man seated behind them. If not for his calm demeanor, I would have guessed that the office had been ransacked.

"Mickey," Karl said, "this is Franklin Aubury."

"Good to meet you," I said.

Aubury stood, rising to a height of about five-eight, and we shook hands. "My pleasure. Karl has told me quite a bit about you." The lawyer's speech was clipped and precise, and his appearance was equally fastidious, although not fashionable. His stark black suit and stiff-collared white shirt were so similar to Karl's that the two of them might have shared the same tailor. They were also similarly devoid of hair, Karl having lost his to nature while the lawyer's head was shaved. Besides skin color, and the fact that Aubury had some muscle under his, the most noticeable difference between the two men was in their choice of spectacles: Aubury wore gold pince-nez that made him appear older than the thirty or thirty-five years I estimated him to be.

He gestured to a couple of chairs and invited us to sit down. Karl and I had to clear off so many newspapers and journals before we could that I wondered when Aubury had last had a client in his office.

"What kind of law do you practice?" I asked. "Karl mentioned you work for the NAACP."

"I work *with* them on certain issues," he said. "But I do not work *for* them. I work for all people of the colored race, and with anyone who shares our goals. Lately, my efforts have been directed primarily toward passage of antilynching legislation."

He and Karl not only dressed alike, I thought, but they both spoke in the same humorless tone.

Aubury removed his pince-nez, and methodically cleaned

the lenses with his pocket handkerchief. "But let us talk baseball for a moment, if we may. I'm quite a fan—I even played a bit myself back in college."

I glanced at Karl, who I knew was utterly devoid of athletic ability, and smiled, relieved to hear that there was a difference between these two. "I'm always happy to talk baseball," I said.

Aubury leaned back. "Do you know when the League of Colored Base Ball Clubs was organized?"

"Two years ago, wasn't it? 1920."

"No, that's the Negro National League. The first professional league for Negro players was the League of Colored Base Ball Clubs—in 1887."

"Huh." I had no idea they'd organized a league that long ago.

"Have you heard of Sol White?" he asked next.

I shook my head no.

"He published the first history of colored baseball back in 1907. White was also a fine player in his time, and still coaches." Aubury adjusted his glasses. "How about Frank Grant—do you know of him?"

Strike three. "Did you want to talk baseball," I replied, "or give me a history test?"

Karl cleared his throat at my bluntness.

Aubury flashed a surprisingly warm smile. "Point taken." He let his chair spring upright. "What I would like you to understand is that colored baseball is not a recent development. Baseball is part of our culture, and important to our community. It's almost as important as church—in fact, some colored churches change the times of their services when they conflict with scheduled ball games. Colored boys dream of becoming baseball players the same as white boys do, and a Negro League ballplayer is as much a hero to our people as a Babe Ruth or a Walter Johnson." Aubury pressed his fingertips together in a peak. "That brings me to Slip Crawford."

From the first time Karl suggested that I meet his friend, I knew it was primarily because of the pitcher's death. "What about him?" I asked.

"Slip Crawford was a local hero. He grew up in a shanty in East St. Louis, and played semipro baseball with the old Imperials there. Last year, he made it to the Negro National League, pitching for the Indianapolis ABCs—struck out twenty batters in his second game. And this season his pitching would have given the St. Louis Stars a shot at the championship." Aubury paused. "Unfortunately, his pitching was *too* good. He beat a white team, and they hanged him for it."

"You know for sure it was the Elcars?" I asked. "I got to believe it takes a better reason than losing a baseball game to kill a man."

Aubury held out the back of one hand; with the other, he pinched a fold of dark brown skin. "Here is all the reason they need."

I wished I could argue, but I knew that what he said was all too often true. I shot a look at Karl; he'd said almost nothing since we arrived, and I had the feeling that the direction the conversation was taking came as no surprise to him.

Aubury's next words confirmed my suspicion. "Karl and I have had some discussions," he said. "We believe that you would be the ideal person to look into Crawford's lynching."

"All I did was play in one ball game with the Elcars," I said. "That doesn't mean I know anything, or have any idea how to find out anything."

"Having played with Enoch's club," Aubury answered, "you have a legitimate reason for contacting the Elcars again. And they might assume you share their racial sympathies." He waved off my protest that I didn't. "I don't mean to suggest that such an assumption would be accurate. But if they're inclined to believe it is, they might be more forthcoming with information." He looked to Karl. "Also, Karl tells me you've been involved in a couple of murder investigations in the past, and had some success with them. Equally important, he vouches for your sense of justice."

I knew it was intended as a compliment, but I didn't feel like thanking Karl for trying to draw me into this. "Those were murders, not lynchings," I said, recalling Karl's explanation of the difference. "Even if I do learn whether it was ballplayers or Klansmen behind Crawford's killing, it was a mob of them, not one person. Do you really think I can track down everybody who took part? Or that the police would arrest them all if I did? What's the point of me putting my neck out if there's no chance it's gonna do any good?"

Aubury considered my argument before replying, "This isn't about bringing Crawford's killers to justice. I know *that's* not going to happen. But I do want to prevent any additional deaths—to people of either race."

Karl spoke up. "Our concern is that there's going to be retaliation for Crawford's death, and then whites will retaliate for that, and so on and so on, until the whole damn city's at war."

"We do not want a repeat of 1917," Aubury said. "Hostilities escalated for two months before culminating in the riot."

I hadn't known that there was a buildup to the riot; I thought they usually erupted suddenly. "How did it start?" I asked.

"With a city council meeting," Aubury answered softly. He began another ritual cleaning of his eyeglasses. "The United States had entered the war, and industries were short of workers. Some of the companies in East St. Louis recruited Negroes from the South, and they moved up here in droves—factory jobs are far more lucrative than picking cotton in Mississippi. But a lot of their new neighbors didn't like the idea of colored folk taking 'white' jobs.

"So, at the end of May, a mob of whites showed up at a city council meeting demanding that all Negroes be driven out of town. They found a friend in one of the local politicians, Alexander Flannigan, who said he agreed that 'East St. Louis must remain a white man's town.' Then he pointed out that the citizens could do the evicting themselves because 'there's no law against mob violence.'

"They took his advice. The mob left City Hall and ran out to the streets, pulling colored people from streetcars and beating them. Then they went to Negro homes and set them on fire. For three days, whites went on a rampage, trying to drive the colored population out. Some of the Negroes did leave, crossing over to this side of the river.

"Fortunately, no one was killed. But over the next weeks, white agitators spread rumors that the colored people who remained were arming themselves for a Fourth of July massacre of white people. Newspapers picked up the rumors and published them as if they came from credible sources. Soon all of East St. Louis was living in fear.

"Shortly before the holiday, a group of white men decided to make a preemptive attack. They drove through a colored neighborhood spraying the houses with bullets. Some residents fired back ... a couple of whites were killed. And then—'' Aubury looked from Karl to me. "Well, if you two have time, perhaps I can take you on a little tour."

Karl and I waited at the intersection of Broadway and Collinsville Avenue in East St. Louis, not far from City Hall. We huddled in our overcoats against the chilly, overcast day.

"I never noticed about the streetcars before," I said.

"Some things are hard to see," he replied thoughtfully. "When you're dining in a restaurant, you don't bother to think about whether the waiter has had a chance to eat."

It took a moment until I got Karl's point. "Guess you're right."

Franklin Aubury couldn't travel with us because he'd had to wait for a "colored" streetcar. And since St. Louis didn't have nearly as many trolleys for Negroes as it had for white passengers, he still hadn't arrived.

"Besides," Karl said, "a lot of these Jim Crow laws are new. Ten years ago, we could have ridden together. But now it seems there are more kinds of segregation in the Midwest than there are in Dixie."

It was another ten minutes before Aubury stepped off an overcrowded streetcar. When he joined us, he made no mention of the delay. He simply straightened the knot of his necktie, adjusted the brim of his derby, and picked up the conversation as if we'd never been separated. "This was where the killing started, gentlemen," he said. "Right at this intersection."

There were no visible signs that anything had happened there, no indications of burning or destruction. People of both races bustled about, doing their shopping and filing in and out of office buildings.

"On the morning of July 2," Aubury continued, "white workers gathered at the Labor Temple, a couple of blocks from here, for a protest meeting. What they were protesting was the fact that colored people had had the audacity to defend their homes and families the night before. What they decided was to drive the Negroes out once and for all.

"They marched down here, and when a colored man stepped off a streetcar on his way to work they shot him. Once they got their first taste of blood, they wanted more—and they proved insatiable."

Aubury started walking east on Collinsville, Karl and I on either side of him. "For the next two hours, blood flowed all over this street. Trolleys were stopped and all Negroes—men, women, and children—were pulled out. The lucky ones got a quick bullet. The others were clubbed, or stoned, or kicked to death—and it often continued after they were dead, until they could no longer be recognized as human. The white mob grew as the killing went on; even women and children joined in, using hatpins and penknives on their victims. And spectators lined the sidewalks, cheering the massacre."

I couldn't have said anything if I'd wanted to; my throat felt like I was trying to swallow a chunk of broken glass.

When we reached Illinois Avenue, Aubury said, "It continued all the way to here. By then the mob was so large, it split up into smaller gangs, who started rampaging through the rest of the city." He led us around the corner, and then turned on Fifth Street, back toward Broadway.

I was finally able to croak out a question. "What about the police?"

"Most remained in their station houses," Aubury answered. "Of the officers who did venture onto the streets, few did so for law-enforcement purposes. Some of the police egged the mob on, thinking it was fine entertainment to watch Negroes die." His tone was matter-of-fact, and I didn't know how he could sound so calm. Then I saw how tightly clenched the muscles were in Aubury's jaw. "With the police useless," he went on, "the mayor belatedly called for the National Guard. The militia began to arrive by early afternoon, and I will give them due credit: Most of the Guardsmen tried to restore order and stop the killing."

"But not all of them," Karl put in.

"No, not all. There was one incident in which a Guardsman came upon a gang of whites beating a colored man. When they saw the soldier, they stopped, and asked him if his rifle was loaded. He demonstrated that it was by shooting the Negro to death."

The tightness in my throat had spread to my stomach, and

I was hoping the tour would conclude soon; I didn't want to learn any more about how cruel humans could be to each other.

We crossed Broadway, and continued to Brady Avenue, then turned toward the river. This was the area Margie and I had seen from the trolley on our way to Cubs Park. A few dozen wood shanties were scattered throughout the otherwise desolate section of town, and Negro children played in the street. Beyond the shanties was the railroad yard, with the Mississippi River past the tracks.

"This is where most of the colored people lived," Aubury said, "in homes like these. Then the mob came to eradicate them." He pointed to the railroad tracks. "The whites who had guns took position over there, while the rest of the mob went to work with torches, setting fire to the homes. The Negroes who ran out of their burning homes were shot down as they fled for the river. For the whites, it was as easy as flushing quail." Gesturing in the opposite direction, he said, "A contingent of Guardsmen formed a line over there, but not to protect the citizens whose homes were being destroyed. No, what they did was fix their bayonets and drive any escaping Negroes back into the hands of the mob. The colored folk who lived here had a choice: burn alive in their homes, be impaled on bayonets, or die in a hail of bullets. Most opted for trying to get past the gunmen. Not many of them succeeded."

I tilted down the brim of my straw boater and ducked my head so my eyes couldn't be seen.

Aubury went on. "The arson spread to other buildings as the mob tried to burn out every single Negro. White gangs ran wild throughout the city, looting and burning any colored homes they found. They even torched the Broadway Opera House when a group of colored people sought refuge there. Everyone inside died as it burned to the ground."

The lawyer started walking back toward Broadway. "The city's firefighters were the only ones who did their jobs that day. The mob threatened to kill them if they put out the fires, but they took the risk and attempted to save whatever homes they could. When their water hoses were cut, the firemen tried to continue with a bucket brigade, but it was hopeless.''

He drew to a stop at Broadway and Fourth. ''By nightfall, the city was lit up from the flames—they could be seen for miles—and the gangs started to gather here, still screaming for blood. Somebody shouted, 'Southern niggers deserve a Southern lynching', and a rope was produced. They found a colored man who'd survived the fires, and strung him up on a telephone pole. The crowd—more than a thousand—started chanting, 'Get a nigger! Get another!' More ropes were found and more Negroes brought in to be lynched. If the ropes were long enough, they hanged them from telephone poles and left the bodies dangling. If the rope was too short to get over a pole, they tied it to a car bumper and dragged their victim to death in the street.'' Aubury's voice was hoarse and fading; it didn't sound like he'd be able to say much more.

As we started walking back to the trolley line, Karl took over the account. ''Nobody knows the final death count. One hundred, two hundred . . . we'll never know for sure. A lot of the bodies were burned beyond recognition, and others had been so mutilated they couldn't be identified. Some of them were dumped en masse in Potter's Field, and many were thrown into Cahokia Creek. There's a fairly accurate count on the property damage though: sixteen blocks and more than two hundred homes burned to the ground.''

''What happened to the people responsible?'' I asked.

Karl answered, ''The county prosecutor claimed that his investigators were unable to find any witnesses to the riot. He also claimed that since the riot reflected 'public sentiment,' it would be impossible to obtain grand jury indictments anyway. Later, the state stepped in, and did obtain indictments and some convictions. Altogether, nine whites were sent to jail—as well as twelve Negroes 'to keep things balanced.' "

Franklin Aubury found his voice again. "When the riot occurred, the colored population was not able to organize any resistance to the mob; it was all they could do to try to get their families away to safety, over the bridge to St. Louis. But as a result of the riot, we now know we cannot rely on law enforcement or the justice system to protect us. And we are prepared in the event that anything like that should start again." Aubury concluded emphatically, "No one is going to be given free rein to kill colored people. There might be a war, but there will not be a massacre."

CHAPTER 8

Franklin Aubury's account of the 1917 East St. Louis riot had left my mind reeling, my stomach queasy, and provided the grist for more than one nightmare. If his intent was to illustrate what an escalation of hostilities could lead to, he'd succeeded. If he wanted to motivate me to look into the Crawford lynching in the hopes of heading off such an escalation, he'd succeeded there as well. But he'd also left me overwhelmed; I had no idea of what to do or where to begin.

It took a couple of days until it hit me that that's exactly what I should be looking for: the starting point. Whether it's a batter charging the pitcher's mound to trigger a bench-clearing brawl, or a politician telling an angry mob that street violence is the solution to their grievance, there's always an *individual* who sets things in motion. I might never identify everyone who was involved in killing Slip Crawford, or learn who tied the noose or who put it around his neck, but maybe I could at least find out who instigated the lynching.

The fact that Crawford had been hanged in the Cubs' ballpark suggested to me that he was killed because of the game with the Elcars. It could have been the Klansmen who'd watched the game, infuriated that he had beaten a white team.

Or Enoch's ballplayers, frustrated that they could do so little against Crawford with their bats.

I decided to try the Elcars first, specifically the one player besides me who might have felt most humiliated by the colored pitcher.

My phone call to the Enoch Motor Car Company was answered by a squeaky-voiced female who relayed the message to Roy Enoch that I wanted to talk with him.

"Can't take more than a hundred off the price," he greeted me. "And that's pretty darned generous, if you ask me. After all, you only played for us once, and you were hardly an asset." I hadn't said a word yet, and Enoch already sounded irritated with me.

"I wasn't calling about the car, Mr. Enoch—but I am still thinking about it. And as far as the game, I know you were expecting a lot from me, and I'm sorry I let you down."

Sounding somewhat mollified, he replied, "Well, truth be told, we weren't expecting all *that* much—Tater Greene told us you were no Babe Ruth."

I was tired of apologizing for my performance, and annoyed to learn that they hadn't thought I'd be much of a help anyway. "Then why did he ask me to play for you?"

"Our regular second baseman got his hand caught in a fan belt. Greene thought you'd be an adequate replacement. He also said you were unlikely to be recognized as a major leaguer, and we figured that on a utility player's salary you could probably use the extra ten bucks."

And to think I'd felt flattered at being recruited. I quickly moved on to the purpose of my call. "I'm interested in one of your other players: J. D. Whalen."

"You won't find him here," Enoch snapped. "And he doesn't play for me anymore."

"I know. Greene told me you fired him. Thing is, I heard

from a fellow I used to play ball with before the war. He's managing a minor-league team in Des Moines, and he's looking for a third baseman. I thought of Whalen; he played a pretty good third base against the Cubs, and since he's out of work now, I thought he might be interested. You know where I could get in touch with him?''

"For one thing, he's not out of work. And for another, I'm not looking to do that snake any favors.''

"Why? What did he do?''

"He—'' Enoch sighed sharply. "Never mind what he did. I'm just glad he's out of here.'' The line was silent for a moment. "Oh, what the hell. I'd just as soon have J. D. living in another state, so go ahead and tell him about the Des Moines job if you want.'' He then transferred me back to his secretary, who gave me the name and address of Whalen's new employer.

J. D. Whalen desperately needed a tailor. The vest of his gray-flannel suit was stretched over his barrel chest, the jacket sleeves were too short for his arms, and the cuffs of his trousers were bunched atop his scuffed oxfords. He also needed a barber; his pasty round face was topped by a full mane of bristly brown hair.

"What can I do for you?'' Whalen asked brightly. The office of Waverly Motors was so tiny that I was almost on top of him, but he showed no sign of remembering me. Of course, all ballplayers look different out of uniform, and I probably wouldn't have recognized him on the street either.

"I thought I could do something for *you*,'' I said.

A look of caution veiled Whalen's dull green eyes.

"Don't worry, I'm not a salesman,'' I said. "Name's Mickey Welch. Played with you against the Cubs a couple weeks back.''

"Oh, sure, second base.'' He stood up from behind his schoolboy-sized desk. "Why don't we step outside? I can use some air."

The office was dense with the smell of oil and exhaust from the adjacent service area, so I readily agreed.

As we walked outside onto the rutted dirt lot at the corner of Waverly Avenue and Thirty-seventh Street in East St. Louis, Whalen called to a burly mechanic, "Clint! I'm takin' five. Get the phone if it rings."

Waverly Motors was a smaller, shabbier version of Enoch's auto dealership. The lot had only a dozen used automobiles for sale, and a single gasoline pump. I had the impression that most of the business was done in the wood-frame garage that still bore signs of its carriage-house origins.

Whalen lit up a cheroot which smelled worse than the fumes inside the building, and tilted back his pug nose to savor the smoke. "What is it you think you can do for me?"

I gave him the same tale about my manager friend in Des Moines needing a third baseman. Whalen looked young enough for the story to be plausible; he was pushing thirty, I estimated, though I couldn't say for sure from which direction.

He look pleased that I'd thought of him, but responded, "Hell, I'm no third baseman. I'm a pitcher."

Every ballplayer in the world thinks he can pitch. From Whalen's relief appearance in the Cubs game, I'd seen little evidence that he could, however. "Guess it doesn't matter, anyway," I said. "I see you already got another job."

Whalen leaned against a 1912 Maxwell that was missing both front fenders. "Ain't a 'job,'" he said. "I'm a partner in this place." He looked proudly at the array of broken-down cars. "Finally got my own business. Mine and Clint's, anyway."

"So you quit Enoch's dealership to start this one? I heard you were ..."

"Fired." He puffed on the cigar. "I was. But I was intending to leave anyway. Enoch just hurried me along. He caught me writing down names and addresses of his customers, and claimed I was 'stealing' from him. Damned old miser. It's not like I was taking money or cars. Anyway, I can build my own business now. We're planning to expand, get some more used cars and maybe a line of new ones. I'm thinking Hudsons—you like Hudsons?''

"Sure. I hear good things about them." I didn't mention that I actually didn't even know how to drive a car. "You know, I thought maybe Enoch let you go because you didn't do so good in that ball game."

Whalen paused to peel a shred of tobacco off his tongue. "I worked for him for five years; he wouldn't have fired me for one game. Hell, if he fired everybody who ever had a bad game, there wouldn't be nobody working there no more."

"It did go pretty bad all the way around," I said. "But it could have been worse—looked like it was gonna turn into a war for a while there. When Crawford brushed you back, and you went out after him, I thought both benches were gonna empty."

"I didn't think about what it might turn into. All I had in mind was bustin' his skull with my bat."

"What made you stop?" I almost said "back down," but "stop" seemed a more diplomatic choice. "It looked like Crawford said something to you."

Whalen tossed down the cigar. "He did. Sonofabitch said 'Sorry, it got away from me.' Took me by surprise, him apologizing like that, and I guess it kind of froze me." He ground out the smoldering cheroot with his heel. "Couldn't charge him again after that, so I went back to hit. Then he froze me again with that goddamn curveball of his, and . . . he beat me."

"He did have a helluva curve," I said.

"Yeah, but by the end of the game I was starting to read it pretty good." Whalen shook his head. "I was real sorry to hear about him getting strung up. I'd have liked to get another shot at him."

It looked like I'd struck out with J. D. Whalen. I had thought that if he'd lost his job because of a poor performance in the ball game, he might have blamed Crawford and wanted to take revenge on him. Or that he might have wanted to kill the pitcher because Crawford had made him look bad after their encounter at the mound. But it sounded like Whalen had the same attitude Tater Greene and I had: You get your revenge on an opponent by beating him the next time.

"Well, good to see you again," I said. "I'll tell my friend in Des Moines you're not available."

Whalen slowly surveyed the seedy lot, looking from the battered cars to the ramshackle garage. "You know, Clint's been doing all right without me so far. I'll bet he could manage on his own for a while longer." He turned to me, his eyes suddenly aglow. "Tell your friend I'm interested in playing ball for him. And tell him I got good experience—played against some top-notch teams when I was pitching for Aluminum Ore. Never got any higher than semipro, but I bet I can hold my own in the minors."

I felt guilty about my ruse. Sometimes I forgot how much an amateur ballplayer will cling to even the slightest hope of making it to pro ball.

After promising Whalen that I'd recommend him to my fictitious friend, I left the car lot. I vowed to myself that I'd call him soon to report that the team had already signed someone else; and, I thought sadly, to snuff out the false hope I'd given him.

Frank Ellerbe's throw from third to second bounced a foot in front of the bag. Marty McManus still should have been able to catch it easily, but the ball handcuffed him, skimming off the heel of his mitt and out to center field. It would have been an error, except that we were only taking pregame practice.

I trotted over to McManus. I thought part of his problem was that, at almost six feet, he was simply too damn tall to be an infielder. Of course I couldn't suggest that he shorten himself, so I was going to offer what I hoped would be more useful advice.

Before I could get a word in, the kid grumbled, "I sure muffed that one."

"It was a tough hop to handle," I said, although it really had been fairly routine. "Here's the thing to remember: A thrown ball is gonna bounce higher than a batted one, so you gotta adjust." I held out my glove, trying to demonstrate the difference in height. "You're gonna get a lot of hops like that, especially when the catcher throws down on a steal."

"Why are they different?"

The answer that came to mind was "Because they are," but I opted to give him a more detailed explanation. "When a batter hits a grounder, he topped it, so it's spinning forward. A thrown ball spins backward. Different spin makes for a different bounce."

"But why?"

What am I, a scientist? "Because it does."

On my way back to the dugout, Lee Fohl cut me off. The former catcher was the strong silent type of manager, who rarely spoke a word to his players. So it came as a surprise when he addressed me. "Helping out McManus there?"

"Doesn't need much help," I said. "The kid's a damn good ballplayer."

"Well, you been making him a better one. Don't think I ain't noticed. And you deserve some playing time of your own. You'll be starting at third for a couple days."

"Thanks. I—" But Fohl was already walking away. This had been about as lengthy a conversation as he ever had.

And it was the best news I'd had all season. I only wished I'd known yesterday so I could have invited Margie to come and watch me play.

The silver-haired waiter placed a steaming dish of chicken fricassee in front of Margie, and served me a plate of roast duck and rice. Pierce House, an intimate restaurant on Euclid Avenue, was noted for excellent food, romantic atmosphere, and courteous service. This waiter was one of the best I'd ever seen; he fawned just enough, without being intrusive. After checking that we had everything we needed, he silently vanished, leaving us to our conversation.

I launched into another report on my three-for-four performance in our win against the Indians. Margie listened as attentively as she had the first couple of times. "Are you sure you can come tomorrow?" I asked.

"I wouldn't miss it," she answered with a smile. "I only hope I don't jinx you. What if you go hitless—will you blame me?"

"Of course not. I'll put the blame where it belongs: on the bat."

Margie laughed and brushed away a lock of hair that had almost fallen into the chicken. "I had a good day, too," she ventured somewhat tentatively.

"What did you do?"

"I went to Washington University; they have a program with City Hospital for training nurses. I know it might sound a little crazy . . . but I'm thinking of enrolling."

It sounded like a splendid idea to me. "What's crazy about it?"

I rarely saw Margie uncertain about anything, but she was now. "I barely finished high school," she said. "And I've never had a serious job. I've always just playacted. In the movies and on the stage, all I did was play. Nursing school is going to be a challenge." Her voice dropped. "And I'm not sure I can do it."

"Are you sure you *want* to?"

Her answer was unequivocal. "Yes."

"Why?"

Margie put down her fork and knife. "Maybe because of all the playing that I've done. It's time for me to do something useful, something that helps people."

"I have no doubt you'll be a terrific nurse," I said. "And I know you'll do just fine in school." I was happy for her that she'd found something she wanted to pursue. I was also encouraged that she intended to stay in St. Louis, and thought it boded well for my plan to settle down together.

As we continued the meal, Margie talked excitedly about the school and the hospital. This year was starting to look awfully promising, I thought, both at home and at the ballpark. With Ken Williams belting home runs almost every day, the Browns were heading into the end of April locked in a tie with the Yankees for first place. And if I kept hitting like I had today, I might be playing third base for quite a while.

The only lingering cause for disquiet was the death of Slip Crawford, and I wondered if I should simply drop that matter. I couldn't be like Karl Landfors, fighting one injustice after another, with always another battle on the horizon. I hadn't wronged anyone, so why should I feel obligated to correct the wrongs of others?

I looked at Margie, and thought that all I wanted to do was play baseball and build a life with her.

When we'd finished the main course, the waiter cleared away the dishes and returned to tell us his suggestions for dessert.

While he waited for us to make our decisions, Margie asked me, "What do you think?"

I promptly answered, "I think we should get married." It

took a moment before I realized that I'd said it aloud, and I felt my face start to burn.

Margie smiled, but didn't reply.

The waiter cleared his throat. "I'll give you a few minutes." Like a ghost, he was gone.

I started to stammer an apology for not asking the right way.

Margie put her hand over mine. "It's the sweetest thing you could have said to me."

I waited for her to utter the word "yes."

A touch of sadness came into her eyes. "And I think it would be wonderful . . . someday."

Someday? What about yes? "Is that a— You mean— Is that a no?"

"It means can we just keep things the way they are for a while longer?"

The waiter returned with several pieces of cake and pie and placed them before us. "Compliments of the chef," he said, "with his best wishes for your happiness." Then he looked at me, and the expression on my face caused him quietly to disappear again.

When I found my voice, I answered Margie's question. "Sure."

I poked at a piece of cheesecake. It had never occurred to me that Margie wouldn't want to marry me. And "someday" sure felt like "no."

I tried to prod her for an explanation, but all she would say was that things were fine the way they were.

We then talked about the dessert, although neither of us did much more than go through the motions of eating.

By the time the waiter came by with the bill, we weren't saying anything at all.

CHAPTER 9

At the plate for Cleveland was Smokey Joe Wood, once my teammate on the 1912 Boston Red Sox. He'd been a pitcher then, with a blazing fastball that earned him thirty-four wins in one of the most spectacular seasons in baseball history. Wood's arm burned out soon after, however, and he converted to a right fielder. Although his pitching arm was long dead, he remained a threat with his bat.

Dixie Davis threw an inside fastball to the former hurler, and Wood ripped it, pulling a hard chopper up the third-base line.

Since I was playing him to pull, I had only to glide over a couple of steps to field the ball. It took a clean bounce, knee-high, easy to catch. Except that I somehow failed to get my glove in the path of the ball.

I still managed to stop it. With a resounding crack, the baseball smacked into my kneecap and bounced toward the coach's box. I felt no pain, only panic and embarrassment at my miscue. I scrambled after the ball, far too late to make a throw to first base. But that didn't stop me from trying. There's some law of nature that if you botch a play with your glove, you have to try to compensate by making a strong throw—

even if the runner is already standing on the base. And there's a second law that virtually guarantees every such throw will end up in the stands. Mine did, passing several feet over George Sisler's extended glove. Joe Wood was awarded second base, and I was credited with two errors on one play.

I'd provided Marty McManus—and three thousand spectators—with a perfect demonstration of what not to do in fielding a ground ball. My head hanging, I tugged and poked at my mitt, trying to find the spot where the hole had opened up to let the ball through.

Lee Fohl shuffled out of the dugout. "Leg okay?"

"Yeah, just let me walk it off." I limped to the outfield grass and back. Pain had started to erupt in my knee, and the joint wasn't bending as easily as it should.

"You want to come out?" the manager asked.

"No." It would have looked like I was being removed for muffing the play. I at least wanted some sympathy from the crowd for playing hurt.

With a 7–1 lead, Fohl decided it was safe to leave me in for the moment, and went back to the dugout. The fans gave me a smattering of pity applause.

I was sure that one of those clapping was Margie, but I avoided looking in the direction of her seat. She was, after all, the reason I blew the play. More so than any flaw in the construction of my glove, at least.

This was the third game I'd been in the starting lineup, and Margie had come to the last two. I'd have preferred that she hadn't. It was difficult enough for me to play baseball with a void in my chest, but with the woman who'd ripped out my heart sitting there watching me, I was barely functional and playing poorly. Which made me angry at myself; I should have been professional enough to forget about personal problems and focus on the ball games.

Those were the thoughts that kept ricocheting around in my head as the game went on.

We continued to run up the score, ending with a 13–2 win that gave us a sweep of the series. Marty McManus contributed a home run. I helped keep the ball game from going too long by grounding into a double play and striking out twice.

Spirits were high in the clubhouse. Word had come that the Yankees had lost to the Philadelphia Athletics, so the Browns were starting the month of May in sole possession of first place.

The team was playing stronger as the season progressed. Pitcher Elam Vangilder, a native of Cape Girardeau, Missouri, who'd had only a 10–12 record last year, was off to a 4–0 start. Ken Williams, already one of the best sluggers in the game, had ended April with an unprecedented nine home runs, earning him a new phonograph in a pregame tribute "because he was making new records." Urban Shocker was pitching as well as expected, and the bats of George Sisler and Baby Doll Jacobson were also helping to power the club.

All of the players took part in the locker-room revelry. Except me. I remained apart from them; not only hadn't I contributed to the success, my thoughts were occupied with other matters. As I lingered in a hot shower, Margie was still on my mind. She'd been extra attentive the past few days, trying to pretend that things hadn't changed between us. They had, though. Although we didn't discuss the subject, the fact that she'd rejected my proposal changed everything—for me, anyway. I had been certain she would say yes—as certain as I was that the Dodgers played in Brooklyn.

I was uncomfortable being with her now. The fact that she was trying to remain close—to "keep things the way they are," as she'd put it—only made me more uneasy. As far as I was concerned, the Browns' upcoming road trip to Detroit couldn't come soon enough.

I finally dressed and met Margie outside. She greeted me with a kiss and a worried expression.

"Sorry it took so long," I said. "Had to ice down the knee."

"It's not broken, is it?" She put her hand in the crook of my arm, and we started toward the trolley.

"Don't think so." It had swollen considerably, and lost much of its flexibility, but didn't seem permanently damaged. "If it's still bad in a couple of days, I'll see a doctor."

"Sure you will." Margie shook her head, knowing full well that I would never go to a doctor as long as I could walk at all. "Well, you should stay off your feet at least. Let's get you home, and I'll put an ice pack on it."

I couldn't bring myself to say so, but I didn't want her to nurse me.

It was almost a relief when I saw Tater Greene approaching. He wore the same rumpled Norfolk jacket that he had when he met me in this same location a little more than three weeks ago.

Greene tipped his tweed cap to Margie, and I made the introductions.

He bobbed up and down on the balls of his feet a few times before asking me, "Can I talk to you a minute? Just us?"

"Yeah, I guess." I excused myself from Margie, who said she didn't mind waiting.

Greene again tipped his cap to her before ushering me a few steps away. His head low and voice hushed, he said, "We got trouble."

"Who does? What kind of trouble?"

"Enoch's cars got trashed last night. Almost every one had its tires slashed, and windows and headlights busted. Most were dented up pretty bad, too—with baseball bats, we figure."

"Sorry to hear it," I said, although I really didn't care about

Roy Enoch's automobile business. "But why are you telling me?"

"It was coloreds that did it. And it was because of Crawford getting killed."

"Hell, Tater, it could have been anyone. How do you know it wasn't J. D. Whalen wanting to get back at Enoch for firing him?"

"It wasn't Whalen. It was a gang. They tied up the night watchman, and he heard them talking."

"And they said they were getting revenge for Crawford?"

"No, but he could tell from their voices they was colored. It must have been because of that pitcher. Why else would they want to smash up the lot?"

Maybe because of that stupid *"Komplete Kar Kare"* slogan on the sign, I thought. Then I realized Greene might have a point: Crawford had been lynched after defeating the Elcars, so it made sense that Enoch's club would be suspected in the killing. And that could make Enoch's business a target for someone angry over Crawford's death.

"Anyway," Greene went on, "we're gonna teach them niggers a lesson. Make damn sure they don't try anything again."

I didn't like where Greene was going with this. "What do you have planned—another lynching?"

"Hey!" He wagged a finger at me. "I told you we didn't have nothing to do with that."

"Who's the 'we'? The team or the Klan?"

"Neither. I mean both." He rubbed his stubbly cheek. "I mean it wasn't the team *or* the Klan that killed Crawford."

"And you know that because . . ."

"Look, I don't mind telling you: I'm in the Klan. And it ain't nothing like what they have in the South. It's a respectable organization up here—no lynching, no branding, none of that crap. I'd have heard about it if there was." He shook his head.

"Hey I'm trying to do you a favor here. Give you a chance to join us."

"The *Klan?* I'm not joining the Ku Klux Klan."

"No, you sap. I told you this don't concern the Klan. This is about the team. We got to stick together—it's a simple matter of self-defense. We're gonna get them for bustin' up the cars. Then they're gonna come after us again. When they do, we all gotta be ready. They could go after any one of us."

"They won't be coming after me," I said. "I only played one game, and it wasn't under my real name." I suddenly remembered the Cubs' catcher, Denver Jones, picking up my bat and reading my name. Okay, so maybe I wasn't as anonymous as I'd have liked, but I still didn't see myself as a target. "Tater, I'm not having anything to do with this."

"But we—"

I cut him off and tried to talk some sense into him. "Why don't you guys just stop it now? Some cars are ruined, but so what? At least nobody got hurt. Leave it be, before somebody does."

From the expression on Greene's face, I might as well have been trying to convince John McGraw not to argue with an umpire.

After a couple more brief exchanges, Greene left, visibly unhappy that I wouldn't be joining the Elcars in whatever mayhem they were planning.

I rejoined Margie and gave her a rundown on the conversation. Then I asked her to wait for me again, because there was somebody else I needed to tell about it.

Back inside the Browns' clubhouse, I placed a call to the home of the writer friend Karl had been staying with since he'd arrived in St. Louis. No answer.

Then I had the operator connect me to the law office of Franklin Aubury. His secretary put my call through immediately, and the lawyer got on the line. "Mr. Rawlings," he said. "A pleasure to hear from you."

"You might not think so when you hear what I called about."

"And that is?"

"Looks like you're right about things getting worse," I said. "Last night, a bunch of cars on Enoch's lot were smashed. They think it was a colored gang getting back for Slip Crawford being killed."

"How unfortunate." Aubury didn't sound particularly sorry to hear the news. Nor did he sound surprised.

"There's more. Enoch's guys are gonna get revenge for that now. Don't know how they're going to find out who busted up the cars, but when they do, they're gonna get 'em."

Aubury said dryly, "I doubt that they'll bother to find out who was truly responsible. They'll simply strike at any colored person who happens to be convenient."

"Well, I just thought you might want to know." I had no idea what he could do with the information, but hoped I'd accomplished something by passing it along. At least it was out of my hands now. Before hanging up, I said, "If you see Karl, or hear from him, could you ask him to give me a call?" There was a different matter I wanted to talk to him about.

"He's here now," Aubury answered. "One moment."

When Karl got on the line, I asked what he was doing there.

"Working on the antilynching bill. I'm trying to get labor endorsements." Karl launched into another one of his speeches, "See, we have plenty of support from Progressives and intellectuals. If we can show support from union members—working-class white people—then we can—"

"She said no, Karl."

"What? Who said—Oh! You mean Margie?"

"Yeah. I proposed and she said no."

"I am sorry to hear that. And surprised. I'd always assumed—"

"So did I. Well, she didn't come out and say no, exactly, just that we should keep things the way they are for a while."

"That's not bad, then!" Karl tried to sound optimistic. "Perhaps she merely wants some time to get accustomed to the idea."

"Could be," I said. "She has been acting real nice, so I don't think it's that she doesn't care for me. Maybe it was the way I asked her—I just blurted out that I thought we should get married. You think maybe I should have got on my knee and all that?"

Karl hemmed and hawed. "I don't know," he finally decided.

"Or do you think maybe she's planning other things that don't include me?" I asked. "She's starting nursing school. Maybe she wants a life of her own."

Karl again said he didn't know. I had to give him credit; that wasn't an admission he made often, and for him to say it twice in the same day was probably a record. Then he suggested, "Why don't you ask her?"

"*Ask her?*" I resisted the impulse to ask him if he was nuts. "No. If she wants to give me a reason, *she* should bring it up."

"So you're going to speculate instead of speaking to the one person who can give you a definitive answer?" Karl sounded like he thought I was the one who was nuts.

"Yeah, that's what I'm gonna do."

After getting off the phone with Karl, I went back outside to Margie.

At the sight of her, I almost did blurt out the question, "Why don't you want to marry me?" Instead I suggested that we get something to eat and then catch the Gloria Swanson double feature playing at the Orpheum.

She agreed, and we went to dinner, where we talked little. Then it was off to the movie theater, where we barely talked at all.

While watching Swanson lounging about in the sort of opulent boudoirs and bathrooms that only existed in Cecil B. DeMille pictures, I did use the time and relative solitude to think.

One of the things I thought about was why my gut was so set against asking Margie directly why she'd turned me down. What I concluded was that I might be afraid to hear her answer. It occurred to me that perhaps the reason she didn't say yes to my proposal had nothing to do with the way I'd asked, or because of any other plans she had. Maybe she simply didn't want me for a husband.

CHAPTER 10

I left Sportsman's Park after Wednesday's game and limped a couple of blocks to LoBrutto's Florist, where I bought a dozen long-stemmed yellow roses. They were Margie's favorite flowers, and her favorite color. I brought her that same arrangement before every road trip; it was one of the many small traditions that we'd shared in the last couple of years.

I thought about that once I'd boarded a Grand Boulevard trolley. I loved the way things had been between Margie and me, and maybe she felt the same way. It could be that she was simply worried marriage would change something that was already pretty terrific. I only wished she would tell me if that was indeed the case; so far, she hadn't volunteered any explanation for declining my proposal.

As the trolley rolled south, Karl's suggestion to ask her directly kept popping into my head. Every time I'd dismiss it as one of his dumber ideas, it would rear itself again. And each time it did, I began more and more to think it made sense. Tonight would be my last night with Margie before the Browns headed to Detroit, and I didn't want to leave town without knowing exactly where things stood between us.

First I fortified myself with more flowers, stopping at a

small shop on Delmar for another dozen roses and a bunch of white carnations. By the time I arrived home, I was feeling optimistic. Maybe it was due to the heady fragrance of the blossoms, but I'd become convinced that romance would prevail.

When I entered the apartment, Margie called from the kitchen, "How's the knee?"

"Okay. Fohl kept me on the bench." Since it was obvious that my bruised knee would keep me out of the lineup, Margie had stayed home from the game.

She came into the parlor, wearing a silk skirt the same color as the roses and an embroidered white blouse. Her hair was in the old-fashioned style that I preferred, like a Gibson girl's, and she was wearing the cameo lavaliere that I'd given her on her last birthday.

Margie's eyes lit up at the sight of the flowers. "Why so many?" There was no indication in her tone that she had any objection to the quantity.

"Well, you know, we're going on the road tomorrow. And . . ." I handed her the paper-wrapped bouquets. "Can we talk for a minute?"

She nodded, and went over to the sofa, cradling the flowers in her arms.

The notion of getting on one knee briefly crossed my mind, but instead I sat next to her. Once again, I hadn't planned what to say. Should I ask her to marry me, or just ask what she thought of my earlier proposal? While I went over the possibilities, Margie bit her lip and waited patiently.

I finally asked, "When you said you wanted to keep things the way they are, did you mean no to getting married? I mean, I know I didn't ask the right way—it wasn't a proper proposal— but I did mean it about wanting to marry you." Damn, I thought, never mind flowers, I should have brought her an engagement ring.

Margie said softly, "There was nothing wrong with the way you asked." She ducked her head slightly. "And I do love you. But I can't get married yet."

"What do you mean you can't?"

"I mean"—her voice caught—"I mean I hope you'll ask me again someday, but I can't say yes right now."

"I don't understand. Why not? What do you mean *can't?*"

She took a deep breath and looked up at me. "I would need to get a divorce first."

If she'd slammed a baseball bat over my head, I couldn't have been more stunned. "You mean you're . . ."

Margie nodded. Tears welled in her eyes. "It wasn't anything serious—"

"You don't think being married is *serious?*" I was rapidly getting angry.

"Yes, of course. But this wasn't—"

I cut her off. "So you have a husband, and you're living with me?"

"No, not a husband. I was—"

"Who is he?"

She put her hand on my arm. "Let me explain."

I pulled my arm away. "Go ahead. Explain."

"It happened when I was in Hollywood. A friend of mine, another actress, was going to Mexico to get married. I went along as maid of honor. Before the ceremony, she and her fiancé suggested that the best man and I get married, too, and make it a double wedding. And we did, but it was just a lark."

"So you and him never . . ."

Margie took a moment to answer. "Like I said, it didn't mean anything. Just one of those crazy things you do sometimes. But it is legal, so I'd have to get a divorce before I could marry you."

"Why didn't you ever mention this?"

"That was years ago. I hardly ever thought about it until the other night."

So I'd been living with a married woman. Whatever the circumstances, I didn't like that fact. "You should have told me."

"I didn't think it—"

"I don't care. You should have told me."

Margie continued to explain and apologize. But I was no longer listening. The only thing that diminished my anger at her was annoyance at myself for taking Karl Landfors's stupid advice.

CHAPTER 11

The last time I'd played in Navin Field, two seasons ago, I'd worn the home uniform of the Detroit Tigers. Now, I sat in the opposing dugout, staring out at my former teammates. In the batting cage was the ferocious Ty Cobb, who last year had assumed the managerial reins while still holding down the center-field job. With him at the helm, some newspapers now referred to the Detroit team as the "Tygers." Behind Cobb were his fellow outfielders Harry Heilmann and Bobby Veach, two of the players who'd been friendliest to me when I was with the club. Warming up along the foul line was Howard Ehmke, slated to pitch against our young left-hander Hub Pruett.

I wouldn't get to do more than look at the Tigers today. Lee Fohl had told me that I would again be idle. He even told me to skip batting and fielding practice until my knee was better. It was just as well, because I wouldn't have been able to concentrate on the game anyway.

My gaze kept drifting from the diamond to a box seat behind the Tigers' dugout. It was the spot where Margie used to sit. Detroit was the city where we'd first started sharing a home.

Marty McManus abruptly blocked the view. "Hey, Mickey, anything tricky about playin' in this park?"

"How the hell should I know?" I snapped.

He blinked. "I thought . . . I mean you used to play here, so I thought you might have some tips."

I shook my head, and he quickly found a spot at the far end of the bench from me.

When the game started, Ty Cobb promptly launched into a sustained verbal assault on Hub Pruett. A week ago, the Tigers had been humiliated when White Sox rookie Charlie Robertson hurled a perfect game against them. Pruett was making his second big-league appearance, and Cobb wanted to make sure the youngster was so off-stride that he wouldn't come close to repeating Robertson's feat.

It worked. Pruett was clearly rattled and gave up two runs in the first inning, while we went hitless.

Before Marty McManus went to the on-deck circle in our half of the second, I walked over to him. "They soak the ground in front of home plate," I said. "It's called Cobb's Lake and it's to help him lay down bunts. Early in the game, a ball will really die in the mud. You might want to try laying one down yourself." It was as close to an apology as I could give him for my earlier behavior.

When McManus followed my advice, and plopped a bunt single, I knew the apology was accepted. The world would make a whole lot more sense, I thought, if women could communicate as well as men did.

I spent the rest of the game thinking about Margie. In two days, I'd found no way to feel better about her deceiving me. No matter how often she repeated that her marriage was merely a weekend lark, I still believed that not telling me about it was the same as lying to me.

It was true that we had never asked each other much about whatever romances might have been in our pasts. But for her to have a *husband*, however nominal, was something important enough that she should have told me.

Maybe I'd see about getting some female companionship after the game, I thought. Why not? It's Friday night, I'm away from home . . . and I'm single.

I didn't find a girl—not that I looked very hard—but I did find a speakeasy on Beaubien Street, near the waterfront. It was no great feat to find a drinking establishment in Detroit; the city almost flowed with illegal booze, ferried across the river from Canada by a small navy of bootleggers. This was better than most, though—clean, well-appointed, with a superb ragtime piano player and an extensive selection of fine liquors.

Usually, I drank nothing stronger than beer, but this night I was in the mood for the hard stuff. I downed shots of Canadian whiskey until almost midnight. That was the team's curfew, and I knew I'd be in trouble if Lee Fohl spotted me coming in late. But I convinced myself that it would be worse to show up drunk than late, and decided to remain in the speakeasy a while longer to give myself time to sober up. Since I continued to sip whiskey while waiting for the earlier drinks to wear off, it turned out to be a losing strategy.

Shortly after two in the morning, I teetered into the expansive lobby of the Statler Hotel, my brain clouded by an alcohol-induced fog. After successfully negotiating my way to the front desk for my room key, I embarked on the long journey across the lobby to the elevator. I'd made it only a few steps before I noticed the Browns' manager in an overstuffed chair, an open newspaper on his lap. I quickly looked to see if there was another route to the elevator. There wasn't; I would have to pass by Fohl. Since he appeared to be dozing, I thought I might have a chance.

Walking as steadily as I could, I worked my way forward, watching where my feet were stepping, and occasionally glancing at Fohl to see if he'd spotted me.

I'd made it halfway across the lobby when I saw that the

manager was on to me. He made a show of checking his pocket watch, then folded the paper and stood up.

In a flash of inspiration, I remembered my bad knee and figured I could use it to disguise any peculiarities in my gait. I promptly tried to affect an exaggerated limp—and almost collapsed on the first step.

Fohl frowned so hard that his eyebrows almost looked like a mustache. I had no idea what he would do to me. The brawny former catcher had such a reputation as a disciplinarian, that I'd never heard of anyone challenging his rules, so I'd never seen what kind of punishment he could mete out.

He waited patiently until I'd reached him, then he blocked my path. "You have trouble telling time, son?"

I opened my mouth to give him an explanation, and saw him wince after I'd only gotten two words out. Damn. I should have taken a mint or something for my breath.

He held up his hand to cut me off. "Don't talk, son. Just listen."

Listening would be the easy part; remaining vertical was the challenging task. I kept shifting to match the way Fohl wobbled in front of me.

The manager's fleshy face relaxed somewhat, but his dark eyes remained stern. "You got a good reputation, kid," he began. "Never been any trouble that I know of, and you're a team player."

"Thanks, Lee. I—"

He held up his hand again. "I'm gonna tell you three things. You better listen, and you better remember."

I nodded, my lips firmly sealed.

"First," he said, "I can smell that you been putting rubbing alcohol on that bum knee."

"It's not—" I cut myself off this time, realizing that he knew full well it wasn't rubbing alcohol he smelled.

"My point is, that ain't gonna help it heal any faster, so I don't ever want to smell it on you again."

I nodded that I understood.

He went on, "Two: When you got a bad leg, don't walk so far from the hotel that you can't get in by curfew. I don't want to see you coming in this late again. If I do, I'm gonna fine you."

I nodded again.

"Three: Whatever that bug is that crawled up your ass, you better get rid of it. You been ornery for days now, and it's gonna end. Get your head back on baseball. Got it?"

I was starting to feel too dizzy to risk nodding again. "Yes," I said meekly.

"Good. Now hit the sack." With that, Fohl spun about and headed for the elevator.

I was grateful that he was giving me a second chance. But I wished he hadn't turned around so fast, because I almost lost my balance from watching him move.

I didn't have another drink for the rest of the time we were in Detroit. In fact, the headache I woke with Saturday morning caused me to swear off anything stronger than ginger ale for the rest of my life—a vow which I fully intended to keep at least until my head cleared up.

I made sure that I arrived early at the ballpark every day and early to the hotel every evening. The only outings I made were to the movie theaters, and only to pictures that didn't involve love stories—I didn't want to be reminded of Margie.

My company for the weekend was limited to my roommate Marty McManus. The lessons I was supposed to give him weren't limited to the playing field. As the veteran, I was also supposed to give him tips on life on the road and warn him of the temptations that were better avoided—like the one I'd succumbed to Friday night. Lately, it seemed that some of the best lessons I was giving McManus were in what not to do.

We dropped two out of three to the Tigers and were packing for the return trip, when I finally called Margie to let her know when my train would be getting into St. Louis. I hadn't phoned her once during the road trip and hadn't returned the several calls she'd made to the hotel.

I apologized for not calling earlier, claiming that McManus kept getting in trouble and I had to keep getting him out of it. She had the graciousness to accept the fib and the apology, and said she was looking forward to my return.

So was I. Because although I'd straightened out my behavior in Detroit, what was bothering me couldn't be remedied until I got back to St. Louis.

CHAPTER 12

There are always fans on hand to greet a ball club when it arrives in a city, especially when the city is the club's hometown. On the road, welcoming committees tend to be small, mostly young ladies willing to provide short-term companionship for visiting ballplayers. Returning home, crowds are larger and predominantly male, with boys seeking autographs and men wanting to get in a few words of encouragement—or criticism, depending on the team's most recent performance.

The Browns' train pulled into St. Louis too late for many boys to still be up, but a dozen or so men were gathered at the end of the platform as we trudged our way, suitcases in hand, into majestic Union Station.

I barely gave the fans a glance. When I first came to the big leagues, I used to search the crowds as eagerly as they looked for the star players; I'd even dawdle and try to look approachable, hoping to be asked for my autograph or have somebody call my name. Not anymore. I was still more than happy to talk with a fan or sign a ball on the rare occasions when I was recognized, but I'd given up on acting like a puppy in a pet-store window.

It wasn't until I was almost upon them that I noticed Tater Greene and a horse-faced man who looked like a smaller, older version of Connie Mack standing at the edge of the crowd.

They appeared to be studying each member of the Browns as he passed by. I tried to hide behind Baby Doll Jacobson, who at six-foot-three and more than two hundred pounds, was probably the largest "Baby Doll" in the world. But he wasn't big enough to keep me out of view.

"Mickey!" Greene called, exposing his stained gums in a smile.

I stopped and grunted hello. At least my unhappiness about Margie had kept my thoughts off the Slip Crawford lynching for a few days. The sight of Tater Greene now brought it freshly to mind.

Greene introduced the man with him. "This is Buddy Vaughn, a good friend of mine."

A ready smile cracked Vaughn's long, craggy face. "Pleasure to meet you, Mr. Rawlings," he said in a soft Southern drawl. "I'm a big baseball fan."

We shook hands, his grip proving stronger than I expected from his appearance. Vaughn's lean build was clothed in a blue-seersucker suit, with a high, tight collar and a small polka-dot bow tie. A fringe of white hair was visible under his Panama hat.

"I hate to impose," Vaughn said, "but do you suppose we could chat for a minute?"

I shifted my suitcase to my other hand. "Wish I could, but I really got to be getting home." My eyes were on Greene, trying to discern what this encounter was about.

"Of course," Vaughn said. "I understand." Then he sighed, and added, "But I sure would be grateful if you could give me just a few moments of your time." He made it sound like his dying request.

What the hell; I wasn't going to learn why they were here from looking at Greene. "All right," I said.

Greene and I followed the older man into the station's magnificent central pavilion. The interior of the hall was as ornate as its castlelike exterior. Frescoes and ornamental moldings decorated the walls, a splendid pictorial window was above the north staircase, and an enormous chandelier, twenty feet across, hung in the center of the arching chamber.

Because of the hour, there were relatively few people in the pavilion. Vaughn pointed to an empty bench near an elaborate marble sculpture. We didn't need to sit if it was really going to be only "a few moments," I thought, but I joined them on the seat.

The three of us had barely sat down when Vaughn turned to Greene. "Say, Tater, I got a hankering for a good cigar. You mind going to see what kind of stogies they have here?" Greene promptly hopped up and headed off to the tobacco stand. "Take your time, son!" Vaughn called after him.

He'd already used up more than a few moments. "Why'd you want to talk to me?" I prompted him.

Vaughn smiled benignly. "First, allow me to complete the introduction. Tater told you my name, but not who I am." He paused for effect. "I'm an officer with the Invisible Empire, Knights of the Ku Klux Klan."

He wasn't invisible enough for my liking. "Like I said, I got to be getting home."

"I'm a kleagle, son."

I had to stifle a laugh, both at his reverential tone—as if "kleagle" was the equivalent of pope—and at the word itself. To me, it sounded like a Klan name for a beagle.

"And," he went on, "it is my pleasure to offer you membership in the Empire. I think you'd enjoy being one of us."

"No," I answered. "I'm sure I wouldn't. Just because I played one baseball game for a team that's owned by a Klansman—and I wouldn't have if I'd known about it—that doesn't mean I believe the same things you do." I was about to let loose and tell this kleagle what I really thought of his organization, but I knew that would accomplish nothing. Instead, I said, "See, the only people I hate are the New York Yankees, and they're about the only group you're *not* against."

Vaughn chuckled good-naturedly. "We don't hate anyone, son. We simply believe that people are happier with their own kind. Prevents ill feelings and keeps life peaceful."

Okay, I couldn't make light of this. "Running around in hoods terrorizing people, burning their homes, lynching them— that's a real peculiar way of keeping things peaceful."

"We don't terrorize anyone," Vaughn said. "We simply have our little ceremonies and rituals same as the Freemasons or Odd Fellows or Elks or any other fraternal organization. If some folks misinterpret our costumes and ceremonies as something sinister, that is not our fault. As for lynching, we're not killers. The Empire has a few hotheads, I admit, but when they get out of hand, we take care of them. You see, we have respectable men among our ranks: ministers, police, judges, doctors, businessmen—and baseball players." He smiled. "You wouldn't be the first big-league ballplayer to join us. And I'll make you the same offer I made the others: We'll waive the ten-dollar klectoken and give you a free membership."

"Why?"

"I'll be honest," Vaughn said. "Because it's an attraction for others who might be interested in joining. Doctors and lawyers are all well and good, but baseball players are *heroes.*"

"I'm not interested in helping you attract more members."

"It's to help yourself, too, son. We don't advocate violence, but we do believe in protecting our own. And that might come in handy for you with the trouble that's brewing in East St. Louis. Like you said, you played for a team sponsored by a Klansman—and that might make you a target for our enemies.

So you might as well join us and enjoy the protection and other benefits that come with membership.''

I was more interested in what he'd said about ballplayers. ''What major leaguers are in the Klan?''

Vaughn smiled. ''You'll find out when you join.''

''If you intend to use ballplayers as drawing cards, you're gonna have to say who they are.''

''All in good time,'' the kleagle answered. ''But for now, I will tell you that one of the biggest stars in St. Louis is a Knight of the Ku Klux Klan. And Tater Greene pointed out a few more of your teammates who might be good candidates.''

I stood. ''Well, it's been real nice talking to you,'' I said facetiously, ''but you're not going to sell me on this.''

He tugged at the sleeve of my jacket, then reached inside his own coat and pulled out a couple of pamphlets. ''Just take a look at these sometime, Mr. Rawlings.'' He put the papers in my pocket. ''Might clear up some of the misapprehensions you have about who we are.''

I knew it would be pointless to argue with him or to tell him what I really thought of his group. ''I'm just not a joiner,'' I said, and walked away.

On my way out of the station, I stopped at the cigar stand where Tater Greene was standing idly. ''You can go back,'' I said. ''He's finished his sales pitch.''

''Sorry, Mickey. This wasn't my idea. Vaughn's all het up on the idea of recruiting ballplayers.''

''What the hell is a 'kleagle' anyway?''

''A salesman, basically. There's a couple hundred of them around the country signing up new members. Buddy Vaughn is one of the important ones, from what I hear. Came in from Evansville a couple days ago to build up membership in the St. Louis area.''

Although Greene and I had never been particularly friendly, I'd always thought he was basically a decent guy, if not a bright one. "What are you doing with these people, Tater? You really believe in what they say?"

"Some of it." He fidgeted uncomfortably. "I go along with the parts I agree with, and I ignore what I don't." Greene smiled weakly. "Kind of like religion, I guess."

I shook my head, at a loss to grasp the attraction of the Klan. "It just doesn't make sense to me, Tater."

"It's good to be part of something," my former teammate tried to explain. "When I was in baseball, I was always part of a team. Once I wasn't in the big leagues no more, I was just me again—and that was the same as being nothin'. I ain't even got a wife or kids." He rubbed his stubbly chin. "You know how I got the name 'Tater'?"

I shook my head no, although I'd assumed it was because his head looked like one.

"A little over a year ago," Greene said, "I was working on a farm, picking sweet potatoes in Georgia. After twelve years as a major leaguer, I wasn't no better than a sharecropper. Then Roy Enoch came through town on a business trip. He saw me play in a pickup game and hired me for his dealership so I could play for him. Now I got a good job, I'm playing baseball . . . and I belong again."

I still didn't understand the appeal of the Ku Klux Klan, but I could sympathize with the desire not to be alone.

For now, at least, I still had somebody to go home to.

I flagged a taxi on Market Street, eager to see Margie again. I still hadn't forgiven her for not telling me about her marital status, but the hurt and anger were no longer as acute.

When I got home and saw her curled up on the sofa, all I felt was affection. Margie was fast asleep, using my old flannel bathrobe as a blanket.

I brushed her hair from her face and kissed her awake.

"What time is it?" she asked sleepily.

"Late. I'm sorry; the train got delayed in Indiana." I didn't mention my meeting with Buddy Vaughn and Tater Greene.

"S'okay." She rubbed the sleep out of her eyes. "How's your knee?"

"Back to normal."

"So you might play tomorrow?" Margie adjusted the robe around her, and I noticed she was wearing only a chemise underneath.

"Huh?"

"Are you playing tomorrow? I'll come to the game if you want."

"Oh, no. I have a feeling Fohl is gonna wait a while before letting me start again." I didn't explain why.

We talked a little while longer. Then, when we were both sufficiently awake, we went to bed and did our utmost to pretend that there wasn't anything wrong between us.

CHAPTER 13

Lee Fohl had to put me in the lineup sooner than I expected. In the fourth inning of Wednesday's game against Boston, Marty McManus got beaned by a Jack Quinn fastball that left him with blurry vision. I was sent in to pinch-run, and immediately proved to Fohl that my knee was fully healed by stealing second and then third before scoring on a Johnny Tobin single.

The rest of the game, a 9–2 rout of the Red Sox, was equally successful; I went 2-for-2 at the plate, including a triple, and made no errors in the field. More importantly, McManus turned out to be all right; by the ninth inning his vision was back to normal, and he complained only of a headache.

In the clubhouse afterward, as we stripped out of our uniforms, I gave McManus some more helpful advice. "Never take a fastball to the head," I told him. "Always jump up so it hits you in the ass instead."

The kid must have still been woozy, because he actually considered that for a moment before he realized I was pulling his leg.

I was about to hit the shower when a high, whiny voice asked, "Excuse me, but can I trouble you for an interview?"

There was Karl Landfors at my elbow, the last person I ever expected to see in a locker room. "What are you doing here?" I asked, too surprised to come up with a more courteous greeting.

Under his breath, he answered, "I need to speak with you."

Must be important for Karl to come into the clubhouse, I thought. His natural environment was a musty library or a museum. Judging by his wrinkled nose and sour expression, the rank locker-room atmosphere wasn't agreeing with him.

"How'd you get in?" I asked.

"I still have newspaper credentials. I came in with the other writers." The usual sportswriters were in the clubhouse talking with the usual stars. How Karl passed for one of them amazed me; credentials or not, he didn't look any more like a sportswriter than he did a baseball player.

I cinched a towel around my waist. "Okay. What's the problem?"

Karl took a notepad from inside his standard black jacket and pretended to be interviewing me. Keeping his voice low, he said, "There's been more trouble in East St. Louis. The home of Denver Jones was burned to the ground. He's the—"

"Cubs' catcher." The fellow who'd picked up my bat. "Is he . . . ?"

"He's fine. The Cubs were on the road, so he wasn't at home. His wife and children were, but they were driven out of the house before it was torched."

"Who did it?"

Karl started to answer, but hesitated when George Sisler came within earshot. Trying to maintain the pretense that he was a sportswriter, Karl asked loudly, "Why don't second basemen play right next to the base the way first and third basemen do?"

Sisler burst out laughing when he heard this. When he could speak again, he asked Karl, "Who the hell do you write for—

the *Ladies' Home Journal?*" Still chuckling, the Browns' first baseman went to the showers.

Karl asked me, "That wasn't a good question?"

"At least you didn't ask how many stitches there are on a baseball." I glanced around to check that no one was in listening range. "So who burned his house? Do you know?"

"A gang of white men wearing pillow cases with eyeholes. There were no burning crosses or KKK insignia."

"Still could have been the Klan," I said. "Or guys working for Enoch who wanted to hit back at somebody for the cars' being damaged."

"That's what we're trying to ascertain," Karl said. "Could you come with me to see Franklin Aubury again?"

"I guess. When?"

"Soon as you have your clothes on."

I agreed. But I left Karl with a warning as I headed to the showers: "Don't try to interview any of the other players."

He agreed on the condition that I later answer his question about second base.

I explained it to him on the trolley down to Compton Hill, a racially mixed neighborhood on St. Louis's near south side. Karl admitted to me that while I was in the shower, he did pass the time by counting the stitches on a baseball, and found there were 108. That discovery virtually doubled the sum total of his baseball knowledge.

When we arrived at the Aubury home, a narrow, two-story redbrick house overlooking Compton Hill Reservoir, Franklin Aubury greeted us at the door. "Thank you for coming," he said. "Sorry to take you so far out of your way, but I decided not to go to the office today; after the news about Denver Jones, I wanted to remain with my family."

Aubury's family consisted of his short, buxom wife Ethel and two pretty daughters, ages about four and six. The girls were clearly enjoying having their father home, and stayed close on his heels.

After the introductions, Ethel said, "Ten minutes till dinner. Hope you're hungry."

While she went back to the kitchen, Aubury led Karl and me into the parlor, the girls following. From the enticing aroma that filled the house, I was glad that we were meeting here instead of at the law office.

We talked about that day's ball game while we waited to be called in to supper. Aubury's younger daughter stayed close to him, playing with his watch fob. The older girl developed a fascination with Karl; to his obvious discomfort, she kept trying to peer up his cavernous nostrils. I egged her on by telling her that he kept spare change in his nose.

Ethel's announcement that dinner was ready came none too soon for Karl. We all filed into the small kitchen and sat down around an oak dining table laden with thick pork chops, baked apples, green leafy vegetables, and pitchers of lemonade and iced tea.

It was rare that I had a family meal, and I enjoyed watching and listening to the interactions of the Auburys. I'd like this for myself someday, I thought, a home with a wife and children. I began to picture myself with Margie and a couple of kids, but the image shattered when I suddenly wondered if maybe she already had children, too, that she hadn't told me about.

"Go on, eat your greens," Ethel said.

I looked up and was relieved to see she was talking to the girls, not me. I was planning to hide as much of the vegetation as I could under the pork bones and apple skins.

"Look at Mr. Rawlings," she went on, trying to convince the girls. "He's a baseball player, and he eats them."

So much for my plans. With the girls' eyes upon me I dug into the greens, and tried to pretend that I liked them. Karl watched also, with great amusement; he knew that popcorn was the closest thing to a vegetable that I would normally eat.

After we'd all cleaned our plates, Franklin Aubury pushed back his chair. "Shall we adjourn to the den, gentlemen?"

I asked Ethel, "Can I help with the dishes?"

She laughed, "Well, there's a first!" More to her husband than to me, she added, "Never heard a man ask to help with dishes in *this* house before. Thank you, Mr. Rawlings, but you all go ahead into the 'den'—and if you find any straight pins, it's because that used to be my sewing room."

Whatever the tiny room was called, it looked like a smaller version of Aubury's law office, and was similarly packed with books and papers. "I do some work here when I'm home," he explained.

There was barely space enough for Karl and me to wedge ourselves into a couple of straight-backed chairs. Aubury half sat, half leaned against a sewing-machine cabinet that served as a desk.

Karl spoke first, "I told Mickey about what happened in Brooklyn."

"Brooklyn?" I asked.

"Not the one with the Dodgers," said Aubury. "It's a village north of East St. Louis, almost entirely Negro, and where Denver Jones and his family *used* to live."

"Franklin and I have been talking," Karl said. "We're wondering if somebody is going after the Cubs' team. Slip Crawford beat the Elcars and he was lynched. Franklin tells me that Jones performed well in that game, and now his home gets burned down—"

Aubury put in, "No doubt he would have been killed, too, had he been there."

"You think somebody's trying to wipe out their entire lineup?" I was skeptical of that notion.

"Do you have another idea?" Karl asked.

Not really, but that didn't stop me from speculating. "Tater Greene told me there was bad blood between the teams for a couple of years. Maybe the attacks are over something that happened a long time ago."

"I suppose that's a possibility," Karl said.

Aubury removed his pince-nez and rubbed the indentations they left on his nose. "A slim one," he said. "Remember, Crawford was never part of the team; he only pitched that one game for them."

I considered the theory that Cubs' players were being targeted because of the game. "If they're going after the best players first," I said, "I can guess who's next on the list: Bell, the center fielder. Fast as lightning."

"Jimmy Bell," said Aubury. "He's actually a pitcher, not an outfielder; he was moved to center for that game because of Slip Crawford being brought in to pitch. The ironic thing is, with Crawford being killed, the St. Louis Stars have signed Bell to take his spot on their pitching staff."

I thought a bit more and decided the idea of the entire Cubs' lineup being knocked off was too far-fetched anyway. "My guess," I said, "is that Jones's house being burned down wasn't part of any big plan. More likely, the Elcars just wanted to get back at somebody for bustin' up their automobiles; they didn't know who was really responsible, so they put the blame on the Cubs."

"I suppose that would be a simpler explanation," said Aubury, and Karl agreed.

It occurred to me that the two of them probably never placed any stock in the other theory; they just wanted to draw me into discussing it—and into getting further involved, no doubt. "What is it you want me to do?" I asked.

Aubury said, "We'd like you to make some further inquiries—about the arson at the Jones house. It may not be clear exactly what the connection is between that incident and Crawford's lynching, but it seems likely that there is *some* relation. Whatever information you can obtain about Jones's home being burned down might also be helpful in solving the Crawford case.''

"The other side's trying to recruit me, too," I said.

"The Elcars?" Aubury asked.

"The Klan." I gave them a report on my encounter with kleagle Buddy Vaughn. "Vaughn didn't come just to talk to me," I added. "He came from Evansville to build up KKK membership in St. Louis."

"Damn," Aubury said. "This is one of the few cities in the Midwest where they haven't been able to establish a foothold. I was hoping it would remain that way."

"I have an idea," said Karl. "Perhaps Mickey should join the Klan. It would be a good way of finding out what they're up to."

I immediately said, "No. I won't do that." Hell, I couldn't even keep my identity secret playing as a ringer in a baseball game; I certainly wasn't going to risk going into the Ku Klux Klan as a spy.

Karl and Aubury both tried to convince me, but I remained adamant. "You know," I said, "I don't even understand what the goal of all this is."

"What do you mean?" asked Aubury.

"Suppose I do learn who burned down Jones's house, or even who killed Crawford. What does that accomplish? Are they going to be arrested? Will they be brought to trial and put in jail?"

Neither Aubury nor Karl answered.

I went on, "If mob action is legal, what's the point of investigating it like it was a crime?"

After a few moments' thought, Aubury said, "I wish we had antilynching statutes. And I wish we had police and prosecutors who would enforce them. But we don't. All we can do for now is attempt to remain informed—and use what information we can garner to try to prevent further violence. Perhaps we can get a warning to an intended victim. Or put one or two of the mob agitators out of commission.'' He didn't specify what he meant by that last sentence, and I wasn't going to ask.

"All right," I decided. "I'll do some more asking around. But I'm *not* joining the Klan."

"Fair enough," said Aubury. "Whatever you can do, and whatever you can learn, will be appreciated." He then squeezed between Karl and me and pulled a short stack of newspapers from a bookshelf. "These might be useful to you. There isn't much about colored issues or colored baseball in the white newspapers. You might want to read these and get some background information."

I saw that the publication was the *St. Louis Argus.* "Thanks," I said. "I'll take a look at them when I get—" Oh, jeez. I'd forgotten to call Margie to tell her I'd be late.

From the fire in her eyes, I could tell that Margie was on the brink of exploding. But she restrained herself, waiting to see if I had a good explanation.

"Sorry I'm late," I said. "I got tied up with Karl and Franklin Aubury."

Her eyes flared a little brighter, suggesting I'd better elaborate.

"Somebody burned down the house of a Cubs' player— he was the catcher in that East St. Louis game. Nobody died, but Karl and Aubury think that was just a matter of luck. They expect there's more trouble coming, and they wanted to talk to me about it."

"All right," Margie said, visibly calmer. "I wish you had called, though."

"I really didn't have a chance. Karl was in such a hurry to tell me, he came right into the clubhouse after the game."

Margie turned toward the kitchen. "Dinner's been ready for a couple of hours. I'll heat it up again, and then we can eat."

"Not for me. Aubury's wife fed us."

She spun back. "You didn't have a chance to call, but you had time to eat? He doesn't have a telephone?"

I realized too late that I should have forced myself to eat a second meal. "I just *forgot*. I'm sorry."

"How could you 'just forget'?"

"It happens sometimes."

"Only lately—like when you were in Detroit."

"What are you so upset about? I'm late for dinner once, and you're mad?"

"That's not it. You've been grouchy for more than a week now."

"Look, I forgot to call. So what? It's not like I forgot to tell you I had a wife somewhere."

Margie took a step backward, staring daggers at me. "I knew you were still mad about that. Tell me now: Are you planning to hold that against me forever?"

"Maybe."

"Fine." Margie went to the sideboard and got her purse and hat. "I'm going to have a peaceful dinner someplace else." She slammed the door behind her.

Let her go, I told myself. If she's going to be irrational, I'd rather have the house to myself anyway.

Grabbing the evening edition of the *St. Louis Times,* I settled into my Morris chair. I proceeded to stare at the paper for ten or fifteen minutes without reading a single word, waiting for a sound at the door. I had assumed Margie would change her mind and come right back. Once again, I'd assumed wrong.

I tossed down the newspaper. Then I glanced at the sideboard, where I'd put the stack of papers Franklin Aubury had given me, and began to review my conversation with Aubury and Karl. I was almost grateful to have something other than my spat with Margie to occupy my mind.

It seemed likely to me that Tater Greene would know something about Denver Jones's home being torched, especially since he'd told me that the Elcars were planning some kind of retaliation for the destruction at the car lot. I decided to give him the impression that I was *sure* he knew something, and went to the telephone.

Greene answered with a grumpy, "Yeah, what?"

"You lied to me, Tater," I said. "You told me you guys aren't involved in violence."

"What do you mean?"

"You know what I mean. Burning down a man's house is violence in my book." Then I fibbed a bit. "After what you and Vaughn told me about the Klan, I was starting to think about joining. But now . . ."

"Hey, it wasn't the Klan," Greene said. "Enoch and Vaughn really *don't* want any violence. This was just some of the boys getting back for the cars being smashed."

"Why Jones?"

"Because it was the Cubs who busted up Enoch's lot."

"You *know* that for a fact?"

"Stands to reason. They thought we killed Crawford—which we didn't—so they hit Enoch's place."

Some reasoning. Franklin Aubury was right, I thought; the Elcars had simply pinned the blame on whoever was most convenient. "But why go after Jones? Why not the others?"

"He's the only one we were able to find out where he lived."

"Does that mean you're still going after other Cubs?"

"Not unless we have to. This should have been enough to teach 'em a lesson."

The we's Greene kept using confirmed he was involved. "You *were* there last night," I said.

"Sure. I *had* to be—you know how it is. But I didn't do nothin'. I just stood by. It's the other fellows who torched the place."

"The 'place' was a home," I said. "His wife and kids were there."

"We got them out first. Didn't hurt 'em a bit." Greene breathed deeply. "Hell, Mickey, I didn't want to be part of anything like this. I even tried to talk the guys into burning down the ballpark instead if they were dead set on burning something, not somebody's home."

"Were the guys who burned Jones's house the same ones who lynched Crawford?"

Greene said firmly, "I told you before, I don't know who was mixed up in that. And I'll tell you something else: We all agreed beforehand that nobody was going to get hurt last night."

"If Jones had been home, he'd have tried to stop you," I said. "Somebody *would* have got hurt. And now his wife and kids don't have a roof over their heads—that's being hurt, too."

"You ever seen them shacks in Brooklyn?" Greene asked. "It wasn't much of a house anyway."

I changed my mind about Tater Greene. I used to believe he was a basically decent man.

I continued to think about Greene after we hung up. Since he admitted being involved in the arson at the Jones house, maybe he was telling the truth when he said he didn't know anything about the Crawford lynching. Then I realized there was one major difference between the two events: Nobody died last night.

* * *

Margie had been gone for a couple of hours. If she only went out for a meal, she should have been back by now, I thought. But I wasn't going to worry about it.

I went into the kitchen for a drink and noticed that the dinner Margie had made was lasagna, one of my favorites. I started to put the dish away in the icebox, then decided to try a plateful. I wasn't at all hungry, but I didn't want her to think that our argument had diminished my appetite any.

Back in the parlor, I picked up the stack of the *Argus*. The newspaper was a slim, weekly publication with the masthead slogan, "Published in the Interest of Colored People." The issues Aubury had given me covered most of the last six months. It was a six-month chronicle of atrocities.

I didn't get past the front pages. A banner headline in the most recent issue read: *Three Men Burned at Stake in Texas*. The three were Negroes accused of assaulting a white woman, and the mob that killed them came from several counties to join in "the fun." The headline of the week before was: *Colored Boy Burned at Stake in GA*. This victim was fifteen years old, and was tortured over a "slow fire" before an enthusiastic crowd of several thousand onlookers; the mob then shot more than two hundred bullets into the boy's body.

A front-page article headed *Bloody Record of the Ku Klux Klan* summarized a number of similar outrages against Negroes. A dentist in Houston was castrated in front of his wife; a man in Dallas was branded with acid spelling out *KKK* on his forehead; and in North Carolina, the United States senator from that state, Lee Overman, along with two congressmen, was among the spectators when three Negro men were hanged by a lynch mob.

I read of numerous incidents of stoning, branding, and tar-and-feathering, mostly in the South. Colored colleges were routinely being set afire, and a church in Texas was dynamited.

Other articles in the *Argus* reported that the Klan was getting more violent as the antilynching bill moved through Congress, as if to demonstrate that they would not be stopped by legislation. Klansmen had also recently adopted burning-at-the-stake as their preferred method of lynching because hanging killed their victims too quickly. The *Argus* dubbed the fire-loving KKK the "Knights of the Kerosene Kan."

There were also front-page editorials condemning "Negroes who ape lawless whites," and urging colored people to work peacefully for passage of the antilynching law instead of retaliating against whites with violence. The St. Louis Board of Aldermen made no similar urging to the city's white population, however, and refused to condemn the Klan.

I was horrified by what I read, and incredulous that there was so little coverage of the atrocities in the major white papers. When I couldn't absorb any more of the horror stories in the *Argus,* I put the papers away. Maybe that's why the white papers didn't print the stories, I realized; people might get upset if they read them.

Then I went over to my desk and pulled out the pamphlets Buddy Vaughn had given me. They portrayed the Ku Klux Klan as a patriotic group in favor of the Bible, Prohibition, purity of womanhood, and "100 percent Americanism." The organization was opposed to "bootleggers, gamblers, and moral degenerates." These innocuous generalities sounded like they could have been put out by the Women's Christian Temperance Union. What a difference between what the Klan claimed and what they actually did, I thought.

I was startled when the front door opened, and Margie came in. I quickly hid the pamphlets under a *Sporting News;* I didn't even want to be seen reading Klan literature.

But I needn't have worried. Margie barely gave me a glance.

"How was dinner?" I asked.

"Fine." She stalked off to the bedroom without another word.

I stayed up a little longer, and briefly debated whether I should sleep on the sofa. I opted for the bed, though. There'd be plenty of space, I knew, especially between Margie and me.

CHAPTER 14

There was even more space when I woke up in the morning. Margie's side of the bed was empty. I felt reassured when I heard her moving about in the kitchen; at least she was still in the house.

I groggily remembered our argument of yesterday, although the reasoning behind it escaped me. The aroma of brewing coffee sparked some life in my brain, but even with my head clearer, I couldn't grasp exactly what Margie and I had been angry about. As I listened to the sizzle of frying bacon, a hunger stirred my stomach. Then I realized I might have to end up making my own breakfast; just because Margie was cooking didn't mean she was cooking for both of us.

I pulled my robe around me and shuffled into the kitchen. Margie shot me a look, and a curt, "Good morning."

"Morning." I could be just as terse as she.

I continued on to the bathroom. When I got back, I saw she'd set two cups of coffee and two plates of eggs and bacon on the table. At least we'd be having breakfast together.

As we sat down, I said, "Sorry about yesterday."

"Me too," she replied.

Neither of us had much conviction in our voices, though, and we began eating in silence.

I broke first. I gave Margie a report on my meeting with Franklin Aubury and Karl Landfors. "It doesn't look like things are going to blow over peacefully," I concluded.

"Thank heaven no one was killed in the fire, at least," Margie said.

"Not this time." I poked at the eggs with my fork, breaking the yolks. "But there'll be more."

"Is that what Karl thinks?"

I nodded. "And Aubury." My talk with Tater Greene had also left me convinced that should there be any retaliation for the arson, the Elcars would strike again, even harder. "I'm going to do whatever I can to try to stop anything else from happening."

"You think you can?"

Realistically, no, I had to admit to myself. "Maybe not *stop* it," I said. "But slow it down some. I hope." I looked at Margie. "I gotta try anyway."

"Why?"

There were several reasons. One was that I'd read in the *Argus* to what horrific extremes the violence could escalate. I briefly considered showing the articles to Margie, but decided against it; the way they'd remained in my mind, I knew she would be even more upset by them. Besides, maybe it wasn't what I read about incidents in Texas or North Carolina that affected me. I had the feeling it was more because I'd looked into the faces of Slip Crawford and Denver Jones, and had imagined them in every story I'd read. "I just have to," I said.

"This isn't like anything you've been involved in before," Margie said. "You'd be up against a *lot* of people—not only those who might have been part of the mob, but those who sympathize with them."

"I'll drop it if I think I'm in too deep, or if I'm not getting anywhere."

Margie rolled her eyes; she knew me better than to believe my last statement. Then she offered, "I'll help—if you like."

"No." My answer came out sharper than I'd intended.

She tried again. "I think I know a way to get some information that you might not have—"

"No. Like you said, this is going to be tougher than anything before." I thought again of the atrocities the Klan committed. Even though they claimed to be protectors of womanhood, I had little doubt that anyone who opposed them, of either gender, would feel their wrath.

Margie pushed her half-eaten meal aside. She wasn't happy at my reaction to her offer. "Maybe there are other things for you to be paying some attention to."

I knew full well what she meant, but I asked, "Like what?"

"Like the problem we've been having. I think we should talk about it."

I dug into the eggs, as if to show that I was too occupied to talk right then. "Okay," I said. "Maybe later."

"Why not now?"

"I don't want to right now."

"Things can't continue the way they are," she said. "And the sooner we . . ." Her voice trailed off when she saw me shaking my head no. "Excuse me." She got up from the table.

"Where are you going?"

"To get dressed. I have an appointment at the nursing school."

"Are you still going to enroll?"

"I don't know," she muttered as she went into the bedroom.

I guess she didn't want to talk after all.

After Margie left, I was tempted to try to get a bit more sleep before going to the ballpark. I'd had little rest during the night; my thoughts kept bouncing around from the argument with Margie to the stories I'd read of Klan brutality to the recent violence in East St. Louis. I didn't get anywhere trying to figure out what was going on with Margie and me, but I did have an idea about Slip Crawford's death.

Instead of going back to bed, I took a long shower, then called Franklin Aubury. He was back at his office, and I made an appointment to meet him there after the game.

I got there a little after four o'clock. To my disappointment, Aubury didn't ask how the game went; I was eager to tell somebody that I'd hit two doubles while filling in for Marty McManus.

"Karl couldn't be here," the lawyer said. "He's been detained in a meeting at Congressman Dyer's office."

"That's all right," I said. Karl wouldn't have thought to ask me about the game either. "I read those newspapers you gave me, and I had a couple of ideas."

A hint of a smile indicated Aubury was pleased that I'd already read them.

"There's a difference," I began, "between the lynchings and violence in the South and what's been going on here. In most cases, the Klan is open about what they do—not open about who they are under the hoods, but about the fact that the Klan is behind the lynchings. They even brand some of their victims with 'KKK,' like signing their work. They *want* people to know it's them, don't they? To show how powerful they are?"

Aubury nodded.

"But here, even if some of the men involved in lynching Slip Crawford and burning Jones's house are *in* the Klan, they don't want anyone to think it was done *by* the Klan."

Aubury's eyebrows arched above the rims of his glasses. "Do you know something about who was responsible for burning down Denver Jones's home?"

"Yes, I talked to one of them last night." I didn't give Tater Greene's name. "He tells me it wasn't officially a Klan activity. This was a bunch of guys who blamed the Cubs for damaging Enoch's cars, so they wanted to hit back at a Cub player."

"Not *officially* a Klan activity," Aubury said. "They publicly disavow violence, but secretly encourage it."

"I don't know. The fellow I talked to said the local Klan leaders gave strict orders not to do anything violent."

"If so, that's only for the time being. Most likely they want to keep their reputation 'clean' until their membership has increased. Then, when they have police officers and potential jurors as members, they can commit whatever crimes they wish to with impunity." Aubury removed his pince-nez. "Did your friend tell you anything about the Crawford lynching?"

"He's not a 'friend,'" I corrected. "He says he wasn't there when Crawford was killed and doesn't know anything about it."

"Do you believe him?"

"I'm not sure. I *think* he told me the truth, but I wouldn't bet my life on it." As I said it, I told myself that was probably something I should keep in mind. "Anyway, since the Klan is publicly claiming they're not behind the violence—and for now they are telling their members to keep things peaceful, according to my contact—then maybe they really *weren't* behind the Crawford lynching."

"You think it was the Elcars' players, then?"

"Could be. But I expect most of them are in the Klan. I don't think they'd risk getting their leaders mad at them by doing anything that could be pinned on the Klan. And they had to know the KKK would be suspected in the lynching, even if it wasn't officially a Klan action."

"Then what *do* you think?"

"Maybe it was somebody who wanted to murder Slip Crawford for a personal reason. And he figured by making it look like a lynching, he could get away with it.''

"You mean to say you believe *one* person killed him and staged it to look like a lynching?"

I considered that for a moment; from the circumstances, I doubted that one person could have handled Crawford alone. "I guess it had to be more than one."

"So several people wanted to murder him and collaborated on it?"

That didn't make much sense either. "Or," I said, "one person got a mob incited against Crawford and basically used the mob as a murder weapon."

"With all respect," Aubury said, "perhaps you simply *want* to believe that there has to be a *motive* for Crawford to have been killed. That's not the way it is. I've lived my whole life knowing that a colored man can be beaten or killed because some white men don't care for his pigmentation."

I couldn't argue with Aubury's experience, but the news reports did support my belief. "From what I read in the *Argus,*" I said, "there usually was some reason given for what the Klan did, even if it was a piss-poor one." Most often, the justification was that their Negro victim was suspected of insulting or assaulting a white woman.

"That's true," Aubury said. "But I don't know what cause there could have been for killing Slip Crawford, other than the fact that he'd won a game from a white team."

I asked Aubury what else he knew about the dead pitcher. He told me that Crawford had a wife Hannah who owned a hair salon in St. Louis, and that the two of them were among the many who'd crossed to this side of the Mississippi after the East St. Louis riot. Most of what he knew about Crawford involved his baseball career.

Maybe I should find out more about Crawford, I thought.

"I'd like to talk to some of his teammates on the Stars," I said. "Maybe they'd know if somebody had a quarrel with him."

"They won't be in town for some time," Aubury said.

"Hasn't their season started yet?"

"If you'd read the sports pages of the *Argus,* you'd know that they're playing the first two months on the road."

"I didn't get past the front pages," I admitted.

From the satisfied expression on Aubury's face, I had the feeling he'd given me the papers primarily to learn about the atrocities, not about colored baseball. "This is the Stars' first season," he explained, "and they don't have a home ballpark yet. Ground was broken last week, but it won't be ready until the end of June."

I was still thinking of the stories I'd read, and they gave me an idea. "For whatever reason, the Klan wants to pretend they're not violent, right?"

Aubury nodded.

"Why? Because people won't join if they think the KKK is about killing and torturing. So they keep quiet about that and try to present themselves as some kind of patriotic society."

He nodded again.

"Then why don't we get some stories into the local papers— the, uh, white papers—saying that the Klan is suspected in Crawford's death and the house-burning."

"And what will that accomplish?"

"Maybe they'll crack down on their members to keep them from doing anything more for a while." I wished Karl was there; he knew the newspaper business. "I'll bet Karl has contacts he can use to plant some stories," I said.

"What about your earlier theory—that the Klan *wasn't* involved? That would make the planted stories lies."

"I'm not worried about giving the Klan a bad name," I said.

Judging from their literature, they didn't care about presenting themselves accurately, so why should we?

Aubury flashed a smile. Even though he was an attorney, I don't think he was worried about libeling the Ku Klux Klan either.

CHAPTER 15

I didn't think it was possible, but over the next day and a half, things between Margie and me only got worse. We barely spoke, barely even acknowledged each other's presence.

When I awoke in an empty bed Saturday morning, there was no aroma of breakfast in the air, just the same chilly atmosphere that had permeated the apartment for the last several days.

I heard Margie moving around, but the sounds weren't the usual. I propped myself up on my elbows and listened closely. There was no clatter of kitchen utensils, no running water in the bathroom. The noises were coming from the parlor.

Glancing around the bedroom, I saw a wide gap on her side of the clothes closet. Her nightclothes and robe weren't on the corner chair where they usually lay either.

I got up and quietly walked to the parlor doorway. Margie was packing an oversize leather trunk and a canvas satchel with clothes. I stood for a few moments, watching. To my surprise, I was more relieved than upset. Then she looked up at me with red, swollen eyes. And I immediately felt guilty that I *wasn't* upset by her leaving.

Margie put down the middy blouse she'd been folding. In

a hoarse whisper, she said, "I think we need to be apart for a while."

"Yeah, I guess that's probably a good idea."

Margie looked as if I'd stabbed her, and I realized that I'd agreed too promptly. She started crying in ragged sobs.

I rushed over and tried to put my arms around her. "I didn't mean—"

She stepped back. "Get away from me."

I stopped in my tracks. What do I do now? Stand here and watch her cry? That seemed cruel, somehow. Go to the kitchen and brew some coffee? No, too callous.

While I debated with myself, Margie got her tears under control, blew her nose, and waved me away. "Go get dressed or something."

I did as she said. While I put my clothes on, I overheard Margie call a cab company for a taxi. She didn't give a destination.

Fully dressed, I went back to the parlor, where Margie had resumed packing. "Where are you going?" I asked.

"I'm not sure."

"When are you coming back?"

"I don't know."

I almost asked, "*Are* you coming back?" but I knew she had a lot more stuff still in the apartment. She'd at least have to come back to get it all.

Margie had finished fastening the suitcase straps when a cab pulled up in front of the apartment. I wasn't sure if I should offer to carry the luggage for her—if I did, it might give the impression that I was eager for her to go.

Fortunately, the driver came to the door and took the bags to his Model T.

Margie pinned a small straw bonnet over her hair. "I'm sorry about . . . everything." She choked down a sob.

"Me too."

I went over to her again; this time she didn't back away. We hugged tight and long, and she kissed me, leaving my cheek moist from fresh tears. Then she left.

The cab probably hadn't gotten more than two blocks before I changed my mind about her leaving. I suddenly did *not* think it was a good idea anymore.

I hoped Margie would come to the same conclusion just as quickly. I even held off taking my morning bath, so that I could greet her at the door.

I kept waiting until I had to leave for Sportsman's Park. And, as I walked out of the apartment, I realized that Margie didn't need to come back for the rest of her things—she could simply send for them.

This morning might have been the last time I would ever see her.

After the game, I hurried back to Union Boulevard to find that what yesterday had been a home was now only an apartment. Margie hadn't returned.

I paced around for more than an hour, listening to the telephone not ring and watching the front door not open. My eyes noted everything of Margie's: the bronze mantel clock, her collection of old photographs on the wall, the silver candlesticks, and a dozen decorative knickknacks. At first, I found their presence comforting; Margie would have to contact me again even if only to have them shipped to her. But soon they only served as reminders of her, reminders that she'd gone.

I got a wooden crate from the back porch, and went through the parlor, taking down everything of Margie's. I put the filled crate in the closet, and even wheeled her Victrola into the pantry.

With nothing of hers visible in the parlor, I settled into my Morris chair with a ginger ale and the latest *Police Gazette* to enjoy the solitude. But the soft drink proved to be tasteless, the magazine merely smudges of ink, and the room was stark and lonely.

I had an impulse to go out somewhere, if only to a picture show, but didn't want to miss Margie in case she did come back.

As a last resort, I called Karl Landfors.

"Karl," I said when he got on the line, "I know it's short notice, but you want to come over for dinner tonight?"

"I wish I could," he said, "but I'm writing a piece for *McClure's*. I need to have it in by Wednesday."

"You got plenty of time, then. Take a break."

"Well . . . I haven't eaten yet. So I suppose I could—"

"Great! How soon can you be here?"

"Half an hour. Less if Margie doesn't mind dirty shirt cuffs."

"She won't mind. She's not here anymore."

"What?"

"Margie left this morning."

"Why? What happened?"

"We've been arguing some." I tried hard to sound indifferent. "But that's okay, doesn't matter. Oh—could you do me a favor, Karl?"

"Sure. What is it?"

"Bring dinner. And some beer."

When the taxi pulled up, I thought for a moment it might be Margie returning. It was Karl, lugging a bundle of groceries and a bucket of illegal beer.

When I let him in, Karl looked quizzically around the parlor. "What happened?"

"I put away some stuff that was cluttering up the place."

He handed me the bucket. "I meant what happened with Margie."

"I told you. She left."

Karl hung his derby on the hat rack and followed me into the kitchen. "What happened *before* she left, you dolt."

"Oh, she was mad that I didn't call her when I went with you to Aubury's house."

"I suspect there was more to it than that."

"Then you'll have to ask *her*. Damned if I know why she was acting the way she was." I unpacked the grocery bag, happy to see that Karl shared my notion of what constituted a balanced meal: Swiss cheese, boiled ham, and a loaf of bread. From the icebox, I added a jar of mustard and half an apple pie to the dinner spread.

We sat down and began to eat, Karl washing his sandwich down with Moxie, and me quaffing beer.

Karl refrained from asking more questions, but when he finished his first sandwich, he said, "I always thought you two were meant for each other."

"Looks like you were wrong." I pushed my plate away. "And so was I, because I thought the same thing."

"Perhaps she'll—"

I cut him off, "I'm just glad I found out now instead of later." Pouring another glass of beer, I asked, "What's the story you're writing about?" The best way to divert Karl was to give him a chance to make a speech.

He obliged, telling me every detail of his article on the status of the antilynching legislation.

Although I found his discourse less than riveting, I did marvel at his passion for the issue. "How do you do it, Karl?" I asked. "Ever since I've known you, you've been fighting battles—against sweatshops, for the suffrage amendment, in defense of Sacco and Vanzetti, and now for this antilynching law. You hardly ever win, and even when you do, you just go on to another fight. Where the hell do you get the energy?"

He pushed up his glasses. "It's the battle that counts, not winning or losing. Take this bill, for example. Even if it never becomes law, the struggle to pass it will accomplish a great deal—by focusing national attention on a problem, exposing the Klan's activities, getting public leaders to speak out against lynchings. Of course, if it does pass, that won't be sufficient to solve the problem, either; there would still be a struggle to get the law enforced and have violators prosecuted and convicted." He shrugged his bony shoulders. "So I have to keep fighting because the battles never end."

"Don't you ever get tired? Don't you ever want to forget about changing things, and just make things as good as you can for yourself? At least relax a while?"

"Sometimes," Karl admitted grudgingly, as if it was a sign of moral weakness. "But then I learn about a problem that makes me want to fight on. Not to solve something necessarily, but to fight for something."

One of the things that amazed me was that he could fight so hard for things that would never benefit him personally. "You ever feel like an outsider?" I asked. "Like with this law—it's mostly colored people working on it, right?"

"Yes, but should I stay out of it because I'm white?"

"No, that's not what I mean." I wasn't sure how to explain what I meant. "They know it will help them, but how do they know what your interest in it is? You're not one of them, so do you think they trust you?"

"I'd like to believe that anyone who gets to know me comes to trust me. It's true that some might initially be skeptical or suspicious of my motives, but eventually . . ." His brow furrowed. "To tell you the truth, I don't know how accepted I am. I think Franklin Aubury accepts me and trusts me—I've certainly never given him cause not to—but you can never know for sure what's in someone else's heart."

We talked about the Crawford lynching, and the Klan, then about Prohibition. We kept talking into the night. Margie's departure didn't come up again, but Karl seemed to catch on that I didn't want to be by myself. He eventually said he was too tired to go back home and asked to spend the night on the sofa.

I went to bed, grateful that Karl had come over, but I'd have preferred that Margie Turner was with me instead.

Even when I knew I wasn't going to be in the starting lineup, I was always among the first to arrive at the park. Sometimes I showed up more than an hour before any of the other players. In ballparks of both leagues, I'd coaxed ushers into playing catch with me, groundskeepers into throwing me extra batting practice, and peanut vendors into shagging fly balls. I needed all the extra practice I could get, but more than that I simply loved being on a major-league baseball field.

In the days after Margie left, though, I spent every moment I could at home. I barely made it to the park in time to suit up, and was the first player to leave once the games were over. Not that there was a reason to remain at home—Margie didn't contact me once.

By the time I got to Sportsman's Park Tuesday, most of the other Browns were already on the field. I tossed my boater onto the locker shelf and was in a battle with the knot of my necktie when Lee Fohl bellowed to me from his office.

It wasn't much of an office—a baseball manager doesn't exactly have a whole lot of paperwork to do—and I barely fit inside.

"Close the door," Fohl said.

Jeez. I'm being released. Nobody tells you to close the door when it's good news. The manager's sagging face looked even droopier than usual, another sign that all wasn't well.

"Sorry I been coming late the last couple of days," I said. "But I—"

"It's not that." Fohl picked up a couple of baseballs and began rolling them around in his huge paw. "I've been told that three days before the season started, you played with a semipro club in East St. Louis. That true?''

I answered promptly, ''Yes. But I didn't take any money for it. I just wanted some game practice to be ready for the season.''

Fohl kept his eyes on the horsehides. ''I know you weren't getting much playing time, and I can understand you wantin' to get in a game. But the point is, you knew you weren't supposed to. Isn't that right?''

''Yes.''

''And, whether you played or not, you were well compensated. You didn't play an inning in the exhibition series with the Cards, but Mr. Ball still gave you the same hundred-buck bonus he gave everybody else.''

I bit back the impulse to say that I'd have paid the Browns' owner a hundred dollars to let me play. Silently, I waited to hear my punishment. Fohl still wouldn't look at me, so I had the feeling it was going to be severe.

''I'm gonna have to suspend you,'' he finally said. ''Fifteen days.''

I was actually relieved to hear that I was still with the club.

''Ruth got a thirty-day suspension,'' the manager went on, ''so you're getting off light. And it's because I *like* the fact that you're so eager to play.''

At least I finally have something in common with Babe Ruth, I thought. Then I remembered that the Babe's suspension had come from Commissioner Landis. ''Am I being suspended by the team, or by Landis?'' I asked.

''By Mr. Ball. But we had to run it past the commissioner. Especially since the team you played against was colored.''

''That matters?''

''Not to me, it don't. But it sure does to Landis. He won't say so publicly, but he don't want major leaguers playing against coloreds—makes us look bad when we lose. He's probably gonna issue some rules on it later this year. Anyway, that's why we made it fifteen days—any less and he might have tacked on a lot more. As it is, he figures we're handling it okay, so he won't take any further action.''

"If you don't mind me asking," I said, "how did you find out I played in East St. Louis?"

"I heard from Mr. Ball. Don't know how he heard about it."

Enough people knew about me playing with the Elcars, I thought, that it could have been almost anyone involved in that game. "When's the suspension start?"

Fohl put down the baseballs with a thump. "Already has. Go home."

As I went back to my locker for my hat and coat, I thought at least now I could spend twenty-four hours a day waiting for Margie to come back.

CHAPTER 16

The Capital Theatre on Chestnut Street was almost empty Thursday afternoon. Most people were at work, and those with the day off were probably at Sportsman's Park watching the Browns play the Philadelphia Athletics. I was among the handful sitting in the dark watching Douglas Fairbanks cavort about in *Robin Hood*.

Soon after Lee Fohl gave me the opportunity to spend all my time at home, I found I couldn't stand to be there. For the last two days, I'd been avoiding the apartment, spending most of my time in moving-picture theaters and living on popcorn and ginger ale.

The movies were a mental escape for me, a way to avoid thinking about Margie or the Browns. They'd both abandoned me, so why shouldn't I purge them from my thoughts? Unfortunately, without Margie or baseball, there wasn't much left in my life. So I watched the shadow lives of celluloid characters whose problems were always happily resolved in the final reel. I'd seen *Foolish Wives, Orphans of the Storm,* and the latest Buster Keaton and Harold Lloyd comedies. They were a distraction, but reality kept nagging at me from the recesses of my brain.

All of a sudden, while Fairbanks dueled the Sheriff of Nottingham, I decided I'd had enough of watching people who didn't exist. It was time to do like Karl Landfors, and get back in the fight, back to trying to find out who killed Slip Crawford and why.

At least, with my present situation, I was freer to do so. The question, once again, was where to start.

I decided to concentrate on the possibility that the lynching could have been a cover for murder. That meant find a motive. I had to talk to people who knew Crawford and find out who might have had a grudge against him.

The first person I thought I should speak with was Crawford's widow Hannah. But I didn't know what to say to her—"Excuse me, ma'am, but do you know why anyone would want to kill your husband?" Maybe I should start with Crawford's teammates from the St. Louis Stars or the Indianapolis ABCs. Often teammates know a player better than his family does. But the Stars were on the road and wouldn't be back for more than a month.

I was stuck for a plan to learn about Slip Crawford, but I did have an idea for getting more information on the Klan's possible role in his death. It was time for another visit to East St. Louis.

Morning sunshine glinted off the shiny new automobiles on the lot of the Enoch Motor Car Company. It was a different selection from what I'd seen last time, with many new ones to replace the cars that had been vandalized.

Brian Padgett looked the same; the little shortstop was again dressed like a vaudeville comic. He was outside the sales office, with a pretty young lady in an ankle-length summer frock. Her flaming red hair was brighter than any of the automobiles, and she held a lacy parasol to protect her fair skin from the sun. From the way she and Padgett were talking and laughing together, I assumed she was the Doreen that Tater Greene had mentioned. Whoever she was, Padgett was certainly intent on impressing her—he kept trying to lift the rear end of an Auburn roadster, undeterred by repeated failures.

"Can I help you, sir?" Another salesman, older and more tastefully dressed than Padgett, had come up behind me.

"Just looking, thanks."

"We have quite a few new models just in. I'm sure we could put you behind the wheel of exactly the right—"

"Hey!" Padgett yelled, as he came running over. "This is *my* customer," he said to the other salesman. "You better not even think about poaching."

"I didn't know he was yours. Besides, you're on lunch."

"Well, now *you're* on lunch."

"Fine by me." The other salesman threw up his hands and walked to the office, shaking his head.

"Pushy sonofabitch," Padgett muttered.

I thought Padgett the pushy one. "You're sure devoted to your job," I said. "If I was you, I'd have stayed with her." I nodded toward Doreen. "She's a pretty girl."

"Yeah, she sure is." From the grin on his face, I could tell he was thoroughly smitten by her. "But don't get any ideas," he added. "She's spoken for."

"I wasn't thinking anything. Besides I have a—" I remembered that, no, I didn't anymore.

Padgett launched into his sales pitch. "That Hupmobile you were interested in is gone. Coloreds came and busted up most of the cars on the lot. We could have had them refurbished, but we only sell the best. Speaking of which, let me show you a choice Essex Coach we just got in."

As he led me to the green-and-black sedan, I said, "Damn shame somebody would destroy fine automobiles like that."

"That's how them niggers are. Don't got no appreciation for property."

"At least you got back for what they did," I said. "I hear Denver Jones's house got burned down."

Padgett smiled. "Yeah, I heard the same thing."

"That's why I'm here."

A scowl darkened his face. "I thought you wanted a car."

"Oh, I do. But I also wanted to find out about this trouble with the Cubs. I mean, what if they do something now to get back for Jones's house being burned?"

"We'll take care of ourselves."

"I hope so, because I might want to be part of that 'we.' Buddy Vaughn asked me to join the Klan. He says we all got to stick together."

Padgett tilted back his porkpie hat. "For one thing, I didn't hear nothin' about the Klan being involved in torching Jones's place. Was probably just a group of concerned citizens. But why you asking me?"

"It's no secret that most of the guys here are Klansmen," I said. "And I'm starting to think joining might not be a bad idea. Jones just caused me some trouble, too, and if there's any more coming, I don't want to be on my own."

"What'd he do?"

I didn't believe that it was the catcher who'd told the Browns about me—more likely it was the Klan wanting to pressure me to join—but I said, "My name's Mickey Rawlings, not Welch. I play for the Browns. When I played for you guys, I used my own bat, and Jones saw my real name. A few days ago, *somebody* told the Browns about me playing as a ringer, and now I'm suspended."

Padgett shook his head sympathetically.

I went on, *"I* didn't have nothing to do with burning his house, so why'd he have to do that to me? Anyway, like I said, if there's gonna be any more trouble, I'd rather have some friends on my side."

Padgett's eyes suddenly lit up. "Hey, what am I doing

showing you an Essex? A big-league ballplayer should go first-class. We got a Paige 6-44 over here, a five-passenger touring car—more than you ever wanted in an automobile."

"And you get more of a commission?" I ribbed him.

He laughed. "I can use it. Saving up to get married."

It bothered me to hear that; not long ago, I had assumed that I would be in the same circumstance.

As we walked across the lot, I returned to the topic of the Ku Klux Klan. "At first I was bothered by what I read about the Klan being violent," I said. "But I'm all in favor of self-defense. Sometimes you *got* to make a show of strength."

"Exactly!" Padgett clapped me on the shoulder. "Don't know why some people can't seem to understand that. If somebody's acting up, you got to send him a message he'll understand—and you got to make it convincing enough that he won't try to answer back."

"*How* convincing?" I asked. "Self-defense is one thing, but I don't want to get mixed up in anything like the Crawford lynching. I'm not going to kill anybody over a ball game."

"Hell," Padgett scoffed. "I don't know *anybody* who'd kill over a game. And I never heard nothing about the Klan being behind the Crawford hanging anyway." He smiled. "I don't mind admitting I'm a member. I'm *proud* to be a Knight of the Ku Klux Klan. And you'll be, too, if you join us." He then went on to point out the features of the Paige—leather upholstery, cord tires, and a six-cylinder engine that could go from five to twenty-five miles an hour in nine seconds flat.

I found myself getting tempted by the luxury automobile. A shiny new car might be just the thing to cheer me up—even though the $1,495 price would set me back about half a year's salary.

Padgett said, "Tell you what: It's a beautiful day for a drive. Why don't you take her out for a test spin? See what fifty horsepower *feels* like."

Too embarrassed to admit that I didn't know how to drive, I tried to think of an excuse to decline his offer.

I was saved when Padgett spotted the other salesman chatting with Doreen. "Sonofabitch," he hissed. "I'll be right back."

Although there was no indication that their conversation was anything but proper, Padgett ran over and railed at the other man until he retreated inside the office.

The sign above the office again caught my eye: *Komplete Kar Kare*. I couldn't remember if there was a similar slogan at J. D. Whalen's garage.

When Brian Padgett returned, I said I'd have to take a rain check on the test drive because I had a dentist appointment in St. Louis.

A brief trolley ride later, I was still in East St. Louis, but on Waverly Avenue, staring up at the shoddily painted sign of Waverly Motors. There was nothing on it that could be construed as a KKK endorsement.

I knew that there were other slogans, more subtle, that meant the same thing. Karl had told me of some he'd seen in Kentucky that read "TWK": Trade With a Klansman. I walked closer to the garage, treading carefully over the rutted earth, to see if there were any such signs. Again, nothing.

The fellow J. D. Whalen had called Clint lumbered out of the garage wiping his greasy hands on a rag. "Can I help you?" He was wearing only denim overalls, no shirt. Even if the day had been cool, he wouldn't have needed anything more than the thick black fur on his body to keep warm. He looked like a grizzly bear, only stronger.

I didn't want to admit that I was only looking at his sign. "Is J. D. here?" I asked. "I talked to him about three weeks ago."

Clint ran the rag across his cheek, making a rasping sound

on the dark stubble that covered much of his broad face. "He's over the river, trying to make a deal on some cars. Anything I can help you with?"

"I was just at Enoch's dealership," I said. "I'm in the market for a new car, and I thought I'd see what you and J. D. had before I made a decision. J. D. mentioned you might be getting some Hudsons."

Clint chuckled. "One day he's talkin' Hudsons, the next day it's Studebakers. Today, he's looking at Gardners—figures since they're made in St. Louis, we'll get a lot of customers wanting to support local industry. I don't know what we're gonna end up with. How soon you lookin' to buy?"

"No hurry. I can wait a while and see what you get." I pushed the charade further. "I figure I'd rather give you my business seeing as how you're just getting started."

"Appreciate it," Clint said. "It'll mean a lot, especially to J. D.—he's got a lot invested in this place." He grinned. "And he sure would love taking a sale away from Roy Enoch."

I pointed up to the Waverly Motors sign. "You don't have the same advertising advantage as Enoch."

"What do you mean?"

"His sign says, 'Komplete Kar Kare'—so he'll be getting business from the Klansmen around here."

Clint grunted. "Yeah, I know. And the way the Klan's growing, that kind of advertising's probably a good idea. But all I want to do is work on cars." He studied me a moment. "You a Knight?"

I wanted to sound neutral until I determined where *he* stood. "Not yet, but they been after me to join."

"Take my advice: Think it over before you do. Ten dollars to join, then they sell you the robes and books . . . comes to a lot of money."

"I don't have to pay," I said. "Not the membership, anyway. I play for the St. Louis Browns, and they're looking to recruit big-league ballplayers.''

Clint's eyes widened. ''The Browns? You for real?''

I nodded.

He began flexing his right arm as if loosening up to throw. ''I *love* baseball. Used to play myself—and wasn't half-bad. I was J. D.'s catcher when he pitched for Aluminum Ore.'' His arm dropped to his side. ''Seems like a million years ago. I've hardly played at all since the riot.''

''With what's going on between the Elcars and the Cubs,'' I said, ''it looks like there could be another riot soon.''

''Nah.'' He leaned back against an old Nash. ''The Klan'll keep things under control.''

''From what I read in the papers, Klansmen are the ones who get *out* of control.''

''Remember,'' said Clint, ''there was no Klan during the 1917 riot; it was a *mob* that did the killing and burning. A lot of good men got caught up in it and did some awful things they never would have dreamed of normally. But now the Klan will keep order and keep the hotheads in line—like the ones at Enoch's place. I'm glad J. D. is out of there.''

''They cause a lot of trouble?''

''Don't know if they *cause* it, but they're always looking for a scrap. Especially with the coloreds. One of their salesmen got killed in the riot, and they won't ever forget it.''

That came as news to me; Aubury had mentioned that a couple of whites were shot in the days before the riot, but not during the killing spree. ''I thought it was only Negroes who were killed,'' I said.

''Most of the dead were colored, but there were a few whites who ended up the same way. Some of the Negroes fought back, and I don't blame them. I'd have done the same thing. You know, I got nothing against coloreds. Never did. And I hate what was done to them in 'seventeen. I think the Klan will stop anything like that from happening again.''

It seemed a safe guess, but I thought I'd ask. "You in the Klan?"

"Well, I joined, but I'm not active."

"Why not?"

Clint slid down to sit on the Nash's running board, which squeaked in protest at his weight. "Basically, I agree with the goals of the KKK—patriotism, clean living, good old-fashioned values. And I like the fact that they'll punish people who need it—like bootleggers and wife beaters. By the way, the Klan mostly keeps *white* men in line; it don't go after coloreds much—not in this part of the country anyways."

"If you joined the Klan, and believe in it, why aren't you active?"

He spit. "I knew a couple fellows who needed to be taught a lesson; one of them let his family go hungry while he drank his paychecks, and another one used his wife for a punching bag. So I went to a Klan meeting, and joined up. There was a whole ceremony—naturalization, they call it—to initiate new members. Everybody was in hoods and robes, and it was real fancy. When it was over, everybody took off their hoods. Turned out the men I wanted straightened out were Klansmen. I ain't been back since."

"You still think the Klan is going to keep order if guys like that are in it?"

He spit again, targeting a radiator cap that was lying on the ground a few feet away. "To tell you the truth, I'm not sure anymore. Guess if I was, I would have put a slogan on the sign by now."

"How about J. D.—is he still active?"

"We're not supposed to say nothing about other members."

"All right. Well, thanks for the talk. I'll hold off on buying a car till I see what you get in." Before I left, I added that if he ever wanted seats to a Browns' game to let me know and I'd leave him a couple of passes.

When I got back home, I tried to sort out all the conflicting information I'd gotten during the past month. There were so many disparities, and they were so extreme, it seemed an impossible task.

The Ku Klux Klan, for instance: I saw no way to reconcile the atrocities I'd read about with the claims that the KKK was dedicated to *preventing* violence. Was the difference simply a matter of geography, with a Southern Klan that openly tortured and killed Negroes and a Northern faction that instead enforced "morality" among whites and disciplined their own members? If so, did that rule out the possibility that East St. Louis Klansmen were behind the lynching of Slip Crawford?

What about the Elcars' players: Were they a bunch of racist hotheads capable of killing Crawford for beating them in a ball game, or were they a proud team of better-than-average baseball players who only wanted another chance to beat him in a game? And, if most Elcars were also Klansmen who'd been ordered *not* to use violence, would they be reckless enough to defy their leaders over a ball game?

I kept coming around to the idea that the motive for Slip Crawford's murder was personal.

Since the St. Louis Stars wouldn't be in town for some time yet, I wouldn't be able to question his teammates. I hoped there might be some information on the pitcher in the back issues of the *Argus* that Franklin Aubury had given me.

I checked the old newspapers, for the first time getting beyond the front pages. The sports section provided a wealth of information on Negro baseball, which got little notice in white newspapers and was completely ignored by *The Sporting News*. I was astonished to read how many organized colored clubs there were. In addition to Rube Foster's Negro National

League, there was the Southern League, a minor league for colored players, and many industrial and amateur leagues. Local Negro teams included the St. Louis Tigers, a Southern League entry, and the semipro Compton Hill Cubs, Union Electrics, and Kinloch Stars.

I learned that a new major league, to be called the Eastern Colored League, was being formed in the northeast. Its organizers were owners of independent barnstorming teams who believed Rube Foster was too dictatorial. One thing both black and white leagues have in common, I thought, is that the owners are never happy.

There was little information on Slip Crawford useful for my purposes, however. According to the *Argus,* he'd had a terrific 1921 season with the Indianapolis ABCs, and was expected to be a mainstay of the Stars' pitching staff this year. The paper contained nothing about his personal life, and there was no mention of any problems on or off the field.

Out of curiosity, I began to flip through the other sections of the papers. There were numerous articles attributed to the Associated Negro Press, most on national political issues. There was also social news; I learned that colored people had their own Greek letter college fraternities, such as Alpha Phi Alpha, and fraternal organizations such as the Pythians. Along with advertisements for Dr. Fred Palmer's Skin Whitener and Strait-Tex hair straightener, were ads for "all-colored" vaudeville shows, motion pictures, and phonograph recordings such as those of Black Swan Records, which featured "exclusively colored voices."

Colored baseball, colored movies, a colored news service . . . There was an entire civilization here, one that was hidden from white Americans—or overlooked by them.

CHAPTER 17

With a few minor modifications, I kept to my usual Sunday morning routine. I started with a large breakfast, but since I didn't have Margie's talent at the stove, bacon, eggs, and pancakes weren't on the menu. Instead, I consumed most of a peach pie from the bakery, washing it down with black coffee. Then I settled into my Morris chair by the parlor window to read the newspaper. Again, I deviated somewhat from standard practice; rather than the *Post-Dispatch* or *Globe-Democrat*, the paper I chose was the latest issue of the weekly *Argus*.

I began at the back of the paper, with the sports section. The main headline read: *Bell Wins Game For Stars*. Jimmy Bell, the speedster formerly with the East St. Louis Cubs, had pitched the St. Louis Stars to their first victory of the season in Chicago. The team he beat was Rube Foster's American Giants, reigning champions of the Negro National League. I was delighted to see that the kid was making good, and I looked forward to seeing him play again when the Stars' ballpark opened in St. Louis.

According to the *Argus*, construction on the park was progressing so well that it was expected to be ready in five weeks.

Until then, the Stars would remain on the road, playing series in Indianapolis, Pittsburgh, and Kansas City.

That reminded me of the road trip I was missing. Today, while I sat idle in St. Louis, my teammates were in the Polo Grounds, where Babe Ruth would be making his first appearance of the season. Ruth's suspension was over; mine had another ten days to run.

I closed the newspaper, and twisted around in my chair to look out the window. It was a beautiful day for a ball game—sunny, warm, and clear. Imagining the Browns and Yankees about to do battle in New York, I ached to play again. Or at least take my usual spot on the dugout bench. Hell, I'd even settle for a seat in the bleachers.

No sense wishing or waiting, I finally decided, neither for the Browns to let me play baseball with them again nor for Margie to return. I picked up the *Argus* again and checked the Stars' schedule. I *would* go to a ball game—in Indianapolis.

By the after on, I was still excited about the prospect of a trip, but didn relish the idea of traveling by myself. I'd had enough of being alone lately.

I called Karl Landfors and asked if he'd like to take a little vacation.

"A *what?*"

I should have known that vacation would be an alien concept to Karl. "I'm going to Indianapolis," I said. "I was wondering if you might want to come along."

"Indianapolis? Why on earth would you want to go there?"

"The St. Louis Stars will be there, playing the ABCs. I want to talk to both teams about Slip Crawford." I didn't mention that I also just wanted to get away for a while.

"I'm sorry, Mickey, but I can't right now." He sniffed. "As a matter of fact, it's an idea of yours that requires me to remain here."

"Huh?"

"You suggested to Franklin Aubury that we try to get articles in the newspapers linking the incidents in East St. Louis to the KKK. That's what I'm working on."

When I recovered from the astonishment that he'd taken my suggestion on something, I asked, "Are you getting anywhere with it?"

"The *Post-Dispatch* is interested. Last year, the *New York World* ran an exposé of the KKK. It was picked up by a number of other papers around the country, including the *Post-Dispatch*. I'm trying to convince one of the editors that a story on local Klan activity would be an important follow-up to that piece."

"All right. Well, good luck with it."

I was disappointed that I'd be traveling alone, but I was still going to go.

Early Monday morning—so early that I considered it night—the telephone in the hallway shattered my sleep.

I hopped out of bed and ran to pick it up, bumping my shin on the dresser. The sound of a ringing phone still triggered the hope that it might be Margie calling.

The voice was male, with the crisp diction of Karl Landfors, but without his nasal whine. "Mickey Rawlings?"

"Yeah, this is me."

"Franklin Aubury here. I understand from Karl Landfors that you are planning a trip to Indianapolis."

"Yeah, that's right."

"May I ask when you were planning to leave?"

I answered groggily, "Not until after I wake up."

Aubury laughed. "I apologize for phoning so early, but I wanted to be sure to catch you before you left." He paused. "Would you mind some company on the trip?"

Company was exactly what I wanted. "Not at all. Who?"

"Me. I'd like to meet with some associates in Indiana who are monitoring Klan activities there."

"Sure, I'd be happy to go together."

"Karl also tells me you are planning to talk with some of Slip Crawford's former teammates. If you like, I would be happy to make some introductions for you; I'm acquainted with some of the players."

I'd actually never thought how I would go about approaching the colored players. "That would be great," I said.

We agreed to leave the following day.

CHAPTER 18

The last time I'd been in the central pavilion of Union Station, I was getting a sales pitch from Buddy Vaughn, a kleagle for the Knights of the Ku Klux Klan. Today I was with Franklin Aubury, a Negro attorney working for legislation to abolish one of the Klan's favorite practices.

The change in mood from two weeks ago was as striking as the change in company. Since this would be one of the rare journeys I'd be taking that wasn't dictated by the baseball schedule, it had the feel of a vacation outing. I dressed casually for the excursion, in a sky-blue Palm Beach suit, with a burgundy necktie and traditional straw boater.

From his dress, I thought Franklin Aubury might be viewing the trip the same way. He'd abandoned the formal black-and-white costume he usually wore in favor of a tailored, three-piece tan suit and a brown derby. A green bat-wing bow tie bloomed from his high collar, and a gold watch chain was draped across his vest.

Fifteen minutes before the train was scheduled to pull out, we gave our suitcases to a baggageman and boarded. Aubury pointed to a couple of seats in the middle of the half-empty car. "Would you care for the window?" he offered.

"No, you go ahead." I'd made dozens of train trips across the Midwest in the past ten years, and I was pretty confident there wouldn't be anything new to see.

Once we'd settled in, Aubury began chattering about the Indianapolis ABCs with as much enthusiasm as a Brooklyn fan on his way to Ebbets Field—but with much better diction.

I interrupted to ask, "Does 'ABC' stand for anything?"

"American Brewing Company. There is no longer any affiliation, of course, but the team was initially organized as a promotional tool for the brewery. The club would travel throughout the state of Indiana playing ball games, taking on local teams, and samples of beer would be distributed to the fans." He smiled. "From that beginning, about twenty years ago, the ABCs developed into one of the premier colored teams in the country, and their rosters have included some of the best players in history."

Strutting down the aisle came a bloated conductor with a bushy black beard and shiny red face. The brass buttons on his navy uniform were tarnished, as was the badge on his cap. I held up my ticket for him to punch.

He directed his attention at Franklin Aubury, who was reaching into a pocket for his ticket. "You must be confused, boy. This ain't your seat."

I said, "We bought tickets."

The conductor gave me a dismissive frown. "Ticket means you ride; it don't say where you sit. *I* say where you sit." He turned to Aubury again. "And your car is in the back."

I started to protest, but Aubury said calmly, "It's all right." He flashed his teeth apologetically at the conductor. "I must have misunderstood the porter's directions." Though his mouth was smiling, I saw rage and pain in his eyes.

Aubury slid past me and headed toward the rear of the train.

I asked the conductor, "If he can't sit here, can I go back where he is?"

"No." He punched my ticket. "This ain't a complicated system, son: Whites ride in the white car, coloreds in the colored car. You look white to me, so here you stay."

After he moved on to the next passengers, I moved over to the window seat. The engine fired to life, and the familiar rumble of the rails shook through me as we rolled out of the station. I stared out the window, thinking that this trip was sure off to a lousy start.

A couple of hours later, the train pulled into a way station in Effingham, Illinois. The conductor announced that passengers had eighteen minutes to stretch their legs or get something to eat. I needed to do both.

The rustic depot was nothing like the magnificent one we'd departed from in St. Louis. It was little more than an oversize shed housing a waiting area, a ticket booth, and a lunch counter. I first used the men's toilet, then got in line for a sandwich. As I waited my turn, I looked around for Franklin Aubury, assuming he'd have gotten off the train, too, but I didn't see him. In fact, I didn't see a single colored person in the depot. As the line moved along, I finally noticed the sign on the cash register: *Whites Only*. There was no corresponding lunch counter for colored people.

I immediately left the line and went outside. I found the lawyer among a couple of dozen Negroes gathered near a stand of beech trees behind the depot. Some were snacking on food they'd brought with them, others were talking, and a few were using the shrubbery for toilets.

I caught Aubury's eye, and he came over to me. "You want a sandwich or something?" I asked. "My treat."

"Thank you, no. I'm not hungry."

"A soda pop?"

He shook his head and glanced back at the Negroes he'd been speaking with. I had the impression he was eager for me to go away. I didn't understand; was it against the rules for us even to talk to each other?

I gave up. "All right. See you later."

I went back inside the station, but didn't return to the line. My impulse was to protest, at least silently; if they wouldn't serve everyone, then they wouldn't get my business, either.

When the warning whistle from the train blew, I reconsidered. My refusing to eat wouldn't do a thing to feed the people outside. I took a couple of steps toward the lunch counter, but then turned around and left because I found I no longer had an appetite anyway.

It wasn't until we'd crossed into Indiana, and stopped again in Terre Haute, that everyone on the train was able to buy food and use indoor bathrooms. The two races weren't allowed to use the same ones; but this station was larger than the last, and provided separate facilities for Negroes and whites.

Before we went inside, Franklin Aubury and I talked briefly, agreeing to eat quickly and meet again outdoors.

After wolfing down a ham-and-cheese sandwich that I suspected was older than I was, I went back outside, sipping a flat ginger ale. Aubury was seated alone on a bench, looking at a carefully folded newspaper.

"What time do we get into Indianapolis?" I asked, sitting down next to him.

"Five-twenty, according to the timetable." He held the paper out to me. "Interesting advertisement."

It was folded back to a quarter page ad that read:

*Ku Klux Klan and Women's Auxiliary
invite all 100% Americans to a*

DECORATION DAY CELEBRATION

One Dazzling Day of Diversified Delights!

Parade—Barbeque—Rodeo
Brass Band—Fireworks—Patriotic Speeches
Imported Texas Cowboys—High Wire Walking

Bring the Kiddies!

Sponsored by Evansville Klan No. 1

"Jeez. They sure are open about it."

"In Indiana, they can be," Aubury said. "The Klan is well on its way to taking over this state."

" 'Taking over'? You got to be exaggerating."

"I wish I were. They're as strong here as in any Southern state, and growing every day."

I remembered that Evansville was where Buddy Vaughn had come from, and mentioned that fact to Aubury.

"Let's hope that Vaughn doesn't prove as successful in St. Louis as he has here." He cleared his throat. "If you are willing, perhaps on the return trip, we can go back via Evansville— and you can go to this picnic."

"I told you I won't—"

He held up his hand. "I know: You won't join the Klan. I am not asking you to do so. I only ask that you go to the picnic—it's open to the public—and perhaps you'll hear some things that might be helpful to know."

Decoration Day was a week away, so it could fit into the schedule, I thought. As I considered the idea, I flipped the paper over and noticed it was an Evansville newspaper dated a week earlier. "You didn't just find out about this, did you?" I said.

The lawyer looked guiltily down at the ground. "No, I've been aware of it for some time."

"Is that the real reason you wanted to go on this trip—to talk me into going to a Klan picnic?"

"No, I do have people to meet with in Indianapolis. I simply thought the Evansville gathering would also be a useful means of acquiring information."

"Why didn't you ask me sooner?"

"I thought if I asked you to do something like this, you might change your mind about going to Indiana."

"So you wait till I'm here, and then spring it on me." I shook my head. "I don't like being played."

"I'm not twisting your arm," Aubury replied. "I'm merely asking."

"Then ask up front. Don't play me."

He nodded. "Understood. Sorry."

"Okay." I handed him back the newspaper. "Let me think about it."

The whistle blew for us to board the train, bringing the conversation to an end.

I stared out at the flat farmland rolling past me. It was the same view as an hour ago, which was no different from the hour before that. This is crazy, I thought, to have to sit here by myself.

I suddenly decided I wasn't going to participate in the craziness any longer. I bolted up from my seat and walked briskly toward the rear of the train.

Standing in the aisle at the back of the car was the black-bearded conductor. "You lose your way?" he asked.

"No." I brushed past him.

Two cars farther back, I came to one occupied entirely by colored people. I stopped at the door and looked for Franklin Aubury among the packed seats. When I spotted his pince-nez glittering behind a newspaper, I waved my boater to get his attention. Others in the car noticed my gestures first, and there were some surprised murmurs that caused Aubury to look up. When he did, I beckoned with my hat. He came to the front of the car, a bewildered expression on his face.

I stood in the doorway of the white car, and he stopped a couple of feet from me, just inside the colored car.

"Speaking of the ABCs," I said, picking up our conversation from Union Station, "I saw them play the Cincinnati Cuban Stars last year in Redland Field."

A smile slowly spread over Aubury's face as he caught on to what I was doing. "You remember who pitched?" he asked.

"Dizzy Dismukes. Threw a two-nothing shutout."

"He's one of the best."

"I believe it. I've been to some other Negro League games, too. I went to Stars Park in Detroit a few times, and saw Rube Foster once."

We were interrupted by the conductor. "What the hell do you think you're doing?" he demanded.

"Talking," I answered. "Something wrong with that?"

His face flushed a deeper red. "I thought I explained it to you before."

"You did. And we're sticking to the rules. I'm not in the colored car." I nodded at Aubury. "And he ain't in the white car." I leaned against the edge of the doorway and crossed my arms, making it clear that I intended to stay.

The conductor tugged at his beard, obviously at a loss. He finally walked off, muttering, "What the hell do I care what kind of company you keep."

Aubury and I both grinned broadly, but we had sense enough not to let our smiles turn to laughter—no point provoking the conductor into coming back.

"I read in the *Argus*," I said, "that there's plans for an

Eastern Colored League. What's Rube Foster gonna think of that?''

"He won't like it," Aubury answered, "but he won't be able to stop it. Foster has limited the Negro National League to the Midwest for now. The East has some well-established teams that want to be part of a league, too. They also have some independent-minded owners who won't relinquish any of their authority to Rube Foster—he maintains tight control of league affairs. They won't submit to him, and he doesn't much care for them.''

"Why not?''

"Some of the Eastern owners are white promoters out to profit from colored labor. Others are affiliated with enterprises that are not entirely legal.''

"What do you think about them?'' I asked.

"I believe having two leagues would be good for colored baseball. We could have our own World Series.''

I thought about the names of the leagues, one "Negro" and the other "colored," and asked Aubury a question I'd wondered about for some time, "What do you prefer to be called: colored or Negro?''

"It's not what I'm called that matters.'' He looked me in the eyes. "I know when I'm being spoken to with respect. *That's* what I want—to be respected as a man.''

As the train rumbled on, the conversation turned to ballplayers. Aubury talked at length about his favorite stars, not mentioning a single white one.

"Which of the Negro Leaguers do you think would make it on a major league club?'' I asked.

"Dozens of them. But why would they want to?''

"Because it's the big leagues!'' Wasn't it the dream of every ballplayer, of any race, age, or gender, to play on a big-league diamond?

"We have our own big league now,'' Aubury said proudly.

"And, truth be told, playing in yours isn't all that appealing. We've had experience in white leagues, and it wasn't a positive one."

"You have?"

"Do you know who invented shin guards?" he asked.

If this was going to be another quiz like the one he'd given me in his law office, I was happy that at least he was starting with an easy question. "Roger Bresnahan," I answered confidently. "Around the turn of the century."

"Wrong. Bud Fowler and Frank Grant both wore them twenty years earlier. But they weren't catchers. They were colored infielders who played on white minor-league teams. White opponents made a sport of driving their cleats into the 'darkies' legs—so Fowler and Grant fashioned wooden shin guards to protect themselves."

"I had no idea," I said.

"Colored players weren't treated any better by their own teammates. Fleet Walker and his brother Weldy both played *major*-league baseball with Toledo in the 1880s. Weldy was the catcher, but kept getting crossed up by pitchers who refused to take signs from a colored man. You know, there aren't even many photographs of mixed teams because whites wouldn't sit with colored teammates to have their pictures taken."

"I didn't know there were ever Negroes in pro ball," I said. "I thought it was always separate."

Aubury shook his head. "No, the color line in baseball is largely the doing of Cap Anson. When he saw Fleet Walker take the field against his White Stockings, he told the other team to 'get that nigger off the field.' Anson refused to let his team play until Walker was gone. And we've been off the field ever since."

"Damn." I recalled Anson's death at the start of the season. It was too bad that the practice he'd instituted hadn't died with him.

"I know there are some whites who don't agree with segregation in baseball," Aubury said. "John McGraw, for example, sometimes tries to pass Negroes off as Cuban or Indian to get them in. And Fred Tenney tried to sign a Negro for the Boston Braves in 1905—almost succeeded, too."

"Who was the player?"

"William Clarence Matthews, shortstop at Harvard University. He was a damned fine ballplayer, and he *almost* became the first colored man to play major-league baseball this century. But the National League owners wouldn't let Tenney sign him. After college, Matthews played for a while in a Vermont league, then he gave up the game. He went to law school, passed the bar, and became such an outstanding lawyer that President Taft appointed him an Assistant United States Attorney. I met him when I was in law school. William Matthews has climbed about as high as a colored man can go in the legal profession, but he told me he still would have rather been a baseball player. Now that we have our own leagues, Negroes *can* make baseball their profession."

Aubury removed his glasses and began polishing the lenses. "I have a question for *you*," he said. "Why would a ballplayer struggling to remain in the major leagues risk his job by playing a semipro game against a colored team? You knew you were risking suspension. What made it worth the risk?"

I thought for a moment. "Well, I always figured making the big leagues meant I was one of the best. But then I went to a few Negro League games and saw some players who were better than the average major leaguer. I got to thinking that maybe I wasn't among the best ballplayers in the country, just the best *white* ones. So I wanted to play against a colored team to see how I'd do." Over Aubury's shoulder, I spotted a couple of boys running in the aisle of the colored car. "Picking teams sure was simpler when I was a kid," I said. "The captains tossed a bat in the air, worked their hands up the handle, and whoever grabbed the knob got first pick. Then they chose up sides, taking the best players first. Nothing mattered except how good a kid played ball, 'cause all you wanted was to field the best team.''

"It was the same way when I was a boy," Aubury said. "Things sure change when adults get involved."

The conductor came back to us, lugging several bulky suitcases. He put them down between Aubury and me. "We need the space," he said.

This sap must have spent the last twenty minutes trying to come up with a way to separate us, I thought. When he left promising to return with more bags, I asked Aubury, "Any chance of getting the law changed about riding in separate cars?"

"The changes are going in the other direction," he answered sadly. "It only recently became law in Indiana, and it hasn't passed yet in Missouri or Illinois—separate travel statutes are only pending in those states."

"If it's not the law in Missouri, why didn't you argue about it in St. Louis?"

"Because it's considered accepted practice—and opposing it can result in worse punishment than breaking any law. If I fought over every indignity, or every time somebody called me nigger, I wouldn't survive a year. I will not leave a widow and two fatherless children over a seat on a train." He clipped the glasses back on his nose. "I intend to remain alive, choose my battles carefully, and perhaps someday my daughters will get to sit up front."

When the conductor came back with more luggage, Aubury and I went back to sitting in separate cars. "Someday" hadn't come yet.

CHAPTER 19

For one season, in 1914, Indianapolis was home to a pennant-winning major-league baseball club. That team was the Hoosiers, champions of the upstart Federal League, and its roster included such first-rate ballplayers as Edd Roush, Benny Kauff, and Bill McKechnie. Unfortunately for the city, the franchise moved to Newark the following season, a year before the entire league folded.

Washington Park remained, however, now serving as home to both the American Association Indians, one of the best minor-league clubs in the country, and the Negro League ABCs, who were allowed use of the field when the Indians were out of town. The ballpark was on the west side of Indianapolis, near the White River. A slaughterhouse between the river and the ballpark contributed an interesting aroma to the warm summer air, and beyond the outfield fence was a railroad roundhouse where heavy machinery clanged and thundered.

Franklin Aubury and I were among the first to arrive for the game. He was my kind of baseball fan; not only did we have to be at the park for the start of batting practice, it was preferable that we be there early enough to watch the groundskeepers groom the field.

When we entered the park, I briefly wondered if I would have to sit in the right-field bleachers, the same way Negroes were limited to that section of Sportsman's Park. It turned out we were both able to get box seats, but not exactly together: Ropes were strung between seating sections, and fans of different races were not permitted on the same side of a rope. Aubury, though, had arranged to get us seats on one of the borderlines. If we could ignore the rope railing between us, it was the same as sitting next to each other.

Once the two of us started talking baseball, I found it fairly easy to ignore the seating arrangement—at least we were able to sit, unlike on the train. What I couldn't ignore was that I was one of only a handful of whites in the park, and I felt uncomfortably conspicuous. As the crowd kept filing in, growing to several thousand, I remained part of a tiny minority.

"Gonna be a pretty good crowd," I said to Aubury. The Browns had played quite a few games before smaller ones this season.

"This is nothing compared to what they draw on weekends." Aubury pointed toward the railroad sidings behind the right-field fence. "Switchmen will park freight cars out there so even kids who can't afford tickets can watch from the roofs."

When the Stars and ABCs trotted out for warm-ups, I asked, "Which team you gonna root for?"

"I have no particular allegiance," he said. "I generally root for whichever team is losing to make a comeback."

Aubury must share Karl Landfors's fondness for underdogs and hopeless causes, I thought.

After the teams had completed practice, a two-man umpiring crew came onto the field. To my surprise, they were both white, and I commented on it to Aubury.

"We don't have many qualified Negro umpires yet. Whites have the training and the professional experience. And Rube

Foster is giving higher priority to having good umpires than colored ones."

From his tone, I got the impression that the lawyer objected to Foster's policy. "You don't agree with that?"

"No, I don't. If Foster only hires experienced umpires, and only white men have been given the opportunity to become experienced, then colored umpires will never get a chance. Negro baseball is something of *ours;* we should have our own people officiating the game, even if it takes them a while to become proficient at it."

I was happy when the game started, and hitting and pitching became the focus of our attention, instead of racial issues.

Through the first couple of innings, there was more to admire in the pitching than in the hitting, as Dizzy Dismukes of the ABCs and the St. Louis Stars' Jimmy Bell were both hurling shutouts. I had assumed that since Bell ran so fast, his pitches would also have lightning speed, but he didn't have much of a fastball, instead relying on a nasty curve and a dancing knuckleball. Dismukes threw harder, submarine style, and with pinpoint control. I suspected that I would be unlikely to hit either of them.

I said to Aubury, "Bell's slow curve reminds me of Slip Crawford's."

"There are a lot of good curveball pitchers in the Negro Leagues," he replied. "They have to work so many games that fastball pitchers tend to burn out their arms." He marked down Bell's latest strikeout on his scorecard.

I noticed Aubury used a fountain pen, instead of a pencil, which prompted me to ask, "What if you make a mistake?"

He smiled, apparently amused at the notion that he could make a scoring error.

I hailed a passing vendor and bought two soda pops, handing one of them to Aubury. The vendor gave me a disapproving stare. Maybe I violated some kind of rule by crossing the rope barrier, I thought. But no one came to throw me out of the park for the infraction, and I went back to watching the game.

As the innings went by, Aubury told me stories and statistics about most of the players on the field. Many of the Stars had once played for the ABCs, and vice versa. It sounded like Negro League players changed teams more often than I did.

"Does every player end up playing for every team?" I joked.

Aubury's answer was serious. "Almost. That is one of the problems that has always plagued colored teams: instability. The clubs are always strapped for cash. If they miss a paycheck, their players go elsewhere; if they miss a rent payment, they have to find another park to play in. There are a couple of teams who play their entire schedules on the road."

"Any Negro League clubs have their own ballparks?"

"No, the closest is Rube Foster's American Giants; they own their grandstand, but not the field. When Stars Park opens in St. Louis, it will be the first to be wholly owned by a colored ball club."

The score was tied 1–1 in the sixth, when Stars' catcher Dan Kennard lifted a long fly to right field, and we both stood up to cheer.

"Go! Go!" yelled Aubury in a most unlawyerly squawk. When the ball carried over the fence for a home run, he screamed, "Yes!" Hometown partisans hurled a few taunts at Aubury, and he sat back down. To me, he said sheepishly, "The Stars are ahead, so now I'll root for the ABCs."

The next couple of innings were quiet, and Aubury returned to the subject of league organization. "Rube Foster is doing his best to bring stability to the game, but the Eastern owners will have a definite advantage in that regard."

"How so?"

"They have more ready access to ballparks. And it's easier to travel in the East; all of the cities have large enough colored populations that players can find places to eat and sleep. In the Midwest, a team can go hundreds of miles with no bed or food, and where the only toilet is the bushes and the only bathtub is a pond. If they—''

An explosion of cheering drowned him out as the ABC's Crush Holloway led off the bottom of the ninth with a line-drive double. Indianapolis now had the tying run on second base. Ben Taylor tried to sacrifice him to third, but Kennard pounced on the bunt so quickly that Holloway couldn't advance. Bell struck out the next batter, but walked the man after that.

With two on and two out, the powerfully built Oscar Charleston strode confidently to the plate. The crowd was on its feet, screaming wildly for the Indianapolis slugger to win the game with one swing of his bat.

Aubury held out his scorecard for me to see. With his pen, he marked a home run for Charleston. ''That is how certain I am,'' he said.

But he forgot to tell Jimmy Bell about his prediction. The wily kid slipped a couple of slow curves past Charleston for strikes, then wasted two pitches. Needing one more strike, Bell went into a twisting windup and delivered a knuckleball that took about five minutes to reach home plate. Charleston swung mightily, but missed, ending the game and giving Bell and the Stars the victory.

Aubury was about to tear up his scorecard, but I asked for it, and he gave it to me. I wasn't going to read about these players in *The Sporting News* or in most daily newspapers, and I wanted something with a record of their names.

''How about dinner later?'' I asked as we filed out of the park.

''I'd better pass,'' Aubury said. ''I'm going to try to set up a meeting with some of the players for you.''

''The ABCs?''

"We'd better try for the Stars tonight. They won, so they'll be in a better mood."

"All right. Gimme a call."

We then parted to go to our separate hotels in different parts of the city.

The speakeasy on Indiana Avenue, in the heart of Indianapolis's most prominent colored neighborhood, might as well have had a sign posted on its front door. Although its brick walls were completely unadorned, anyone walking within half a block of the place could tell what was going on inside. The sound of a jazz band rumbled from within, and automobiles were parked in tight formation all along the curb. Stylishly dressed men and women were clustered outside the club's entrance, waiting to be admitted; several made the wait more tolerable by sipping from pocket flasks.

Franklin Aubury led the way past the crowd, and said a few words to an enormous black doorman. Despite some loud protests from those who still had to wait, we were immediately ushered through the door.

The dimly lit interior was hazy with smoke and sweet with the mingled scents of perfume and hair tonic. A dapper maître d' led Aubury and me across the crowded dance floor to a polished round table near the bandstand. I was acutely conscious of eyes upon me; the low lighting couldn't obscure the fact that I was the only Caucasian in the place.

At the table were three men I'd watched play that afternoon. They'd swapped their baggy uniforms for fashionable suits, and were now celebrating their win over ABCs. Aubury asked if we could join them, and at their assent, the maître d' brought us two extra chairs. The lawyer then introduced me to the Stars: Big Bill Gatewood, manager and part-time pitcher; veteran pitcher Plunk Drake; and young Jimmy Bell.

Gatewood, a round-faced man who fully merited the "Big"

in "Big Bill," corrected the lawyer, "It's *Cool Papa* Bell now. I never seen a pitcher so cool as he was facing Charleston. I thought Oscar was gonna break his back swinging at that knuckleball!"

I had to strain to hear Gatewood's words. The proximity to the bandstand was a place of honor, no doubt given to the Stars because of their celebrity status, but it was also deafeningly loud. The old-fashioned jazz band had a tuba instead of a string bass, and the big horn was so close to my ear that it felt like one hard blast would send me to the floor.

Plunk Drake, smiling broadly, brushed a hand over his high forehead. "Sure was sweet seeing Oscar go down like that. He was with us last year, and was always complaining we didn't have no pitchers."

Gatewood playfully punched Bell in the shoulder. "Well, we got one now." Turning to Drake, he added, "I mean we got *another* one, of course."

It didn't appear that Drake needed any mollifying. He seemed to have a perpetual grin on his face, and his eyes had a squint that I expected was more from smiling and laughing than from any difficulty seeing.

The two veterans proceeded to heap compliments on the rookie, who quietly sipped a soda pop and visibly glowed in the praise. He looked so young, I was tempted to ask if his mother knew he was there.

A waiter came with tall beers for Aubury and me, and we added our own congratulations on that day's game.

Bell spoke up, telling Gatewood, "I'd do even better if you'd let me throw my knuckler more. It's the best pitch I got."

"I told you before," the manager replied firmly, "don't matter how good a pitch you throw if the catcher can't catch it."

Drake said to the youngster, "Bill will teach you some

new pitches, same as he taught me." He jerked his thumb at Gatewood, and explained, "This man only got three pitches: spitball, emory ball, and bean ball. And he taught me that last one real well. He'd pick out a spot on a batter's body, and tell me I got to hit that spot or pay a dollar fine."

Gatewood roared above the music, "Hell, I was just teaching you *control*. A little target practice is the best way to learn it!"

Bell tilted his head toward Drake. "He sure learned it good—they don't call him Plunk for nothing. If he don't hit you, he'll keep you dancing. First game I was with the team, I saw him throw at a batter's head, knee, and hip, to go 3–0 on the count—and then he struck him out on three straight strikes."

I could have listened to them talk baseball all night, but I forced myself to get to the point of the visit. "You had another pitcher on the Stars who was real good," I said. "Slip Crawford."

They all grew somber, even the jovial Plunk Drake, and I was sorry that I'd put a damper on the party. I felt especially bad for Bell; he'd gotten his spot in the Stars' rotation because of Crawford's death, and he squirmed uneasily, as if I'd just reminded him of that fact.

Drake said, "It was a damn shame about Slip."

"A goddamn *crime*, is what it was," said Gatewood.

Aubury and I exchanged glances, but neither of us pointed out that technically lynching *wasn't* a crime.

"You know," Drake said, "he had the best curveball I ever seen." The pitcher started to smile again as his thoughts turned to Crawford's talents instead of his death. "He'd just slip that ball right around your bat. Hitting Slip was like trying to catch a greased pig."

"He sure slipped his curve around my bat," I said. "I couldn't get one hit off him."

The colored players looked at me quizzically.

Aubury spoke up, "Mickey played against Crawford last month in East St. Louis."

"Yeah," I said. "And he made me look as bad at the plate as you"—I pointed to Bell—"made me look in the field with your base running."

"I *thought* I seen you somewhere before." The young pitcher grinned, and his eyes shone brightly. "You're the one who tried that appeal play. You didn't believe I touched second base."

"Hell, I didn't know anybody could run like you do. And even after seeing you run, I *still* don't believe it."

Plunk Drake said, "I room with this boy, and I swear he can turn out the light and be in bed before the room gets dark." His sly smile suggested he might be exaggerating, though probably not by much.

Gatewood was the only one at the table not smiling. He took a long swallow of beer, then said to me, "So you played in that game at Cubs Park."

"Yeah, I did."

"It was after that game that Slip was killed."

Franklin Aubury said, "That's why Mickey is here—he's helping me investigate Crawford's death."

"You a cop?" Drake asked me.

"No, I play for the St. Louis Browns."

Gatewood asked suspiciously, "Then why ain't you with your team?"

"I got suspended for playing against the Cubs."

"The Browns, huh?" said Drake. "*I* pitched a game in Sportsman's Park last year, you know."

"You did?" Since colored fans were limited to the bleachers, I was surprised that a Negro player had been allowed on the field.

"Yep. Exhibition game. St. Louis Giants—that's what we were called before we became the Stars—against the Cardinals.

Against most of the Cardinals, anyway—Hornsby said he wouldn't go on the same field with colored men. Turned out to be one of the best games I ever pitched." Drake smiled brightly at the memory. "They beat me, but it took 'em twelve innings to do it. Not bad, being able to take a big-league club into extra innings."

A large, sultry-voiced woman joined the band and began singing a slow, seductive blues tune. The band played at a lower volume, making conversation at our table much easier.

Big Bill Gatewood was still focused on the Crawford lynching. "You're 'investigating,'" he said derisively. "If you ask me, there ain't much to investigate. The Klan strung Crawford up for beating a white team."

"That very well may be," said Aubury. "But we need to *know* what happened, not merely assume."

"I've already been talking to players on the Elcars," I said, "and I'm looking into the Klan. What I'm hoping *you* can tell me about is Slip Crawford."

There was no trace of a smile remaining on Drake's face when he said, "You mean you want to know what there was about Slip that would make somebody want to lynch him? That's easy: He wasn't the Klan's favorite color."

"What if it wasn't the Klan?" I said. "What if he was killed by somebody else—maybe for some personal reason?" I could tell that the men around the table didn't think there was much chance that it was anyone other than the KKK; and perhaps they didn't like the idea that I might be trying to pin the crime on someone other than the Klan. I pressed on anyway, "Was Crawford tough to get along with? Did he run with a bad crowd?"

Bell answered first. "I only saw him that one game. I didn't really know the man at all."

"I did," said Drake. "If he was alive, he wouldn't be here with us tonight, I can tell you that. Off the field, Slip led a quiet life. Had a good wife in Hannah. She's a hardworking woman—runs a hair salon and writes dreambooks on the side. They made a decent living and had a good life together. No kids, but they were hoping."

"Dreambooks?" I asked.

Franklin Aubury explained, "Little booklets that tell people what numbers to bet on; women who write them claim the numbers come to them in a dream. It's like fortune-telling."

I addressed Drake. "You said off the field he was quiet. What about *on* the field? Did the other players get along with him?"

"All except the ones who had to hit against him—Slip was at *war* when he was stepped onto the diamond. No trouble with his own teammates, though." He started to grin again. "Not like George Scales, our third baseman—that man's not right in the head. I roomed with him for a couple weeks and never got a minute's sleep. Had to keep one eye open all night, 'cause now and then he'd get a mind to try to cut me with a knife. I even took to keeping a gun under my pillow, but still couldn't sleep. Finally had to get me a different roomie."

"Was there any problem about Crawford jumping from the ABCs to the Stars this year?" I asked.

Gatewood answered, "No, we all do that. You play wherever you can get a decent paycheck."

Plunk Drake spoke up again. "As long as you stay within the league, it's okay."

"What do you mean?"

Drake looked at Gatewood as if seeking permission. The manager shrugged and nodded for him to go ahead. "There's another league starting," the pitcher said, "the Eastern Colored League."

"I read about that."

"Well, to have a league, you got to have ballplayers. And

the ECL is trying to recruit Negro National League players to jump to them.''

"Were they recruiting Crawford?"

"Sure were. Some thug named Rosie Sumner—works for a gangster in Harlem—was pushing him hard."

"Was he making any progress?"

"Nah, Rube Foster says he'll blacklist any player who signs with the ECL. Crawford wasn't gonna take that risk."

"Did Sumner talk to any of the other Stars about jumping?"

"To me," Drake said. "But he didn't push much."

Bell shook his head no, and Gatewood said Sumner had only phoned him once.

The band launched into an up-tempo number that started my foot tapping and got Bell drumming along on the tabletop.

Drake polished off his beer and thumped the empty glass down on the table. "No offense, but I came out for fun tonight—and this ain't fun." He scanned the room, and another smile took over his face. "I see a young lady I'll bet is dying to dance with me. Excuse me, gentlemen."

With Drake gone, I asked Gatewood, "Why would Slip Crawford be the only one of the Stars Sumner was applying pressure to? You got a *lot* of good players from what I saw today."

"Yeah, but we don't got *great* players. Crawford was gonna be a great one. He'd been around long enough to prove himself, and was young enough that we all knew he'd get even better." The manager nodded to Bell. "Of course, once the ECL hears about Cool Papa here, they'll come trying to recruit him, too."

Bell grinned at the compliment, but I worried that it might not be a good thing for the youngster to be "recruited" by Rosie Sumner. I asked Bell, "Have you had any problems after the game with the Elcars?"

"What kind of problems?"

"Crawford got killed," I said, "and Denver Jones's house

was burned down, so I was wondering if any of the other players had trouble.''

The youngster shook his head. "I ain't heard nothing from the Cubs—but I been on the road all season. Ain't had no trouble myself, though. And if anybody came to our house, I got four bigger brothers at home who'd protect the place.''

"Okay.'' I was out of questions, so I looked from Bell to Gatewood. "Anything else you can tell me about Slip Crawford?''

Gatewood said, "No, but I got a question for *you*. What if you find out that it *was* the Klan who killed him? What will you do then?''

I had no ready answer to that. I glanced at Aubury for help.

"One thing at a time,'' the lawyer said. "First we must establish the facts. Then we can decide on an appropriate course of action.''

"If you want *action*,'' Gatewood said, "you get Oscar Charleston in on it. He knows how to handle that kind. Outside a ballpark in Florida, a couple of masked Klansmen came up and threatened him. Oscar went over to them, calm as you please, and tore their hoods off. Then he stared them down till they walked away, tails between their legs.''

We all drank a toast to Charleston. Then another one to Slip Crawford.

When the waiter came around to fill our drinks again, I was ready to go, but I could tell Aubury wanted to remain with the ballplayers.

I made the excuse of being tired and left alone. This was their place, and I'd intruded long enough.

It was strange, I thought. When I'd first walked into the speakeasy, I'd been uncomfortable at being the only white person in the place. But while talking with the Stars, I forgot about color. Now, leaving the nightclub, I again felt like an outsider. And it was worse than before, because I no longer had Franklin Aubury with me.

I quickly headed down Indiana Avenue, noticing that every face I passed was dark. Although I didn't know anyone at the whites-only hotel where I was staying, I was eager to see white faces again. I didn't like being a minority.

As I walked, I recalled what Buddy Vaughn had said about people being happier among their own race. I hated to think that he could be right. I was comfortable with Aubury, though, so it wasn't really a matter of skin color. Maybe it was just a matter of getting to know somebody.

I gave up thinking about the race issue, and for the rest of the walk to the hotel I reviewed what I'd learned from the St. Louis Stars.

The only real news was about the Eastern Colored League trying to sign Slip Crawford. This was nothing unusual in baseball; whenever a new league formed, the established leagues were raided for ballplayers. When the American League started in 1901, National League stars were enticed to jump. And both the American and National Leagues had lost marquee players to the fledgling Federal League in 1914.

The difference this time was using somebody like Rosie Sumner to do the recruiting. Why a strong-arm man? Perhaps to threaten instead of entice. The more I thought about it, though, the less I thought Sumner would have actually hurt Crawford. If he wanted him for the new league, he'd need to keep him healthy. Unless, of course, Crawford gave him a firm no; then hurting him would be a blow to the Negro National League.

Okay, I decided, if Sumner was going after the top players, then he must have approached the ABCs—everyone agreed they had some of the best in the game. So let's see if Aubury can set up a meeting with them.

CHAPTER 20

Franklin Aubury was tied up in meetings at the local NAACP office the next morning, so I was free to explore Indianapolis on my own.

I started in the heart of the city, at Monument Circle, where the towering Soldiers and Sailors Monument rose three hundred feet above the ground. After a walk around the circle, I headed two blocks west, where the domed state capital building, a small mountain of limestone, dominated the view. I continued my tour in a widening circle around the center of town, trying to get a sense of the place.

I had never spent much time in Indianapolis. Since the city didn't have a big-league ball club, I'd never thought of it as much more than a place to pass through on my way to a city that did. But as I strolled around the downtown area, I was impressed. The roads and sidewalks were in excellent repair, the parks were green and groomed, and the buildings well maintained. Altogether, the capital of Indiana appeared clean, modern, attractive, and prosperous.

Part of the prosperity was due to the thriving automobile industry, which was second only to Detroit's. Locally manufac-tured automobiles were much in evidence, from luxurious Deusenbergs and Marmons to sporty Stutz Bearcats to the lower-cost cars produced by the National, Premier, and Cole factories.

The city's automobile heritage was also prominently heralded in the numerous posters that advertised the upcoming race at the Indianapolis Motor Speedway. The tenth Indianapolis 500 would be held on Decoration Day—the same day that Evansville Klan No. 1 would be enjoying its "Dazzling Day of Diversified Delights."

It became clear as I walked that Indianapolis had a strong Klan presence of its own. No one wore hoods or robes on the street, but almost every other business carried a KKK or TWK slogan on its sign, and many storefronts displayed placards for a Fourth of July Klan rally on the capital steps.

I kept walking, and continued to wonder why the Ku Klux Klan would thrive in this idyllic part of the heartland. What was its appeal to the men who lived here?

When I checked back in at the Harrison Hotel, the desk clerk handed me a message from Franklin Aubury. The lawyer wanted me to meet him at one o'clock at the corner of West Fifteenth and Holtan Place. He was apparently expecting trouble, because the last line of the note read: *I can use some muscle.*

I had only twenty minutes to get there, so I asked the clerk for the quickest route.

"You don't want to go there," he said, with a prissy shake of his head.

"Why not?"

"That's a colored part of town." He whispered the word *colored* as if one didn't even mention that race in polite company.

"I didn't ask who *lived* there. I asked how to *get* there."

The desk clerk again cautioned me against venturing into "that neighborhood" and I decided it would be faster to take a taxicab anyway. Outside the hotel's front entrance, I hailed a cabby, who proved no more eager to take me to my destination than the clerk had been to give me directions. But for double his usual fare, he agreed.

It turned out there'd been no need to hurry. The location Aubury had given me was a vacant lot. The only trouble he was having was in keeping order as twenty or so colored boys, ages from about eight to fourteen, warmed up for a baseball game.

"What's going on?" I asked him.

"These young men," Aubury said, "are newsboys for the *Indianapolis Freeman*. One of their reporters mentioned to me this morning that they were playing a game today, and I volunteered to umpire."

"Perfect job for a guy who wears glasses," I kidded. "Your note said you needed muscle; I thought you were meeting some tough guys or something."

Aubury smiled. "I *can* use extra muscle." He tossed me a bat. "You mind hitting them infield practice?"

I took off my hat and coat and proceeded to do as he asked. I rapped grounders to half the boys while Aubury, similarly coatless, hit fly balls to the other half.

After practice, Aubury called all the kids in, and announced, "You're in luck today. This is Mickey Rawlings; he's a major-league baseball player, and he's going to give you some coaching today."

I was so flattered that I didn't mind that Aubury hadn't talked to me before volunteering my services.

A small boy in a sleeveless undershirt asked me, "You know Oscar Charleston?"

"No," I had to admit. "But I saw him play once."

Another kid asked, "How about Pop Lloyd?"

"Uh, no. I don't know him, either."

They shouted the names of several other Negro stars, and

I had to keep giving the same disappointing answer. The nature of the questions wasn't unusual for me; most people, when they found out I was a utility player they'd never heard of, asked me about more famous players they *had* heard of. But at least when I was asked about Ty Cobb or Tris Speaker, I could say I knew them. With the Negro League players, I was at a loss.

Aubury tried to come to my rescue. "Mr. Rawlings played in a game against Slip Crawford last month."

One of the boys called out, "You get a hit off him?"

"No. He struck me out three times."

Several cheers went up for the dead pitcher. I took no offense; Crawford was obviously a hero to these kids.

Aubury then appointed the two tallest boys captains and told them to choose up sides. As they did, he said to me, "I love working with kids. You have any?"

"No, I was hoping . . . I thought I might someday, but now . . ." Jeez, I was getting no end of awkward questions today. "What happened was, the girl I thought I was gonna marry left me a couple of weeks ago."

"I'm sorry," Aubury said. "A good woman will make you or break you."

"I'll find another." To myself, I added, "I hope."

The game began, with Aubury umpiring from a standing position behind the pitcher. I piped up often with playing tips for the members of both teams. Now and then, Aubury would stop the game so I could demonstrate a particular point.

I'd never seen the lawyer so relaxed. I was having a great time, too, until one of the boys asked me how he could become a big-league ballplayer. The present reality was that he'd have to change his skin color. What I told him was, "Keep practicing."

For the rest of the game, I kept looking around at the boys, all playing their best. It pained me to realize that with the current state of Organized Baseball not one of them, no matter how hard he practiced or how well he played, would be signed by a major-league ball club. But I continued to give the best playing advice I could, hoping some of them might be able to put it to use someday in the Negro League.

When the game ended, Aubury asked me, "Do you feel like swinging a bat some more?" He flexed his arm. "I've got a pitch or two in me that are dying to get out."

"Sure!" I said eagerly. I remembered he'd mentioned playing in college, but I assumed college boys were all as devoid of athletic ability as Karl Landfors.

Aubury removed his vest and went to the mound, yelling for the kids to go back out on the field.

I grabbed the heaviest bat I could find. I'd batted against lefties and righties, fastball pitchers and curveball artists. This was the first time I would be facing a *lawyer,* and I figured the only challenge would be that, since the kids were sure to be rooting for Aubury, I shouldn't make him look too bad.

I called to him, "You want any warm-up throws?"

When he didn't answer, I stepped to the plate.

The lawyer went into a windmill windup, swiveling his body until at one point in his motion he was facing centerfield. Then he spun around, hurling a fastball directly at my head.

It wasn't much of a fastball, but I was so surprised that I hit the dirt, causing a roar of laughter and cheers from the boys.

"Okay!" Aubury said, smiling. "I'm all warmed up!"

Good, I thought, because I'm all *riled* up. No longer worried about how he might look to the kids, I wanted to wallop every pitch he threw.

It turned out to be no easy task. Aubury was a masterful junk-ball pitcher; he wrapped slow curves around my bat almost as deftly as Slip Crawford had.

I hit some solid line drives and a few towering fly balls off him, but he also made me miss about half his deliveries.

Neither of us would quit. We kept going, both of us huffing

and sweating, and we kept the boys busy running down the baseballs. Finally, he got me to miss three pitches in a row. I dropped my bat and conceded defeat. "You got me!"

While the kids cheered, I walked out to the mound and Aubury came in to meet me. We stood grinning at each other for a moment, then we shook hands.

Aubury and I mopped the sweat from our faces with our pocket handkerchiefs as the kids gathered up their meager equipment. When we'd stopped perspiring, we put our coats and hats back on, said good-bye to the boys, and began walking down toward Washington Park. We strolled slowly, letting ourselves cool down.

"You pitch pretty good for a lawyer," I said.

He chuckled. "It felt great to throw a baseball again. Next time, how about if you pitch to me, and I get to hit some."

"You're on—but be ready to duck on the first one."

"Only fair," he said. Brushing the lapels of his jacket, he added wistfully, "I sure wish I had a son so I could teach him baseball. Don't get me wrong: I adore my girls, but it's not the same."

"If Margie and I had a daughter," I said, "we'd teach her baseball anyway. Margie used to make adventure serials as Marguerite Turner. She'll make sure any daughter of hers knows how to play sports—and probably how to wrestle alligators, too."

"I've seen some of her movies," Aubury said. "Was she the one who . . ."

"Left me. Yeah."

"What happened? If you don't mind my asking."

I gave him a brief account of how unreasonable Margie had been.

He asked dubiously, "If I understand you correctly, you

were angry with her because she did not accept your marriage proposal *quickly enough?*''

''At first. But it's what she told me about her past that was the real problem.''

''The past cannot be changed, not yours nor anyone else's. You have to put it behind you.''

''I guess. But that's easier to say than do.''

He tugged at the brim of his derby, and said as if thinking aloud, ''Too many people continue to fight old battles. That won't lead anywhere. You have to go forward if you want to get someplace.''

I had the impression we weren't talking about Margie and me anymore. ''Old battles,'' I said. ''You mean like the Klan trying to change the outcome of the Civil War?''

''And everyone else who wants to set back the clock—and set back human progress.'' He went on in a soft voice, ''My father was born into slavery, and my mother during Reconstruction, when night riders of the first Klan were terrorizing the South. When I was born, my parents were working as sharecroppers in Louisiana; conditions weren't much better than in slave times, but at least they were nominally free. They made sure I did my studies so that I could get into college, I worked my way through law school, and now I'm an attorney. I still don't have all the rights that are due me, but I'm doing better than my parents. My goal is for my daughters to do better, to live better, than me. I will fight the Klan or the government or anyone else who wants to keep my daughters from being full citizens and having the rights to which they are entitled. And the battleground is here.''

''Not in Washington?'' I asked. ''Or in the South?''

Aubury picked up the pace. ''I am starting to believe that the Midwest Klan is a far greater threat to our liberty than the Southern mobs. At the meeting this morning, I learned that Indianapolis has *ten thousand* Klansmen. Statewide, there are *seventy* thousand, with two thousand more joining every week. They are organized, and they are trying to take over the state. Once they gain political power, more segregation laws will be passed, and Negroes will be further excluded from society.'' His voice rose. ''Disenfranchise the Negro, dehumanize him, and then you can kill him at will.'' He breathed hard a few times, and said more calmly, ''The Klan is already pushing for segregated schools and segregated neighborhoods.''

I said, ''I was thinking about that, about people being happier with their own kind ... I'm not in favor of any *forced* separation, but it does seem whites are more comfortable with whites and Negroes with Negroes. Generally, I mean—in groups, not necessarily as individuals. I'm comfortable talking to you.''

Aubury said, ''*Everyone* is an individual. But I know what you mean, and what you say is largely true. However, it must be a matter of choice.'' He adjusted his glasses. ''And, to be candid, I am not entirely comfortable with you.''

His bluntness took me by surprise. ''Why not?''

''I mean no offense, but there are things about me that you will never truly understand, and things about *you* that *I* will never understand. One can never really know what it is like to live in someone else's skin. There are differences between us, and there always will be. There is no sense pretending otherwise. Negroes are not looking to become the same as white people; we just want to be treated as human.''

''Whatever the differences between you and me,'' I said, ''we also got something in common.''

''What's that?''

''We both play baseball a helluva lot better than Karl Landfors ever will.''

Aubury laughed.

As we neared Washington Park, the parade of people coming

the other way indicated the game was over. We learned from one of the fans that the ABCs had won.

"That's good," Aubury said to me. "You don't want to be around them when they lose. Let me see if we can talk to the players."

I waited outside the park while Aubury went into the clubhouse. He came back shortly to report that we could meet with some of them later in the evening.

Russell's Tonsorial Parlor, in a colored section of the city's near east side, appeared to be more of a social club than a place of business. Of the seven men lounging in the cozy, old-fashioned barbershop, not one was engaged in a shave or a haircut. Near the front window, two ancient black men were hunched over a checkerboard. On a stool by the sink, a lanky young man was playing a battered guitar, sliding the back edge of a closed straight razor along the strings.

One of the shop's two barber chairs was occupied by an elderly man in a white tunic, reading a copy of the *Indianapolis Freeman.* When I walked in with Franklin Aubury, he laid down his paper, and said to me, "I'm sorry, sir, but I can't do nothing for you here. I cut hair at the Capital Hotel on Wednesdays if you want to come see me there."

Once again, all eyes were on me, the only white man in the place, but it was Aubury who answered, "We've only come to talk."

The old barber said with a laugh, "Then you sure come to the right place! More of that going on here than hair cutting."

A powerfully built man, who had the body of a wrestler and the bearing of a king, was enthroned in the second barber chair. With a nod at Aubury, he told the others, "This here is Mister Franklin Aubury, a lawyer from St. Louis. I told him he could come by."

Aubury introduced me to the big man in the chair. He was

Oscar Charleston, "the best baseball player in the history of the world," as Aubury put it. With a twinkle in his eye, the lawyer identified me as "an occasional infielder with the St. Louis Browns and a sucker for slow curveballs."

After Charleston gave me a handshake that nearly turned me into a lefty, Aubury continued the introductions. In a couple of straight-backed chairs across from Charleston were two more of the ABCs, both of them dressed in finer suits than I had ever owned. One was Biz Mackey, a tall man with a serious face, and "the premier catcher in the Negro National League," according to Aubury. The other was second baseman Crush Holloway, a bony-cheeked fellow with wide, innocent eyes.

While the guitarist played a mournful tune, making the strings actually *moan* by sliding his razor, Aubury said to the ballplayers, "I'm sorry we missed the game. How did it go?"

"Don't get them started." The barber sighed. "These boys been braggin' on that game for an hour."

They happily proceeded to give us the highlights. Since Aubury and I had already heard about the game from some fans, I assumed Aubury had asked the question primarily to get the conversation rolling. Nothing makes a ballplayer more talkative than asking him to recount his successes.

Biz Mackey said, "You should have seen the catch Oscar made. Tully McAdoo hit a fly to center field that had 'triple' written all over it. But old Oscar jus' started running back, never even turnin' around to look for the ball. At the last second, he reaches up and catches it like he *knew* where that baseball was gonna come down."

"Wasn't nothing to it," said Charleston. "I could tell by the sound of the bat where the ball was goin'."

The barber gave Charleston a friendly swat with the newspaper. "This boy was *born* to play ball. I've known him since he was eight years old, and he *always* had a glove or bat in his hand. He was such a regular at the ABCs games, they made him their batboy—and even back then, he could hit as good as some of the players!''

Charleston basked in the praise. He was obviously accustomed to receiving such compliments, but that didn't appear to diminish his enjoyment at hearing them.

Crush Holloway said, ''Hey, Oscar, finish that story about the time you got arrested.'' To Aubury and me, he explained, ''He just started tellin' it when you came in.''

The center fielder obliged, recounting a 1915 game against a white semipro team. When the umpire made a string of blatantly biased calls against the ABCs, Charleston objected. He punctuated his argument by decking the ump in front of five thousand fans, and was hauled off to jail. The incident prompted the Indianapolis chief of police to propose a ban on all ball games between white and colored teams.

Holloway chuckled. ''Oscar, you just ain't happy 'less you're having a scuffle with *somebody*. But you oughta know better than to punch out a umpire.''

I said to Charleston, ''I heard you once had a run-in with some Klansmen in Florida.''

''Wasn't much of a run-in,'' he said. ''They backed down quick.'' The big man added emphatically, ''Ain't nobody gonna bully me—especially not some cowards hiding under bedsheets.''

Franklin Aubury, getting to the purpose of our visit, said, ''Speaking of the Ku Klux Klan, we think they might be the ones who lynched Slip Crawford. Mickey's looking into it.''

I eyed each of the players. ''When Crawford played for the ABCs, did he have any trouble with anyone?''

''Like with the Klan?'' Charleston asked.

''With anyone.''

All of them shook their heads, and commented on what a good guy Crawford had been.

''Except when he was pitching,'' Holloway added. ''The

batter was the *enemy* to Slip, and he'd knock him down without a second thought. Got into some fights on the field, and Biz here had to stop more than one batter from taking a bat to Slip's skull, but that's just part of the game. Never heard about him having troubles off the field.''

Biz Mackey pointed to Holloway. ''This man got the exact opposite approach as what Slip had. Crush is always friendly and smilin' to the other team. The thing is, he's about as deadly as they come when he's running the bases—makes Ty Cobb look like a ballet dancer. Crush'll cut a second baseman to shreds or knock a shortstop clean out to left field. But he'll give him a big ol' smile, and say, 'Hey, man, sorry I came in so hard. You all right? Let me help you up.' ''

Holloway mugged for us, demonstrating the apologetic grin Mackey described, and we all laughed.

The catcher went on. ''Slip Crawford, though, never had no apology for knocking down a batter. He figured home plate was his—if you got too close, he'd back you off or stick it in your ear.''

Oscar Charleston asked me, ''This your way of finding out who killed Slip—by talking to his friends? Talk to his enemies—talk to the Klan.''

''I intend to,'' I said. ''I'm just trying to be thorough.''

''Mickey has been working hard on this,'' Aubury said. ''And he is covering all possibilities, the same as I would.''

''*Why?*'' asked Charleston. ''Why are you so interested in who killed Slip?''

Aubury said, ''We are trying to prevent any further violence.''

Charleston gestured at me. ''I'm asking *him.*''

My impulse was to give the same answer the lawyer had. But I opted to give a more personal reason instead. ''I got to play in only one game against Slip Crawford. He struck me out three times, and I didn't get on base once. I wanted another chance at him, to see if I could hit that damned curveball of his. Whoever killed him took that chance away from me. I'm never gonna get a hit off him now, and I'm mad as hell about that."

There were nods of approval and understanding at my answer.

Charleston leaned toward me. "Last year, I was with St. Louis, and Slip was pitching for the ABCs. I faced him maybe twenty or thirty times, and didn't get but a handful of hits off him either." He chuckled. "So don't feel too bad."

The barber climbed off his chair and swatted the leather cushion a couple of times with a towel. "You need a trim," he said to me. "Sit down, and I'll give you one—just don't tell nobody."

I hung up my jacket and took the seat.

As he wrapped the linen cloth around me, the barber called to the old men by the window. "You fellas let me know if you see a cop."

"Why?" I asked.

"This barbershop's for colored only. Can't cut a white man's hair in here."

"But you can at the hotel you mentioned?"

"Of course. The Capital's a white hotel. In there, I can't cut a *colored* man's hair."

"But you can work in either place?"

"Goes by the color of the customer, not the barber." He fastened the cloth around my throat. "I don't make the laws, I jus' try to survive 'em."

I tried to clear my head. I was never going to understand the convoluted logic of segregation laws, nor the people who conceived them.

As the barber began snipping at my hair, I returned to the reason Aubury and I had come. "We were told," I said, "that

Slip Crawford was getting pressured to jump to the Eastern Colored League. Any of you heard anything about that?''

They all said they'd heard nothing about Crawford being recruited. Mackey added, ''He was gone from our team by the time the ECL was getting started.''

''Have any of *you* been contacted by them?''

Oscar Charleston answered, ''A new league is gonna want the best players they can get, and we *are* the best.''

''So Rosie Sumner's been to see you?''

''You know about Sumner?'' Charleston sounded surprised.

''Yeah, he works for somebody in Harlem, right?''

''Alex Pompez,'' Charleston said. ''He's a numbers king who also owns a ball club—the New York Cuban Stars. And, yeah, Sumner's been to see me. Dizzy Dismukes, too, I know. Sumner came to our spring-training camp in French Lick; he was talking up the new league, saying how we'd get out from under Rube Foster's thumb if we jump.''

''What did you tell him?''

''I told him no.'' Charleston looked thoughtful. ''When I played for Rube in Chicago, I didn't much like him as a manager. He's too damn strict—even tells his players how to dress off the field. And now that he's president of the league, he moves me from team to team, wherever a club needs a star to attract the fans.'' Charleston stated this as simple fact, not bragging. ''But the thing is, even though I don't like all his rules, I figure Rube Foster made this league, and he can run it however he wants. I'm satisfied with the Negro National League, at least for now.''

I asked Holloway and Mackey, ''How about you guys?''

Both said Sumner had approached them, and their answers had been that they'd think about it.

''Did he push you?''

''Not then, he didn't,'' said Mackey.

''What do you mean 'not then'?''

Mackey answered, "Rosie Sumner called me again after Slip Crawford got killed. He *suggested* I should go east, where I'd be safe from the Klan."

Jeez. Sumner was using Crawford's lynching as a selling point for the ECL.

Crush Holloway said, "He told me the same thing. What I told him was to go to hell." He added, "Me and Biz come up here from San Antonio, where we played with the Black Aces. In Texas, the Klan hangs or whips a colored man every week. We survived there; we can sure as hell survive here."

"Sumner tried that line on me a couple weeks ago, too," Charleston said. "I told him if I ever saw him again, *he'd* be the one to have to worry about staying alive."

The barber brushed the loose clippings from around my neck and removed the cloth.

I dug into my pocket. "What do I owe you?"

"Not a thing. But if you do find out what happened to Slip Crawford, you let us know, okay?"

I promised that I would.

CHAPTER 21

Over the weekend, Franklin Aubury and I went to both games at Washington Park. The St. Louis Stars had left for the next city on their two-month road trip, but an even better team had arrived in Indianapolis: the Kansas City Monarchs, whose outstanding pitching staff included Bullet Joe Rogan and Jose Mendez. I almost forgot about my suspension and thoroughly enjoyed being able to take it easy and simply be a fan for a few days. I saw some spectacular plays, gorged myself with hot dogs and peanuts, and talked baseball endlessly with Aubury.

After Sunday's contest, I told the lawyer that I would attend the Klan picnic in Evansville. Probably neither of us had much doubt that I would reach that decision, but he sounded delighted to hear it. I also jokingly asked him if he wanted to accompany me, but Aubury said he preferred to sleep on bed linen, not wear it.

Monday afternoon, I was alone on a southbound train, dozing off and on, and sporadically catching up with the sports pages to see what had been happening in the world of Caucasian baseball while I'd been immersed in the Negro League game.

I read with mixed feelings of the Browns' recent fortunes.

My teammates had lost two of three games to the Yankees, and had continued to struggle thereafter. At the time I was suspended, we were in a tie for first place; as of this morning, St. Louis had fallen three games behind New York. Petty though it was, I couldn't help but feel a bit smug that the team was faring poorly without me. On the other hand, I didn't want them to continue losing—I still hoped that the Browns would take me to my first World Series.

The Yankees were riding so high on their success, according to another story, that they were going to leave the Giants' Polo Grounds and build a ballpark of their own in the Bronx. They had already broken ground at the site, and were planning to spend more than two million dollars on a stadium to open next spring. I did some arithmetic, and found that at my current salary I would have to play baseball for more than five hundred years to earn that sum of money.

The latest baseball news, though, wasn't about anything that took place between the foul lines. The United States Supreme Court, through some tortured logic, had just ruled that Organized Baseball was a sport, not a business, and therefore exempt from antitrust laws. Among other things, the court determined that the reserve clause, which bound players to teams in perpetuity, was perfectly legal. I carefully read the reasoning given by the court, but try as I might, it made no more sense to me than segregation laws which specified where a man could and could not get a haircut. So I wadded my jacket into a pillow and took another nap.

So many people had flocked in from nearby towns for the holiday festivities, that I had to try four hotels on Main Street until I found one with a vacancy. When I entered my room, I saw on the washstand a handbill for the Klan gathering, which noted: *All White Gentile Protestant People of Indiana and the Tri-State Territory Are Cordially Invited.* I muttered aloud,

"What the hell is this?" The colored bellboy who'd carried my bags answered that the hotel was distributing the leaflets to all its guests.

With more than an hour until sunset, I took a walk around downtown Evansville, Indiana. Although less than 150 miles from the state capital, the two cities were vastly different.

Indianapolis, with its central location and numerous railroad tracks and highways passing through it, billed itself as the Crossroads of America. It was a modern city with a thriving automobile industry, pharmaceutical manufacturers such as Eli Lilly, and a couple of universities.

Evansville, surrounded by coal country, was less prosperous and more isolated. It was tucked in the southwest corner of the state, on a bend of the Ohio River so sharp that a finger of Kentucky poked into the middle of town. The remote location might have been one reason why entertainment options were limited. I saw plenty of churches, but few movie theaters, only one vaudeville house, and no dance clubs. Judging by the posters plastered all over town, there was only one event worth attending in the city of Evansville: the Decoration Day picnic sponsored by the Ku Klux Klan.

Evansville Klan No. 1 was blessed with perfect weather for its festivities. Late Tuesday morning, soft sunshine bathed the city in warmth and light, and gentle breezes carried the scent of greenery from the surrounding hillsides.

There was no need for me to ask directions when I left the hotel. I merely had to follow all the other people walking toward the river. Many families were making the trek; children talked excitedly about seeing the fireworks, and women chatted about what kind of food might be served. From all outward appearances, these people could easily have been on their way to a Sunday church picnic or a Fourth of July celebration. There was nothing to suggest that they were going to a rally in support of terrorism and bigotry.

Once I arrived at the park, near the riverbank, it became apparent that there *was* something different about this event. Although most people were dressed in ordinary summer clothes, quite a few proudly wore the white robes and pointed hoods of the Ku Klux Klan. On the breast of each robe was embroidered a stylized cross in a circle, with what looked like a red blood drop at the center of the cross. Not many of the Klansmen worried about hiding their identities; the mask of almost every hood was kept rolled up above the face like a little window shade. The outfit wasn't worn only by men. Women and children also wore the hoods and robes, and one family even had a Labrador retriever draped in a white sheet.

I began to stroll through the park and saw that the more traditional costume for Decoration Day was in evidence as well. Veterans of the nation's wars proudly wore their snug old uniforms, adorned with medals and ribbons. Most were younger men who'd survived the Great War, some were middle-aged veterans from the "Splendid Little War" with Spain, and a few white-haired old men sported the ancient blue uniforms that they'd worn during the War Between the States. I wondered how these men who'd fought for the preservation of the Union felt about all the Confederate flags on display.

As I wandered around, I noticed nothing out of the ordinary but the Klan attire. The only fires were in the barbecue pits, and the only ropes were those twirled by the rodeo riders performing tricks in a small arena. Everything was normal holiday recreation; kids ran sack races and played games of tag, a brass band filled the air with patriotic tunes—as well as occasional renditions of "Dixie"—and frankfurters and ice cream were being consumed in enormous quantities.

Around lunchtime, I got a hot dog and lemonade for myself. While I ate, I watched a photographer set up a picture of four men standing in a row. Three of his subjects wore the uniforms from each of the last three wars; the fourth was in Klan regalia, with his mask down. The men were arranged with the Civil War soldier on the left, then the Spanish-American and Great War veterans, and the Klansman on the right. From the sequence, it looked like a prediction that Klan robes would be the uniform of the next war to come.

Unlike many of the veterans in the park, I had never felt the urge to don my army uniform again for the holiday—I'd been too relieved to get out of it. Besides, until this year, I'd never had occasion to wear it, since I'd always spent Decoration Day in the uniform of a major-league baseball team. I wished that I was in my wool flannels now, helping the Browns in their doubleheader against Boston.

My thoughts turning to baseball, I drifted over to the park's diamond, where an informal game was in progress. I wasn't learning anything about the Klan anyway, other than that it could put on a perfectly normal, all-American picnic.

I sat down in the small, wooden bleachers to watch for a while. There wasn't much skill in evidence—to players in these games, the most important thing is usually to avoid spilling their drinks—but at least it was baseball.

I'd barely settled on the pine board when a man behind me reached out with an open paper bag. "Peanut?" he offered.

"No, thanks. Just ate."

Pointing to the batter's box, he said in a weak, tremulous voice, "Look at that fool. How is he gonna run in that outfit?"

A hitter had come to the plate wearing a Klan robe and hood. "Never mind run," I said. "How's he even gonna swing a bat?"

The man got up and moved next to me on the bench. I couldn't tell if he was a Klansman from his dress. He wore faded denim overalls with a white shirt and black bow tie, and a sweat-stained fedora was tilted back on his head. I pegged his age at about sixty, and he had a wrinkle for every one of those years etched on his leathery face.

"Name's Glenn Hyde." He held out a hand impregnated with coal dust. "Haven't seen you around here before."

"Mickey Welch." We shook hands. "I'm just passing through town."

"Where you from?"

"St. Louis. I'm on my way back home from Indianapolis."

"What were you doing there?"

It didn't sound like Hyde was merely passing the time of day. "I'm a mechanic," I lied. "I was learning how to repair Nationals. Got a new job with a garage in East St. Louis, and they want me to be familiar with the latest models." Before he could ask me any details about automobiles, I added, "I've been asked to join the Klan in East St. Louis, too. Hope it's okay for me to be here if I'm gonna be joining a klavern someplace else."

"Of course! Everyone's welcome here. We're glad to have you." He coughed a few times and wiped his mouth with a handkerchief. "Let me tell you, if the East St. Louis klavern is anything like the one we have here, you're gonna find you're always among friends when you're a Klansman."

"You been a member long?"

He chuckled. "Nobody's been a Knight for long, not in Indiana. The Evansville klavern was only organized a year and a half ago, and it was the first in the state. I joined last fall, after I saw the Klan in action."

"What kind of 'action'?" I wasn't sure Hyde would answer this question.

He did, promptly and proudly. "My wife and I were sittin' in Sunday worship one morning at the Methodist church we go to. It's a small congregation, and a poor one; the church is always needing some kind of repair we can't afford. Anyway, this particular Sunday, the pastor is in the middle of his sermon when all of a sudden he stops talking and gets a look on his face like he's seen a ghost. There's whispers coming from the back pews, so I turn around and can't believe what I see: a dozen robed Klansmen walkin' up the aisle. They go up to the altar, and one of them says to the minister, real polite and respectful, 'We're sorry to interrupt, but we thought you might be able to put this to good use.' He hands the minister a bill, then the Klansmen turn around and file out as quiet as they came in. It was a *hundred dollars* they gave. Our pastor blessed the offering, and we all praised the Lord. I joined the Klan at their next meeting."

I wondered about the Klan's less charitable activities. "What else does the local klavern do?" I asked.

"Oh, all sorts of good works. Last Christmas, we took groceries to families down on their luck. And we made a few rent payments for some folks facin' eviction. Tell you the truth, I had to scrape a bit for the ten-dollar membership—that's almost a week's wages around here. But when I see how it gets put to use, I'm real glad I did." He nodded with satisfaction. "Yes sir, Klan is good people."

This wasn't the Ku Klux Klan I'd heard about. "Must be doing something right," I said. "Sure is growing fast."

"By leaps and bounds." Hyde fell into a brief coughing fit; after catching his breath, he went on, "I been a coal miner all my life, same as most men in these parts. I never joined anything before, except the church, mostly 'cause I was never *invited* to join anything—them fancy fraternal organizations want doctors and lawyers and businessmen, not workin' men. That's the great thing about the Klan: They want any good Christian American man, no matter how he earns his living— as long as it's legal and moral, of course."

And it wants his ten bucks, I thought.

Hyde crumpled up the peanut bag and rapped my knee.

"Say, the Old Man is gonna be talkin' soon. Wanna go hear him?"

"Who *is* he?"

"David C. Stephenson, but everybody calls him the Old Man. He's the Exalted Cyclops of the klavern. Rumor has it he's gonna be made Grand Dragon soon—that'll put him in charge of the entire state."

Stephenson was the Klan leader Franklin Aubury had told me about. "Sure," I said. "Let's go."

We left the ball game and headed toward a clearing near the river bend, stopping occasionally when Hyde grew short of breath. Groups of men were walking in the same direction, most of them wearing robes and hoods. Not all the Klan costumes were white, I noticed; a few were brightly colored. When I asked Glenn Hyde about it, he explained that they signified different ranks, including green for Great Titan and red for Grand Dragon. One that Hyde said we wouldn't see today was the purple robe of Imperial Wizard William J. Simmons, who ran the Invisible Empire from his headquarters in Atlanta.

"Why do some have the masks rolled up and others have them down?"

"Well, not everyone understands what the Klan is truly about. So some prefer to keep their membership secret; I know a few whose own families don't know. Others want to be open about being in the Klan. A Klansman is always free to reveal his own membership—but to tell about other Knights is a severe crime." Another coughing fit racked him. "Don't worry, they'll give you all the rules when you join."

"What happens if you do tell who's in the Klan?"

Hyde thought a moment. "Let's just say I don't know anybody who'd risk tryin' it."

I spotted a gold Klan robe tied with a red sash. "Is that Stephenson?"

"No, gold is for national officers, like kleagles—very

important men in the Invisible Empire." He smiled. "I bet you'll be surprised when you get a look at the Old Man."

A flatbed truck was parked at one end of the clearing, in the shade of a giant oak. On the bed of the truck, a gold-clad Klansman spoke through a megaphone, making a lengthy introduction of the featured speaker. Four white-robed comrades, their masks down, stood at attention behind him.

When David C. Stephenson's name was announced, a chubby-faced blond man in a gray business suit emerged from the passenger's side of the truck. He was hoisted upon the truck bed and waved to acknowledge the cheers of the crowd.

Glenn Hyde was right: Stephenson's appearance did surprise me. The Exalted Cyclops was totally unremarkable in his dress and physique. If I'd met him on the street, I would have taken him for a bank clerk or an insurance salesman. I'd assumed Stephenson would have the most flamboyant costume of all, but his sack suit was positively drab compared to the robes around him. I had also assumed that he would be older, but the "Old Man" at the megaphone was probably no more than thirty-five, forty at the most.

He launched into his speech, and it, too, was not what I'd expected. Stephenson didn't rail against Negroes, and he never advocated vigilantism. He spoke in favor of "100 percent Americanism," the sanctity of womanhood, the Bible, the flag, old-time religion, and law and order. He was against immorality, crime, and invasion of America by foreign dictators. Stephenson's delivery was polished and passionate. Sometimes he sounded like one of the moving-picture stars who hawked Liberty Bonds during the war. At other times he sounded like a carnival snake-oil huckster, claiming that the Klan was the cure for all America's ills.

Most of what Stephenson said could have served as the campaign platform for any politician in the country. But he said it all with such vigor and conviction, that the crowd cheered him wildly and applauded his every hackneyed slogan as if it was a profound insight.

The final surprise was that he had the good sense not to go on too long. Waving his fist, Stephenson concluded, "Every gambler, every criminal, every libertine, every home wrecker, every dope peddler, every moonshiner, every white slaver, every brothel madam, every pagan priest, every crooked politician, every shyster lawyer is fighting against the Klan. Think it over. Which side are *you* on—theirs or ours?"

After the applause died down, he gave a friendly wave and encouraged the crowd to have fun, enjoy the barbecue, and come to the parade later that night.

"What did you think?" Glenn Hyde asked eagerly, as we began to walk away.

I tried to sound enthusiastic. "Stephenson made a lot of sense."

Hyde smiled so broadly that I could almost hear new wrinkles crackling on his face. "Let me show you some other things that make sense."

I had the feeling some kind of sales pitch was coming, but I agreed, and he steered us toward the park entrance.

"You know," I said, "the newspapers make it sound like the main purpose of the Klan is to lynch colored people. I was glad to hear the straight scoop from Stephenson's own lips."

"I never even look at the papers anymore," said Hyde. "Only things I read now are the Bible and what the Klan publishes; those are all I can trust to give me the truth."

"Come to think of it," I continued, "Stephenson—the Old Man—didn't say anything about colored people at all."

"No reason he should. We have no quarrel with Nigras— long as they know their place, of course." He wheezed suddenly and touched my arm; I helped him to a bench, where he rested for a few minutes.

We then went on until we reached a row of food stands and merchandise tables. Hyde led me to one table that was covered with Klan literature and popular novels with Klan themes—like *Ku Klux Kismet*, *White Knights*, and Thomas Dixon's *The Clansman*, on which D. W. Griffith had based his motion picture *Birth of a Nation*.

"Mickey Welch," he said, introducing me to the robed Klansman staffing the table, "this is a good friend of mine, Pete Gaffney." Gaffney's mask was rolled up, but he would have looked better with it down; he had a hatchet face pitted with smallpox scars.

Hyde said to Gaffney, "I was just tellin' Mickey here that we don't have nothing against Nigras." To me, he added, "We all keep to our own kind, and that keeps life peaceful for everybody."

"Ain't had no kind of nigger trouble around here," Gaffney agreed. "It's the goddamn Catholics that's the problem. They're trying to take over this country for their goddamn pope."

"They are?"

"Damn right, they are." Gaffney picked at his nose. "Did you know that whenever a Catholic boy is born, they bury a rifle for him in the church grounds?"

"No, I didn't know that."

"Well, it's true. They do it so when he grows up, he'll have a gun ready for when they try to turn America into part of the papal empire." Gaffney wagged his finger. "There's a Roman army in this country right now, and they're just waiting for the pope to give the word." He picked up a pamphlet titled *Traitors In Our Midst.* "Here, take this. You can read about it for yourself."

Yeah, I thought, as if being in print was enough to prove the claim true.

"Give him some other material, too," Hyde said. "Mickey's gonna be joining the East St. Louis klavern." He smiled warmly. "Let's give him an education compliments of the Evansville Klan."

"Good idea," said Gaffney. "Should read up on what the Jews are planning, too—they're almost as bad as the Catholics."

He gave me copies of the official Indiana Klan newspaper, *The Fiery Cross*, and pamphlets entitled *America for Americans, Believe the Bible,* and *The Public School Problem in America*. Finally, he handed me a boycott list of "un-American" businesses, which he explained meant that they were owned by Jews or Catholics.

When my hands were full, I thanked Gaffney, then Hyde suggested we get some barbecue.

I tagged along with Glenn Hyde for the rest of the day. The old Klansman was a rich source of information, open, hospitable, and quick to introduce me to his friends. He seemed to enjoy taking me under his wing. I found that I also enjoyed his company; Hyde struck me as a decent man who happened to genuinely believe that the Ku Klux Klan was the best vehicle for promoting American and Christian ideals.

Late in the afternoon, after another trip to the barbecue pit, Hyde asked, "You mind if we set a spell? I'm runnin' out of wind."

We settled on a bench with a couple of soft drinks. I told Hyde that I'd spoken with Buddy Vaughn in St. Louis, and asked if he knew the Klan recruiter.

"I've met him a couple times," he answered. "Vaughn is one of the top kleagles in the country—really helped build the Invisible Empire. In 1915, when *Birth of a Nation* came out, Vaughn would sign up new members right in the theater lobbies.

And he helped organize this klavern; the Old Man considered him his right-hand man."

"Was he the one in the gold robe who introduced Stephenson?"

"Might have been, but there's quite a few kleagles workin' this part of the country."

I waited a while, then broached the subject of violence again. "There seems to be a lot of beatings and lynchings that the newspapers blame on the Klan," I said. "You don't believe *any* of them are true?"

"Oh, I expect a few are. Every organization has its troublemakers and hotheads. But there isn't nearly as much violence as some people want to believe. And what there is, is mostly in the South. We don't have mob rule in Indiana."

"None?"

"Not by the Klan. We're official agents of law enforcement." He dug into his pocket and pulled out what looked like a sheriff's badge. The five-pointed tin star was stamped *Horse Thief Detective Association*.

"What is this? You go after horse thieves?"

Hyde chuckled. "No, no, that's just the name; it goes back to pioneer days. By organizing ourselves as a Horse Thief Detective Association, the state of Indiana gives us the same power and authority as a constable. We use it to enforce the laws the police don't want to trouble themselves about."

"Such as ... ?"

"Bootlegging, for one. This winter, we had a flood of Dubois County Dew pouring into Evansville—that's a local moonshine. We put an end to it; busted up the stills and turned the moonshiners over to Prohibition agents."

This sounded like something out of the Wild West. "So you're like a posse?"

"Or an auxiliary police force. We also take care of things that maybe aren't spelled out in the law, but ought to be."

"Like?"

"Say a man's not doing right by his family. Gambles away his money, leaving his wife and kids to go hungry. We straighten him out."

"How do you do that?"

He coughed and spit. "Some morning, he might leave his house and find a dozen switches laid out at his front door. That's a warning: It means if he don't get on the straight and narrow, we'll take him down to Possum Hollow, tie him to a tree, and wear out those switches on his back."

"Do they always take the warning?"

"Wish they did, but no. We've had a few we had to take down to the Hollow. Had one last month, as a matter of fact." Hyde smiled. "That fellow's been a perfect gentleman ever since."

"What if the fellow who needs straightening out is a Klansman?" I asked. "I met a guy in East St. Louis who told me he joined the Klan but never went back after his first meeting. He said there were some bad apples in the klavern."

"The fellow we whipped last month *was* a Klansman." Hyde sat up rigidly. "We can't be preaching morality to others if we don't practice it ourselves. The leadership of the Klan expects more of Knights than of anyone else."

I thought Hyde might be getting a little uncomfortable with the direction of the conversation. "Sorry to keep asking about violence," I said. "Seems like you have things real well organized here." Then I decided to push a little further. "But in East St. Louis, there was a colored baseball player who was lynched, and folks seem to think it was Klansmen who did it. I wouldn't ever want to be part of anything like that."

"Me neither," Hyde answered. "But with Buddy Vaughn being the kleagle there, you won't have to worry."

"Why not?"

"Vaughn won't stand for it. Any Knight who got involved in a lynching would be punished—severely."

"A whipping?"

Hyde gave me a look that hinted the punishment would be far worse than a mere whipping.

After dusk, the parade began, with all marchers in full regalia, their masks down. By the flickering orange glow of hundreds of torches, the Ku Klux Klan advanced in disciplined formation, like a regiment of ghosts.

Dozens of Klansmen carrying American flags led the way on horseback, riding mounts that were garbed in white horse suits. Next were the Klan officials, strutting proudly in robes of red, green, or gold. Behind them came the infantry, with row after row of pointed white hoods poking up into the night.

Less organized, but garnering many admiring comments, was a small cluster of hooded children marching under the banner "Ku Klux Kiddies." At the rear of the formation were a marching band and a women's group whose hoods and robes were embellished with some feminine touches.

The flames, the masks, the military precision, and the sheer number of marchers all made for a most impressive display.

The Klan had organized the day well, I thought. First a relaxing picnic to fill the bellies, then some stirring speeches to rouse the emotions, and finally a striking spectacle that would make onlookers wish they were participants. Evansville Klan No. 1 was sure to get many new members after this day.

I had the impression that the Klan's long-term strategy was similar: Bring the members along gradually. First appeal to their sense of patriotism, then get them to carry out some "disciplinary" actions, and finally— That was still unclear. But whatever their ultimate objective, it appeared the Ku Klux Klan would have an army at their disposal, willing to achieve it.

The parade was followed by a rally. Klansmen gathered around an enormous burning cross while rockets and fireworks exploded above. They led the crowd in singing "The Star-Spangled Banner," "America," and the official Klan song, which Glenn Hyde told me was called "The Kluxology."

Afterward, Hyde asked me to join him in seeing *The Birth of a Nation*, being shown in a tent. I knew that Griffith's racist movie was probably the best recruiting tool the Klan ever had, and so inflammatory that the NAACP had tried to have it banned.

I made the excuse that I had to get up early to catch the train, and thanked him for his companionship.

Hyde shook my hand, and said, "I do hope you'll join us. And spread the word—there's a Junior Klan being organized for kids, and Queens of the Golden Mask for women." He slapped me on the shoulder. "The Invisible Empire is going to be something like this country's never seen before."

I feared that he was right.

CHAPTER 22

I tried to squelch it, but despite my better sense and best efforts, my heart was full of hope when I got back to St. Louis Wednesday afternoon.

Even after I went inside the apartment and saw that Margie hadn't returned, a flicker of hope remained, and I grabbed for the small stack of mail that had accumulated during my trip. There was no letter from her, though, and a tour of the apartment proved it to be as bleak and empty as when I'd left.

After I unpacked, I checked the calendar. This was the final day of May, and the fifteenth day since Lee Fohl had suspended me. Tomorrow, I would be an active member of the St. Louis Browns again. At least something in my life would be taking a positive turn.

I spent the rest of the day puttering around the house, waiting for a phone call or telegram from Fohl instructing me to join the team in Washington for the final series of the road trip. When night came, and I still hadn't heard anything, I began to wonder if the suspension was fifteen days, as I'd thought, or fifteen *games*. I checked the team's schedule; a suspension of fifteen games would mean that there were four left to go.

Thursday morning, I could wait no longer. I called the

Browns' hotel in Washington. Fohl wasn't in his room, but I asked for a bellboy to page him in the lobby; most managers are habitual lobby sitters who like to talk baseball with anyone willing to listen.

The next voice I heard was Fohl's. "I was in the middle of a story," he growled. "What do you want?"

I ignored the brusqueness of his greeting. "My fifteen days is up," I said. "I can catch the next train for D.C., if you want."

"Oh, that's right, your suspension's over." The manager paused. "Tell you what: Why don't you just skip this series, and wait till we're back in St. Louis. We don't really need you right now—the infielders are all healthy, and Herman Bronke is doing a good enough job in your spot."

I didn't like the sound of that. "I *am* going to be back on the team, right?"

In a somewhat kinder voice, Fohl answered, "Yeah, don't worry. It's just that there's no sense you making the trip to sit on the bench for three games. Might as well save Phil Ball the train fare."

Since I had no choice, I agreed. I didn't mention how much I hated to miss a series against the Senators. For ten years, I'd been wanting to get a base hit off Walter Johnson, and needed every opportunity to face him.

After hanging up, I thought at least I'd get future opportunities to face Johnson. I'd never be able to bat against Slip Crawford again.

I phoned Franklin Aubury's office, and learned that he was still in Indianapolis. Next, I tried Karl Landfors; I was told that he was out of town and hadn't left word on what town he was in, or when he'd return.

By late morning, I was so restless that I began to feel like a caged bear thrashing back and forth against the bars of his prison. When Margie had first left, I'd wanted to stay in the apartment all the time, not wanting to miss any attempt she might make to contact me. Now, with it clear she wasn't coming back, I wanted to get out of the home we'd once shared and avoid all reminders of her.

I went out to do errands, dropping my dirty clothes at the laundry and stocking up with groceries. Then I spent the afternoon and evening exploring Forest Park, the Missouri Botanical Garden, and a few other areas of the city that I'd never visited before.

Friday morning, after a few hours of fitful sleep, I brewed a pot of coffee and read the morning paper. In a break from habit, I didn't start with the baseball news. I looked in the classifieds for a furnished apartment. I wanted a new home.

When I did get around to the sports pages, I read about the upcoming series between the Chicago Cubs and St. Louis Cardinals in Sportsman's Park. The *Post-Dispatch* played up the historic rivalry between the Cubs and Cards, comparing it to the one between the Brooklyn Dodgers and New York Giants. The Midwestern clubs were a bit more genteel than their eastern counterparts, however, and the annual results of their competition more lopsided—the Cardinals had never won a National League pennant, while the Cubs took the flag almost every year that the Giants failed to win it.

I found myself itchy to get back on a baseball diamond again. In the last two weeks, the only practice I'd had was when I batted against Franklin Aubury on an Indianapolis sandlot. When I did rejoin the Browns, I was sure to be rusty.

That gave me an idea, and I put in another call to Washington. It was early enough that Lee Fohl was still in his hotel room.

"If the Cards let me," I said, "you mind if I take practice with them? I can use the workout." Normally, I wouldn't have asked, but I didn't want to make the same mistake of playing without permission that got me suspended in the first place.

"Go ahead," Fohl answered. "As long as Rickey says it's okay."

"I'll talk him into it."

Fohl laughed. "I expect you will. And practice hard—McManus booted a couple easy grounders yesterday, so it looks like we'll be needing you for the Red Sox series."

That was the best news I'd had in weeks.

I wasn't so confident when I arrived at Sportsman's Park Saturday morning. Cardinals' skipper Branch Rickey had managed the Browns before switching to St. Louis's National League franchise, and I seemed to recall that the parting hadn't been amicable. He might not be inclined to do the Browns, or me, any favors.

The offices of the St. Louis Cardinals were on the Dodier Street side of the park, around the corner from those of the Browns on Grand Boulevard. Typically, a field manager wouldn't be found in a club's front office, but Rickey was also the Cardinals' vice president and part-owner. Rumor had it that the notorious skinflint only managed the team because he wanted to save the expense of paying a real manager.

After a brief wait in an outer office, I was ushered in to see Rickey. The Cardinals' manager wore a tweed suit, spectacles, and a stern expression. The stub of a dead cigar was in his mouth, and as he chewed on it, his thick black eyebrows rose and fell above the rims of his glasses. "What can I do for you?"

I introduced myself, told him of my suspension from the Browns, and asked if I could take pregame practice with the Cardinals.

"Why were you suspended?" he demanded.

That was another reason I thought Rickey might not want to help me. Although he indulged a fondness for cigars, he was otherwise so moralistic that he never managed on Sundays and violently disapproved of any players who drank, ran with women, or broke team rules. I told Rickey about playing against the East St. Louis Cubs, hoping the fact that I hadn't been suspended for bad behavior would count in my favor.

He said sharply, "You played under false pretenses—a ringer. Was it for money?"

"No. I turned down the money. I just wanted to play against a colored team—to see how good they are, and find out how I'd do against them. Playing in the East St. Louis game seemed like the only chance I might get."

Rickey took the cigar from his mouth and rolled it in his fingertips. "How did you fare?" he asked in a gentler tone.

"Lousy. Didn't get a single hit, and made a bonehead play in the field."

He nodded. "Some of the Negro players can be formidable opponents." Staring down at the blotter on his desk, he went on, "When I was a student at Ohio Wesleyan, I helped coach the baseball team. Best player we had was colored—Tommy Thomas. Poor fellow was subject to more abuse than any man should have to endure. I'll never forget the time we went to South Bend, Indiana, to play Notre Dame. The hotel refused to give him a room. After some arguing, I convinced the hotel manager to let him share mine. That night, Tommy broke down crying. He started rubbing one hand over the other, muttering, 'Black skin, black skin. If I could only make 'em white.' Tommy rubbed his hands raw trying to take the black off." Rickey crushed his cigar in an ashtray. "Someday, we'll get them in the big leagues, if I have anything to say about it."

"I hope so," I said. "But I hear Commissioner Landis is against it."

Rickey nodded sadly. "You hear correctly." Then he told me, "Go see the clubhouse man and suit up."

* * *

The uniform was colorful, I'll give it that, but too garish for my taste. This season, the Cardinals had introduced a new design for their jerseys: two redbirds perched on a baseball bat. It was a drastic departure from the typical major-league uniform in which the only decoration is the name of the team or its city. I hoped that next year the Cards would have the good taste to revert to the old style.

When I trotted onto the field, I got some good-natured ribbing from the players, most of it to the effect that I must have forgotten which St. Louis team I was under contract to.

I took infield practice with the Cards' regulars, including veteran first baseman Jacques Fournier, Specs Toporcer, and the premier hitter in the National League, Rogers Hornsby.

Nearby in the outfield was Max Flack, another ballplayer who'd only recently donned the Cardinal uniform. He had come to the Cards in exchange for Cliff Heathcote in one of baseball's strangest trades: They were swapped between games of a double-header, and became the only players ever to appear for two different teams on the same day.

At the start of batting practice, I found the Cards less than willing to let me take part—ballplayers hate to give up any time at the plate. I was finally allowed to hit after they had all finished, and stepped up to bat.

The right-hander on the mound started me off with a soft brushback pitch. Just a little more ribbing, I assumed. The next toss came at my ear. It wasn't fast enough to be a threat, but I wanted hitting practice, not ducking practice. "Hey! What's the idea?" I yelled.

"That was for costing me a ball game!"

I stared at the pitcher for a few seconds. Then I recognized him as Leo South, the Elcars' starting pitcher in the East St. Louis game.

South gestured with his glove for me to get back in the

box, and proceeded to throw me a series of fat pitches down the middle of the plate.

As I smacked the ball around the park, I thought it made perfect sense that the Elcars had brought in a pitcher as a ringer, too. A pitcher has far greater impact on a game than a second baseman. I had been so flattered at being recruited, it never occurred to me that I wasn't the only one.

When he'd thrown his last pitch and walked off the mound, I went to greet him. "Leo South, right?"

He smiled. "Close. Lou North."

"Mickey Rawlings." We shook hands. "I played as Welch. That was some game we had over there, wasn't it?"

"Scared the bejesus out of me," said North. "I thought folks were gonna start shooting."

"Try playing at Ebbets Field in a Giants' uniform," I joked. *"That's* scary. Say, is this your first year?" North looked a bit long in the tooth to be a rookie.

"Nah, I been in the big leagues off and on. Mostly off. That's why the Elcars wanted me to pitch for them—they figured nobody would recognize me as a pro."

"They picked me for the same reason," I admitted.

We talked a bit more, sharing a bond as professional bench-warmers, and walked off toward the Cardinals' dugout. It occurred to me that we might have something else in common, too. "You been approached to join the Ku Klux Klan?" I asked.

"Yeah, but there's no way I'm getting mixed up with that bunch."

"Is Buddy Vaughn the one who talked to you?"

North nodded.

"Me too. He told me there's already a St. Louis player in the Klan." I had assumed the player Vaughn referred to was a Brown, but it could just as easily be a Cardinal. "You know who it could be?"

North appeared uncomfortable, and I wondered if maybe his denial had been a lie. Then I recalled that Buddy Vaughn had said "star," not "player." It must be somebody else. I looked at the Cardinals seated in the dugout, and settled on Rogers Hornsby. The cantankerous Texan, who had the temper of Ty Cobb but without the charm, was the biggest star on the club. And according to Plunk Drake, he wouldn't play on the same baseball field with Negroes.

The pitcher confirmed my guess, whispering, "It's Hornsby."

"I thought the Klan would be too progressive for him," I said, causing North to burst out laughing.

Branch Rickey called all the players in, and my tenure as a Cardinal came to an end.

I did get a seat in the stands and watched the first five innings as the Cards' Jesse Haines dueled Grover Cleveland Alexander. I was glad to be out of Indiana and back in a big-league ballpark. This was the world I knew, and the one that made sense to me.

Most of it did, anyway. I kept glancing at the right-field bleachers, where colored fans sat in the only section open to them. As the innings went along, I stared in their direction more than at the diamond, thinking about all that I'd seen and heard during my recent travels. I gradually realized that the trip might be over, but I didn't have the comforting sense of being back home. What was happening in Indiana wasn't limited to that state. It was going on here, too, and in this very ballpark.

The score was 2–2 in the eighth inning, but I left early anyway. My world wasn't as perfect as I once thought it to be.

From Sportsman's Park, I headed a couple blocks north to Robison Field, the old wooden stadium where the Cardinals played before becoming tenants of the Browns. It was also where I had played when I'd visited the city with the Giants and the Cubs.

I walked along Natural Bridge Avenue, looking up at the Robison Field grandstand, wishing I could go back to those days. It was enough for me then to be a big-league ballplayer myself—I didn't worry about who *wasn't* allowed in the major leagues.

Then I thought that if I'd played forty years ago, I wouldn't be worrying about it either, because that would have been before the ban against colored players. I entertained myself by imagining what it would have been like for me to play in the 1880s. The Browns were the Brown Stockings, then, the premier team of the American Association. They were owned by eccentric Chris von der Ahe, and starred Arlie Latham and a young first baseman named Charles Comiskey.

As I turned onto Prairie Avenue, back toward Sportsman's Park, I recalled Franklin Aubury telling me about Fleet and Weldy Walker, the two Negroes who'd played in the American Association around that time. Those men could have very well played big-league baseball right here. But if they came to the park today, the closest they'd be able to get to the field was a seat in the right-field bleachers.

On racial issues, I thought, the country was going in the wrong direction. Negro players were now barred from Organized Baseball, new segregation laws were being instituted every year, and the rapidly growing Ku Klux Klan was convincing thousands that bigotry was "100 percent American."

I had to admit to myself that, to some degree, I'd bought the "separate but equal" argument that the races were happier apart. But after my trip with Aubury, I wasn't buying it anymore. I'd seen that separate was not equal, and I'd been a whole lot happier talking with Aubury and the Negro Leaguers than I had been with Glenn Hyde and the Knights of the Invisible Empire.

When I reached Sportsman's Park, fans were streaming out of the gate. The game was over, a 3–2 win for the Cubs, according to what I heard.

I walked on to Grand Boulevard, where the streetcars were starting to shuttle people home. Just before jumping aboard, I spotted a long line of Negroes waiting patiently for one of the scarce "colored" cars. A few months ago, I wouldn't have noticed them.

As my trolley pulled away, I had the feeling that from now on I'd be noticing a lot of things that I used to overlook. And I wasn't sure that I wanted to see them.

CHAPTER 23

The first time I'd walked into Franklin Aubury's law office, he'd seemed very much an attorney, with his conservative suit, precise English, and calculated demeanor. By now, I'd eaten in his home, traveled with him, drunk with him, and played baseball with him. When I entered his office late Monday morning, I saw him as a friend.

From the warmth of his greeting, I sensed that he viewed me the same way.

He filled me in on his return trip from Indianapolis while we waited for Karl Landfors to join us.

When Karl arrived, he was harried and out of breath. "Sorry I'm late," he wheezed. "I wanted to drop off some papers at Congressman Dyer's office."

"Quite all right," said Aubury.

Karl took out a handkerchief and patted the beads of sweat from his forehead. He turned to me. "Have you heard from Margie yet?"

"I'll let you know if I do," I said. I didn't mean to sound snappish, but his question hit me the wrong way—it was like asking a starving man if he's eaten yet. "By the way, where were you? When I tried calling, I was told you were out of town."

"I was. And I told no one where I was going."

"Why not? Or is it still a secret?"

"It is, but I trust you to keep this between us." When Aubury and I nodded that we'd keep the information to ourselves, Karl went on, "I've been in Chicago. As you know, I was working on getting newspapers to run exposés of the Ku Klux Klan." He stopped to refold his handkerchief methodically and tuck it away. "The Klan has established a firm foothold in Chicago, and in response a group called the American Unity League has been organized to fight them. One of the League's tools will be *Tolerance,* a new progressive weekly. This newspaper is taking a unique approach to exposing the KKK: It will not only run stories about the Klan, it will also publish the names and addresses of Klansmen."

"But those are secret," I said.

"Yes. That's why it will come as quite a blow when they find themselves unmasked in print."

"I mean, how does the paper get their names if they're secret?"

Karl's lips twitched in a smug smile. "The Chicago offices of the KKK were burglarized last week. Everything was taken, from membership lists to pamphlets to costumes."

Aubury and I both grinned. Neither of us asked how Karl happened to know of the robbery.

Then it was my turn to report. I gave a detailed account of my trip to Evansville and the Klan picnic. I concluded, "I hate to say this, but I got the impression there's some basically decent people joining the Klan because they think it's good for America."

"They may be decent," said Aubury, "but they must also be deaf and blind if they don't realize the Klan's true agenda."

"There was no talk of violence," I said. "And not much

against colored people—they seem more worried about Catholics taking over the country. I brought back some of their pamphlets; thought you might want them."

"Thank you," said Aubury. "I do like to keep tabs on what they publish."

"I'll bring 'em next time I come." The literature, though, would be awfully flat compared to the speeches and spectacle. "The Klan makes a powerful impression," I said. "You should have seen all the marchers, and the torches and everything. It was a helluva show, and the crowd ate it up." I promptly added, "Not that I agree—"

Aubury waved off the explanation. "I understand."

"It was really impressive."

The lawyer nodded. "I'm sure it was."

Karl asked, "Has there been any progress on the Slip Crawford investigation?"

"Not much," I said. I told him it might have been Klansmen, or Elcars, or both, and that I still believed it might prove to be neither—that he was murdered, not lynched. Then I added, "One new thing we found out in Indiana was that Crawford was being pressured by a thug named Rosie Sumner to jump to the Eastern Colored League." I hesitated. On the way back from Indiana, I'd thought of another motive for Crawford's death, but was reluctant to suggest it to Aubury.

He noticed. "There's something else on your mind."

"Yeah, just an idea, probably crazy."

"Well, let's hear it."

"The ABCs told us that after Crawford was killed, Sumner contacted them again and said they ought to come east where they'd be safe from lynchings. I thought it was lousy of Sumner to use Crawford's death as a sales pitch, but what if he did worse than that?" I looked at Aubury. "Could a Negro *stage* a lynching? Maybe Sumner knew he couldn't get *Crawford* to jump leagues, but figured if he killed him and made it look like a lynching, he could get *other* players to move east.''

Aubury answered quietly, ''A colored man can be every bit as devious and evil as a white man.'' He cleared his throat. ''However, the same way that you do not wish to believe that a man can be killed solely because of his skin color, I do not want to believe that someone of my race would lynch another Negro—especially not as a recruiting tool for a new baseball league. It is possible, but highly doubtful.''

''Just trying to cover all bases,'' I said.

Karl spoke up. ''That's the way to do it; you have to consider every possibility.''

At the moment, I was considering what Aubury had said about choosing what we want to believe. It was probably true for Glenn Hyde, too; he simply didn't *want* to believe certain things about the Klan.

''I think we should still pursue the Rosie Sumner angle,'' I said. ''He does work for a mobster, and he did use scare tactics with the ABCs.''

Aubury said, ''The 'mobster' is Alex Pompez, and he runs the numbers in Harlem. That's not like a real criminal— numbers racketeers don't kill or steal. They basically run a lottery that happens to be illegal. It is very popular in colored communities; for as little as a penny, somebody can have a chance at winning a few dollars. The numbers gives people hope, and that is a good thing. There are times when the prospect of hitting the number is the only thing a Negro has to hope for.''

We all sat in silence for a while.

Aubury leaned back in his chair. ''So, gentlemen, where do we go from here?''

Neither Karl nor I had a ready answer.

Karl finally said, "I haven't eaten yet today, so I suggest we go to lunch."

That was the best idea any of us could come up with. But we decided to send out for sandwiches instead when we realized there might not be a restaurant that would permit the three of us to eat together.

CHAPTER 24

As good as it was to have Franklin Aubury and Karl Landfors back in town, I was even happier that the Browns had returned and that I was again one of them.

I was also pleased to have the Red Sox in town—not because I'd once played for Boston, but because they were now one of the easiest teams in the American League to beat. Not a single player remained from the 1912 club of which I'd been a member. Gone was the superb outfield of Tris Speaker, Harry Hooper, and Duffy Lewis, their positions today taken by Nemo Leibold, Pinky Pittenger, and Elmer Smith. Red Sox owners had sold or traded away the club's best players, many of them, including Babe Ruth, going to the New York Yankees. The only reminder of Boston's glory days was Hugh Duffy, their manager, who'd starred with the champion Boston Beaneaters of the 1890s. This season, Duffy was struggling, and failing, to keep his team out of the league's cellar.

There weren't many fans in Sportsman's Park Tuesday afternoon, about two thousand at the most, but to me it felt like Opening Day, because Lee Fohl had put me in the starting lineup at second base.

Once the Browns came to the plate in the bottom of the

first, it was more like batting practice. Red Sox hurler Herb Pennock, one of the few pitchers in baseball who had no fastball at all in his repertoire, had control problems from the start; every pitch was either outside the strike zone or down the middle of the plate. Johnny Tobin led off for us with a single, and Frank Ellerbe walked. Then George Sisler, Ken Williams, and Baby Doll Jacobson each doubled to put us up 4–0. I came up next and surprised everyone, including myself, by belting a triple on Pennock's first offering. The Boston left-hander didn't get out of the inning until we'd batted around.

Our pitcher, young Hub Pruett, held the Red Sox to only a few scattered hits over nine innings, and we romped to a 12–1 win.

The celebration in the clubhouse was boisterous, and I was part of it. I'd gone 4-for-5 in the game, plus a walk. I was slow to strip out of my uniform; it had felt so good to wear it again that I didn't want to take it off.

As George Sisler jokingly asked me for batting tips, one of the stadium cops brought me a note. I was annoyed at the interruption until I read the message. It was from Margie, and it said that she would be at the Jefferson Hotel if I'd like to see her.

I almost ripped my flannels taking them off, and raced for the shower. After a quick soaking, I went back to my locker and started to dress. Then it occurred to me that I might have washed too quickly to be sufficiently clean. To the bewilderment of my teammates, I showered again. Finally, still damp, I fumbled my way into my Palm Beach suit, retied my necktie half a dozen times before I got it right, and ran out of the clubhouse to hail a taxi.

There might as well have been a spotlight on her. The spacious lobby of the Jefferson Hotel was crowded and bustling, but as soon as I went through the revolving door, I saw Margie.

She was seated alone on a divan, dressed in an elegant frock of shimmering yellow silk and white lace.

I was hesitant to approach. For one thing, from her note, I couldn't tell why she wanted to meet—was this to be a reunion, or did she only want to tell me to my face that it was over between us. For another, I found that I was enjoying the opportunity just to drink in the sight of her; I'd been thirsting for it too long.

Margie turned her head in my direction, and I gathered my courage to find out where we stood.

I walked over to her, but the moment I opened my mouth, my mind went blank. I had no idea what to say.

Margie saved me by speaking first. "You could have stretched that triple into a homer easy."

She sure knew how to break the ice and put a smile on my face. "Probably, but with no outs, Fohl would have killed me if I didn't make it."

Patting the cushion, she asked, "Would you like to sit down?"

I'd been hoping for something more along the lines of a kiss or a hug, but I was happy to settle for a seat next to her. "You were at the game?"

"For the first seven innings. Then I left the note for you and came back here. Did you bat in the eighth?"

I nodded. "Singled; drove in two runs."

"You sure had a hot bat today!"

For the first time, I'd had a great game and didn't want to talk about it. "You haven't had time for dinner then?" I asked.

"Not yet."

"Would you like—"

"I'd love to."

We opted to eat in the hotel restaurant. After we'd ordered, Margie said, "I've been checking the box scores, but you haven't played for a while."

"I was off the team for a couple weeks. They found out I played in East St. Louis and suspended me."

"Oh, I'm sorry."

I shrugged. "At least it's over now."

Margie sipped her ginger ale. "So what have you been up to?"

I told her about my trip to Indiana, pausing frequently to allow her to jump in and tell me what *she'd* been doing. She passed up all the openings, and we were half-done with the main course by the time I finished my report. I idly pushed what was left of my food around on the plate. "Actually," I said, "what I've been doing most is missing you. I was a damned fool to act the way I did."

The look in Margie's eyes told me I'd finally said the right thing. "I've missed you, too," she said.

"Where did you go?"

"California. And then Mexico. I didn't expect to be gone so long, but the paperwork was more than I expected."

"Paperwork?"

She reached for her purse. "I got a divorce. It's official." She pulled out a set of papers and offered it to me.

For a moment, I was too surprised to react—but I did think this was the nicest surprise I'd ever had. I started to reach out, then pulled back. "I don't need to see it." I didn't *want* to see it; I didn't want to know the name of the man she'd married. "So with you not being married anymore, that means there's nothing to stop us from—"

"Courting," Margie said.

I thought we were beyond that. "Courting?"

She nodded. "I wanted the divorce so there wouldn't be any obstacle in case you should ask me—"

"What I asked before still holds."

She shook her head. "I was going to say, 'in case you should ask me again someday.'"

"Why not—"

"*Someday,*" she said firmly. "We still have things to think about and talk about."

"Are you coming home?"

"I'm staying here. Let's take things slow and see what happens."

I agreed, although I wasn't sure exactly what "slow" meant. "Would going for a walk be too fast?"

She laughed. "A walk would be lovely."

We skipped dessert and went for a stroll. I had no idea what we talked about or where we went. It was enough for me simply to hear the sound of her voice and feel her hand in mine again.

Back at the hotel, I walked her into the lobby. "Are the, uh, rooms nice here?"

Margie almost burst out laughing at my less-than-subtle question. "Yes, they are. And I'm still tired from my trip." She kissed me good night—on the cheek—and went to the desk clerk to pick up her key. I watched her until she stepped inside an elevator.

So far, "slow" was pretty nice, I thought, but I sure hoped we could pick up the pace soon.

The first thing I did when I got home was take Margie's things out of the closet, and put them back in the parlor. I even polished her mantel clock and dusted her pictures.

I was cranking the handle of her Victrola, when the phone rang. I pounced on it, hoping that she'd decided she wasn't tired after all.

Franklin Aubury's voice put an end to my romantic notions. "I have just learned that Roy Enoch's son was beaten up tonight," he said.

"So? Kids always get in fights."

"It *began* as an innocent fight, from what I understand. But it was with a colored boy. And Enoch's son told him, 'You better not mess with me; my father's a Klansman.' "

"Jeez, that was stupid."

"It was indeed. The boy he was fighting rounded up some reinforcements—all colored—and they gave young Enoch a thorough thrashing."

I vaguely remembered that I'd seen Enoch's kid; he'd kept the scorebook at the game with the Cubs. "Is he hurt bad?"

"I don't know. I certainly hope not. However, whether he is or not, I am certain Roy Enoch will instigate some kind of retaliation."

"And he can claim he's doing it for his kid, not as a Klan activity, so he won't get in trouble with the higher-ups in the Klan."

"Exactly." Aubury cleared his throat, and I knew what was coming. "Do you think you could make some inquiries and see what he might be planning?"

I agreed to find out what I could, and we hung up.

Then I picked up the receiver again to call Tater Greene. No, I suddenly decided, not tonight. I'm not responsible for what happened, and I don't have to jump every time Aubury or Karl Landfors calls me with a problem.

I readily put Roy Enoch out of my mind and spent the rest of the night thinking about Margie.

CHAPTER 25

I didn't call Tater Greene the next day, either. Nor the one after that.

For those two days, Margie and I were almost inseparable, and she was the sole object of my attention. It was almost like when we'd first started dating, back when she was making moving pictures in Brooklyn and I was playing for the New York Giants. I once again felt a giddiness in my stomach and a vacuum in my head.

The two of us met for an early lunch each morning, and went to Sportsman's Park together each afternoon, where I continued to play and play well. Afterward, it was dinner and dancing and long, aimless walks through downtown St. Louis.

Margie remained firm about not moving back to the apartment yet, but she did invite me to stay with her Thursday night.

Soon after we woke Friday morning, I found myself wishing that I had a regular job, one that allowed me to call in sick. Because I didn't want to play baseball; I wanted to spend the day in bed with Margie and do some more reconciling.

But a baseball player can't simply call in sick, especially not a utility player who's coming off a suspension. So I got dressed and left Margie, to meet her later again at the ballpark.

As I departed her hotel, I grumpily thought that if Lee Fohl kept me on the bench, I would be royally pissed.

I caught a trolley for home to get a fresh change of clothes before heading to the park. During the ride to my apartment, I scanned the morning newspaper that I'd picked up in the Jefferson lobby. I was halfway home by the time I saw the small headline on page five:

NEGRO BALLPARK TORCHED
Ku Klux Klan Suspected

Cubs Park in East St. Louis had burned to the ground the previous night, while a wooden cross blazed in the middle of the diamond.

Damn! I wished I had called Tater Greene when Aubury first told me about Enoch's kid getting beaten up. Maybe I'd have been able to do something to prevent this.

At least the newspaper report did pin the blame on the KKK; perhaps Karl Landfors's efforts were paying off. Although, considering the trademark burning cross, it was hardly a journalistic coup to conclude that the Klan was behind the arson.

As soon as I got home, I phoned the Enoch Motor Car Company and learned that Tater Greene had phoned in sick. Lucky bastard, I thought.

I dialed his home number. It took eight rings before he picked up. "What?" he moaned.

"You got what you wished for," I said. "They burned down Cubs Park last night. Or should I say 'you' burned it down?"

"Hey, when I said that about burning the park, I only meant instead of the catcher's house." Greene's speech was slow and slurred. "I didn't mean they should torch a park just because some snot-nosed kid couldn't handle himself in a fight."

"You sick?" I asked.

"Nah, a little hair of the dog, and I'll be fine."

"Were you all drunk when you did it?"

Greene didn't deny being involved. "Stone-cold sober," he said. "Until I got home anyways."

"Did Roy Enoch tell you to burn down the park?"

"I'm not saying who gave the order or who was involved." He made a belching noise. "You think I'm a dope or something?"

"Somebody is," I said. "If the Klan doesn't want to be connected to violence, then it's not real clever to leave a burning cross as a calling card. It's just as dumb as Enoch's boy was, telling the other kids that his father's a Klansman."

"You know about that?"

"Yup."

"Well, that's why we had to leave the cross. Nobody liked Enoch's kid saying what he did, but it was too late. Once he told them not to mess with the Klan, we had to back him up. And we had to let folks know it was us, so we burned a cross. Matter of pride."

"*Pride?*" I said, my voice and anger rising. "You mean if you're going to do something stupid, you should be *proud* and stupid?"

He groaned, in what sounded like a hangover pang. "What are you yelling at *me* for? Wasn't my idea to get mixed up in any of this crap."

"You were forced?"

"Nah, I just— Hell, you ain't never gonna understand. I just wish I never got mixed up with these guys. Be better off if I was still picking sweet potatoes down in Georgia."

No sense beating on Tater Greene, I thought. Part of my anger was at myself, for not calling him before the park was burned. "The Klan got anything else planned?" I asked. "Or will this end it?"

"Ain't nothing more going on that I know of," he said. "But it doesn't ever seem to end, does it?"

That was a point we were able to agree on.

Greene then insisted that he needed to get a shot of rye before his head exploded, and the conversation was over.

I briefly considered phoning Franklin Aubury, but I was too ashamed. I didn't want to admit to him that I hadn't followed up on his Tuesday call.

While I changed into a clean shirt and one of my favorite summer suits, I tried to think if there was anything else I could do, or anyone else I could talk to. I wasn't going to get much from any of the Elcars' players, I was sure, and Roy Enoch was unlikely to tell me anything. Should I go ahead and join the Klan to see what I could learn? No, I couldn't go that far.

The thought of calling in sick to Lee Fohl flickered through my mind again. Not to frolic with Margie, but to head over to East St. Louis. I again rejected the idea of calling Fohl, but realized there was another manager I *should* contact: Ed Moss, of Enoch's Elcars.

I recalled Tater Greene telling me that Moss didn't work at the automobile dealership. He was a cop, a desk sergeant, Greene had said.

With a phone call to police headquarters in East St. Louis, I learned the precinct where Moss was stationed. Another call, to the station house, provided the information that his next shift would be Saturday morning.

CHAPTER 26

Although Ed Moss's short, round body was now clothed in the blue-serge uniform of the East St. Louis Police Department, his demeanor was exactly the same as when he'd worn the Elcars' gray flannels in the coach's box of Cubs Park. He still resembled belligerent John McGraw on one of his bad days.

When I walked into the Bond Avenue station house, Moss was at the front desk, threatening a shabbily dressed old man who was trying to lie down across three chairs. "This ain't a goddamn flophouse, you old puke! Put yer feet down before I come over there and chop 'em off!"

The emaciated man struggled to obey the order. He appeared to be suffering from the same condition that Tater Greene was in yesterday.

Moss stared at him until he'd complied, then he turned to me, muttering, "All we get is rummies and whores coming through here." The sergeant's bloated, red face looked like something that needed to be lanced.

"You ought to see about a transfer," I said. "I hear they get a better class of criminal in Washington Park."

"Huh?" He eyed me closely. "Say, I know you. Mickey Welch, right?"

"Rawlings," I corrected. "But, yeah, I played for you as Welch."

Moss reached into his back pocket and pulled out a wallet. "There's something I owe you." He offered me a five-dollar bill. "This is all I got right now, but I'll get you the other five. Roy Enoch told me you were at his car lot a while ago, and you never let on that I kept your money—that was real white of ya."

"You can still keep it," I said. "You managed a helluva lot better than I played." The way to get on the good side of a man like Moss, I figured, was to flatter him.

He quickly pocketed the money. "Appreciate it."

"I came by because I heard about Enoch's kid getting beat up. Is he all right?"

"Just some bruises. He'll be fine."

"Good! Glad to hear it."

"Unless his father gives him another whupping, of course."

"His father?"

Moss sat down behind his high desk. "Yeah. The beating Roy Junior took from the kids was nothing compared to what his father gave him afterward."

"Because he told the kids about him being a Klansman?"

"Nah, that ain't no secret. He beat the kid for losing a fight to a bunch of niggers."

Jeez. "If he was mad at his son," I said, "why did he order Cubs Park burned down?"

Moss looked at me sharply. "I don't know nothing about that."

"I do. Some of the Elcars were involved—they told me about it." I gave Moss the story of how they were recruiting me for the local Klan, and I was considering joining. "But I wanted to talk to you first, and get your advice."

"Me?" The sergeant was clearly puzzled. "You don't know me from Adam. What do you want *my* advice for?"

"For one thing," I said, "you're a cop, so you know what goes on in this town. And more important, you manage these guys; nobody knows a team's players better than their manager."

From the way Moss puffed himself up, the flattery was working. "Well, go ahead, shoot. What do you want to know?"

"I don't mind them burning down the ballpark," I said. "Nobody got hurt. But that catcher's house getting torched, and, worse than that, the Slip Crawford lynching—I couldn't have anything to do with things like that. And from what I hear, Enoch's boys were behind all of those."

"You think the *Elcars* were involved in killing Crawford?" he said.

"Or the Klan. That's why I'm asking you. Could the team have lynched Crawford because he beat 'em in that game?"

Moss shook his head. "I can't speak for the Klan—I ain't in it, by the way. But as far as the team goes, they're a real good bunch. I been around ballplayers all my life—even played a couple years in the minors—and I guarantee you that the boys I have on the Elcars want to beat a man on the field, not kill him."

That matched what everyone else had told me. Perhaps the Crawford lynching—the event that started all the attacks and counterattacks—really was committed by people who had nothing to do with the ball game.

Moss suddenly grabbed his nightstick, and roared, "What the hell did I tell you?"

I looked behind me and saw that the derelict was listing and about to curl up on the chairs.

Waving the club, Moss warned, "Don't make me come over there!"

I was relieved when the man pulled himself upright on his own.

"Ought to throw his ass in a cell," Moss said.

I tried to recapture his attention. "Whoever started this latest trouble," I said, "if it keeps going the way it is, there could be a repeat of 1917."

Moss sat back in his chair, and let out a long breath. "Nothing could ever get as bad as that was."

"Where you here then?"

"I was walking a beat."

"The night of the riot? I heard that all cops hid in their station houses when it broke out."

"'Hid'?" repeated Moss, with obvious distaste for my choice of words.

"That's the way I heard it," I quickly explained.

"I'm guessin' you only heard one side of the story."

I looked around the waiting area. Other than the one old man, it wasn't bustling with business. "If you got the time," I said, "can you tell me the other side?"

"Sure. I only wish more people would want to hear it." He snorted. "All they seem to 'know' is that the white folks of this city set out to slaughter the coloreds. It wasn't that simple."

"What did happen?"

"A lot of things, all building on each other." Moss paused to gulp some coffee. "It started as a labor dispute. Months before the riot, the workers at Aluminum Ore went on strike. The company decided to break the union and brought up Negroes from the South as replacements. Wasn't the first time white men were put out of work around here—the year before, the same thing happened when Armour and Swift brought in coloreds during a meatpacking strike."

Something rang a bell. "J. D. Whalen used to play ball

for Aluminum Ore, didn't he?'' So did his partner Clint, if I remembered right.

"Until he lost his job," Moss said. "After the strike, he wasn't playing for quite a while—or working, or hardly eating. Lucky for him, Enoch hired him to do body repair in his garage; if Whalen had been out of work any longer, he'd have been lookin' like this fellow here.'' The sergeant lifted his coffee mug toward the old man, who was pulling a tattered overcoat tighter around his gaunt body.

"If the *companies* put these men out of work,'' I said, "why did they blame the Negroes? They were just looking to feed their families, too.''

"Because it's easier to blame a man than a factory, I suppose.'' He took another sip of coffee. "I ain't saying it was right, but the fact is, a lot of white men believed that they lost their jobs because of Negroes moving into town. So they wanted to drive them out. Didn't do much about it for a while though—just beat a bunch of 'em up and maybe shot a couple.''

It sounded like Moss considered those actions more entertaining than criminal.

He went on. "Now here's what you probably ain't heard: The night before the riot, two cops were killed—by Negroes.''

He was right; I hadn't known about that.

Moss could tell from my reaction. "See? I didn't think you heard the whole story,'' he said smugly.

"What happened?''

"There were some white men driving around a colored neighborhood shooting up houses. They were probably just trying to scare the people into moving away, but we sent out a couple of cops to put a stop to it.'' Moss's voice dropped. "Problem was, their car looked like the one that was doing the shooting. When the cops got to the area, the coloreds thought they were under attack again and decided to open fire themselves." The sergeant choked for a moment, then concluded, "We found their car on the corner of Market and Seventeenth, riddled with bullets, and both men dead."

I said, "I'm sorry."

"The riot started the next day," Moss said. "When it did, we were still mourning. And we were angry. We sure weren't about to put our asses on the line again to protect people who were only going to shoot them off. So a lot of cops did stay in their station houses—but they weren't 'hiding.'"

"It sounds like the Negroes didn't know they were shooting at cops," I said. "They were just trying to defend their homes."

"I know that. But at the time, all we could think about was that two of our own had been killed in cold blood. You got to understand what people think, not just what they do. Same with the fellows who work for Enoch; if they got a grudge against coloreds, you got to understand the why."

I was starting to think I didn't understand much at all. "Because of losing the game?"

"Nah. Because one of their own got killed in the riot, too. You probably only heard about coloreds getting killed by whites."

"Weren't there one or two white victims, too?" I asked.

"There were at least half a dozen white men killed by Negroes. One of them worked for Enoch. Tim Lowrey, his name was. In fact, Lowrey didn't just work for Enoch; he was engaged to marry his daughter Jessalyn."

Was that what motivated Enoch to join the Klan, I wondered. Did he blame all Negroes for his future son-in-law getting killed?

Moss was distracted by hacking noises from the old man. "If you don't shut up that goddamn coughing," he warned him, "I'll shove my club down your damn throat."

When Moss had calmed down, I said, "Five years later, Enoch and his guys are still mad?"

"Hard feelings die slow," he answered. "But most people are being pretty sensible now, I think. See, you got to look at all sides of what happened. Now me, I can understand the coloreds wanting to move up here for better jobs. But I can also see the whites resenting them for it. And I can see coloreds defending their homes when somebody's shooting at them. But I can understand cops being angry when two of their own get killed as a result of it."

"It seems to me," I said, "that what's happening now is a lot like what you say happened in 1917—one thing leads to another, and it just keeps building. You really don't think there can be another riot?"

"Nah. Most people involved in the 'seventeen riot were decent people, and they've been ashamed of what they did ever since. They'd never let it happen again."

"Not even the hotheads?"

"The Klan will keep them in line. And if they don't, we will. Law and order will be preserved."

So even a police officer had bought the notion that the Klan was a force for peace. "Are you keeping order now?" I asked. "Has anyone been arrested for killing Crawford or for burning Denver Jones's home or Cubs Park?"

"That's for the detectives," Moss snapped. "It ain't my problem." The answer was clearly no.

It was also clear that Moss didn't like the tone of my last questions. He informed me that he had some official duties to attend to and that I would have to go.

As I left, he went back to yelling at the old man. The East St. Louis Police Department might not be interested in solving a lynching or arson, but they would do their utmost to ensure that derelicts didn't cough in the station house.

I stood in line at the batting cage, waiting my turn at the plate, while Ken Williams rattled the outfield fences with a succession of line drives. It was an awesome display, but it failed to hold my interest.

I was still mulling over my morning conversation with Ed Moss. It hadn't left me with much cause for hope. If Moss was representative of official law enforcement, and the Ku Klux Klan was considered the leading civilian instrument for preserving law and order, then East St. Louis was no safer from violence today than it was in 1917. Hope wasn't the only thing I lacked; I was also without any idea what my next step should be.

Williams capped his batting practice show with a towering shot that left Sportsman's Park over the centerfield wall. As he headed back to the dugout, a sportswriter for the *St. Louis Globe-Democrat* stopped the slugger and asked for a baseball for his son. Williams happily obliged, picking up a stray practice ball and tossing it to the writer.

That gave me an idea. I might not get much further in finding out who killed Slip Crawford, and I was sure I'd never understand the racial hatred that had led to so many deaths like his, but I now had a plan for what to do next.

I began implementing it during the game. Lee Fohl had put Marty McManus back in at second base, so I sat on the bench and calculated what the East St. Louis Cubs would need to replace what they'd lost in the fire. Between innings, I cornered some of the Browns' staff and coaxed donations out of them. Our equipment manager agreed to give me some bats and balls, the clubhouse man offered some old uniforms he had stored away, and the groundskeeper said I could have three old bases.

I became increasingly excited, delighted that I finally had a way to make a tangible contribution. I'd had enough of asking questions and sorting through stories for a while; I wanted to do something I *knew* would help.

By game's end, I had enough material piled up that I would need to get a car to transport it. It still wasn't enough to equip an entire ballclub, though, so I also stopped in at the Cardinals' office to ask if they could contribute. Branch Rickey was on the road with his team, but his secretary promised to give him my request.

Before leaving the park to meet Margie for dinner, I called Franklin Aubury. It was a nice change to have something positive to report.

"I got a bunch of equipment," I told the lawyer. "And I might have some more coming. I wanted to give it to the Cubs to replace what they lost in the fire. Is there anything else I can do to help?"

He answered, "All they need now, then, is a ballpark."

"Isn't there another park they can use?"

"Yes, but they won't. The first priority is to rebuild Cubs Park—immediately. We cannot allow the Klan to succeed; what they destroy, we will restore."

"Do you know when the rebuilding is gonna start?"

"Tomorrow morning. The Cubs are unable to afford contractors, but donations of lumber and supplies have been coming in, and volunteers will start construction tomorrow."

"I'm pretty handy with a saw and hammer," I said. Years ago, I'd worked and played ball for a number of industries, including a furniture manufacturer and a shipyard. "Of course, I'm not sure if they'll want a white guy helping, considering what happened."

Aubury said, "We need hands. It doesn't matter what color they are."

CHAPTER 27

S ince Sunday was my last day in town before a road trip to
Cleveland, I had originally intended to idle it away with
Margie on pursuits that didn't involve construction tools. She
agreed that helping to rebuild Cubs Park was a better idea,
though. And we would still get to spend the day together,
because she insisted on coming along.

Early in the morning, the two of us were again on a trolley
crossing Eads Bridge, taking the same route that we'd taken
on our way to the Elcars' game in April. This time, we avoided
looking at the devastated section of downtown East St. Louis
when we passed by.

Once we reached Cubs Park, however, there was no way
to miss seeing the destruction there. The two-story building
that had housed the club's offices was gone, reduced to scattered
piles of ashes, out of which jutted some charred beams and
plumbing fixtures. Even less remained of the wooden bleachers.
A burnt smell lingered, and ashes were kicked up by sporadic
breezes.

Dozens of volunteers were already gathered near the spot
where the park entrance used to be. As Margie and I joined
them, I saw that Franklin Aubury was right about all helping

hands being welcome. During the game in April, there had been strict separation of the races. Today, a surprising number of white men, as well as a few women, both black and white, were joining together for the rebuilding effort.

Several of the Cubs' players were present, including their catcher, Denver Jones, who appeared to be in charge.

I approached the big, moon-faced catcher, and introduced myself. "Thought you might be able to use a couple workers," I said.

"Glad to have you." With a hint of a smile, he added, "Not going by 'Welch' anymore?"

"No, that 'Welch' guy couldn't hit for beans. I do a whole lot better as Rawlings."

A laugh rumbled from deep within Jones's belly. "Well, let's see how you do with a saw and hammer."

I told him Margie wanted to help, too, and asked what we should do.

"First we're gonna sort out what all needs to be done. Waitin' for a couple of carpenters to come by and give us their advice."

I looked around at all the people who'd gathered to help rebuild this baseball park, and wondered if any had thought to help Jones build a new house. I hadn't, and I felt bad about that. "I'm sorry about you losing your home," I said.

"Thanks," he said. "But I didn't lose my home, just a building. My family's together, and that's 'home.' And we'll be movin' into a new house soon."

Jones then excused himself to organize some cleanup squads that began raking up ashes and cinders. Margie helped with that task, while I joined some men in carting away the burnt beams.

I was trying to pry a charred four-by-four out of the rubble when Karl Landfors showed up. "Would you care for some assistance with that?" he asked.

It took a moment before I could answer yes. Karl's appearance had me stunned. He was dressed completely out of character, in dungarees, a flannel shirt, and a cloth cap tilted at a careless angle. The clothes looked stiff and new; I had the feeling he'd bought them specifically for today's labor.

As we tugged at the wood, Karl told me between grunts that Aubury had wanted to come but was instead working on getting more funds for building materials.

After most of the large pieces of rubble were cleared away, a couple of trucks arrived with fresh lumber, wire fencing, nails, and paint. Denver Jones and a contingent of men strolled around the park, trying to determine what to do first.

I joined them in surveying the site. The building and bleachers obviously needed to be completely rebuilt, but it was less clear what to do about the fencing. The wire fences in front of the bleachers had been scorched, but were still intact; Jones decided a coat of paint was all they needed.

The backstop, from which Slip Crawford had been lynched, triggered some discussion. The wire mesh had been burned through in spots, but the frame was still intact and standing. While the other men debated whether to replace all or part of it, I imagined the pitcher hanging there. I was happy when they decided to tear it all down, to get rid of the gallows from which Crawford had been hanged.

No one had an idea what to do about the grass in center field. The burning cross had toppled at some point, scorching the grass where it lay. Although the fragments of wood had been removed, the image of the Klan's calling card remained seared on the turf.

We then split up into work groups, Karl and I joining the one assigned to rebuild the first-base bleachers.

I was happy finally to put my carpentry talents to use, but soon found that they weren't as strong as I'd thought. The factories where I'd worked had paid me primarily to play ball for the company teams, so I never really had to develop industrial skills. I never had much of a chance, either; as soon as I started to learn one line of work, I'd be off to some other factory that needed a second baseman.

At least I was doing better than Karl. Within a matter of minutes he'd been taken off sawing detail when it became apparent that he might amputate his own fingers. He was doing no better trying to nail boards together.

"You hammer like lightning," I told him. When he smiled, I added, "You never strike twice in the same spot."

That caused him to miss another one. After he'd built up a small pile of bent nails, Karl was sent to join the children and women raking debris from the field.

I continued to work on the stands and talked with the men. I learned that some of the white workers were regulars at Cubs Park. They liked to watch good baseball and wanted the park rebuilt so they could see the games again.

There were others in the neighborhood, I suspected, who didn't feel the same way. A number of spectators had gathered on the sidewalk and automobiles slowed down as they drove past. I wondered how long it would take before local Klansmen knew that a ballpark was rising from their ashes.

While the office and bleachers began to take shape, the Klan's handiwork was also being erased in the outfield. Karl Landfors had figured out what to do about the cross branded on the turf. He dug up plugs of grass near the cross and replanted them in the burnt area; by the time he'd finished, the ground looked spotty, but at least the Klan trademark was barely discernible.

After we'd been working for a couple of hours, Jones called a break, and we all dug into the coffee, sandwiches, pies, and cookies that some women from the neighborhood had brought by.

While we were resting, the panel truck I'd hired to deliver the baseball equipment from Sportsman's Park arrived. I was astonished to find it packed with far more gear than I had collected. Branch Rickey had donated additional bats, balls, and gloves, as well as a dozen pairs of spikes and last year's uniforms.

A crowd gathered around as I handed out equipment from the van. Once it was all unloaded, I told Denver Jones the material was compliments of the Browns and the Cards.

The big catcher beamed. "All that's missing," he joked, "is a genuine 'Mickey Rawlings' model bat." Then he added, "Tell them thank you. We'll sure put this all to good use."

One of the other Cubs' players picked up a bat, hefted it, and took a few swings. "Can't wait to use this," he said.

Karl Landfors piped up, "The field's all clear."

I wasn't sure if it was a progress report or a suggestion, but Jones took it as the latter. "All right," he said. "Let's play an inning."

Those who wanted to play gathered around, and the Cubs' catcher appointed two young colored boys captains. They proceeded to choose up sides, taking Denver Jones as first pick. The other Cubs' players were next, then a brawny white man was chosen. Next were a couple more Negroes, and another large white. I realized that the kids were picking sides primarily based on size, not race. This was going to be a game between mixed teams.

As they kept picking players, passing me over, I wanted to yell out that I was a big-league ballplayer; if they kept going in descending order of size, I'd be one of the last chosen. I glanced uneasily at Karl Landfors. If he got picked ahead of me, I vowed, I would have to kill him.

To my relief, I was selected two players ahead of Karl. When both teams were rounded out, we grabbed up the equipment and took the field. We agreed to play just one inning, with each batter allowed to swing until he hit the ball.

It was a completely unremarkable game—just a bunch of men and boys playing ball and having fun. The highlight for me was hitting a solid double down the left-field line, my first base hit in this park. Karl managed to get a hit, too, which was probably the first in his life.

After the inning, we all went back to work so that soon a more competitive game could be played on the site.

As much as I hated to be the first to quit, I still had to play in Sportsman's Park in the afternoon.

I went over to Denver Jones, who was working on the frame for the main building. "Sorry to go," I said, "but I got a game today, and we're leaving for a road trip tomorrow."

"You done plenty," the catcher answered. "We're obliged for your help—and for the equipment."

"Wish I could do more," I said, looking around at the progress. The bleachers were almost finished, the field was all cleared of ashes and debris, and the framework of the office was coming together. It was already a striking difference from that morning. I hoped that I might have a chance to play there again when construction was completed. If only Slip Crawford could do the same, I thought sadly.

I waved to Margie to join me, then turned to Jones again. "Can I ask you something?"

"Sure," he said.

"Why did you guys bring Slip Crawford in as a ringer? You already had Jimmy Bell, who could have pitched. I saw him in Indianapolis—he beat the ABCs, and even struck out Oscar Charleston. In fact, they're calling him 'Cool Papa' now because of the way he handled Charleston."

"I always knew Bell was gonna be a good one," said Jones. "As for Crawford, we didn't bring him in. He *asked* to play.

Slip used to live here in East St. Louis until the riot, and he wanted to come back and do something for his community."

Another carload of white men drove by. I could swear it was the same Studebaker that had passed a couple of times before. I said to Jones, "The Klan isn't going to like seeing this. What if they come back tonight and destroy what was done today?"

"Don't worry," he answered confidently. "This neighborhood is being patrolled. Won't nothing happen here again."

I was pretty sure it wasn't the police department that was going to be doing the patrolling.

CHAPTER 28

The series in Cleveland was only four games, and I played a total of only three innings, with only one at bat, but I didn't remember ever having a better road trip.

I was buoyed by the satisfaction that I'd done something positive in helping out at Cubs Park. During one of my calls to Margie from Cleveland, she told me that construction was progressing so well that the Cubs would be playing their first game in the rebuilt park on Saturday.

Also boosting my spirits was the Browns' continued success. We'd been winning so regularly, and attracting so many fans, that Phil Ball announced plans to add thousands of bleacher seats to Sportsman's Park to accommodate the growing crowds. He didn't mention, but we all knew, that he also expected to need the extra seats for the World Series in October. We were consistently maintaining a several-game lead over the Yankees, and although it was still only mid-June, the team and the fans were becoming convinced that this would be the year the Browns would win a pennant for St. Louis.

I was starting to believe it myself, and even began monitoring the National League standings to predict who our opponents would be. I was pleased to see that we would most likely be facing John McGraw's New York Giants, whose lineup included my old friend, and former Dodger, Casey Stengel.

The primary reason for my good mood, though, was Margie. I'd brought her a dozen yellow roses before leaving on the trip, and phoned her every morning and every evening while in Cleveland. From our conversations, I was optimistic that she'd agree to move back in with me soon. We hadn't talked any more about marriage, but I would be content for a while simply to be together again, sharing a home.

The Browns' train pulled into Union Station shortly before eleven o'clock Friday night. Margie had invited me to come directly to her hotel, but I decided to stop at home first. After the eight-hour trip, I wanted to wash and change into clean clothes before seeing her. One of the drawbacks of not being married yet was that I still had to pay attention to my grooming.

The taxicab made such good time to my apartment that the detour wasn't going to set me too far behind schedule; I figured I'd be able to shower and change and be at the Jefferson Hotel around midnight.

After giving the cabby a hefty tip for his speed, I hustled to the door with my suitcase and dug into my pocket for the key. I never got it out.

I didn't notice the sound of rustling bushes until a gruff voice barked, "Grab 'im!" My suitcase fell to the step as my arms were pinned behind me. Then my head was covered with a coarse cloth.

I twisted and jerked, trying to get out. No luck. Then I tried the other extreme; I remained still for a moment to collect my senses and try to figure out what was going on. At least two men were holding me. Neither of them spoke, though; the only sound I heard was two nearby automobile engines suddenly roaring to life.

The same voice I'd heard before ordered, "Get 'im to the car."

As they started dragging me toward the sound of the engines, I resumed my struggle to get free, and yelled, "What the hell are you—"

"Shut up!" A punch to my head sent me reeling; with my eyes covered, I'd had no way to duck or brace myself.

Don't let them get you in the car, I told myself. "Let me go!" I shouted at the top of my lungs, hoping a neighbor might hear.

Another blow to my head put an end to my yelling—it was all I could do to remain conscious. I was half-carried the rest of the way and tossed onto a backseat.

Three doors slammed shut, and the car squealed in a tight turn as it peeled away from the curb. The second car followed close behind.

Okay, now what? I remained quiet and motionless, listening for any clue that might tell me who I was with or why I'd been grabbed or where I was going. The only thing I could tell for sure was that this was no friendly prank.

Still encased in the sack, almost gagging on the damp burlap, I oriented myself as best I could to determine my exact position inside the vehicle. Then I waited.

When the car slowed for a turn, I reached out blindly for where I thought the door handle would be. It wasn't there. As I fumbled to find it, I was yanked away from the door before I could open it.

"You'll be out soon enough," said a smug voice.

It was only another five minutes before we pulled to a stop, and the driver killed the engine. The car behind us did the same.

Now I struggled to stay *inside* the automobile as the men tried to drag me out by my feet. I figured whatever they wanted me to do, it was in my best interest to do the opposite.

It was another losing struggle. In a matter of minutes, I was lying facedown on the ground, the heel of a boot pressed on the back of my neck.

Through the sack I heard the repeated rustling of cloth, then a voice I hadn't heard before drawled, "Everybody ready?" The others must have indicated that they were, because he went on, "Good. Get him on his feet."

I was immediately pulled upright, and the burlap was ripped from my head, scraping the bruised skin of my face.

The sight that greeted me made me wish my eyes were still covered. Six men garbed in the white robes and masked hoods of the Ku Klux Klan stood around me. Two of them gripped my arms, and two others carried rifles. In the moonlight, they all looked like ghosts. If they were trying to throw a scare into me, they'd succeeded thoroughly. I only hoped that scaring me was all they wanted to do.

Glancing away from them, I saw we were in a dark, wooded area of what I assumed to be Forest Park. The cars, I noticed, were two black sedans, pulled off the dirt road, near a giant elm.

The man with the drawl said as if pronouncing sentence, "Mickey Rawlings, you are a traitor. The only thing worse than an uppity nigger is a white man who betrays his own race."

I couldn't tell from his statement what he meant by "betrayal." Was it the fact that I'd helped rebuild Cubs Park? Or did he mean my association with Franklin Aubury? Or maybe it referred to my inquiries about the Klan and its possible role in the lynching of Slip Crawford. But I didn't much care which of these "betrayals" he meant right then, and I wasn't going to ask. All I was thinking about was how I could get away. Try as I might, I couldn't break the grips of those who were holding me.

Momentarily giving up, I relaxed again to conserve my strength.

The Klansman in charge drawled even more slowly, perhaps enjoying the taste of the words, when he next ordered, "Get the rope."

My knees buckled; if not for the men holding me, I'd have collapsed. I'm going to be *lynched?* I almost blurted, "You can't!" But a mental image of Slip Crawford hanging from a backstop flashed before me, arguing back, Yes, they can.

One of the Klansmen got a length of rope from the back of the second car.

This isn't a swamp in Georgia, I thought. They're going to lynch a white man in the city of St. Louis?

Rage suddenly coursed through me, and I twisted and squirmed again. My goal wasn't escape. I wanted to pull the hoods off these bastards—if they were going to kill me, they were going to have to do it with me looking at their faces, not hiding behind masks.

"Tie him up!"

Still trying and failing to grasp one of the masks, I was dragged to the elm and slammed facefirst into the trunk. My arms were extended to encircle the tree, and my hands tied together. I started to hug the tree tightly, thinking that they couldn't hang me if they couldn't pry me off the tree trunk.

When they ripped the coat and shirt off my back, I realized that lynching wasn't their intent. At least not their immediate intent.

A crack like a rifle report split the air. I twisted my head to see the group's leader brandishing a bullwhip. "You associate with niggers," he said, "you get treated like a nigger."

The next crack of the whip tore into my bare shoulder. The one after that stabbed the base of my spine.

Egged on by the others, he continued the whipping, taking a long pause between each lash to let the pain fully register.

My goals were twofold: One was to stay alive, and the other was to deny them the satisfaction of hearing me cry out. As he kept snapping the whip, I bit the inside of my mouth so hard I tasted blood.

The other Klansmen grew quiet; I probably wasn't giving them the fun time they'd expected. Eventually one of them grumbled, "Is he dead?"

"Nah," huffed the one with the whip. "He's still flinching. See?"

Another lash came, and I tried to remain completely motionless. I couldn't avoid a slight flinch, but I still remained silent.

"That should be enough to teach him a lesson." The Klansman walked up to me and growled in my ear, "Tonight we're letting you off with a warning. If we got to talk to you again, you won't survive it."

He headed back to the others, and one of them asked, "Should we cut him loose?"

"Nah. Come sunup, somebody'll find him. Let them do it."

There were some laughs, then car doors slammed, and they roared off into the night.

I let my muscles gradually relax, and took slow, deep breaths. The panic and fear began to subside. With the immediate threat over, I took a sensory inventory of my body, trying to assess the damage. The worst, I knew, was to my back: My skin burned from the lashing, and electric spasms jolted my legs and spine whenever I moved the wrong way. I could also feel warm blood trickling down my back; the waistband of my trousers was soaked with it. The only other injuries were minor, as far as I could tell, including a bruised face that stung where salty tears had flowed into the scrapes.

Okay, now to get out of here. I was not going to wait until sunup. Oddly, it was the idea of someone finding me this way that bothered me most. To be tied up and whipped was *humiliating,* like I'd been punished for doing something wrong.

I began to pull at the ropes, trying to break them. I kept yanking harder and harder, but all I accomplished was to strain my shoulders and cut off the circulation to my hands.

As I struggled, I was subjected to new torment: Flies and mosquitoes lit upon me and began to feast on my bloodied back.

Pulling hadn't worked, so I next tried going the opposite way. I pressed my chest into the biting bark of the tree in an attempt to put some slack in the rope. That worked; I was able to get my hands close enough together to pluck at the knots.

The picking became more urgent as insects buzzed around my head, crawled over my skin, and dug into every open wound. When the rope finally slipped free, I didn't think I'd ever felt a greater sense of relief.

I collected my tattered clothes from the ground, not wanting to leave any evidence of what had happened to me. Holding what was left of my jacket around me, I began the long, agonizing walk home.

When I got to the apartment, my suitcase was still on the steps. I left it there and went inside to call Margie.

I told her briefly what had happened, and after a few questions to determine how badly I was hurt, she promised to be right over.

After hanging up, I lay belly-down on the sofa. Then I pulled one of the pillows to my mouth and screamed into it. I kept screaming, again and again, sometimes from pain, more often from rage.

Margie didn't arrive alone. Despite the hour, she had persuaded the hotel doctor from the Jefferson to come with her.

The brisk young doctor examined me closely, and determined there was little he could do. "A few of these cuts need stitches," he said, "but there's not enough good skin left around them to sew into. Best just to keep it all clean and hope it heals okay on its own."

The two of them then began to clean the wounds, Margie gently working on my face, and the doctor cleaning the more serious cuts on my back. As they worked, the doctor asked me what had happened.

"Some guys whipped me," I said.

"I didn't think it was a dog bite. Did you call the police?"

"No."

"Why not?"

"Not much to tell them." I hadn't recognized any of the men's voices, and would be unable to give any more identification than "six Klansmen in two dark sedans."

The doctor said, "I'll give you some bandages and a poultice for your back. It needs to be changed several times a day."

"I'll do that," Margie volunteered. "Show me what to do."

He instructed her on how to prepare the poultice and apply the bandages, then made the first application himself to demonstrate. Then he gave me several days' worth of sleeping powders so that the pain wouldn't keep me up nights.

After the doctor left, Margie removed my clothes and gently gave me a thorough sponge bath on the areas that weren't bandaged. When she finished, she sat at the end of the sofa by my feet, and I could sense that she was staring at my back.

Suddenly Margie said in a choked voice, "I'll be right back."

I heard her run to the bathroom, then I heard her start to cry. The sound of her sobbing pained me far more than the lashing had.

CHAPTER 29

"Don't tell me you're planning on going somewhere," Margie said.

"Got a game today." I continued to rummage through the dresser drawer. "I have to go."

"After what happened last night, you're going to the *ballpark?* You can't play *baseball.*"

She was right about that. If I even tried to swing a bat or throw a ball, my back would split wide open. But I had to show up and let the team trainer make his evaluation. I explained that to Margie as I slipped a gauze undershirt over the fresh bandages she'd put on. She then helped me into a loose-fitting silk shirt.

I continued to dress with her assistance. Although my skin was still on fire, the shooting pains up my spine had ceased, and I was able to walk without much difficulty. Once I was fully clothed, the only visible reminders of the previous night were an ugly bump on my forehead, a split lip, and a scraped cheek.

I asked Margie, "Why don't you stay here, and maybe take a nap? It was a hard night for you, too." The lack of sleep was apparent in her eyes.

"I want to do some shopping first. The doctor gave me a list of some things we'll need. And I thought I'd pick up a few groceries." She kissed me on my good cheek. "Not all of us can live on coffee and cookies."

Although the trolley was less than half-occupied, I remained standing during the ride to avoid pressing my back against a seat. Except for a few times when other passengers brushed against me, the trip was relatively pain-free.

I was the first to arrive at the Browns' clubhouse, as I'd intended. I wanted a chance to suit up alone, before the other players could see my mutilated body.

First I went to the trainer's room, where old Doc Quinn was stretched out on the rubbing table, snoring loudly.

I shook him awake. "Doc?"

"Yeah, what?" He rubbed his unshaven jowls.

"Can't play today."

He slowly swung his legs around, and slid off the table to examine me. Like most baseball "Doc"'s, he had no actual medical training, and prescribed liniment for almost any ailment. He took a look at my face, then I showed him my bandaged back.

Fortunately, he didn't suggest liniment; he simply deemed me unfit to play, then climbed back on the table to resume his nap.

I went to my locker and began to remove my street clothes. Although excused from playing, I would still have to watch the game from the bench. By the time Lee Fohl and my teammates arrived, I was in uniform. As I tied the laces of my spikes, I saw Fohl stop in the trainer's room.

Doc Quinn must have failed to convince the Browns' manager that I didn't belong in the lineup, because Fohl soon stormed out of Quinn's office and came up to me. "What's the problem?" he demanded. "I'm tryin' to win a pennant here, and I can't have somebody sittin' out a game unless he can't move." Fohl eyed my bruised face, and shook his head. "That's not enough to give you the day off."

"My back's bad, too."

He appeared unconvinced. "If you can bend it, you can play."

I removed my jersey, and lifted my undershirt to reveal the bandages.

"Goddamn! What the hell happened?"

"Some guys jumped me."

Other players gathered around. I was embarrassed at being the center of attention—especially for something like this.

Fohl asked, "Can I see?"

"Go 'head."

He pulled away a corner of the bandage. Judging by the stunned gasps of my teammates, it was probably a good thing that I couldn't see for myself what was underneath.

Urban Shocker asked, "What did they jump you *with?*"

I turned around and saw my teammates all staring at me. They looked sympathetic, but I still didn't want to admit what had happened. Partly I was embarrassed at losing a fight, even if it hadn't been a fair fight. But my reluctance to speak was mostly because there was something so emasculating about having been whipped. I drew up my courage and said as matter-of-factly as I could, "A week ago, I went over to East St. Louis to help rebuild Cubs Park—that's the colored ballpark the Klan burned down. Last night, after we got back in town, a bunch of Klansmen grabbed me outside my house. They took me to Forest Park, tied me to a tree, and tried to take the skin off my back with a bullwhip."

There was shocked silence for half a minute, then my teammates let loose, cursing the Klan with some spectacular combinations of profanity.

Baby Doll Jacobson said, "You find out who did this, you

let us know. We'll take care of them for you." Marty McManus seconded his offer, as did several others.

I nodded my thanks, too choked up to speak.

Lee Fohl said, "You go on home and take care of yourself. Just give me a call when you're ready to come back."

I gladly accepted Fohl's suggestion and began changing back into street clothes, taking comfort in the knowledge that at least I wasn't going to have to take care of myself alone. Margie had told me that morning that she was moving back in.

After wishing my teammates well in the game, I left the ballpark. On the way home, I made only one stop—to pick up a dozen yellow roses for Margie.

The doctor had suggested that I sleep on the sofa for a while, instead of on a bed, because there was less likelihood that I would roll over onto my back. I was following his advice, dozing on the sofa, when the telephone rang.

I heard Margie run to pick it up before a second ring could wake me, but it was too late.

"I don't know if he can come to the phone," she whispered to the caller.

"I'm awake," I said. "Who is it?"

"Tater Greene."

I went over to the phone stand and took the receiver from her. As she handed it to me, Margie told me softly, "He sounds drunk."

"Mickey!" Greene said, enunciating my name as if it was a hiccup. "I had to call."

"Why the hell didn't you call me sooner—in time to warn me?"

"I didn't know what they was gonna do. Honest, I didn't."

"You knew everything else they've been doing."

"Not this," he insisted. "They pro'ly knew I wouldn't go along with it, on account of you and me bein' friends."

I was tempted to correct him by pointing out that we had never been friends. "All right," I said, "then tell me what they have planned *next.*"

I could hear Greene take a sip of something that probably wasn't going to make his slurred speech any clearer. "They don't let me in on nothin' no more. I don't think they trust me—they know I don't like what's been going on lately."

I pressed him anyway. "There is something that I *have* to know: Who whipped me?"

"Dunno," he moaned. "Like I said, they didn't tell me."

"Then how do you know it happened? You didn't hear it from me, so you must have heard it from one of them."

"Some guys at Enoch's were talkin' about it."

"*Who* was talking about it?"

Greene hesitated. "Brian Padgett. But he didn't say nothin' about being there. He was just tellin' it like it was a funny story he heard someplace."

Funny? Only to a Knight of the Invisible Empire, I thought. "Okay, Tater, do me a favor: If you hear who *was* there, let me know, will you?"

"Yeah, okay." He coughed. "Anyway, I just wanted you to know *I* had nothing to do with it. You hurt bad?"

In case he should pass my answer on to anyone, I said, "Nah. I've gotten worse raspberries from sliding into base."

"I'm glad of that, at least." Before hanging up, Greene added, "I *am* sorry, Mick. About everything."

After we got off the phone, I thought that Greene certainly sounded like he was feeling no pain—a condition I wished I was in. So I prescribed myself a couple of shots of "medicinal" brandy that Margie had picked up, before lying down again.

* * *

By the second day of my confinement to the sofa, doing little but listening to scabs form on my back, I was getting as itchy inside as my skin was underneath the bandages.

I tried to pass the time by reading—newspapers, the latest movie magazines, and Mark Twain's *Life on the Mississippi*—but I didn't get more than a couple of pages into any of them. Margie made numerous attempts to cheer me, but she couldn't hold my attention either. I kept thinking about what had happened to me in Forest Park. Every painful twinge in my back was like another lash of the whip, keeping the memory of that night vivid in my mind. I was determined to get back at whoever was responsible—if I could only determine how to do so.

Sunday night, Margie tried again. "I was thinking," she said. "Why don't we have Karl to dinner? And Franklin Aubury, too."

I was torn; I didn't want them to see me like this, but I did like the idea of Margie and me having dinner guests—it would be nice to show that we were together again. "Sure," I said. "But I don't know when we'd ever get them here on the same night. They're both always working on some cause or other."

"Let me call and see," she said.

I told her where I had their phone numbers, and she first called Karl. "He's free anytime," she reported to me. "How about tomorrow?"

"Fine by me. How about Aubury?"

Margie got through to the lawyer at home. After talking briefly, she called to me, "Tomorrow's okay for him, too. What time should we make it?"

"Anytime." I'd certainly be here, lying in the same spot. "Oh! Could you ask him to bring any books or articles he might have on the Klan?"

She relayed the message.

"And on the 1917 riot," I added.

Margie passed that on, too.

"And on colored baseball."

She spoke briefly to him again, then hung up before the poor fellow ended up agreeing to bring me his entire law library.

As it was, Aubury had his hands full when he and Karl showed up Monday evening. In addition to the reading materials I'd requested, he'd brought a peach pie that his wife Ethel had baked and a small bouquet of flowers. Karl, bless his heart, brought beer.

Neither of them asked for details about what had happened to me. Karl's only comment came when he saw my bruised face. He said, "I suppose that's one bad thing about being white: The black-and-blue really shows."

The four of us sat down to dinner, with me using a stool instead of a chair.

Margie made sure the conversation was kept light. No mention was made of the Klan or the antilynching bill or even of politics—an impossibility, I'd have thought, with Karl Landfors here.

That didn't mean none of us were thinking about those things, though. I certainly was. Looking at Aubury, I remembered when the two of us were talking in Indianapolis. He'd said that there would always be things we wouldn't understand about each other because of our different races. There was one less difference, between us now, I realized. I'd had a fear put in me Friday night that Aubury had lived with all his life. And I doubted that I would ever entirely lose it.

After dinner, we retired to the parlor. Margie, Aubury, and I drank beers while Karl ate the last piece of pie, his third.

The lawyer pointed to the literature he'd brought, which was piled on the coffee table. "Why did you want all of this?"

I leaned over and picked up *Sol White's History of Colored Baseball.* "This is because I'm interested. After our trip, I wanted to learn more about colored baseball." I then tapped the stack of papers about the Klan. "And this," I said, "is because I intend to find some way of getting back at the guys who whipped me."

CHAPTER 30

Over the next few days, my back improved to the point where I asked Margie to stop applying the poultices. It was a week earlier than the doctor suggested, but the pain of having bandages peeled off my tender skin was worse than leaving it untreated.

While I continued to rest at home, I delved into the reading materials that Franklin Aubury had brought me.

I started with some official Ku Klux Klan publications that Aubury had managed to acquire. One of them was a fifty-four-page booklet called the *Kloran*, written by Klan founder William J. Simmons. This, the Klan Bible, included dire warnings that its "sacred contents" were never to be revealed to anyone outside of the Invisible Empire. I'd hoped the *Kloran* would contain information on the Klan's true nature and goals, but it proved a disappointment. Like the pamphlets I'd already seen, this one also presented the KKK as a benevolent fraternal organization. The only secrets in the *Kloran* were regarding their strange vocabulary and elaborate rituals, called Klankraft. The booklet also laid out the structure of the Klan's national organization; the Invisible Empire was divided into eight domains, which were further broken down into realms, provinces, and, finally, local klaverns. Leadership flowed down from the Imperial Wizard to Grand Goblin, Grand Dragon, Great Titan, and Exalted Cyclops. The grandiose organizational scheme and funny names would have been amusing had I not known firsthand that the Ku Klux Klan was no laughing matter.

I then turned to material on the Klan published by the NAACP and in the *St. Louis Argus*. These gave a perspective on the Klan much closer to the one I'd encountered in Forest Park, but didn't provide much new or useful information.

Next, I read more about the East St. Louis riot of 1917. The hostilities still flaring this year seemed to have gotten their initial spark back then. As Ed Moss had told me in the Bond Avenue station house, "You got to look at all sides of what happened." I believed that I needed to look at what happened five years ago.

Much of what Aubury had brought me about the riot was newspaper clippings, which I read thoroughly. Then I opened a few ponderous official reports that resulted from several government investigations. One of the reports was from the Military Board of Inquiry, which had held hearings on the conduct of the National Guard. Aubury must have gone to some lengths to obtain a copy, because according to an attached letter, it was considered too "inflammatory" ever to be released publicly. Since the report concluded that numerous militiamen had actually aided in the killing of Negroes, I could see why the board didn't want that information to become public knowledge.

The congressional report that I read next *was* a public document. It included testimony regarding the actions—and inaction—of local law enforcement during the riot. According to one eyewitness:

> *Two Negroes came out of a house in the middle of the block, on Broadway, between Fourth and Fifth Sts., about half-past seven in the evening. They fell*

> on their knees before some policemen, and begged
> to be saved from the mob. "Keep walking, you
> black——," ordered a police sergeant. Both
> Negroes fled, only to be shot down half a block
> away. An ambulance came, but drove on again
> when the sergeant shouted, "They're not dead yet,
> boys."

It was passages like that one that kept me from reading the material for any length of time. When I needed a break from the accounts of tragedy and turmoil, I picked up the Sol White book Franklin Aubury had brought and read instead about the rich history of colored baseball.

On Saturday, in the company of Margie, Franklin Aubury, and Karl Landfors, I got to witness a new chapter in that history: the grand opening of Stars Park, the first Negro League ballpark owned entirely by colored people.

Although my back wasn't quite healed enough for me to be up and around, it was important for me to be there—both to support the Stars and to show that the Klan wasn't going to scare me off. My only regret was that I wouldn't be able to stay for the game, because I'd have to leave for Sportsman's Park immediately after the pregame festivities. Lee Fohl, I knew, would expect me to attend the Browns game if I was well enough to be at Stars Park.

The Negro National League's newest stadium, at the corner of Compton and Market Streets, wasn't entirely completed yet—tarpaulins were being used as a temporary grandstand roof, and there was no fence in left field—but it was clearly going to be a splendid ballpark. It was filled with more than five thousand fans, of both races, and a stellar array of dignitaries that included St. Louis mayor Henry Kiel and Missouri governor Arthur Hyde. Thousands more had cheered the team during a morning parade through the neighborhood.

When Mayor Kiel began to give a speech at home plate, I noticed there was no segregation in the park's seating, and wondered if that was due to the presence of the mayor and the governor. It wouldn't have looked good to have the white and Negro dignitaries sitting on opposite sides of a rope.

As the mayor droned on, Franklin Aubury leaned toward me, and whispered, "You were interested in Rosie Sumner, the fellow who's recruiting for the Eastern Colored League."

"Yeah, what about him?"

"I have made some inquiries. I assumed that since he was in the Midwest, there was a strong likelihood he might come here."

"And?"

Aubury pointed to a beefy, light-skinned colored man sitting in a box seat not far from our section. "That is Sumner. In the white-linen suit."

I checked my pocket watch. I had to leave for Sportsman's Park in ten minutes at the latest. Then I looked again at Sumner. I didn't want to miss a chance to talk to him, even briefly.

"I better go," I said to my companions. "I'm just gonna talk to Sumner a minute, then I gotta get to the park."

"Want me to come with you?" Margie asked.

I shook my head and got to my feet. "No, you stay here. I'll just be riding the bench today anyway."

Margie seemed content to remain with Karl and Aubury, and I didn't blame her. She would be getting to see the visiting Indianapolis ABCs face Cool Papa Bell, who was slated to pitch the first home game in St. Louis Stars' history.

I edged toward Rosie Sumner, who appeared to be alone. He was fanning himself with a scorecard and studying the players who stood along the foul lines. As I drew near him, I saw that Sumner had the fashion sense of a riverboat gambler and the face and body of a prizefighter.

Leaning on the railing next to his arm, I said to him, "I hear you're recruiting for the Eastern Colored League."

Sumner looked up at me, and I noticed the ugly scars on his squat face. If he *had* been a boxer, I thought, he must have ended up on the losing end of most of his bouts. "Don't think we can use you," he replied in a voice so high and reedy that it sounded like he must have taken quite a few punches below the belt, too.

"You *could* have used Slip Crawford," I said. "You wanted to sign him."

"Of course I did." Sumner had an amused glint in his cold eyes. "Crawford was a top-notch pitcher."

"But he wouldn't sign with you."

"No, he wouldn't. What's it to you, anyway?"

I ignored the question. "Did you try to force him?"

"Convince, not force. What are you, a cop?"

I stared at Sumner for a moment, hoping he might interpret my silence as a yes. "When you couldn't *convince* him, did you decide he wasn't going to play for anyone else then?"

When he realized what I was implying, Sumner squawked, "Hey, you can't—"

"I know you threatened some other players—told them they better sign with you before they ended up like Crawford."

"Hey, that was just talk."

"And I know you work as muscle for a gangster in New York—Alex Pompez."

Sumner slumped back in his seat and worked the scorecard more vigorously. "Let me tell you, I'm a *scout,* not a hoodlum. And Mr. Pompez is a baseball fan first and foremost. If he thought I hurt a ballplayer, *I'd* be the one getting hurt." He shrugged his broad shoulders. "Yeah, I used Crawford getting killed as part of my sales pitch, but that's all I did."

"All right," I said, trying to sound official. "If I have any more questions, I'll be in touch."

My prediction proved wrong. Lee Fohl did decide to use me in the ball game. Although he'd let me skip practice, when he needed a pinch-runner for Frank Ellerbe in the seventh inning, he asked me if I was up to it.

My answer was automatic: yes. I went in, and broke open the scabs on my back sliding into third base on a single by Hank Severeid.

Soon after the game, I was back at home, belly-down on the sofa again. And, once again, I returned to reading about the events of 1917.

What bothered me was the five-year gap between the riot and the violence of this year. I couldn't fill in the time span in a way that made sense.

I could grasp what happened *in* 1917, I thought. Franklin Aubury and Ed Moss had both told me about whites losing their jobs and resenting the Negroes who had taken them.

I could also understand tensions continuing in the aftermath of the riot. Even the anger of Enoch's workers over one of their salesmen being killed by Negroes, which I assumed was why the Elcars and Cubs didn't play a game for the next two years.

But two years ago, the series resumed. That was a sign that the rift was mending. So why would the Elcars wait five years to get back for one of their fellow employees being killed in the riot? That didn't make sense. Certainly it wasn't to build up the klavern—the mobs had managed to kill quite effectively without any formal organization in 1917.

And what about Slip Crawford? He hadn't been in East St. Louis since the riot, and last year he'd played in Indianapolis. So why was he the target of the Elcars or the Klan? Because he'd won a ball game? The Elcars had lost each of the last two games, and no one was killed because of it.

The problems seem to have started with the riot, but there was no continuity from 1917 to 1922.

I went back to the reports to see what followed in the months after the riot. There were indictments against eighty-two whites and twenty-three Negroes for crimes committed during the riot. Of the white men indicted, however, only nine went to jail, and the first of those was convicted of beating another white who had attempted to save a Negro.

As for those in law enforcement who'd abetted the rioters, three police officers were indicted for the murder of Negroes, and four others for rioting and conspiracy. They made a deal with the attorney general, however. Instead of facing the murder charges, three of the officers, chosen by lot, agreed to plead guilty to the misdemeanor crime of rioting. They were each fined fifty dollars as their total punishment, and the fines were paid by the other policemen.

The trials of the Negroes went on into 1919. Most of the charges were related to the killing of the two police officers the night before the riot. The theory which served as the basis of the case was that there had been some kind of colored army being supplied with weapons by gunrunners from St. Louis.

There were extensive investigations of all "known" colored criminals, including a St. Louis numbers racketeer named Ronald Parker. Like most of the others, no evidence was found against him and no charges filed. But what was interesting to me was that his attorney was Franklin Aubury.

CHAPTER 31

It was impossible to tell from the mild weather St. Louis was enjoying that one of the most powerful forces of nature had blown into town. Babe Ruth had arrived with his New York Yankees for a head-to-head battle with the Browns.

Our lead over the Yankees was down to two games, and New York was vowing to sweep the three-game series and topple us from our first-place position in the American League standings. A good part of the population of St. Louis, Margie and Karl among them, was crammed into Sportsman's Park for the opener Monday morning, hoping to see us fend off the Yankee threat. I'd invited Franklin Aubury, too, but he declined, unwilling to be stuck in the colored section of the right-field bleachers.

Pitching chores for both teams fell to a couple of youngsters. Rookie Hub Pruett pitched for us, facing the schoolboy from Brooklyn, Waite Hoyt, of the Yankees.

I began the game on the bench, but spent little time sitting on it. I kept moving around, caught up in the excitement.

When Babe Ruth came to bat in the top of the first, all of Sportsman's Park was on its collective feet. Hub Pruett wasn't intimidated by the Babe's reputation or lethal swing, however.

He struck out the slugger on four pitches, to the wild cheers of the crowd.

Pruett fanned the mighty Ruth in both of his next appearances also, and the Browns were up 3–2 in the seventh inning. I was fidgeting and pacing, trying to attract Lee Fohl's attention without actually saying, "Put me in, Coach!"

He got the hint that I wanted to play. In the bottom of the seventh, Fohl said, "Rawlings! Yer up for Ellerbe."

I grabbed my bat and went to the plate, taking a few easy practice swings. My back was pinched and tight from the way the skin was being pulled by the scabs, and I knew I wouldn't be able to make a good swing.

Waite Hoyt worked me to a two-two count, as I swung lamely and missed a pair of curveballs. Okay, one thing to do, I decided. On Hoyt's next pitch, I laid a bunt up the first-base line; it was risky—if the ball went foul, I'd be out automatically—but it rolled just inside the foul line, and I made it to first safely.

Since that risk had paid off, I promptly took another. With Hank Severeid at the plate, I stole second base, sliding headfirst to avoid landing on my back. I stood up, dusted myself off, and looked around at the packed stands and all the fans cheering my hustle. This was *fun,* I thought, and the only thing that could be more fun would be doing this in a World Series.

Severeid rapped a single to right on the next pitch, and I raced for home. With another headfirst slide, I beat Babe Ruth's throw to put us up 4–2.

My run proved to be the winning run as the Yankees scored once in the eighth. We had a three-game lead now, and New York couldn't overtake us in this series.

In the locker room, we celebrated as if the game had clinched the pennant, and I got plenty of praise for my play. No one was feeling sorry for me now, as they had when they'd first seen my back. Today I was no longer a victim. I was part of the team, one of the guys who helped beat the Yankees.

Margie, Karl, and I celebrated by going to dinner. Initially, all we talked about was the game and the Browns' prospects for winning the pennant.

When Margie left Karl and me alone for a few minutes, though, I shifted to a different subject. "I know why Franklin Aubury was able to identify Rosie Sumner so easily," I said. "It's because Aubury works for a numbers racketeer, too, a fellow by the name of Ronald Parker. Five years ago, he did anyway."

"He still does," answered Karl. "However, he doesn't really *work* for him."

"Then why is he listed as Parker's attorney in 1917?"

Karl thought a moment. "This is confidential, but I'm sure Franklin wouldn't mind me telling you. He is kept on retainer by Parker. There is rarely an occasion when Parker actually needs his legal services, but he wants to support Aubury's civil-rights work."

"Huh?"

"It's a way to funnel money. Numbers racketeers support many community institutions, but they have to be careful about how they account for their money. On the books, Franklin Aubury is paid a monthly retainer for legal services. The legal work he does, however, has nothing to do with Parker's enterprises."

"It may not be that innocent, Karl," I said. "Aubury might be using his connections with the rackets. He always seems to know right away when something happens—maybe it's because he has *advance* knowledge. Maybe he's even using his connections to get revenge on the Elcars."

Karl shook his head. "I've known Franklin Aubury long enough to know he wouldn't do anything wrong." He pointed to the glass of beer next to my plate. "He isn't any more a criminal than you are for drinking illegal beer."

"I know," I said, "that bootleggers hijack, steal, and kill in their business. Maybe numbers racketeers do the same."

"Even if they do, Aubury wouldn't be involved in that end of it. Look, I'm sure he's not happy about having *any* connection with criminals, but what choice does he have? I've always fought for causes that were underfunded because they were against established interests—and sometimes I didn't look too closely where *my* money came from. You take it where you can get it and make good use of it. That's what Aubury's doing."

Could be, I thought. But if he wasn't doing anything wrong, why did he keep it a secret?

I sure hoped Karl was right about Franklin Aubury. Because on Tuesday night, the sales office of Enoch's Motor Cars was burned to the ground. Also torched was the dealership's garage, destroying the cars inside and killing the night watchman, who was found in the backseat of a charred Auburn. According to the newspaper, the name of the watchman was Melvin Greene, once a major-league baseball player.

The only thing I now understood was why he'd preferred "Tater." I didn't know why he was identified as a watchman when he'd been a mechanic. And the paper didn't reveal how the fire started, although since it struck two separate buildings, the police believed it was arson—which with Greene being killed, made it a homicide.

What I wondered was: Who lit it? Greene had mentioned to me that the Klan didn't trust him anymore. Was he killed by the KKK, who then set the fire as a cover? Or was the fire set by Negroes as revenge for Cubs Park having been burned down, and Greene an unintended victim?

Whatever the reason, and whatever he'd done in the past, I felt sad about my old teammate. Especially since the last thing he'd said to me was that he was sorry for everything.

CHAPTER 32

Without calling ahead for an appointment, I showed up at Franklin Aubury's law office early the next morning. Despite Karl Landfors's reassurances, I wanted to talk to the lawyer directly.

Aubury looked like he hadn't slept in days. When I sat down, he took off his pince-nez and rubbed his bloodshot eyes.

"I was reading about the trials from 1917," I began, "and I came across an interesting item: You were the attorney for Ronald Parker. According to the report, he's a kingpin in the St. Louis 'policy' rackets. That's numbers, right?"

"You are correct on all three counts," Aubury answered matter-of-factly. "*Policy* is another word for the numbers, Mr. Parker runs a numbers operation, and I represented him—in fact, I still do."

"I never expected you to be tied up with the rackets," I said.

He spread his hands. "I am sorry to be a disappointment to you. But I have done nothing criminal, and I am not ashamed of my relationship with Mr. Parker."

"Then why didn't you tell me about it before?"

"For what purpose? What business is it of yours who my

clients are?'' For somebody who wasn't ashamed, he was sounding pretty defensive.

''None, I guess. Just surprised me.''

Aubury pushed a stack of papers aside and leaned back. ''When I was in law school, I was determined to help the poor, those who had no voice and no one to defend them. When I started my practice, I took on so many *pro bono* cases, that I wasn't providing for my own family. Mr. Parker wanted to support the work I was doing for the community, so he put me on retainer—it enables me to spend all my time working on the issues that will help our people the most.''

''Not *all* your time. You did have to defend him on the gunrunning charge in 1917.''

''That did not require much effort on my part. He wasn't involved in any such thing, and it never went to trial.''

''I'll take your word for it,'' I said. ''From what I read, it did seem that the cops were accusing just about all colored people of stirring up trouble.''

''They certainly were.'' He put his glasses back on. ''Even before the riot took place. There was no end of rumors about 'gun-toting darkies,' and newspapers were reporting that pawn-shops were doing a brisk business selling guns to Negroes—they'd display them in the windows because we're attracted to shiny things, you know. The police department eventually issued a general order to disarm all Negroes. Patrolmen would stop and frisk colored people who were walking down the street, and pull over and search their cars for no reason. All weapons were confiscated from Negroes, while the whites armed themselves to the teeth against an imaginary colored army. Our people saw it as an attempt to leave us defenseless, and there *were* some colored people running guns from St. Louis over the bridge—transported by light-skinned Negroes who could pass for white.''

''But it wasn't the numbers guys doing it?''

"Not my client. I've told you before, the numbers men are more like bankers than criminals. They generally avoid violence. By the way, Mr. Parker provided the money for rebuilding Cubs Park."

I didn't believe they were quite as innocent as Aubury claimed, but perhaps he wanted to believe that his benefactor had no "bad" criminal involvement. "I was kind of worried," I said. "The thought crossed my mind that if you were involved with Parker, maybe you were passing on information that I gave you on the Elcars, and maybe Parker was using his thugs to get revenge on them."

Aubury rolled his eyes.

I said, "You did seem to know pretty quickly when things happened, or were about to happen."

"I do hear things—I make an effort to remain informed. And I do have some contacts with those in the community who do not have the patience for justice to be achieved through legal means. But I have been using whatever small influence I might possess to urge restraint, not revenge."

"What about Enoch's place being burned the other night— have you heard who was responsible for that?"

Aubury answered sadly, "No. *If* Negroes were involved, I doubt that they intended that anyone should die. So they are unlikely to say anything at all."

There remained three possibilities, then, I thought. The only *impossibility* was that the fires had been accidental. Flames don't accidentally break out in two separate buildings at the same time.

Aubury rubbed his eyes again.

"You look like hell," I said. "Want to get some lunch? My treat."

He laughed wryly. "My wife has been telling me the same thing. Thank you for the lunch offer, but what I need is sleep, not food."

I knew what he meant; I hadn't been sleeping much lately, either.

Only four days after Tater Greene's death, Roy Enoch had a display ad in the *St. Louis Globe-Democrat*. It made no mention of Greene's death, only that the "huge inventory of fine automobiles" hadn't been harmed, and the lot was open for business. He also made a statement of defiance to the Negro community by including his slogan *"Komplete Kar Kare"* at the bottom of the advertisement.

I telephoned the number listed in the notice.

A cheerful female voice squeaked, "Enoch Motor Car Company."

"This is Detective Brown," I said. "East St. Louis Police Department. I'm calling about the fire Tuesday night."

"Oh, I'll get Mr. Enoch. He's out on the lot."

"No need," I said. I preferred to speak with someone who might be less guarded. "I just have a couple of simple questions; there's a minor discrepancy in the report I have to clear up. Is this Miss, uh"—I didn't know her last name—"Doreen, is it? I'm sorry, but I can't make out the last name on the report here. I guess I need to give our officers some penmanship lessons."

She giggled. "That's okay. It's Doreen Uhler." She slowly spelled the last name for me.

"The main question I have, Miss Uhler, is about Mr. Greene's position at the dealership. One of my officers wrote that he was a mechanic, but I have another report here that he was a watchman."

"Oh, I can explain that! He *was* a mechanic, but a week or so before he died, he was made night watchman instead."

"Wasn't a good enough mechanic?" I thought if Greene had been made a watchman, it might be because Enoch wanted him there at night—if he was still a mechanic, there was no good reason for him to be there when the fire was set.

"Well, I think it had to do with something else."

"And what was that?"

She hesitated. "I really think I better get Mr. Enoch. I shouldn't say anything bad about Mr. Greene."

"I can assure you this will be kept in confidence. I only need to complete the report; I'm not looking to damage Mr. Greene's reputation."

"Well . . . he'd been drinking a lot lately. Mr. Enoch is a strict Prohibitionist, and normally he'd fire anyone he knew was a drinker, but he thought Mr. Greene might change if he was demoted to watchman."

"I appreciate your time, Miss Uhler. That's all the questions I have."

It didn't really answer much. From my phone conversations with him, I already knew that Greene had been drinking lately. And that he regretted the things he'd been involved in. One possibility was that he'd set the fires himself—the sales office to harm Enoch, and the garage—well, if he was drunk enough, that might have been an accident. Or if he was sad enough, maybe he wanted to die in the blaze. Then I remembered his body had been found in the backseat of a car; that sounded more like he'd been sleeping when the fire broke out.

The two leading possibilities were that it was a retaliatory attack by Negroes to get back for Cubs Park having been burned down, or it was the Klan, using the fire as a cover to kill Greene, who they might have considered untrustworthy. Although if it was the Klan, burning the garage would have been enough. Why the sales office? That would have hurt Enoch's business. Unless all the important things had been removed first. Maybe that's why they were able to open again so soon.

The only thing for sure was that, no matter who was really

responsible, the Klan would have to act as if they'd been the victims of an attack. Which meant they would be striking back.

I was determined to do what I could to stop the Klan this time—and to get some measure of revenge for what they'd done to me.

The question was where to apply the pressure. I couldn't take on an entire klavern. I had to find a weakness.

The only area I could think of where the Klan might be vulnerable was with regard to the Slip Crawford lynching. That act was the one the Klan most wanted to disavow. Among those likely to have been involved, I thought Brian Padgett was a good choice. He was a hothead for sure. He was also the one Greene had heard talking about me being whipped. So he must have had some contact with those who'd grabbed me.

The next question was how to get him to break the secrecy of the Invisible Empire.

I finally came up with the beginnings of a plan. Then I enlisted Karl Landfors to help me carry it out.

CHAPTER 33

I never thought it would happen, but at midnight, as June turned into July, I was attired in the white hood and robe of a Knight of the Ku Klux Klan. Karl Landfors wore a similar costume, but his was the green outfit of a Grand Titan, a rank higher than that of Exalted Cyclops Roy Enoch.

"Maybe they won't be able to pick him up," I said.

"If he's home, they've got him," Karl said confidently.

The two of us were in an abandoned boathouse on the shore of Horseshoe Lake, north of East St. Louis. We sat a while longer, waiting, in the dim light of a small kerosene lamp, listening to the crickets and owls.

"You sure you know what to say?" I asked.

"We've been over it often enough."

I said nothing more until we heard a car pull up near the boathouse.

We nodded at each other, lowered our masks, and stood up.

In walked two muscle-bound young men in street clothes, prodding along a smaller man shrouded in a burlap sack. From within, came the muffled yelp of Brian Padgett, "Let me out of here! What the hell's the big idea?"

I took some pleasure in watching him endure what I had been through.

The two big fellows donned hoods and robes as white as their skin, then jerked the sack off of Padgett. "Sit," one of them ordered.

Padgett's eyes lit on Karl's uniform, and he was clearly awed by it. He might never have seen such a high-ranking Klansman. A rough shove sent the Elcars' shortstop toward a straight-backed chair next to the lamp. The second man pushed him down into the seat and promptly tied him in place with a rope.

Karl stood a few feet in front of Padgett, I stood behind Karl's shoulder, and the two big men positioned themselves on either side of our captive.

"What is this," Padgett pleaded, "some kind of initiation?"

"No," answered Karl in a surly voice. "This is an inquiry."

"But why'd you drag me—" Padgett squawked as a hard slap to the side of his head sent him crashing to the floor.

"Speak when spoken to," said the man who hit him.

The other man pulled Padgett upright.

I didn't know where Karl had found these two, but they were playing their parts perfectly—they even scared the hell out of me.

Padgett's frightened eyes darted from one to the other. "Okay," he said softly, as if unsure that even this much speaking was allowed.

"First question," said Karl. "Did you, or did you not, take an oath to 'heed all Imperial mandates, decrees, edicts, rulings, and instructions'?"

"I did. But I—" Another blow to the head let Padgett know that he was not supposed to elaborate. I found the sound of a fist on Padgett's head quite satisfying; I only wished it was my fist doing the punching.

"And were you, or were you not, informed that the Invisible Empire does not want its Knights involved in acts of violence?"

"I was."

"Then what in damnation was the idea of lynching that darky pitcher? We have bigger plans than lynching a nigger over a baseball game!"

"We didn't—"

Karl held up his hand to interrupt. "Before you say anything more, I have another question: Have you read your *Kloran?*"

"Yes."

"Then you know the penalty for lying to an officer of the Invisible Empire."

Padgett nodded meekly.

"Good," said Karl. "Now, bearing that in mind, you may answer."

"We didn't kill him because of the ball game."

"Then why?"

"He insulted a white woman."

"How?"

"After the game, the nigger was bragging he was gonna celebrate by screwin' one of our women."

"You heard him say that?"

"No. Another player did—J. D. Whalen. And J. D. told us Crawford pointed to my fiancée when he said it." Padgett was starting to display the anger that he must have felt when he heard Whalen tell him that. "We *had* to do it. Got to protect the women, right?"

That was the usual excuse the Klan gave to justify the most vicious violence: protecting American womanhood.

Karl said, "So you took it upon yourself to lynch Crawford without permission from your Exalted Cyclops?"

That was one of the questions I had: Did Roy Enoch order the lynching, or was it an unsanctioned act by some hotheads?

Padgett squirmed. "No sir. We wasn't gonna lynch him at

all. We just brought him to the ballpark, to give him a beating and teach him a lesson. But he wouldn't admit to what he said.'' He added with some admiration, ''Pounded the hell out of him, but he swore he never said nothing about any white woman.''

Apparently, it never occurred to Padgett that Whalen was lying.

''Go on,'' prodded Karl.

''Then somebody said 'hang him.' ''

''Who said it?''

''I dunno.'' One of the men next to Padgett cocked his fist. ''Really, I don't!''

Karl shook his head, and no punch was thrown.

Padgett appeared grateful. ''Guys were yelling all along— 'Hit him again,' 'Kick him'—and we kept doing it. Then somebody said, 'Hang him,' and all of a sudden there was a rope.''

''So you strung him up.'' Karl's voice cracked, and I feared he might give himself away.

''You know how it is,'' Padgett whined. ''Who's gonna say, 'No, let's not'? So we went ahead and hung him.''

By then, Padgett seemed more pathetic than evil.

Karl looked at me, and I nodded slightly toward the door. If we asked too many questions, Padgett would get suspicious; we had to limit ourselves to what we could pretend we knew.

In the most ominous tone he could muster, Karl said to Padgett, ''Consider yourself warned: If there are *any* further actions that could reflect badly on the Invisible Empire, *you* will suffer the consequences.''

With that, Karl spun about to make a regal exit. The two large men and I followed. When we got to the Buick sedan, we could hear Padgett yell, ''You can't just leave me here!''

''How's he gonna get out?'' I asked as we got into the car.

The driver said, ''Depends. If he's smart, he'll realize he

can slip the rope off the leg of the chair. If he tries to untie the knot, he'll be there all night."

He'll be there all night, I thought.

The four of us removed our robes and hoods, and then we drove away, the big men sitting up front and Karl and me in the back.

As I folded the robes, I asked Karl, "You got to get these back to Chicago?"

"Yes, perhaps they'll come in useful again." He stuffed the robes and hoods into a leather satchel.

"By the way," I said, "what *is* the penalty for lying to an officer of the Klan?"

"I have no idea."

"But you asked Padgett if he read his *Kloran*."

"He didn't strike me as the reading type. So I figured if I bluffed, he'd assume the worst."

The two men dropped Karl and me off downtown near Union Station, where they'd picked us up a couple of hours earlier. "They did a helluva job," I said. "I didn't know you knew any muscle guys, just college boys."

Karl smiled. "They *are* college boys—and the pride of their school's football team."

"You sure you can trust them to keep quiet about this?"

"Oh yes. The college they play for is Notre Dame. Catholics are no greater fans of the Klan than the NAACP is."

I smiled, but a pang shot through me that caused me to feel less cocky about what we'd done. "Do you realize, Karl, that we just committed a *kidnapping?*"

He rubbed his long nose. "Yes, I suppose we have." After a moment of thoughtful silence, he added, "But I can live with that."

I decided I could, too.

Then I looked at Karl, who had really impressed me this night. I'd had to let him do the talking at the boathouse since

Padgett might have recognized my voice, but I'd worried whether Karl could pull off the impersonation of a Klan official. He'd sure thrown himself into the role, though, and Padgett never showed any sign of suspecting the ruse.

Just before we split up, I said, "You know, if you ever want to get into acting, I'll bet Margie still knows some people in Hollywood. You did great, Karl."

He doffed his cap and made an elaborate bow.

CHAPTER 34

Although I'd gotten in late from my outing with Karl Land-fors, the experience had me too energized to get much sleep. Shortly after dawn, I was awake for good, while Margie still slept soundly.

For a while, I just lay next to her, enjoying the fact that my back had healed to the point where I could once again join her in our bed. Almost all that remained from the whipping I'd received was that I would have some ugly scars. But since I couldn't see them, I wasn't going to worry about how they looked.

As Margie shifted on the mattress and purred softly into her pillow, I had one of those brainstorms I get sometimes when I haven't had enough sleep. I thought it would be nice to repay her for the way she'd taken care of me by making her Sunday breakfast.

I slipped out from under the covers and went out to the kitchen, where I began to gather all the utensils I assumed were involved in preparing breakfast. I was familiar with the coffeepot; the rest might as well have been chemistry equipment.

After spreading a fair number of pots and pans on the kitchen table, I stepped back and decided that it might be better to take Margie out to breakfast. I began putting them back in the cupboard, when I knocked an iron skillet to the floor. It sounded as if an automobile had run into the house. I remained motionless for a moment, hoping Margie hadn't awoken, then began putting them away again.

"What are you doing?" she asked sleepily from the doorway.

I confessed, "I was going to make you breakfast."

She stifled a laugh. "That's so sweet!" Looking over the mess I'd managed to create before I'd even started on the food, she added, "Can I help?"

"Maybe you could give me some hints on what to do."

Ten minutes later, Margie was preparing eggs, toast, and pancakes, while I manned the coffeepot. As I waited for it to brew, I filled Margie in on what Karl and I had learned from Brian Padgett.

She said, "You don't believe that Slip Crawford really said something about Padgett's girlfriend, do you?"

"Not for a minute. J. D. Whalen must have lied about that."

"Could I have the butter, please?" After I handed it to her, Margie asked, "But *why* would he lie?"

"The way I figure," I said, "is that Padgett probably has the worst temper on the Elcars' team. I saw it when we almost had a fight during the game, and then again at the car lot when another salesman was talking to Doreen. If Whalen wanted to get the Elcars riled up against Crawford, the best way to do it would be to claim to Padgett that Crawford had said something about Doreen."

"But why would he want to get the Elcars to attack Crawford? Because he beat them?" Margie sounded as perplexed as I'd felt most of the night.

"Maybe because Crawford embarrassed him during the game. Whalen looked awful bad, first backing down against him when he went to the mound, and then striking out in a critical spot." I poured a couple mugs of coffee. "It might fit with what happened to Denver Jones, too. Jones plowed into Whalen during that game, so maybe Whalen got the Elcars to torch his house."

"That sounds awfully extreme to me," Margie said. "Ballplayers look bad in games all the time. They don't kill or burn down a house because of it."

"I know. It doesn't really make sense to me, either."

Margie flipped the pancakes over. "Maybe Whalen instigated things but never expected them to go as far as they did."

"Could be. Padgett did say they only intended to beat Crawford, not kill him." Unless, I thought, Whalen was the one who'd said, "Hang him." Maybe he did want the pitcher killed all along.

After we sat down and began eating, Margie asked, "What's the next step?"

"I don't know," I admitted. "Seems like I've run out of ways to get information. Tater Greene is dead, and none of the other Elcars will talk to me now. I can't pretend I'm interested in joining the Klan; they won't buy that story anymore."

"Brian Padgett told you quite a bit last night. Maybe you could try him again."

"I think we got as much as we can out of him. He only talked last night because he thought Karl Landfors was a Grand Titan in the Klan. If I show up asking questions, he'll just be suspicious—and he won't tell me anything."

Margie paused from stirring sugar in her coffee. With a look of concern, she asked, "Aren't you worried about the Klan finding out that somebody impersonated them?"

"It will be a while before they find out. Padgett will be too embarrassed by what happened to him to want to tell anyone." I know I certainly had been.

We worked on the food for a while, then Margie suggested, "If you're out of leads, why don't you let me try something?"

I thought of what the Klan had done to me in Forest Park. "I really wouldn't like for you . . . it's too dangerous."

Margie pushed her plate to the side. "A couple of months ago, I told you I had an idea for getting some information and you wouldn't even hear me out. At least listen to me now—please."

Eventually I learn. "Of course," I said. "What's your idea?"

She smiled slightly at my response. "You remember during the Elcars' game, I sat with the other women in the stands?"

I nodded.

"Most of them were wives or girlfriends of the players. Doreen was there, and so was Enoch's daughter Jessalyn. Let me talk to them."

"That's a great idea, but if you show up asking questions, they're sure to get suspicious."

"I don't have to question them, and they don't have to know who I am," she said. "I'll just go to their next game, and sit near them again. They spent most of the game gossiping, so with a little nudging, I'll bet I can learn a few things."

That did sound like a good idea. "I'll find out when their next game is," I said.

This meant, though, that Margie had something to do, while I was still at a loss for my next step. I wondered if perhaps I should take the risk of talking to Whalen directly to find out why he'd lied to Padgett about Slip Crawford. I thought it over, and suddenly realized that Whalen had told me a lie, too.

I got up and refilled Margie's and my coffee cups. I told her, "When I asked Whalen why he backed down after Crawford threw at him, he told me Crawford *apologized* for the ball getting away from him. But when Franklin Aubury and I were in Indianapolis, the ABCs players told us that Crawford would knock down his own mother without saying he was sorry."

"Maybe he mellowed when he joined the Stars?" Margie suggested.

"No, I don't think so. Plunk Drake—he pitches for the Stars—he told us that Bill Gatewood orders his pitchers to throw at batters for target practice. Crawford would have probably become even tougher with the Stars, not softer."

I began to clear the dishes. What had Crawford really said to Whalen, I wondered. Was it something that would make Whalen want to kill him?

It wasn't until I'd settled into my parlor chair with the morning newspaper that I thought of a way to find out. Now Margie and I both had something to pursue.

The village of Brooklyn, north of East St. Louis, on the Mississippi River, was nothing like the one in New York. There was no Coney Island, no Ebbets Field, no Greenlawn Park. Virtually the only structures were small houses and shacks, occupied entirely by Negroes. One of the larger houses—about the size of a bungalow—was the new home of East St. Louis Cubs catcher Denver Jones.

He greeted me warmly when I arrived at his doorstep Monday evening. I'd asked Franklin Aubury to call him for me, so the big catcher was expecting me.

When Jones invited me inside, I looked around the simple parlor. It had a cozy feel, but there seemed to be something missing. "You all settled in?" I asked.

"Pretty much," he answered. "But I'm missing the wife and kids. Ain't really a home without 'em."

"They're not here with you?"

"Sent them to live with my sister in Chicago for a while. Until things calm down around here." He offered me a seat in an overstuffed chair. "Oh, thanks again for the help at the ballpark—and for the gear. It helped get us back in business."

"Glad to do it," I said. "As for things calming down, I'm trying to help with that, too, if I can."

"Mr. Aubury mentioned that. Says you're one of the good guys." A smile lit up his broad, round face. "But I already knew that—I seen how you worked at the park."

"Thanks. You probably thought different when you first saw me in an Elcars uniform, though."

"Sure did." He handed me a beer. "But opinions change."

I leaned forward. "Let me ask you about that game. When Slip Crawford threw at J. D. Whalen, Whalen started out to the mound to go after him. But Crawford said something that made Whalen back down. You were right on Whalen's tail, ready to break up a fight if it came to that. You must have heard what Crawford said."

"Yeah, I did." Jones shifted in his chair. "But it didn't make no sense to me. Slip must have known what he was doing though—he got Whalen shook-up enough to strike him out easy."

"What exactly did Crawford say?"

"He asked Whalen a question: 'You don't got a tire iron with you this time?' "

"What does that mean?" Was it some kind of colored slang that I was unfamiliar with?

"I got no idea," said Jones.

Great, I thought. Now all I have is more questions to answer.

CHAPTER 35

The new bleacher seats had been added to Sportsman's Park, and every one of them was occupied. More than thirty thousand fans were on hand for the Browns' Independence Day doubleheader against the visiting Cleveland Indians.

Any other year, this occasion would have been one of the highlights of the season for me. A major-league baseball game was as much a part of a Fourth of July celebration as fireworks and flags, and it was always something special to play on the nation's birthday. It was impossible for me to get excited about these games, though.

For one thing, Lee Fohl was putting the Browns' pennant drive into high gear, which meant he was relying primarily on the regulars. My role would be limited to coaching Marty McManus from the bench.

I was also distracted by the situation in East St. Louis. I had no doubt that Roy Enoch's klavern—with or without his blessing—would be planning some action to get revenge for the dealership being burned down. I only hoped that I could find a way to get things resolved before we left on our next road trip.

Most of my hopes rested with Margie. She was in Collinsville, at an Elcars' semipro game, to find out what she could from their female fans.

"The game itself was terrific," Margie reported. "The other team was also white, so there was a completely different atmosphere from the game with the Cubs." She took a bite of her hot dog and washed it down with soda pop. Dinner was informal, on a picnic blanket in Fairgrounds Park, while we waited for the holiday fireworks display.

"Who won?" I asked, hoping it hadn't been the Elcars.

She smiled. "Collinsville, five–four." After tossing a piece of bread to a nearby pigeon, she said, "I learned some things from the women there. I don't know if any of it's useful though."

I still had concerns about Margie being involved in this. "Were they suspicious about you asking questions?"

"I hardly had to *ask* anything!" Margie laughed. "All they did is gossip—they barely paid attention to the game. Jessalyn Enoch and Doreen Uhler were both there, and they seemed happy to have another set of ears around to listen to their talk."

"Did you find out anything about Whalen?" Before she'd left for the game, we agreed she should focus on him, since he'd lied about Slip Crawford.

"Some, but I don't know if it's helpful." Margie refolded her legs and smoothed out her skirt. "J. D. Whalen started pursuing Jessalyn soon after her fiancé Tim Lowrey was killed in the riot. I don't know if it was his idea, though. He might have been encouraged by Jessalyn's father. Roy Enoch promoted Whalen from mechanic to Lowrey's sales position, and seemed to be grooming him to take over the business."

I asked, "Was the falling-out between Enoch and Whalen a couple months ago because of Whalen starting his own garage or because of something between Whalen and Jessalyn?"

"I don't know. Whalen pursued her off and on for a few years, but she never warmed up to him, from what I gather."

"You don't think she and Whalen were involved earlier—while she was engaged to Lowrey?"

Margie shook her head. "The other girls at the park filled me in on Jessalyn when she went to the ladies' room. She's not likely to attract many suitors—neither her appearance nor personality is terribly pleasant. The girls seemed to think Roy Enoch was essentially bribing Whalen to court his daughter with the better job and more money."

"And it didn't work?"

"No, I think she loved Tim Lowrey, and no one was ever going to replace him for her. That's another odd thing, though: The girls all agreed that Whalen would have been a 'better catch' for her than Lowrey. After Lowrey was killed in the riot, he became something of a martyr, but he wasn't well liked when he was alive. Doreen told me she'd heard that Lowrey was always bragging to the other workers that he had it made because he'd be marrying the boss's daughter."

"Hm. Did you learn anything else?"

"Nothing new. Doreen did mention Padgett's temper, but you already knew about that. She said, 'With his temper, he should have my hair color.' She also said he never got angry with her, but *would* get into a jealous rage at any man who showed her attention."

I thought over what Margie had told me. She was right; there wasn't much we didn't already know.

"Do you think it was worth me going there?" Margie asked.

I smiled. "At least you got to miss seeing us play against Cleveland." We'd lost both ends of the doubleheader, shrinking our lead over the Yankees to one game. "I'm not sure where to go from here."

"Well," Margie said, "what about talking to Hannah Crawford?"

I didn't really want to question Slip Crawford's widow, but I had to concede that it was a sensible idea.

Once again, I'd called Franklin Aubury, this time to set up a meeting with Crawford's widow; I didn't want to show up unannounced and start asking her questions about her dead husband. I'd also told the lawyer about Karl's and my interrogation of Padgett, and that I thought we were making some progress. I didn't tell him yet that it looked like J. D. Whalen had instigated the lynching.

Margie and I arrived at Hannah Crawford's spacious Olive Street apartment Thursday afternoon. Mrs. Crawford was a pretty, shapely woman with skin almost the same shade as her black hair, which was straightened and cut in a Dutch bob. She greeted us graciously and ushered us into a pristine parlor.

"I sure appreciate what you're trying to do for my Sherman," she said. "You just tell me anything I can do to help."

As she poured us tea from a silver pot, I looked around and saw the photos of her husband on the mantel. Many of them were formal portraits of Sherman Crawford wearing a suit and tie; others showed "Slip" Crawford in the baseball uniforms of the Indianapolis ABCs and St. Louis Stars. On the wall above, was a color-tinted wedding portrait of the two of them together.

I began, "I understand you and your husband used to live in East St. Louis."

"Until the riot," Hannah Crawford answered. "Our house was one of those that was burned down. We moved to St. Louis right after, and never went back across the river again."

"But Slip went back to pitch in the Cubs' game. Why did he do that? Why go back to East St. Louis to play in a semipro game?"

"The city had been our home for several years. Slip always felt bad about the way we left, and he wanted to do something for the community. He figured pitching that game against the Elcars was one of the best things he could do for the colored people of East St. Louis. Nothing's ever going to make up for what happened to us during the riot, but every time we get some small victory against the whites, it's something for us to cheer about."

"Were you at the game, too?"

"Sure was. Afterward, we had dinner with some friends who used to be neighbors."

"Did your husband say anything after the game?"

She hesitated. "About what?"

"You remember when one of the Elcars' batters—J. D. Whalen— started to go out to the mound? Slip said something to him, and Whalen backed down. Did he tell you what he said?"

Hannah Crawford thought for a while. "Mr. Aubury says I should feel free to tell you anything. This is the first time I've told anybody what I'm going to say to you, and I want *your* promise you won't use it in any way to hurt the memory of my Sherman."

I promised that I had no intention of harming her late husband's reputation.

She said, "The day the riot started, I was home, and Sherman was over in St. Louis trying out for the St. Louis Giants. When word started to spread about what was happening in East St. Louis, he came back over Eads Bridge—almost had to fight his way back, because of all the people going in the other direction trying to escape. Sherman didn't know it, but I was one of them, along with our next-door neighbors. I figured Sherman was already safe, being in St. Louis; I didn't know he'd try to come back to check on how I was.

"Well, by the time he got to where we lived, our house was already up in flames. So he started to search for me, all the while having to avoid the whites who were shooting colored folk like it was target practice. The city was crazy—killing, burning, looting. One of our neighbors was even killed for a pair of shoes.

"Anyway, Sherman kept looking for me. As he did, a couple of white men passed near him, and went into an alley. Sherman hid until they passed. But apparently, these men weren't hunting colored people. One of them knocked the other on the head with a tire iron."

"Was he killed?" I asked.

"Sherman wasn't sure, but he thought so. Said the man's skull cracked as loud as a gunshot. He never checked though—soon as the man who'd hit him left, Sherman took off before he ended up getting blamed for it." Hannah Crawford looked down at her folded hands. "He always felt a little cowardly about what happened—that he didn't try to help the man, and that he left town never to come back. I suppose that's another reason he wanted to play for the Cubs that day."

And that's when he saw the man who'd swung the tire iron that night: J. D. Whalen. I asked, "So what did your husband tell you after the game?"

"He recognized the man who killed the other fellow in the alley. It was the one who went out to the mound. When he did, Sherman said something to him like, 'You better have another tire iron with you.' " She shook her head, then almost screamed, "That damned fool! Soon as he said that, he was as good as dead."

Margie said, "I don't understand. Why would your husband let Whalen know that he recognized him?"

"I think I can answer that," I said. "Crawford was in a tight spot and he wanted to get Whalen off-stride. And it worked—he struck him out."

Hannah Crawford nodded. "That's what he told me. He didn't really *plan* to say anything; it just came into his head and out his mouth. He didn't think of any consequences beyond the ball game.'' She began to weep. ''We sure started to worry about it afterward though.''

With good reason, I thought.

CHAPTER 36

I pored over the thick transcripts and depositions of the 1917 trials in the basement of East St. Louis's City Hall. As I did, I wondered how Franklin Aubury had managed to stay awake in law school if he had to read this kind of stuff. It was all in a dry legalese that made it tough to tell if any of it meant anything.

It took a couple of hours, but I sorted through the material until I'd found the coroner's reports on each of the six white men who'd been killed in the riot. Most had died of gunshot wounds. The only one who'd been killed by bludgeoning was Tim Lowrey. He'd suffered a fractured skull from "a blunt object, perhaps a metal pipe."

It looked like the connection between 1917 and 1922 was confirmed. Slip Crawford had never gone back to East St. Louis until the game against the Elcars. That's when he saw J. D. Whalen again. And that's when Whalen learned that there'd been a witness to his murder of Tim Lowrey—and when he'd decided to make sure Crawford could never tell what he saw.

But after five years, and with the only witness to the crime dead, how could I prove what Whalen had done?

* * *

I knew there was no way to get Whalen for Crawford's lynching—the only witnesses were Klansmen—so my best chance to nail him was for the murder of Tim Lowrey.

The main question about that, I thought, was whether it was a planned murder or a spontaneous act. Whalen might have been able to get a mob riled up against Crawford to do his killing for him, but he certainly didn't start the riot in 1917 for the sole purpose of providing cover for his murder of Lowrey.

Okay, start with the basics, I told myself: means, motive, opportunity. The means was a tire iron. Opportunity was the riot—in the mayhem of the burning and the killing and the looting, with few police on patrol, it was easy for Whalen to add one more victim to the toll. No one would investigate it as a murder, and the blame would be placed on Negroes.

But what was his motive? He'd pursued Jessalyn Enoch after Lowrey's death—was *she* what he wanted?

There was one person who might be able to give me more information.

I placed a phone call to Waverly Motors, and asked for Mr. Whalen.

"You got him," he said.

"This is Mr. Lockhart in the tax office at City Hall," I said. "We have a bit of a mix-up on your paperwork here. Right now, your business is only listed as a garage, and we need to correct that to include automobile sales."

"Oh. Okay, what do I have to do?"

"Just fill out a couple of forms. Can you be at City Hall tomorrow at ten?"

"I suppose."

"It will only take a few minutes. Come to room 142 and ask for Lockhart."

At ten o'clock the next morning, I arrived at Waverly Motors, where I was greeted by the hirsute Clint.

He said, "Hey, you guys are playing real good. Looks like you're gonna take the pennant."

"Don't jinx it," I joked.

"I been thinking of taking you up on that ticket offer. Haven't been to a ball game in ages."

"Anytime," I said. "Just let me know, and tickets will be waiting for you."

"Thanks. Oh, J. D.'s not here, if you come looking for him."

I knew that. "I wanted to talk to *you*, if you have a minute."

"Sure, but I promised some guy to have his car done by noon. You mind talking inside?"

I followed Clint into the service bay, where he resumed work on the engine of a Chevy coupe.

"You mentioned about all the good people who got caught up in the riot," I began. "Was J. D. one of them?"

"No reason to go digging up bones. Let it be."

"The bones keep coming to the surface," I said. "That might be why this problem with the Elcars keeps getting worse." I tried to make it sound like I wanted to keep Whalen out of trouble. "Wouldn't want J. D. to get hurt in whatever happens."

"Don't see why he should."

"He *was* involved in the riot, wasn't he?"

"All the fellows at Enoch's were. But they didn't start nothing. When they heard about it, they just grabbed tools or whatever else they could use as weapons and started patrolling."

"Patrolling?" So that was how Whalen and Lowrey happened to be together in an alley that night.

"Yeah, there was rumors that coloreds were coming over from St. Louis, and it was gonna be out-and-out war."

"But that didn't happen."

"Hell, there was rumors flying around like you wouldn't

believe. Made people crazy, but hardly any of 'em were true. Can't blame J. D. or any of the fellows at Enoch's for getting caught up in things—there weren't a whole lot of cool heads that day. And they've all suffered enough. That's why I say it should stay buried.''

''They've *suffered?*''

''Sure. Felt like idiots for what they did, and then to lose Tim Lowrey because of their foolishness. Good people can do stupid things sometimes.''

''Yeah, they can.'' And at least one of those ''good people'' did an evil thing.

CHAPTER 37

By Friday night, I felt I needed the evening of dancing that Margie and I had planned. Despite the Marquette Hotel's terrific band, though, I couldn't get into a dancing mood. While other couples danced nearby, Margie patiently sat at the table, listening to me go on about J. D. Whalen.

"The problem," I said, "is that I know what happened, but I don't have any idea what to do about it. There doesn't seem to be any way to nail Whalen for either murder. There's no witness to him killing Lowrey anymore, and the only witnesses to Slip Crawford's lynching are Klansmen—they sure won't testify against Whalen."

Margie suggested, "Maybe you should talk with Franklin Aubury. He's a lawyer; he should know what you'd need to make a case against Whalen."

"I don't want to tell him that Whalen had Crawford killed by the Klan and got away with it because lynching isn't a crime." I took a sip of the champagne, which suddenly had a sour taste. "Whalen found the perfect murder weapon: a mob."

"What about talking to Karl?"

"He might tell Aubury. And if Aubury decides there's no legal recourse, maybe he'll tell some of his 'contacts' about

Whalen and let them take care of him. That will only cause more violence." There appeared to be no hope of convicting anyone for Crawford's death, so I considered Lowrey's again. "Was there anything else you heard in Collinsville," I asked Margie, "that might explain why Whalen killed Tim Lowrey?"

"No . . . Just that he started pursuing Jessalyn Enoch soon afterward."

I tried to piece together what Whalen had been doing around that time. "Ed Moss—the cop who manages the Elcars—told me Whalen was practically starving after losing his job in the Aluminum Ore strike. But then Roy Enoch gives him a job in the garage, where he keeps hearing Lowrey brag about having it made by marrying Jessalyn. The riot breaks out, Enoch's workers join in, Whalen finds himself alone in an alley with Lowrey, and kills him."

Margie wrinkled her face. "Doesn't sound like much of a plan."

"I doubt if it was a plan at all. Whalen didn't know there'd be a riot that day, and with all that was going on—the killing and looting and burning—he couldn't have been thinking clearly. He just saw an opportunity and took it. But why? Was he jealous of Lowrey, or tired of his bragging, or did he figure by getting Lowrey out of the way he could get Jessalyn for himself?"

"Maybe a little of everything," said Margie. "Remember, Hannah Crawford told us a neighbor of hers was killed for a pair of shoes. If Whalen got it into his head that Lowrey had something he wanted, either his job or Jessalyn, maybe he simply decided to take advantage of the opportunity."

No matter how close I thought I came to understanding what had happened, I could still see no way of putting it to use. The authorities certainly wouldn't reopen the 1917 killing of Lowrey, especially with no witness. And they wouldn't view the Crawford killing as "murder" at all.

At a complete loss on what to do next, I polished off a glass of champagne and asked Margie to dance.

There was one person, I decided, who didn't have to be convinced what happened. He already knew everything about it, both the what and the why. All I had to do was convince him that he wasn't alone in possessing that knowledge.

Saturday morning, I was again walking over the rutted dirt lot of Waverly Motors, toward the small office off the garage.

J. D. Whalen spotted my approach and met me outside. "Sorry I missed you yesterday," he said sarcastically. "Somebody sent me on a wild-goose chase over to City Hall." He pulled a cheroot from his jacket pocket and lit it up. "Heard you talked to Clint, though."

I had no doubt that he believed I was the one who sent him on the wild-goose chase. Nor did I doubt that he knew what my questions to Clint were about. So there was no sense being other than direct with him now. "You're a killer, J. D.," I said. "And there are people who know it."

He exhaled a stream of smoke. "That a fact?"

"You killed Tim Lowrey in 1917. There was a witness— Slip Crawford—so you had him killed, too. Whoever was involved with lynching Crawford knows that you're the one who egged them on. You got to turn yourself in."

Whalen took a leisurely drag on the cigar. "Assuming that what you say is true, then as far as killing Lowrey, it'd be my word against a nigger's—and a dead nigger at that. So I don't see any reason why I should worry myself over that. Besides, everybody knows that it was niggers who killed white men in the 'seventeen riots—it says so in the official reports. As far as Crawford getting strung up, that was because he insulted a white woman."

"But you're the only one who claims to have heard him."

"I can get a dozen men to swear they heard him. Hell, I can get a hundred to swear to it."

He could be right, I thought. I looked around at the crummy car lot. "Tell me something," I said. "Was this worth it? You killed Lowrey, and this is all it got you. You didn't get Jessalyn, you didn't get Roy Enoch's money, all you get is this."

He answered contentedly, "I had five years of good living, and I put enough money away to build my own business. This place'll make Enoch's look like a shoeshine stand someday."

That was close enough to an admission, that I ventured one more question. "*Why* did you kill Lowrey? Did you plan it, or did it just happen?"

He looked around and chewed on his cigar. In a low voice, he answered, "Wasn't plannin' nothing. He had things that I didn't—money, good job, a girl—and he was always rubbin' my nose in it. I never thought to do nothing to him, though. But when the riot hit, and everything was crazy, I just—I just looked at him, and decided I hated him. Everything was fair game that night—shooting, burning, stabbing—so it didn't seem like nothing to take a swing at Lowrey's head. Wasn't till after he was buried that I thought I might try to get what he had for myself." Whalen smiled slyly. "Now, I'm no lawyer, but I know you can't do nothing about what I just said. Your word against mine."

I wasn't looking for a confession to take to the police, only to clear up in my own mind what he had done, and what I might elect to do about it. "Doesn't matter what I know," I said. "There's other people who know what you did. Slip Crawford talked to people. And your pals in the Klan know who set them on to Crawford. If local Negroes or the Klan officers find out what you did, prison could be the safest place for you."

He shook his head, appearing totally unconcerned. "If you believe I'm a killer," he said, "you got to be pretty stupid to come here like this. Don't you think I'd be willing to kill you, too?''

"I'm not worried," I answered. "You don't have a mob here to do your killing for you."

He smiled again. "I can get one."

After two days of looking over my shoulder, and worrying about Margie's safety, I decided what I had to do. There was almost no chance of bringing J. D. Whalen to legal justice for the deaths of Tim Lowrey or Slip Crawford, and I had to give up that idea. The most I could hope to achieve would be to prevent further violence, and there was only one way I could see to bring that about.

Monday morning, the day before we were to leave for our road trip, I went to the Enoch Motor Car Company to have a conversation with Roy Enoch.

At first he was unwilling to see me, but I convinced first Doreen and then Enoch himself that it was important. I was sufficiently convincing that Enoch told the secretary and the two salesmen in the office to go outside so we could talk in private.

I then gave him the story of J. D. Whalen killing Tim Lowrey and using the Klan to cover it up by lynching Slip Crawford. As I spoke, Enoch's stony face betrayed no sign of whether or not he believed me. Throughout, I forced myself to sound respectful toward the Exalted Cyclops, which was the most difficult part of the task. I omitted mention of Hannah Crawford and Denver Jones, to avoid putting them in danger.

When I finished, Enoch asked in his flat twang, "Why are you telling me this?"

"Because you run the Klan in this town, and you have the power to put an end to more violence. I'm betting you didn't know about the Crawford lynching until after it happened. I know the Klan doesn't want a reputation for violence, and you can stop it.''

''You're interested in preserving our reputation?''

''No,'' I answered honestly. ''I'm just saying it's in everyone's interest to have the killing stopped.'' I leaned forward. ''I've read your pamphlets, and I've met some of your members who truly believe that the Klan is nothing more than a patriotic, Christian fraternal society. I'm hoping that's what you believe and that once you know how your klavern's been used to cover up personal crimes, you'll make sure there's no more attacks on colored people—or on me. There's one person responsible for what's happened here, and that's J. D. Whalen.''

''Why should I take your word for all this?''

''You don't have to. Talk to your own members, and the fellows who work for you. Think over what you know about Whalen and what you knew about Lowrey. Maybe talk to Jessalyn, too. And definitely talk to Whalen. Then make up your mind.''

A thoughtful nod was Enoch's only answer.

I don't know how much of an investigation Roy Enoch did, but he made up his mind in only a few days.

The Browns were in Philadelphia when Margie called me at the hotel with the news. J. D. Whalen had been killed in a tragic train accident, found crushed on one of the many railroad tracks that ran through East St. Louis. Good way, I thought, to cover up any injuries he might have had ahead of time—if he'd even been alive when he was put on the tracks.

I didn't believe for a moment that it had been an accident, but it was smart of Enoch to make it appear that way. If the Klan had made it an obvious murder, other Klansmen might have thought he'd been killed by Negroes, and the revenge attacks would have only continued to escalate.

CHAPTER 38

After a two-week eastern road trip, I was back in St. Louis, in the cluttered law office of Franklin Aubury, talking with Aubury and Karl Landfors.

The lawyer reported that there had been no further outbreaks of violence in the city while I'd been gone, and that he'd helped spread the word that the man behind Slip Crawford's lynching was now dead himself.

While Aubury and I spoke, Karl remained oddly silent for some time. He finally blurted, "Dammit! I don't like what you did, Mickey. You used the Klan to kill Whalen the same way Whalen used them to kill Crawford. That's not justice."

"It's not the same," I said. "One difference is I told the *truth* about what Whalen did. When he got the Klan to lynch Crawford, he did it by *lying*. For another thing, I did not go to Roy Enoch hoping they would *kill* Whalen. I just thought that if he knew what had really happened, he'd put a stop to any more violence."

Karl scoffed. "You mean to tell me you had no idea Whalen would end up being killed?"

"I'm saying that wasn't my *hope*. But I guess it did cross my mind as a possibility."

Growing more agitated, Karl went on, "We had a unique opportunity here to demonstrate the danger of mobs—by charging Whalen for murder and exposing his use of a lynch mob to carry it out. You ruined that chance by resorting to the same tactics as the Klan."

Franklin Aubury spoke up, asking Karl, "What world do you inhabit?"

Karl turned to him. "You *agree* with what Mickey did?"

"When you have limited recourse," the lawyer answered, "you take the best options available."

"I still don't like it," said Karl.

"I don't *like* it, either," I said. "But I can live with it."

"Are you sure about that?" Karl asked. "You don't think the Klan will come after you now?"

"No, I had a phone call soon after I got back home. Anonymous, but it sounded like Roy Enoch. He said the Klan does take care of punishing their own, and told me the matter is closed."

"You believe him?" asked Karl.

"I'll be watching my back for some time," I admitted. "But I'm hoping it's over."

We sat in silence for a few minutes, then I added, "One thing I'm glad of is that Crawford was killed for a reason other than his skin color."

Franklin Aubury said, "The unfortunate fact is that if *that* had been the reason, Whalen would have gotten away with it."

CHAPTER 39

I turned out to be right about John McGraw's New York Giants taking the National League pennant. On October 4, the Polo Grounds was all decked out for the opening game of the 1923 World Series. Unfortunately, their American League opponents were the New York Yankees, who beat out the Browns by one game in the final standings. Once again, I had missed out on a Fall Classic.

The last couple of months featured a number of victories and defeats. Although it was a severe disappointment to come so close to a pennant only to lose it on the final day of the season, there was cause to celebrate the achievements of some individual Browns players. Ken Williams had bested Babe Ruth in the slugging race, breaking the Babe's string of home-run crowns, and George Sisler ended the year with a phenomenal .420 batting average to take the hitting title.

There were ups and downs off the field, too. The federal antilynching bill died in the United States Senate, but public outcry against mob rule was rising, and the bill's proponents were confident of passage next year. In East St. Louis, an uneasy calm had settled over the city; the Klan continued to grow, but there had been no more violence. And in St. Louis, there was no sign that the Invisible Empire was establishing a foothold.

At the same time that the Yankees and Giants were battling in New York for the World's Championship, I was playing baseball, too. Commissioner Landis had decided to permit an "all-star" team of major-leaguers to play an exhibition series against the St. Louis Stars. Landis was firm, however, that the big-leaguers could not appear in major-league uniforms or use the names of their professional teams.

So on a Saturday afternoon in early October, I was in Stars Park, temporarily a member of a team called the Wabadas, about to face a Negro League ball club. In the stands were Franklin Aubury, rooting for Stars; Margie, rooting for me; and Karl Landfors, probably rooting for the umpires.

My eagerness to play in the game was dampened only by the thought that I wouldn't have the chance to bat against Slip Crawford.

Once the game started, I didn't think much about Crawford. Another player from that April game in East St. Louis dominated the action: Cool Papa Bell, the Stars starting pitcher. He tripled and scored in the first inning, while holding our team hitless.

In the second, I got my first chance to face the young pitcher. I thought, as I walked to the plate, of how he'd handled Oscar Charleston in Indianapolis. What chance did I have against Bell, I wondered, if Charleston couldn't hit him?

I took my stance, and looked at Bell's baby face. Then I backed out of the box, and quickly came up with a plan. I could use his age against him.

In the Indianapolis night club, Bell had insisted that the knuckleball was his best pitch, and wished Bill Gatewood would allow him to throw it more often. I knew that he'd be using it a lot today, with or without Gatewood's permission. A rookie pitcher will *have* to use his best pitch, especially if he wants to impress a big-league club. It's the ego of youth, and Bell won't be able to resist going with what it orders him to do.

I stepped back in the box, ready now to take advantage. Bell first threw a fastball which I let pass. Then came the pitch I expected: a slow knuckler. I scooted up in the box to hit it before it broke, and caught the ball solid, sending it to the gap in left-center. Racing around first, I almost skidded, but righted myself and made it into second base with a double.

Dusting myself off, I looked around the ballpark, at the fans both black and white, and at the players. Then I caught the eye of Bell; he gave me a slight nod in salute. This wasn't the same as getting a base hit off Slip Crawford, I thought, but it would do. And I had the feeling that getting a hit off Cool Papa Bell would be something to brag about someday.

AUTHOR'S NOTE

By 1924, more than four million Americans were members of the Ku Klux Klan, among them the governors of Texas and Oregon, the mayors of Atlanta and Denver, five United States senators, a future Supreme Court Justice, and future Hall of Fame baseball players Rogers Hornsby and Tris Speaker. The Invisible Empire was strongest in Indiana, where one out of every three white Protestant men was a Klansman, including the governor and the mayor of Indianapolis. The rapid rise of the Klan was followed by an even faster decline. After the 1925 conviction of Grand Dragon David C. Stephenson for the rape and murder of a young white woman, membership in the Ku Klux Klan plummeted, and the organization soon lost its political power.

In the 1920s, 281 blacks were lynched in the United States, while the NAACP continued to press for the passage of anti-lynching legislation. The federal bill to outlaw lynching never became law.

After 1922, Judge Kenesaw Mountain Landis forbade major leaguers from playing in major-league uniforms or using major-league team names in games against Negro League clubs. He later ruled that only ''all-star'' white teams could play Negro

Leaguers. When the all-star teams still failed to win often enough, he tried to prohibit such games entirely. During his twenty-four-year tenure as baseball commissioner, there was no progress in integrating baseball.

The Eastern Colored League began operations in 1923. Alex Pompez, owner of the New York Cuban Giants and organized crime figure, was one of the men who negotiated the truce with Rube Foster and the Negro National League that led to the first Negro League World Series in 1924.

James "Cool Papa" Bell, who began the 1922 season as a pitcher with the semipro East St. Louis Cubs before joining the St. Louis Stars, went on to play Negro League baseball for a quarter of a century. He was widely hailed as the fastest man to ever play the game, and was inducted into the Baseball Hall of Fame in 1974. Oscar Charleston's baseball career spanned half a century, from his playing debut with the Indianapolis ABCs in 1915 to managing the 1954 Indianapolis Clowns, winners of the Negro American League championship. Considered by many the greatest all-around ballplayer in Negro League history, Charleston was elected to the Hall of Fame in 1976. Neither Cool Papa Bell nor Oscar Charleston ever played a game in the major leagues.

In 1944 Sportsman's Park became the last major-league park to desegregate. That same year, the Browns won their first and only American League pennant, losing to the St. Louis Cardinals in the World Series. Ten years later, the Browns' franchise moved to Baltimore and was renamed the Orioles.

In 1946 former Cardinals' manager Branch Rickey signed Jackie Robinson to a contract with the Brooklyn Dodger organization. When Robinson took the field in 1947, he broke the color barrier that had stood for more than sixty years.

Please turn the page for an exciting preview of
ISLAND OF TEARS by Troy Soos.
A Fall, 2001 Hardcover release from Kensington Publishing.

CHAPTER
ONE

December, 1891

The double eagle glowed like a miniature sun, a solitary beacon amid the murky shadows of the Hole. The saloon actually had no formal name—"The Hole" wasn't advertised on any signs, nor was it registered on city license rolls—but Bowery locals all knew the illicit dive by the same name used for the most notorious jail cells. The comparison to a dungeon wasn't quite a fair one, however. Prisons generally had better ventilation than the fetid Hole of Hester Street, and they certainly had a more reputable clientele.

Marshall Webb pried the twenty-dollar gold piece from the scarred table top, where it had mired in a paste of stale beer and old cigar ash. He held the coin tightly against his palm for a moment, as if trying to absorb some warmth from its luster, before slipping it into his vest pocket.

Across the table, Lawrence Pritchard eyed Webb with a look of concern on his drawn face. "We *had* agreed on twenty dollars, hadn't we?"

Webb shrugged, then continued to hunch his shoulders trying to shake off the winter chill. The temperature of the Hole was maintained at the optimal level for business: a little warmer than the December air outside to attract customers, but cool enough so that once inside they would have to warm themselves internally with whiskey and gin. "Yes, twenty," Webb said with a cough. Smoke and dust hung thick in the low-ceilinged room, providing the ambience of a coal celler.

"You don't look happy about it," said Pritchard with a frown that caused his Dunlap derby to duck low across his forehead. There was no hat or coat rack in the Hole since anything hung there would disappear faster than pickled eggs at a free lunch counter.

The flickering gaslight from behind the bar was feeble, but Webb could see enough of his companion to notice that Pritchard was the one who didn't look happy. The middle-aged man's bony face, with sunken eyes and clean-shaven pale skin, had a spectral quality that was even eerier in the shadows. The occasional glint from his pince-nez was the liveliest aspect of his appearance. Webb reminded himself that Pritchard didn't look much different in any other venue, generally giving the impression of a nervous ghost.

After one last wriggle of his shoulders, Webb nestled within his overcoat. "The twenty is fine—it's what we agreed to for the last one." He toyed with his whiskey glass debating whether to empty it at one gulp or make it last for two. "But the next one will cost you more—considerably more."

Pritchard hesitated before answering, "I'm a reasonable man. You know I have no objection to paying a fair price."

Webb stifled a laugh; to those in their trade, "fair" was often a matter of vigorous contention. He ended his debate about the drink by downing it at once, straining it through the thick mustache that overhung his lip. Immediately, he launched into another debate about whether to exceed his customary limit of two drinks.

"The last one did very well for us," continued Pritchard. "If the next is at all comparable . . ."

"The next will be a *peach*." Webb dabbed his tongue at the drops of rye clinging to his mustache. "I'm going to have some fresh material in three days."

Pritchard's expression instantly changed from nervous to eager. "Care to give me some idea of what I can expect?"

"You've heard about Ellis Island?"

"One of Harrison's dumber decisions." Pritchard rolled his eyes. "What kind of idiot puts an immigration station where the water's too shallow for boats? Political, that's all it was— a way to get the Navy's munitions dump off the island and placate those New Jersey dunderheads who thought it would blow them all up some day." He shook his head. "Need to get Grover Cleveland back in the White House. Next election—"

Webb cut him off. "I don't care *why* the place was chosen. The point is: Ellis Island opens January first, and there are going to be thousands of immigrants coming in every day . . ." His attention drifted to a nearby table, where two plug-uglies in shabby clothes of no discernible color or style were stealing glances at them. Webb discreetly looked around the rest of the place. About a dozen other men—little more than shadowy figures in the dim light—were drinking the afternoon away, five of them at the bar and the rest at small rough-hewn tables. The two nearby weren't the only ones watching Webb and Pritchard with interest.

Murmuring to himself, Pritchard was going on, "The whole idea of transferring immigration from state to federal control is nonsense—"

Webb suddenly slammed his palm on the table, and leapt up from his chair, yelling at Pritchard, "You ever try something like that again and I'll cut your heart out!" He reached into his jacket pocket, as if going for an implement to do exactly that.

Pritchard almost tumbled from his own seat, and his pince-nez fell into his lap as he jerked his head back. The look on his face was as shocked as if he'd already been stabbed.

With one hand on the tabletop, and the other still in his pocket, Webb leaned forward until his face was inches from Pritchard's. He then hissed as softly as the gas jets, "No offense, but I don't want anyone here thinking I'm an easy mark. There's men in this place who'd kill for a pair of old shoes without giving it a thought. Putting that twenty on the table the way you did was like waving red meat before a starving cur." Webb let go of the fountain pen that he'd hoped made a knife-like bulge in his pocket, and sat back down. "Good," he said in his normal voice, "now we understand each other."

When he'd recovered enough to speak, it was Pritchard's turn to whisper, "*You're* the one who insists we meet in places like this."

"In order to avoid being seen together. If you go attracting attention, that defeats the purpose, doesn't it?"

Pritchard paused to clean his glasses, then wiped the handkerchief across his forehead, having managed to break a sweat despite the cold. "You're quite right," he stammered. "I'm sorry." He neatly refolded the cloth and tucked it into his breast pocket and took a moment to compose himself. "So . . . tell me about your plans."

Webb settled back in his chair, satisfied that he'd given any potential muggers reason to reconsider their plans. "As I was saying, Ellis Island opens Friday. People from all over the world coming in. Some of them will be girls, on their own, expecting to find jobs as maids or cooks."

Pritchard shook his head with disapproval. "What kind of family sends a young girl alone across the ocean?"

No answer was expected, but Webb replied, "A poor one—

perhaps a family that can only afford steerage for one. So they send a daughter to start her off on a better life in the new world. Maybe later they'll send a son, and if they can afford it, the rest of the family will follow." He smiled. "Anyway, that's the kind of girl I'm looking for: Thirteen or fourteen years old—maybe as old as sixteen but no more. Young, alone, and eager, that's what I want." An orphan would be ideal, he thought to himself—no one to help her in the strange new country, and no family to which she could return.

"Pretty?" asked Pritchard.

"Of course. And if nature didn't make her that way, she'll be a doll by the time I finish with her." He smiled again. "I can do a lot with the right kind of girl. I guarantee you'll be happy with the result—*and* you'll be happy to pay."

The door to the Hole creaked open, letting in a gust of cold air and two ragamuffins, each about nine years old. Webb and Pritchard both watched as the boys made their way directly to the bar, their bare feet squishing in the swampy mixture of tobacco juice and sawdust that covered the floor. The taller of the two held open a small burlap sack, and began negotiating to sell the three live rats squealing inside.

"For the lunch spread, no doubt," said Pritchard in a rare attempt at humor.

Webb shook his head. "For the rat pit tonight." He then listened as the boys settled for two nickel beers a piece instead of the eight cents per rat they'd asked for initially. The saloonkeeper managed to convince them that they were coming out four cents ahead on the deal.

"I thought pitting dogs against rats was outlawed," said Pritchard. "Didn't the SPCA get that stopped?"

"For one thing," Webb answered, "neither the SPCA nor the law has any control over what goes on in here. For another, there are no dogs involved."

"It's just rats against rats? I can't imagine that would be very entertaining."

"No, its *man* versus rat. A man wearing boots steps in against a hundred or so rats, and he's got to stomp as many as he can before they bite through to his feet."

Pritchard's derby lurched up. "You can't be serious!"

Webb nodded solemnly. "A good terrier takes at least half a year of training, and the top ones can cost more than a hundred dollars." He gestured toward a group of toughs standing at the bar. "A man can be gotten for next to nothing."

Absently touching the vest pocket that held the gold piece, Webb thought of the new immigration center opening at Ellis Island. In a few days, human life would be even cheaper as a fresh supply poured into the city. It was a simple matter of supply and demand, and in New York City, as 1891 drew to a close, a human being could be had for less than the price of a good ratter.

BOOK YOUR PLACE ON OUR WEBSITE AND MAKE THE READING CONNECTION!

We've created a customized website just for our very special readers, where you can get the inside scoop on everything that's going on with Zebra, Pinnacle and Kensington books.

When you come online, you'll have the exciting opportunity to:

- View covers of upcoming books
- Read sample chapters
- Learn about our future publishing schedule (listed by publication month *and author*)
- Find out when your favorite authors will be visiting a city near you
- Search for and order backlist books from our online catalog
- Check out author bios and background information
- Send e-mail to your favorite authors
- Meet the Kensington staff online
- Join us in weekly chats with authors, readers and other guests
- Get writing guidelines
- AND MUCH MORE!

Visit our website at
http://www.kensingtonbooks.com

Get Hooked on the
Mysteries of
Jonnie Jacobs

__**Evidence of Guilt**
    1-57566-279-5 $5.99US/$7.50CAN

__**Murder Among Friends**
    1-57566-089-X $4.99US/$6.50CAN

__**Murder Among Neighbors**
    0-8217-275-2 $5.99US/$7.50CAN

__**Murder Among Us**
    1-57566-398-8 $5.99US/$7.50CAN

__**Shadow of Doubt**
    1-57566-146-2 $5.50US/$7.00CAN

Call toll free **1-888-345-BOOK** to order by phone or use this coupon to order by mail.

Name _____

Address _____

City _____ State _____ Zip _____

Please send me the books I have checked above.

I am enclosing	$_____
Plus postage and handling*	$_____
Sales tax (NY and TN residents only)	$_____
Total amount enclosed	$_____

*Add $2.50 for the first book and $.50 for each additional book.

Send check or money order (no cash or CODs) to:

Kensington Publishing Corp., 850 Third Avenue, New York, NY 10022

Prices and Numbers subject to change without notice.

All orders subject to availability.

Check out our website at **www.kensingtonbooks.com**